"LOOK AT ME, MY BEAUTY."

Hesitantly, Bliss forced her eyes upward. The face above hers, illuminated by the silvery moonlight glistening on the pristine snow, was sharply planed, brutally handsome. The eyes, deep-set, were dark, shaded by arching brows.

His eyes moved slowly, lingeringly, over her face as his hands held her by the waist. "Gad," he breathed, "but you are beautiful."

The desire in his voice, his face, was plain even to Bliss's innocent eyes. She trembled, drawing as far from him as she could. "Please," she whispered. "Don't."

"I won't hurt you," he promised. "As I told you, sweetheart, all I want from you is a kiss."

Bliss gasped as he drew her hard against him. The force of his kiss, the savage, demanding plundering of her mouth by his set her senses awhirl.

> "Sandra DuBay fulfills
> all her readers' fantasies!"
>
> —*Romantic Times*

NIGHTRIDER

SANDRA DUBAY

LEISURE BOOKS   NEW YORK CITY

A LEISURE BOOK®

June 1991

Published by

Dorchester Publishing Co., Inc.
276 Fifth Avenue
New York, NY 10001

Prologue: The First

Lady Bliss Paynter walked along Whitehall Palace's Stone Gallery on her way to the King's chambers. A page had come to her door and told her the King desired her presence at once.

She smiled as she threaded her way through the hustle and bustle that was the life blood coursing through the gallery which was the main artery of the sprawling palace. Bliss loved living at court. She'd been here since the death of her father, the Earl of Barthorp, a loyal and trusted friend of King Charles II. She had been left a ward of the crown upon her father's death and the King had allowed her to keep the apartment in the palace that had been her father's.

She watched, envious, as a pair of young,

7

pretty maids of honor, their beribboned heads close together, hurried past on their way to the Queen's rooms. She wished she could be one of them; she'd dreamt that one day she would be appointed. But she knew there were no vacancies now and so she had to believe this sudden summons could mean just one thing: the King had found her another guardian.

It was a common practice, she knew, the sale of guardianships. The highest bidder would win the right to control her fate, to oversee her estates and her fortune, and to arrange her marriage. In the process there were many opportunities for the guardian to profit from the arrangement. He could use his ward's money to invest in ventures from which he, himself, would reap the greatest reward. He could sell her into marriage in much the same way he had become her guardian—by auctioning the pretty heiress to the potential bridegroom willing to pay the most for a wealthy, landed wife.

Bliss had hoped the King would retain her guardianship for she knew he was a kind-hearted man with a well-known weakness for pretty girls. She knew that if he decided upon a husband for her and she did not like the man, she had only to weep and beg and the King, unable to bear a woman's tears, would relent and choose someone else.

But her hopes, she was sure when she'd received the summons to the King's chambers that early-winter afternoon, were about to be dashed. Dutifully she went to his rooms, and her skirts, of somber black brocade with only the slightest hint of golden lace to enliven it, whispered as she made her curtsy to her guardian, the King.

"Come here, child," the King invited, holding out a hand whose long fingers were laden with rings. "You look very pretty today."

"Thank you, sire," she replied, coming to take the chair he indicated near his own.

"There is someone I want you to meet. Chiffinch!"

The King's Keeper of the Privy Closet, William Chiffinch, opened the door and conducted a gentleman into the room. Then, bowing to the King, he melted away with all the silent discretion that made him the King's most valued servant.

The gentleman who had entered the room and bowed low to the King was a spare, hollow-cheeked man of middling height. His forehead had long since receded to the crown of his head and the remainder of his hair, pale brown peppered with gray, was worn cropped short beneath his plain periwig.

"Sir Basil Holme," the king said. "This is Lady Bliss Paynter, daughter of the late Earl of Barthorp, a close friend and trusted advisor. Bliss, Sir Basil is to be your guardian."

Bliss felt a quiver of misgiving. Sir Basil's face was the very picture of dour ill humor. His clothes, though obviously well made of good quality and expensive materials, were plain with none of the braid and ribbons and laces that decorated most gentlemen of fashion. She knew instantly from the way his small eyes swept over her, that he did not approve of her gown, of the bright, golden touches that lifted some of the somber air that would otherwise have surrounded her.

Rising, she swept him a deep curtsy. "My lord," she said softly.

"Lady Bliss," he replied, with the shallowest of bows. "You are still in first mourning, are you not?"

Blushing, Bliss's fingers plucked at the golden lace trimming her ruffled sleeve. "Aye, my lord," she admitted, "but—"

"Come now, Sir Basil," the King interrupted, taking pity on Bliss. "She is so very young. What are you, my dear, eighteen, isn't it? She's so lovely, much too lovely to look like some dull, black crow."

"It shows a lack of respect, sire," Sir Basil ventured to disagree.

"Be that as it may," the King went on. "Bliss, I want you to come to the masked ball tonight in something bright and beautiful. For this one night." Seeing her delighted smile, his wide, sensual mouth curved in a lazy smile that extended up to his long, exotic, dark eyes. "You are far too young and much too lovely to be condemned to black and to shut yourself away from pleasure and people for a year. I want you to dance tonight and laugh. That is a command."

Flushing happily, Bliss bobbed him a curtsy. "As you wish, sire," she acquiesced most willingly.

"You may leave, my dear. I wish to speak to Sir Basil now."

"Thank you, sire," Bliss said fervently. Putting her fingers into the King's outstretched hand, she found herself drawn forward to kiss the King's cheek.

And then she was gone, hurrying back to her chambers to have the final fitting on the costume she'd already had made for the ball. She had known the King would not object to it; his "command" had only been for Sir Basil's benefit. Now, with the King's permission, her new guardian could not forbid her wearing the lovely emerald-and-gold gown and matching mask trimmed with paste jewels. Gold and green plumes would decorate her titian hair and she would, she was determined, be the belle of the ball. For it was certain that with Sir Basil Holme as her guardian, there would be no more such nights for a long time to come.

Hours later, as she watched her maid threading green ribbons through her hair, she felt a mixture of anticipation and misgiving. Anticipation because the night would be aglitter with beautiful bejeweled ladies and gallant, satin-clad gentlemen to dance attendance upon them. Everyone would be masked and no one's identity would be revealed until midnight. Until then a girl could dance with whomever she pleased, let a particularly dashing gentleman steal a kiss, or an embrace, without worrying that he might think less of her the next morning.

Her misgiving had a deeper cause. Tonight, she knew, she enjoyed the King's protection. But Sir Basil was her guardian and she knew without being told that he would brook no nonsense. He would not be the fond, lenient guardian the King had been. Once she was in his control, she had no doubt she would be forbidden balls, beautiful gowns, and glittering jewels until her year of mourning was done. And by then, she supposed, he would have decided on a husband for her and she would pass from his control to the control of yet another stranger.

And so, for this one night, as the King had said, she was going to laugh and dance and, she thought with a shiver, kiss some gallant gentleman before the hour of unmasking arrived and she was forced to bend to the stern will of Sir Basil Holme. For this one night she would banish those daunting thoughts that had plagued her since she'd met her new guardian.

Smiling to herself, she held the mask up to her face while her maid tied the ribbons over the golden caul that confined her titian hair. With a wink at her maid, Bliss left her rooms and made her way along the packed corridor toward the Queen's presence chamber where the ball was to take place.

NIGHTRIDER

The gallery, wide though it was, was thronged with courtiers and ladies and mere spectators who crowded into the palace to watch the dazzling spectacle of the nobility at play. Sweet, heavy perfumes competed with the odor of unwashed bodies, silks and taffeta brushed against plain cloth, jewels sparkling in ears, on arms, bosoms, and necks were reflected in the greedy eyes of those who would have liked nothing better than to pocket them.

The presence chamber was lit with candles and flambeaux, and it was ablaze with color, for not only the women but the men as well wore flashing silks and taffeta looped with ribbons and lace in a rainbow of hues.

Only a few were recognizeable. The King, of course, taller than anyone with his tumbling black curls and rich, rolling laughter. No mask could disguise him. And the Queen, as petite as her husband was tall, with her olive complexion so different from the pink-and-gold coloring of the English women. She wore a gown of dusty pink and silver that was very beautiful indeed, but it was not the fashion to admire the "little Portuguese" and so no one bothered to tell her she looked unusually pretty, not even the unfaithful husband she adored.

The King's premier mistress, too, was easy to pick out of the crowd. Barbara Palmer, Countess of Castlemaine, rapacious, voluptuous, insatiable bitch that she was, she was also the most breathtakingly beautiful woman in England and no mask, no costume, could disguise that remarkable beauty.

Bliss paused on the threshold and gazed with rapt enchantment at the scene before her. Bless the King for letting her come tonight! she thought fervently. If she had to be immured in some crepe-draped chamber for months to come, she would at least have this night to remember.

And it was all so unnecessary, she thought. As if dressing in starkest black and shutting one's self away in a darkened room meant she grieved more for her father. Mourning, she believed, was done with the heart and it was what was in the heart that mattered, not the trappings with which one surrounded one's self.

She steadfastly believed that her father, who had loved her so much, who had pampered her after her mother's death, would have wanted her to laugh and dance and enjoy herself. And that, she resolved as she plunged into the crowd, was what she meant to do with a vengeance!

The tall, slender blond man in the suit of violet silk had attached himself to Bliss's side early in the evening. He plied her with glass after glass of sweet wine, flattered her outrageously, danced with her, and teased her until she giggled uncontrollably.

She pushed his hands away as he tried to tug at the ribbons of her mask. "No, you mustn't!" she chided, a giggle in her voice that was caused half by amusement and half by the wine she had consumed that evening.

"But it's nearly midnight," he protested, his pale blue eyes admiring her through the slits in his purple velvet mask. His hair of cornflower yellow tumbled to his shoulders and rolled over into great natural ringlets. "Let me see your face, my beauty," he coaxed.

"How do you know I am a beauty?" Bliss challenged. "You cannot see my face."

"I know by the curve of your delectable lips," he purred, his own lips brushing her ear. "How I long to kiss them!"

"You judge a woman's beauty by the shape of her lips, then?" Bliss asked.

"And by the sparkle of your beautiful eyes," he whispered. "How I long to see them glowing with desire!"

"So it is by her eyes and lips that you judge a woman?" Bliss prompted, a strange quivering in her stomach.

"And by her body." His fingers tips brushed, as if by accident, over the creamy swells of Bliss's breasts above the lacy edge of her neckline. "How exquisite you are. I long to hold you, to caress you, to be your lover."

Bliss clutched her fan with a sweaty hand. She thought she knew who this rash young man was, a young viscount who had succeeded to his title but recently. He was busily cutting a swath through the ranks of the females of the court and it was whispered had been entertained by

Castlemaine herself. He was vain, self-centered, conceited and unutterably handsome. Bliss had often seen him courting this lady or that. He was far from the dashing, tall, dark, masterful stranger she dreamed of in her girlish fantasies, but he was known to court only the most beautiful women at Whitehall and therefore to be singled out for his attention was something of a coup.

"You are too bold, sir," she breathed, her eyes demurely averted.

"I would be bolder still," he replied, one hand sliding comfortably into the curve of her waist.

"People are staring," she told him, conscious of the envious eyes of more than one lady who, like Bliss, had divined the identity of the blond man in violet. It was a heady feeling, to be pursued by one of the most sought-after men at Court, and Bliss reveled in it.

"Come with me, my sweet," he coaxed. "This crowd . . . How can we get to know one another?"

"I should not," Bliss hesitated, her heart pounding. "It is nearly midnight—the unmasking."

"We can have our own unmasking. Do come."

Bliss was sorely tempted. She knew she should not. The man was a rake, a seducer of the first order. And yet . . . Across the room she saw Sir Basil. Clad in somber gray, he was surveying the room with an air of absolute disgust and disapproval. She knew she would not see another night like this one for many months, possibly not until her guardian had arranged her marriage. And by then she could well belong to some sour-faced, puritanical old man who would not allow his beautiful young wife to frequent the licentious, bawdy court of Charles II.

"I . . . I . . ." Bliss was befuddled. The heat of the room, the glass after glass of wine, the stirring of her own senses made her mind a dizzying whirl of utter confusion.

"Come," the young viscount cajoled, drawing her by the hand toward the door.

Bliss went with him out of a mixture of defiance and curiosity. They made their way along the Stone Gallery to a door that opened at the viscount's touch. Inside was a small, elegant sitting room. Bliss wondered if it were the viscount's room but she did not ask as he drew her down beside him on a crimson-and-gold brocade sofa.

The viscount reached for the ribbons of her mask but Bliss leaned away.

"Don't," she whispered. "It's best not to spoil the illusion."

Seeing her there, a vision of beauty in emerald and gold, the viscount felt he would agree to almost anything if only it meant he could touch her. He sensed an innocence in her that stirred him. His fingers itched to feel that soft, creamy flesh, his arms ached to hold that lush, lovely body, his lips tingled at the thought of kissing her pretty, pouting mouth.

"As you wish," he replied softly, reaching out, his hands slipping into the curve of her waist and drawing her with him down . . . down onto the curved, silky sofa.

Bliss melted into his arms. She'd never been kissed this way before. Oh, there had been stolen pecks on the lips, teasing kisses in shadowy corners, but nothing, nothing like the hot, demanding onslaught of the viscount's mouth on her own.

He kissed her lips, her throat, working his slow, sensuous way down to the cleft of her breasts at the lace-trimmed edge of her neckline. Bliss gasped, lips parted, as he caressed her flesh with his lips, his tongue, his hands. But when he started to lift her skirts, when his hand groped for her legs while his upper body held her back against the sofa, she began to panic.

"No!" she cried. "Let me go!"

"Don't be frightened, my sweet," the viscount rasped, his voice husky.

"No!" The haze of wine dissipating, she saw clearly the danger she had placed herself in. "No, please, I want to go!"

"And so you shall," he told her, his blue eyes glinting with anger and desire. "But not until I've shown you how foolish are your fears. You'll love it, sweetheart. All women do. They merely pretend they don't."

"I'll scream!" she threatened, struggling to free herself from him.

"Scream," he invited. "Do you think anyone could hear you with all that noise coming from the ball? And even if they did, they'd merely think you were screaming with—"

"Take your hands off her, you varlet!" a deep, outraged voice shouted.

Bliss and the viscount leapt to their feet. Sir Basil Holme, his small, close-set eyes ablaze with fury, pointed to the door. "Go to your rooms, girl! Now!"

Bliss fled quickly through the door.

"See here, sir," the viscount protested. "This is none of your affair!"

"I am the lady's guardian, sirrah," Sir Basil told him. "She is a particular favorite of the King. It will not go well with you to be accused of raping her!"

The viscount gulped. The King! He knew the King suspected his affair with the Countess of Castlemaine. Were he to be accused of accosting a young girl who stood high in the King's favor, he could well find himself banished from the court. Then he would be faced with a deluge of bills, for his creditors could only be held off by his continued high standing at Whitehall.

"I apologize, sir," he said quickly. "I meant no harm. The lady came here of her own free will."

"Much as I hate to believe you," Sir Basil

replied, "I suspect you are telling the truth. And so, I will bid you good night. I do not think the King need hear of this."

"Thank you, sir," the viscount said, sagging with relief as Sir Basil left his rooms.

Bliss swung on Sir Basil the moment he appeared in her sitting room.

"How dare you, my lord!" she demanded, her eyes glinting dangerously. "How dare you spy upon me!"

"How dare I!" Sir Basil's hollow cheeks flushed. "I am your guardian, madam, and one of my duties is to see that you behave as a gentlewoman and not as a slut!"

"Slut!" Bliss breathed, the hot blood of fury pounding in her ears.

"What would you call it? Alone, with a man in his rooms, lying together?"

"He was trying to force himself upon me!" Bliss argued.

"But you went there with him! Can you deny it?"

Bliss averted her eyes. "No, my lord, I cannot. But . . ."

"What did you imagine he wanted? Why do you think he was taking you to his rooms? Surely you're not so stupid as all that!"

"I'm not stupid!" Bliss shouted.

"I'm not so sure," Sir Basil disagreed with maddening calm. "I suspected from the first that you have been given far too much freedom.

NIGHTRIDER

But that is at an end. In the morning your belongings will be removed to the Barthorp townhouse here in London. You will remain there, under my supervision, until I can arrange for you to be taken into the country."

"The country!" Bliss breathed. She, like many who enjoyed the glitter and excitement of London and the court, did not relish the prospect of a long, lonely winter in some drafty country house. "You cannot!"

"I assure you, I can. And I will. Now, give me your key."

"My key?" Bliss asked. "Surely, my lord, you do not mean to—"

"Your key!" Sir Basil blustered. "At once!"

Her hand trembling, Bliss handed him the key to her rooms in the palace. "Please, sir," she asked, "do not do this!"

"I do not trust you, madam," he told her frankly. "If you will go willingly to the rooms of a man, how do I know you will not bring men to your rooms?"

"That is not fair!" she cried. "It's never happened before. I've never . . . before tonight . . ."

"I have only your word for that," her guardian told her bluntly, "and I do not put much faith in your word. If you will not guard your good name, then I must; that is my responsibility as your guardian."

He held out his hand and Bliss dropped her key into his outstretched palm. She watched, torn between fury and chagrin, as Sir Basil left the room and locked the door behind him. She was a prisoner in her own rooms. And, she feared, she would remain Sir Basil's prisoner wherever she might be for as long as he remained her guardian.

Prologue: The Second

The old man was dying. The stone-and-thatch cottage in which he lived was a world away from the turreted castle where he'd once held sway as lord and master. The tiny chamber within whose walls he would soon breathe his last would have fitted, unnoticed, into one corner of the soaring, cavernous chambers where he had once entertained royalty, meted out justice, and honored his illustrious ancestors whose origins were lost in the swirling mists of history. The rough-hewn bed where he lay beneath a scratchy quilt was a far cry from the grand, carved bed with its velvet counterpane embroidered in gold with his family crest where he had once lain beside his now-dead but still beloved wife.

But the look in the old man's rheumy blue eyes as they found the face of his only child, his son, his heir, was the same as it had always been, filled with love . . . and regret.

He reached a skeletal hand toward him. It trembled until his son enfolded it between his own. "Forgive me," he said, his voice scarcely audible, his tone quavering.

"Father . . ." the son sighed, his broad shoulders and ruddy wind-and-sun roughened complexion a startling contrast to the drawn, parchmentlike skin stretched taut over his father's fragile old bones. "Rest now. Don't try to talk."

The old man, the Baron de Wilde, shook his head faintly. He reached out with his other hand and another old man, the baron's faithful valet, leapt out of the shadows and came to the bedside with a dented metal cup of water.

Propping his master gently in the crook of one arm, the aged valet let a trickle of the cool water run down his lord's throat. The Baron gestured for him to stop and then was laid back on his pillows to rest from the exertion.

"Christopher," he breathed, once more turning his attention to his son. "I was wrong all those years ago. All I could see was the corruption of the Court—the Queen with her priests and her favorites, the King, weak, allowing himself to be influenced by toadies and unscrupulous villains whose fine clothes and polished manners masked their villainy . . ."

"Father, please," his son begged. "This is not necessary."

The old man did not hear him, he was lost in his own misgivings and regrets. "I believed," he went on, "that England had had enough of the Divine Right of Kings, of setting any fool upon the throne and thrusting kingship upon him simply because he was his father's son."

"Father, there is no need for this," Christopher insisted, seeing his father's strength waning before his eyes.

"There is. There is!" his father assured him, his eyes awash with tears. "It is important that you know why . . ." He closed his eyes, his fragile hand clutched at the bedclothes.

"I thought Cromwell was a good man, a brave man, an honest man. I thought he would bring the country to order, instill the fear of God, make life better for those who, until then, had been at the mercy of the lords who bled them dry to support a life at Court. I did not know . . ."

He shuddered, remembering the Roundhead soldiers, Cromwell's soldiers, defiling beautiful old churches, destroying them, proclaiming them temples of idolatry. They swept through towns, burning ancient manors that had stood for generations, looting, killing. And after . . .

He remembered the repressive Puritanism that had swept England after the execution of Charles I and Oliver Cromwell's accession to the title "Lord Protector."

"Witch finders," he whispered. "Good English men and women accused of sorcery and burned alive. Good God!"

"It's over now, Father," his son reminded him, wanting to draw the old man away from those terrible memories.

"I did not know they meant to kill the king," he insisted, seeing once more the small, brave figure of Charles I as he stepped out of the Banqueting House window onto the scaffold where the executioner waited to behead him.

"I thought they would exile him, perhaps to France. His queen, after all, had been a French princess . . ."

"Father, please, please!" Christopher begged, tormented by the sight of his father's anguish.

But his father went on, lost in his memories and his guilt. "When at last Cromwell died and his son succeeded him as Lord Protector, it became apparent that England had had enough of Puritanism. They longed for the old ways, the feasts, the laughter . . . the Court. I was glad when the Prince of Wales—now Charles II— was recalled from his exile. I did not know . . . I did not realize he would still, after all these years, seek to avenge himself on all who had failed to support his father."

Christopher remembered the day the summons came. His father had been called to London to answer for his "treachery" in supporting the dead king's enemies. He had been stripped of his lands, his possessions, cast out to find his own way in the world. After the elegant, if somber, grandeur of Chatham Castle, his ancestral home, the confines of the thatched-roofed cottage had taken on the aura of a prison.

"My mistake," he whispered, his voice growing noticeably weaker, "cost me my lands, treasures that had been in our family for centuries. And it cost you your inheritance. I have cheated you, my son, of everything that should have been yours. I cannot die without your forgiveness. Can you give me that, Christopher?"

His son, tall and strong and brave though he might be, drew a tremulous breath. His dark eyes glittered with unshed tears.

"With a full heart, Father," he answered softly. "You must not torture yourself with this any longer."

"When I die," the old man went on, "you will be Baron de Wilde. It is all I have left to leave you but it is a proud title, my finest possession, and not even King Charles could take it from me. Do it justice, my son. Honor, duty, these must be your watchwords."

"Father," Christopher pleaded, "rest now, I beg you. I forgive you everything. Now please, save your strength."

Exhausted, the old man lay back against the pillows and closed his eyes. He had no strength left to conserve. With every breath that left his body, he could feel his life ebbing away. Before the night was out, he knew, he would be dead and his son would be the new Baron de Wilde. He would leave to him nothing but an ancient, dishonored, title and this tiny cottage deep in the forest, a forest that had once belonged to him as master of Chatham Castle but now belonged to another.

Three days later, on the night of the old Baron's funeral, Christopher, now Lord de Wilde, led the torchlight procession to the ancient Norman church that dominated the village of Chatham. There, in the crypt, his father would be interred along with his ancestors whose effigies, some depicted in the chain-mail and armor of medieval times, nearly filled the crypt beneath the church they had built as lords of this region.

Christopher and the coffin were accompanied by the inhabitants of the village and the servants from the castle who, although now the minions of another lord, carried in their hearts a loyalty they had inherited from their ancestors just as Christopher and his father and his father before him had inherited the title of baron.

Afterward Christopher sat in the warm sitting room of the man who had been like a second father to him, his father's former head groom, a short, compact man whose diminutive stature belied a formidable strength.

NIGHTRIDER

Isaac had retained his position as head groom after Lord de Wilde's disgrace, had remained at Chatham Castle out of a concern for the excellent stables he had over years developed for his master. Those horses belonged to someone else now, to the new lord of Chatham, but in Isaac's mind and heart they were his children and he had to stay to see that they were well cared for.

Christopher did not consider Isaac's remaining at Chatham a betrayal of loyalty to his father or himself. Like Isaac, he had watched over the years the building of Chatham's stables into something special. Like Isaac, he knew all that work would be for nothing if the stables fell under the sway of a less competent man. And he knew, above all, that whomever Isaac worked for—whatever the title of Chatham's new master—Isaac's first, best loyalties would lie with the de Wilde family.

Now, in the low-ceilinged sitting room of the quarters Isaac occupied adjoining the stables of Chatham Castle, Christopher sipped a mug of ale and tried not to think of his father, lying in the darkness of that cold, damp crypt.

All evening long the inhabitants of the village and the servants still at Chatham Castle had trickled through Isaac's rooms. One by one, two by two, sometimes whole families, they had knelt before Christopher, had kissed his hand and sworn their allegiance to him, the new Lord de Wilde.

It was all highly improper, of course. Their allegiance should have been pledged to the new master of the castle, but they cared little for machinations, politics or the whims and grudges of the king. They were simple people who did not give their loyalties lightly and all they knew was that their ancestors had served Christopher's ancestors, that for generations they had looked to the Barons de Wilde for guidance and protection, and they would not easily abandon that tradition.

Eyes heavy with fatigue, Christopher drained his mug. He waved Isaac away as he would have refilled it.

"I should be going home," he said, his weariness apparent even in the tones of his voice.

"You are welcome to stay here tonight, milord," Isaac offered, thinking he might prefer to put off his return to the cottage where his father had so recently breathed his last.

Christopher shook his head. "Not you as well, my old friend. No 'milords' between us. Call me Kit as you always have."

The old groom smiled then groaned as yet another knock sounded on the door connecting his rooms with the stables.

"I thought we'd seen the last of them," he said, rising.

"So did I," Christopher agreed. "Well, let them in, Isaac. And then I'll be leaving."

The old groom opened the door and two

elderly women appeared. One, stooped, fingers gnarled with arthritis, leaned heavily on the supporting arm of the other.

Christopher gallantly rose as they entered. "Come, sit down, Mag, Kate," he invited.

"Oh, we couldn't, milord," the older, arthritic woman demurred for them both.

"I insist," Christopher told them, an edge of gentle command in his voice.

The two women obeyed and Christopher could see that there was more to their visit than simply wishing to pay their respects to the new Lord de Wilde. Their wrinkled cheeks were flushed, their eyes filled with worry. Old Mag's hand trembled as it gripped her companion's arm.

"Tell me," Christopher invited. "What has happened?"

"A letter came, my lord," Kate, once the personal maid of Christopher's mother, replied. "The new lord of Chatham, the Earl of Barthorp, died some weeks ago."

Christopher and Isaac exchanged a glance. The King had bestowed Chatham Castle, the village of the same name, and the forests surrounding both, upon the Earl of Barthorp who had remained loyal throughout the King's long exile following his father's death. If the Earl was dead, might it not be that the King would restore Chatham to Christopher? After all, it had been Christopher's father who had sided with the former King, not Christopher.

"Did he leave an heir?" Christopher asked urgently.

"Aye, milord," Mag, once a seamstress of renown whose arthritis had robbed her of her livelihood, replied. "A girl-child."

"A girl?" Isaac repeated.

"Aye."

"And?" Christopher prompted.

The two old women looked at one another, both reluctant to go on. Kate, at last, replied, "The King has bestowed her father's holdings upon her. She will inherit everything but his title."

Sighing, Christopher sagged in his chair. Everything, Chatham Castle, the village, the lands, now belonged to some mere slip of a girl.

"But that is not why we have come, my lord," Kate went on, a quaver in her voice.

"There is more?" Christopher asked, not at all sure he wanted to know.

Kate nodded, the lappets of her muslin cap bobbing on her bony shoulders. "The King has appointed a guardian for the girl. Sir Basil Holme. The letter was from his man of business. He is sending his own servants to Chatham. Only a few of us are to stay. Isaac"—she nodded toward the groom—"and a few others. The rest of us, Mag, me, most of the rest, are to pack our belongings and be out in two days' time." Tears shimmered in her tired old eyes. "We have nowhere to go, my lord. We have always lived in the castle. I have no family to take me in, nor has Mag. We'll starve, my lord. With winter here, we'll freeze like beasts in the field."

Christopher looked at their terrified faces and remembered the long years of faithful service both had given to his family. Leaning toward them, he took one of each of their hands in his own.

"You will not starve," he told them. "You will not freeze. I'll see that you, and all the others, have places to stay and are taken care of. Will you trust me for that?"

"Aye, milord," the two old women whispered, grateful and immeasurably relieved. "We'll tell the others."

They kissed his hands despite his efforts to stop them. Then they took their leave, their gratitude and relief almost painful to see.

When the door closed behind them, Christopher looked at Isaac. His disgust was plain in his chisled, handsome face.

"Just like that!" he muttered. "Get out! For years those two old women and all the others have worked faithfully! And with a letter they are cast out. They have nowhere to go, no one to care for them."

"Their years of faithful service were to the Baron de Wilde," Isaac reminded him. "Not to the Earl of Barthorp."

"Even so. What kind of person would be so

callous? I'd like to get my hands on this little heiress who thinks people are clothing, to be used until they are old and threadbare then discarded without a backward glance!"

"The letter came from the guardian," Isaac reminded him.

"She must have known. She must have approved." Christopher shook his head. "No, this little bitch cares nothing about these people. Doubtless she's been raised at the Court and thinks of nothing but gowns and jewels and her own wants and needs. I'd like to teach her a few things—"

"Whatever may be the truth of it," Isaac interrupted, "the fact remains that you have promised to provide for all the servants dismissed from the castle. How do you plan to do that?"

Christopher blew out his breath in a long, drawn-out sigh. "I did promise, didn't I?" He smiled a smile full of self-mockery. "Me, a lord without a castle, a baron who doesn't know where his own next meal is coming from." He turned to Isaac, his dark eyes shining with fierce determination. "But I will provide for them," he vowed. "I will keep my promise to them even if I have to beg, borrow, or steal the means. I will see that those people are cared for!"

Rising he went to lean on the fireplace where a small fire burned, banishing the winter chill from the chamber. "Chatham has belonged to my family for centuries, Isaac, and somehow, some way, I will get it back. I'll die before I let some careless chit ruin it. Someday, Isaac, the name de Wilde will be revered, honored, as it always was. And a de Wilde will once more be the lord of Chatham Castle!''

Chapter 1

The great black traveling coach jolted and swayed as it rolled through the gathering darkness falling over the cold, wintry countryside of Kent. Inside, swathed in blue velvet, a wolfskin lap robe tucked about her, Bliss rode in sullen silence.

Beside her, his presence and attempts at conversation stubbornly ignored, was Sir Basil. Bliss stole a furtive glance at him. Though nearly three weeks had passed since the night of the masked ball, she had not forgiven him for bursting in upon her and the viscount. Her cheeks burned with humiliation whenever she thought of it. Though she'd been struggling to get away from the viscount's groping hands, she'd felt like a chastised child when her guardian had ordered her to her room.

How could the King have sold her to such an ill-mannered, arrogant, unfeeling man? She thought wistfully of her father. A gentle, kindly man, he had spoiled his daughter, his only child, since her infancy as if to compensate for the loss of her mother in childbirth. But for all his gentleness, for all that he had always been happiest living a quiet life in the country away from the hustle and bustle of the court, the Earl was a passionate monarchist. He had distinguished himself fighting for the late, lamented Charles I and then for his son, Charles II. In return, the restored monarch had given him back the estates that Oliver Cromwell had confiscated—Barthorp Hall in Yorkshire and the London townhouse—and presented him as well with Chatham Castle, an ancient country estate dating from the Middle Ages nestled in the heart of Kent.

It was to Chatham Castle, long the ancestral home of the Barons de Wilde, that Bliss and her guardian journeyed. The first Baron de Wilde had come to England with the Conqueror six centuries before. The last Baron had sided with Cromwell and the Roundheads and so, upon the Restoration, had found himself dispossessed of his lands. Bliss had heard he had recently died, broken and penniless, the rich lands that had been in his family for so long given as a spoil of war to another.

Hearing the soft snore of the man beside her,

Bliss rolled her golden eyes heavenward. Sir Basil was not a cruel guardian, though he held very definite views as to the future of his pretty young ward. But Bliss resented his presence in her life. She was eighteen, she reasoned, surely old enough to see to her own affairs. But when Sir Basil bought her guardianship, he had secured control over all Bliss's affairs, including every detail of her personal life.

And so, Bliss reflected sourly, she found herself carted off into the depths of the country in the middle of winter to some strange, ancient castle. Chatham Castle, so she'd heard, had been left in the hands of servants since the former owner's disgrace. One wing of the sprawling building had been burned and was nothing more than an empty, tumbledown ruin. As for the rest, Sir Basil had sent his own servants ahead to clean and prepare for their arrival. She could only hope for the best.

Spying the lights of an inn glimmering in the darkness, Bliss realized how cold her fingers had grown in her fur-lined muff. Her toes inside her fur and velvet boots were nearly numb, the warmed bricks placed in the coach in London having long ago lost their heat.

"Might we not stop, sir?" she asked, nudging her guardian dozing beside her.

"Eh?" Sir Basil awakened with a frown. "What was that?"

"There is an inn ahead," Bliss told him, nodding toward the lights in the distance.

"Might we not stop? If not for the night, at least to warm—"

"No, no," Sir Basil interrupted, shaking his head. "It cannot be much farther now. We may as well drive on through."

Sighing, Bliss snuggled deeper under the lap robe that afforded precious little comfort against the biting cold. They would have reached the castle earlier had not a broken wheel cost them several hours of daylight. Now they had to travel after nightfall, a dangerous business given the number of highwaymen haunting the roads near London.

Bliss felt for the diamond-and-ruby brooch that fastened her blue velvet cloak. Her father had given it to her for her eighteenth birthday and she cherished it as his last gift to her. If they were so unlucky as to fall prey to a highwayman. . . .

As though her thoughts had invoked him, a man appeared astride a rearing horse. He blocked the road, forcing the coachman to haul at the reins and bring the coach to a rocking stop. Cloaked in the dark shadows of the overhanging branches, the highwayman brandished a horse pistol and ordered the trembling coachman down from the box.

"Everyone get out of the coach!" he shouted next. "Throw down your weapons!"

Fearfully, the coachman dropped a knife that was his only protection. The two footmen, having descended from their perch on the rear of the coach, meekly threw their own pistols to the ground in plain view of the robber.

Sir Basil, seeing that his cowardly lackeys had so easily surrendered, knew that for his own protection and Bliss's they, too, would have to descend and place themselves at the highwayman's mercy.

Bliss took her guardian's hand as she descended from the coach. The winter-chilled wind whipped at her tumbled red curls and she drew up the fur-lined hood of her velvet cloak.

Ignoring the coachman and lackeys who stood well behind their master and his ward, the highwayman went first to Sir Basil. Stripping several costly rings from his fingers, the highwayman helped himself as well to the emerald in the folds of Sir Basil's jabot. Holding his pistol in plain sight, the robber roughly searched Sir Basil's pockets and found the leather purse fat with gold.

Then he turned to Bliss. Her eyes were wide, more with fascination than fear, for she knew that few highwaymen killed their victims. Though robbery on the King's highway was punishable by hanging, a wily villain could often buy an acquittal if no one had been killed during his robberies.

The darkness of the night and the wide brim of his plumed hat hid the highwayman's face from his victims. Only a glint of dappled moonlight and the flickering light of the coachlamps showed Bliss the barest suggestion of a strong, square jaw and a sculpted column of a throat that disappeared into the turned-up collar of his billowing black cloak. Bliss trembled as a large, leather-gauntleted hand reached out and tipped her head back until her hood fell.

"Good evening, my beauty," he said, his voice low and smooth with a hint of steel. One fingertip stroked Bliss's cool, alabaster cheek. "All I'll claim from you is a kiss."

He leaned toward her. Bliss's heart pounded in her breast until she thought it must burst. But as his lips neared hers, as she felt the first warm wisp of his breath on her chilled skin, as her own lips quivered in unconscious anticipation, the highwayman swung away.

From the corner of his eye he had seen Sir Basil's tentative movement toward one of the pistols that lay on the ground. The highwayman brandished his own weapon in the older man's direction.

"That was a mistake," he told Sir Basil, moving warily toward his horse. Seeming never to take his eyes from Bliss's guardian, he swung himself up into the saddle. "I'd caution you not to touch those weapons until I'm well away, or else . . ."

"Or else?" Sir Basil growled. "Would you murder us, then, in cold blood?"

"Not at all," the highwayman assured him. "But if you try to shoot me, you might hit your pretty daughter here."

Spurring his horse forward, the highwayman

leaned from the saddle as he passed Bliss. One steely arm snaked about Bliss's waist and pulled her into the saddle. Before Sir Basil could move, before he could snatch up a pistol from the ground, the horseman and his precious burden disappeared into the all-enveloping darkness of the forest.

Bliss leaned back against the man who held her with an iron grip about her waist. The winter cold bit at her cheeks, the wind, whipping past them as they galloped through the forest, took her breath away. She closed her eyes, certain they must surely crash into the trees that grew so thickly there but the horse and rider seemed to know the forest with the certainty of some night-stalking beast of prey.

They were well away from the road and Sir Basil when the highwayman reined in the great, prancing horse and swung down to the snowy ground. Reaching up, he pulled Bliss from the horse and stood her on shaking legs before him.

Bliss trembled, not daring to look up at him. Sir Basil would not rescue her this time. She was completely at this man's mercy. "What," she asked tentatively, "will you do with me?"

"I mean you no harm," he assured her, his tones amused, as though he knew that visions of ravishment and murder must be dancing in her mind. "Look at me, my beauty."

Hesitantly, Bliss forced her eyes upward. The face above hers, illuminated by the silvery moonlight, was sharply planed, brutally handsome. The eyes, deep-set, were dark, shaded by arching brows.

His eyes moved slowly, lingeringly, over her face as his hands held her by the waist. "Gad," he breathed, "but you are beautiful."

The desire in his voice, his face, was plain to see and hear. Bliss trembled, drawing as far from him as she could. The sheer, powerful masculinity that seemed to emanate from him frightened her. "Please," she whispered, "don't . . ."

"I won't hurt you," he promised. "As I told you, sweetheart, all I want from you is a kiss."

Bliss gasped as he drew her hard against him. The force of his kiss, the savage, demanding plundering of her mouth by his sent her senses awhirl. Bliss felt as though only the strength of his arms about her kept her from falling. Her small, half-frozen hands pushed at his arms to no avail. She arched away but his body curved over her, his arms tightened, molding his body against her in an embrace that made her experience in the viscount's arms seem like the awkward dalliances of a schoolgirl.

When he released her, Bliss had to grasp at the folds of his cloak to keep from stumbling. She heard the low chuckle rumbling deep in his throat and flushed crimson with embarrassment.

"Easy, sweetheart," he said softly. "Tell me, where were you and your father bound?"

"He's not my father!" Bliss hissed. "My father

is dead. He is my guardian. And why should I tell you where we were bound?"

"Because then I can take you there. And you will be safe and warm, when he arrives."

"Oh." Bliss was a mass of conflicting emotions. She was freezing, her fur-lined leather boots were no match for the snow, and her cloak, though full and warm, could not protect her from the night's chill. On the other hand, she had never had an adventure like this and she was loath to see it end.

Seeing that he was waiting for her answer, Bliss told him: "We were bound for Chatham Castle."

The highwayman started visibly. "Chatham! Then you must be . . ."

"Bliss," she told him. "Lady Bliss Paynter, daughter of the late Earl of Barthorp."

The chill of the night was nothing compared to the ice that suddenly glinted in the highwayman's dark eyes.

"Come then, my lady," he snarled. "We must get you to your castle, mustn't we?"

Bliss found herself being nearly dragged to the highwayman's horse that waited nearby. He pulled her roughly into the saddle before him and kicked the horse into a gallop.

As they rode silently through the forest, Bliss could feel the anger radiating from the man who held her. She was confused. He had called her beautiful, he had kissed her. She knew he desired her. But then, like lightning, all that admiration, all that desire, had vanished and been replaced by such bitter dislike that Bliss feared for her safety.

After what seemed an eternity, they emerged from the forest. A great castle loomed before them, its crenellated walls and tall, hexagonal towers rising toward the wintry night sky.

The highwayman reined in his mount and set Bliss down on the ground. "There you are, milady," he said coldly. "Go to the gate. The gatekeeper will let you in. Just tell him you are mistress of the castle."

Bliss opened her mouth to reply but it was too late. With a flick of the reins, the highwayman's horse leapt forward and disappeared back into the all-concealing depths of the forest.

Confused and upset, Bliss pulled her cloak tighter and made her way to the gatehouse. She did not understand what had happened; her mind was full of questions. But the darkness and the cold drove her toward the lights of the castle and the warmth they promised.

Ushered through the arched stone gateway where a spiked portcullis was raised to allow her entry, Bliss found herself in the central courtyard. Around her, the walls of Chatham Castle shone silver in the moonlight. Its many towers rose in stark silhouette against the black sky.

The footmen posted at the door admitted
Bliss, their surprise at her arrival unconcealed.
She was led into an anteroom where the arms
and pennants and ancient family armor of the
Barons de Wilde had been replaced by those of
the Earls of Barthorp.

A maid relieved her of her cloak, another
knelt to remove her snow-caked, fur-lined boots
and replace them with slippers warmed by the
hearth. Mrs. Lonsdale, the housekeeper who
had worked for Bliss's father, came to press a
mug of mulled wine into her young mistress's
hands.

"Where is Lord Holme?" Mrs. Lonsdale
asked, leading Bliss into a small chamber where
a fire blazed in a peaked stone fireplace.

Wearily Bliss sank into a chair. "The coach
broke a wheel," she told the woman who had
raised her after her mother's death. "And then
we were . . . were . . ."

Bliss's eyes filled with tears and she set aside
her wine. Mrs. Lonsdale held out a handkerchief
and Bliss took it and dabbed at her eyes.

"Oh, my darling child," the older woman
murmured, "what can it be?"

"A highwayman," Bliss managed. "He
stopped us on the road."

"Did he hurt you?" the housekeeper demanded, her grey-blue eyes swiftly skimming
Bliss from head to toe. "He did not . . . harm
you?"

Bliss shook her head. "He took me away from Sir Basil. He pulled me onto his horse and we rode into the forest. He—" Bliss felt her cheeks flushing. Her voice dropped to a near whisper. "He kissed me."

"The blackguard!" Mrs. Lonsdale hissed.

"And then he brought me here and left me at the gate," Bliss finished.

Mrs. Lonsdale made a face. "This would not have happened had you not been traveling at night. Why did Lord Holme not stop at an inn after the coach wheel broke?" She did not wait for Bliss to answer but grumbled, "Too miserly to pay for a night's lodging, doubtless."

Bliss said nothing aloud. Except for Mrs. Lonsdale and a few others who had survived the purge of Lord de Wilde's faithful servants, the staff at Chatham Castle were servants of her guardian. Bliss wanted no disparaging remark to reach his ears and perhaps make an already unpleasant situation even worse. But in the privacy of her own thoughts she could not have agreed more.

"Sir Basil should be along soon," she told Louise Lonsdale. "I think I'll go up to bed before he gets here. You can assure him I am safe and unharmed. Is my room prepared?"

"It has been for days, my sweet," the housekeeper told her. "Since your baggage arrived from London. 'Tis the best room in the castle— Lord de Wilde's own, I'm told. If only the windows did not face the west wing."

"What is wrong with the west wing?" Bliss wanted to know.

"'Twas burned, by Royalists, during the war."

"Ah." Bliss nodded. "I'd heard that part of the castle was in ruins. I did not notice it when I came into the courtyard."

"The walls are still standing," Mrs. Lonsdale clucked disapprovingly. "The old banqueting hall, so I'm told. It should be pulled down before it falls."

"I'll speak to Sir Basil about it," Bliss decided. "If it's dangerous, it should be—"

"So you're here!" Sir Basil had arrived. He seemed to fill the small, cozy chamber where Bliss had taken refuge. "Did that varlet lay—"

"He did nothing to harm me," Bliss informed him quickly. "He only used me to shield himself in case you fired. He brought me to the castle gate and left me."

Sir Basil smacked a fist into the palm of his hand. "By God, I'll see that bastard on a gibbet on Tyburn Hill, damme if I don't! I'll show him he can't steal Basil Holme's gold and get away with it!"

Weary, Bliss bade her guardian good night and, accompanied by her housekeeper and friend, made her way up the ornately carved staircase to her room. A maidservant waited there to help her out of her clothes and into her nightrail. Bliss dismissed her with a wave of her hand and lay back against the pillows of the great tester bed.

Sighing, she let sleep overtake her and soon found herself in a world of dreams—restless, troubling dreams of a handsome, powerful man who seemed to desire her and detest her with equal fervor.

Chapter 2

The chill morning air raised gooseflesh on Bliss's bare arms as she pushed back the heavy velvet coverlet on the tester bed whose hangings still bore the elaborate coat of arms of the previous occupant, the late Baron de Wilde. Though a servant had crept into the chamber while Bliss slept and built up the fire in the ancient carved stone fireplace, the flames did little to warm the cavernous chamber.

The furnishings of the room were exquisitely carved, and the old tapestries covering the stone walls were beautiful creations worked by generations of de Wilde women. Thick carpets lay on the flagstone floor. The candelabra placed here and there were tall and ornate, mostly of silver, though Bliss suspected that a pair atop the mantel were of gold for they bore the royal cipher of Henry VIII and seemed to be presentation pieces, a reward for some long-ago service to the King.

Bliss remembered that the old Baron de Wilde had died a broken man, having seen the lands, the castle, and all its beautiful contents stripped away as a punishment for his stand against Charles I. Looking at the beauty that surrounded her, admiring it, calculating its worth, she could understand how the loss of so many centuries' accumulation of family treasures could take the heart and soul out of any person. She felt a twinge of guilt as she sat there on the edge of the bed. Her father had been given all of this, handed over to him as a reward for being on the right side in the dispute between Royalist and Roundhead. King Charles II, the so-called merry monarch, was not above wreaking vengeance on those who had helped bring about the downfall and death of the father whose memory he revered.

The muffled sound of shouts caught Bliss's attention. Pulling a fur-trimmed mantle over her nightrail, she slid her feet into high-heeled mules and went to the oriel window overlooking the courtyard.

With a fist she scrubbed away the frost etched on the diamond panes. Peering down, she saw Sir Basil's traveling coach drawn up before the door. The horses were shifting restlessly in the traces, the coachman and postillions were stamping their booted feet, impatiently awaiting the descent of their master.

Whirling away from the window, Bliss fled from her room. She ran to the curving stone staircase that led to the great hall below. There she saw, as she neared the bottom, Sir Basil giving last-minute instructions to the servants.

He turned, hearing the clatter of her heels on the stone stairs. A glimmer of some indefinable emotion flickered in his deep-set eyes as he saw her there, her red hair tumbled in glistening disarray, her cheeks flushed with the cold.

"Ah, Bliss," he said, drawing leather gauntlets onto his hands and tugging their wide cuffs over the cuffs of his heavy coat. "I thought you were still asleep."

"The noise in the courtyard woke me," she told him. "Why did you not send someone to waken me earlier?"

"Why?" he asked, his dark brows drawing close over his eyes.

"So I could make ready," she replied. "I can hardly leave like this." She plucked at the heavy velvet of her mantle.

"You are not leaving," he told her bluntly. "I am returning to London, but you are to remain here."

"Here!" The color drained from Bliss's cold cheeks. "Surely not!"

"Do you dislike the castle?" her guardian asked, his tone not concerned but merely curious. "It seems perfectly well appointed to me.

Not the height of London fashion, perhaps, but—"

"The castle is fine," Bliss interrupted, "but I don't see why I must remain behind while you return to London."

"The court is no place for a gently bred young heiress," he answered, not bothering to hide his impatience to be on his way. "There is always the danger that some disappointed suitor will take matters into his own hands and abduct you. Your reputation would be ruined and with it all chance of making the brilliant match I intend to arrange for you."

"But if you mean to look for a husband for me," Bliss reasoned, "should I not be there?"

"To what end?" Sir Basil snapped. "You must know I would not consider anyone unsuitable."

Bliss bit back a sharp retort. "Do you not think," she asked, each word clipped and hard, "that gentlemen interested in courting me might wish to meet me before offering for my hand?"

Chuckling, Sir Basil clapped his hat onto his head. "My dear, look about you. This castle and the treasures it houses are but a fraction of the inheritance your father left you. With your wealth you could be a toothless hag and still have men dueling over you."

His laughter echoed among the intricate tracery that crisscrossed the vaulted ceiling of the great hall. Bliss stood there, frozen to the spot, staring after him, her hands clenched into white-knuckled fists. To think that her future, her fate, lay in the hands of that insensitive boor!

She glanced around suddenly aware that the servants Sir Basil had been lecturing still surrounded her. "Go back to your work," she told them softly, embarrassed that they should have witnessed the conversation.

They turned to leave and Bliss spotted her maid, Mercy, among them.

"Mercy," Bliss called. The girl returned and curtsied before her. "I want a bath. Have water brought to my rooms."

The maid hurried to obey as Mrs. Lonsdale appeared, coming to her mistress. "Will you have something to eat, child?" she asked solicitously.

Bliss shook her head. "Nothing," she said shortly. "I've no appetite." The sound of hooves and coach wheels leaving the courtyard brought an angry flush to her cheeks. "I'll tell you something," she said tersely, her golden eyes blazing on the startled housekeeper. "I'll not marry some well-bred buffoon nor some doddering old duke just to satisfy that villain! 'Suitable' or no, I'll not marry a man I cannot love, however much my guardian wants the match!"

Turning in a swirl of fur and velvet, Bliss stalked off toward the stairs. Louise Lonsdale watched her, love and concern in her eyes. She realized that Sir Basil considered his ward an empty-headed child to be disposed of as he saw fit, but she knew better. There was steel beneath that cloud of titian hair and alabaster skin—that red and golden beauty masked a will of iron, a stubbornness that occasionally drove Bliss to recklessness. If Sir Basil were not such a self-important fool he would have seen it. Just let him arrive at Chatham Castle with the wrong suitor in tow and he would see a side of young Lady Bliss he'd never suspected existed!

Bliss brooded for days over Sir Basil's decision to return to London while she remained at Chatham. In the dark privacy of her velvet-hung bed she railed at the injustice of it all. She was eighteen—had she been born male she would have succeeded to her father's title upon his death. She would have been Earl of Barthorp with full rights of ownership over her inheritance. But because she was female she could not inherit the title. And the lands and riches that made her such a desirable wife were controlled by her guardian, held in trust for the day when she would wed and her fortune would become the property of whatever titled fool Sir Basil married her to.

Yet even as she lay there she knew it was futile to curse her fate. It was the way of the world. And, to be fair, she was more fortunate than some, she knew. Stories abounded of aged and greedy guardians who married their young wards to possess their fortunes. At least Sir Basil, for all his insensitivity, harbored no such avaricious ambitions.

Sighing, Bliss rolled over and pulled the covers up tight under her chin. She hoped, as she drifted off to sleep, that things would work out for the best—it had become almost a ritual, replacing her bedtime prayers—and she would not allow herself to consider that she might, in the end, be disappointed.

The air was crisp and cold the next morning. The sun shone in a sky of pale blue and illuminated the intricate, feathery patterns of frost on Bliss's windowpanes. The snow that had blanketed the ground during the night glistened, sparkling like diamond dust on the silvery stones of the castle walls.

Tired of languishing indoors, Bliss wrapped herself in heavy fur and ventured out to explore the castle that was now her home. In particular she wanted to examine the eerily beautiful ruins of the west wing.

Leaving the courtyard through the arched stone gateway, Bliss picked her way around the tumbled rubble half-buried at the base of the soaring walls. The tall lancet windows were empty, the lead and wooden tracery that had once held their diamond panes having been destroyed in the heat of the fire. The beautiful wooden vaulting had burned and collapsed—only charred timbers, burned pendants and blackened braces remained, littering the floor of what must once have been a magnificent chamber.

Amidst the rubble Bliss saw the glitter of ruby glass. Brushing away the dirt and ashes, she picked up a piece of what appeared to have once been a window containing the de Wilde coat of arms. A rampant lion, exquisite in gold, reared in a square of blood-red glass. Bliss laid the pane back among the ruins. It was sad to contemplate the downfall of such a proud, ancient, and noble family. Old Lord de Wilde had stood up for his beliefs and his principles and had lost everything.

Moving on, Bliss spied the octagonal tower at the far corner of the wing. The castle's towers, rising a story higher than the outer walls, stood one at each corner with another pair flanking the main gate. All of them opened onto the interior of the castle. All, that is, but this one. An iron-banded, rough-planked door opened toward the forest that grew nearly to the base of the castle's rear walls.

Curious, Bliss made her way to it. The door was weathered, the iron rusted. She stretched out a hand toward the latch.

" 'Tis not safe, milady," a soft masculine voice warned from behind her.

Bliss gasped. Whirling around, she found a short, elderly man in rough working clothes standing beside her.

He jerked his head toward the tower. " 'Tis not safe," he repeated. "You should not go in there."

"Who are you?" Bliss demanded.

"Isaac, milady," he replied. "I am the head

groom." He looked again at the tower's door. "The floors be burned through, milady, and the stairs have crumbled. You could fall."

Bliss frowned. "The wing should be pulled down. And the tower. They could fall. They could—"

The curt shake of the old man's head silenced her. "They won't fall. The walls are strong. 'Tis the timbers that are burnt. The wing—and the tower—could be restored." His pale blue eyes took on a distant, wistful look. "'Twas beautiful once."

"Were you here then?" Bliss asked. "Before the fire?"

"Aye, milady," he confirmed. "I was born here, at the castle. I wanted to stay. After the others were sent away."

"The others," Bliss told him, repeating what Sir Basil had told her, "refused to swear allegiance to me."

"Some don't give their loyalty lightly, milady," he told her.

"But you do?" she asked.

The old man shrugged. "The castle is my home. I know no other."

Bliss looked up at the high, silver-gray walls. "So you knew Lord de Wilde, did you?"

"Aye, milady, that I did. A fine gentleman. A man of honor."

Bliss imagined she saw a glimmer of disapproval in the old man's eyes. He had seen his former master, a man he obviously admired, cast out of his ancestral home. He must view her as an interloper.

"It was very sad," she murmured, not knowing what else to say.

Isaac shrugged. "Fortunes of war, milady," he replied.

"I suppose so," she acknowledged. Feeling awkward, she rubbed her gloved hands together. "I think I'll go in now. It's very cold."

"Aye, milady, that it is," the groom agreed.

With a small, uncertain smile, Bliss turned and retraced her steps along the base of the castle wall. She did not look back as she went; she did not see that Isaac had entered the very tower he'd warned her away from.

That night as she was preparing for bed, Bliss stood before the oriel window of the bedchamber. Absently she drew an ivory-backed brush through the cascading titian curls that fell nearly to her waist. Outside the moon was bright. It bathed the castle in its silvery light, making it shine with an almost unearthly glow.

She was about to turn away when a movement caught her eye. A shadowy figure moved among the ruins of the opposite wing. The moonglow threw deep shadows into the hollow, ruined banqueting hall, and Bliss strained to see who could be there, moving so surely, so confidently among the treacherous rubble of the burnt-out wing across the courtyard.

A light tap on the door was followed by the

appearance of Bliss's maid, Mercy. The girl, daughter of a family who lived in the nearby village of Chatham which belonged to the master of Chatham Castle, bobbed a curtsy and awaited her mistress's orders.

"Mercy," Bliss said urgently, her eyes leaving the opposite wing for the briefest of moments. "Come here."

She looked back as the maid joined her. But across the courtyard there now was nothing, no shadowy form, no movement, no sign of life.

"What is it, milady?" the girl asked.

Sighing, Bliss turned away. "I saw something —someone—moving among the ruins. I'm certain of it!"

"They do say . . ." the girl began, then stopped.

"What do they say?" Bliss prompted.

"They say the wing is haunted, milady," the maid replied. "Haunted by the ghost of himself —Milord de Wilde." The maid's pretty, dark eyes widened. "They say he cannot rest until Chatham Castle's re—" She broke off, her gaze falling in mortification.

"Until the castle is once more in de Wilde hands?" Bliss finished for her.

Chagrined, the girl nodded. "Forgive me, milady, I should not have told you.

Bliss shook her head. Releasing the velvet draperies from their golden hooks, she let them fall across the towering window. "It's all right," she told the maid. "I shouldn't be surprised if people hereabouts say such things. They were very loyal to old Lord de Wilde, weren't they?"

"Aye, milady, they were," Mercy confirmed.

"That will be all," Bliss told her. "You may go."

The girl bobbed another curtsy and turned to leave. Behind her, Bliss drew aside the drapery once more and gazed out at the gaping, empty windows of the ruined wing. It was as still, as silent, as . . . she shuddered at the thought . . . as the grave.

Bliss felt icy fingers snaking along her spine making her shiver. Was it possible, she wondered, that the Baron de Wilde's unquiet spirit really did roam the ancestral home that had been taken from his family?

"You're imagining things," she told herself sternly as she made ready to go to bed.

But even as she comforted herself with that thought, she left one candle burning to dispel the shadows in the bedchamber that had once belonged to the dead Baron de Wilde.

Chapter 3

It was after midnight when Mercy shook Bliss awake. "Milady!" she cried. "Please, you must get up!"

Yawning, Bliss pushed back a lock of her red hair and looked up at the maid who stood over her clad in her nightrail. Mercy's own dark hair was disheveled, hanging down her back. It was evident that she, too, had been abruptly roused from her bed.

"What is it, Mercy?" Bliss demanded. "Is the castle afire?"

"No, milady. There's three travelers below. They're asking for shelter. They say they've walked ever so far."

"At this hour? How do they look? What sort of

people do they seem to be?"

"They're very elegant, milady. They told Mrs. Lonsdale their name was Villiers. Lady . . ." The maid frowned. "I don't remember her first name, but—"

"Villiers? Good God. Run down, Mercy, and tell Mrs. Lonsdale to make them welcome. Say I'll be down in a moment."

The maid left and Bliss threw back the coverlet and felt on the floor for her mules. If they were members of the Villiers family they could well be related to both the Duke of Buckingham —the King's boon companion and one of the most powerful men in England—and the Countess of Castlemaine—the foremost of the King's many mistresses. It would not be wise to turn their relatives out into the cold—or to keep them waiting.

Pulling a dressing gown over her nightrail, Bliss took only enough time to brush out her tumble of red curls before she left the relative warmth of her room and went to meet her unexpected guests.

The three of them stood huddled around the gaping fireplace in the great hall, their hands outstretched toward a fire that had been hurriedly kindled. There were two women—one middle-aged and one about Bliss's own age— and a gentleman. All three were dressed richly, their silks and velvets of excellent quality, sumptuously embroidered and edged in fur, frothed with heavy cream lace. It was apparent at a glance they were people of breeding and consequence, and Bliss wished they had arrived at a time when she could meet them as chatelaine of the castle rather than as a young woman dragged from her warm bed in the middle of a cold winter's night.

The gentleman noticed her first. He was tall and broad-shouldered with thick, light brown hair that fell in luxuriant waves to his shoulders. He was dressed in royal blue velvet edged with heavy lace shot through with golden threads that caught the firelight and glittered as he moved. He smiled as Bliss appeared in the doorway, his full lips parting over glistening teeth. With the sweep of one lace-frothed hand, he bowed to her as grandly as if they had met in a Whitehall gallery rather than the draughty hall of a winter-shrouded country castle.

"I must beg your pardon on behalf of my mother, my sister, and myself," he told her. "You are no doubt unaccustomed to such inopportune arrivals."

"You are welcome, all of you," Bliss told him, smiling at the two women who turned toward her. "I am Lady Bliss Paynter. This is Chatham Castle."

"I am Stephen, Lord Villiers," he replied. "These ladies are my sister, Letitia, and my mother, Lady Daphne Villiers."

Bliss curtsied to the elder of the women. They

were remarkably alike, the mother and daughter. Slender, they had the same light brown hair as Stephen, but their narrow faces had a brittle, feline quality. Their green eyes slanted, with a calculating, cold, haughty expression that spoiled their chances of being called beautiful.

Bliss invited them into the small anteroom where the fire just kindled in the hearth did more to blunt the biting cold than the blaze in the cavernous hall. A servant entered with mugs of mulled wine and a quickly assembled platter of cheese, cold meats, and bread.

"Tell me," Bliss said when they had all been seated and served, "how did you come to be stranded on such a cold, wintry night?"

"We were robbed!" Letitia Villiers cried. "What is the world coming to when honest people cannot travel without risking their very lives?"

"I hardly think our lives were in danger," Stephen corrected, casting his sister an impatient look. He turned his attention to Bliss. "We were stopped by a highwayman. The wretch took what he wanted from us and rode away. I took up a pistol and shot at him. Our coach horses were frightened. They bolted. The coach overturned; one horse had to be shot. The others scattered after the traces broke. With no way to right the coach and no horses to pull it, I'm afraid we had no choice but to seek shelter for the night. I can't tell you what a relief it was to see lights and smoke rising from the chimneys here."

"In the morning I will send men out to see to your coach and to find your horses," Bliss told them. "The most important thing is that you are all safe and uninjured."

"I doubt that villain of a highwayman can say the same," Lady Daphne sniffed, examining a piece of cheese as though unable to decide if it was edible. "My son is too modest. He told you he shot at the varlet; he did not tell you he hit him."

"Indeed I did," Stephen confirmed, obviously pleased. "I'm certain of it."

"I hope he's lying somewhere in the cold, bleeding his life away!" Letitia hissed.

Bliss could not suppress a shudder at the thought of such a gruesome, lingering death. She wondered if the highwayman who had robbed them was the same man who had taken her into the forest and kissed her. Though the thought of him evoked troubling memories, she could not help hoping Stephen Villiers had not hit him after all.

"I was surprised," Lady Daphne was saying, "to find the mistress of the castle at home. Most of the great country houses are closed at this time of year. All the fashionable world is in London for the winter."

"I'm certain they are," Bliss agreed, feeling a budding dislike for the dowager Lady Villiers. "I should be there as well, but my guardian bade me stay here."

"Your guardian?" Stephen asked.

"Sir Basil Holme. He became my guardian after my father's death."

"And who was your father?" Lady Daphne asked pointedly.

"The Earl of Barthorp," Bliss replied.

"You have no relations to see to your well-being?"

Bliss shook her head. "None. I am the last of my family."

"The Earl of Barthorp," the handsome Lord Villiers mused. "Surely your country seat is to the north."

"Yorkshire," Bliss agreed. "Barthorp Hall is there. But Lord Holme considered it too far from London. The King gave my father Chatham Castle and its lands."

Bliss did not miss the furtive look that passed from Lady Daphne to her son. Their minds were working in tandem, clicking like abaci, working out an estimate of the wealth inherited by the red-haired beauty in whose home a quirk of fate had landed them.

"Surely you are betrothed?" Lady Daphne asked, none too subtly.

"I am not," Bliss replied. "My guardian is even now in London seeing to the choosing of a husband for me."

Her visitors let the subject drop, but Bliss

knew she had not heard the last of it. Nor, she suspected, would she have seen the last of them when the Villierses took their leave of Chatham Castle.

At first light a party of men was dispatched to see to the Villierses' coach. When Bliss came down to the dining room she found Stephen alone seated at the end of the long table—in the great carved chair reserved for the lord of the manor—enjoying a hearty breakfast.

He rose when Bliss appeared. His green eyes swept from the top of her head—where her red hair was piled up and threaded with heather-blue ribbons—to the tips of the blue brocaded shoes that peeped from beneath her rippling blue skirts and white quilted silk petticoat.

"You must allow me to tell you," he said as she sat down not far from him, "that you are even lovelier now than you were last night. Though I'd hardly have thought that possible."

Bliss murmured her thanks. She thought: His mother has spoken to him. Court this young heiress, she'd doubtless told him. She may well be a prime candidate to be the next Lady Villiers.

And what, Bliss wondered, would Sir Basil think of such a match? It depended. Certainly a mere baronet was hardly a brilliant match for the daughter and only heir of a rich earl. Still . . .

She waited until she had been served her own breakfast, then asked:

"Tell me, sir. Are you perhaps related to the Duke of Buckingham or my Lady Castlemaine?"

"We are," Stephen confirmed with unmistakable satisfaction. "We are cousins—second cousins. I am happy to say both His Grace and her ladyship favor us with their friendship and interest.

That clinched it, Bliss knew. Stephen, Lord Villiers, might be a mere baronet but his ties to the two most powerful people at court would make him the favorite in Sir Basil's eyes. For after all, if Bliss were ensconced in the bosom of the illustrious Villiers clan, what benefits might not Sir Basil reap for bringing such a fortune into the hands of such a notoriously avaricious family?

There was a rustling in the hall and Lady Daphne swept into the room with her daughter Letitia in her wake. She smiled her tight, curiously condescending smile at Bliss and took her place at the table gesturing impatiently for her daughter to do the same.

"Well, now," she said, motioning for the footman standing near the buffet to bring her her breakfast. "Have you spoken to her yet?"

"Not yet, Mother," Stephen replied tightly. "I was about to . . ."

"No point in dallying," she interrupted. "Surely it will not be unexpected." She turned her light green eyes on her young hostess. "My son intends to seek out your guardian when we return to London, my dear. Will his suit be well received, do you think?"

"This seems very hasty, madam," Bliss said, flushing. "Lord Villiers and I hardly know—"

"Come now, child," Lady Villiers broke in. "I think we can dispense with all this maidenly modesty. What I am asking is: How would your guardian receive such an offer?"

Bliss gazed at her. That was the real question. How would Sir Basil receive it. It did not matter how Bliss felt about the marriage. In the end it would be arranged between Sir Basil and this hard-eyed, haughty woman.

"I'm certain Sir Basil would find such a match worthy of consideration," she said honestly. "But you realize, my lady, that I would need to become better acquainted with any man my guardian put forward before I could—"

"Of course, my dear," the older woman said quickly, a complaisant smile on her narrow lips. It was clear she had no doubt that Bliss, like her own children, would do as she was told in the end.

Bliss bit back the words that sprang to her lips. She had vowed she would not marry a man she could not love, and she did not care what schemes and plans Lady Villiers might hatch with Sir Basil—she intended to keep her vow!

* * *

NIGHTRIDER

Bliss was far from displeased when her servants came back with both the Villierses' coach and their three surviving horses. The coach had suffered no irreparable damage in overturning, and Bliss was only too happy to lend them a horse to complete the team that would take them away from Chatham Castle and out of her sight.

Wrapped in velvet and fur, Bliss stood near the gateway of the castle watching as the repaired coach grew smaller and smaller, disappearing into the distance. She breathed a sigh of relief. Lady Daphne had not endeared herself to her hostess—she had roamed from room to room with an appraising eye as though calculating Bliss's worth by the value of the castle's furnishings. Letitia, though saying little, had eyed the jewels and sumptuous gown Bliss wore, and Bliss had the uncomfortable notion that the girl was imagining the riches that would be theirs once Bliss's fortune lay securely in the family's coffers.

As for Stephen, Lord Villiers, he was undeniably handsome, but it was clear he thought himself a cut above all others because of his relationship to the Duke of Buckingham and Lady Castlemaine. He might be a courtly suitor, he might dance attendance on a girl and woo her with sweet words and wistful kisses, but Bliss had the impression that one crossed him at one's peril.

71

Sandra DuBay

Pulling the hood of her rose velvet cloak up over her head and burrowing her hands deep inside the silk-lined depths of her fur muff, Bliss wandered awhile in the park that surrounded the castle. The forest was near—occasionally a skittish doe or a proud, beautiful stag wandered into the open and stood for a moment before bounding off into its woodland home. Before Bliss realized where she was, she had walked into the edge of the forest, moving toward the tower at the back of the ruined banqueting hall.

Kicking at the fluffy snow as she walked, Bliss watched it fall, glittering, in her path. The snow was pristine, unmarked here, fresh and new, and . . .

It was the hoofmarks marring the snow that first caught Bliss's attention. They trailed toward the castle, the prints of a single horse. Bliss followed them until suddenly she saw a splotch of crimson marring the pure, shimmering white.

Bliss gasped. Hurrying forward, she found another stain, and another. Whoever had ridden the horse, whoever had come toward the castle in the night, had been bleeding. With her eyes Bliss followed the trail toward the castle. It led . . .

She stepped quickly behind the thick trunk of an ancient oak. The door of the tower—the same tower she'd been warned not to enter—was opening.

72

NIGHTRIDER

As she watched, Isaac, the old head groom, appeared. He carried a bundle of rags and a pail of steaming water. Glancing around, he put down the rags and poured out the bucket, sending a stream of pink-tinged water over the snowy ground. Then, collecting his rags, he stuffed them into the now-empty pail and set off.

Bliss waited until he was out of sight, then went quickly to the tower. The ground where he had poured the water was bare now—the warm water had melted the frosting of snow. Only a circle of wet brown earth remained.

Bliss glanced toward the front of the castle. There was no one. She tried the latch of the tower door. It gave beneath her hand and she pushed the door open and stepped inside.

Arrow slits in the thick stone walls afforded a weak grey light that allowed her to see. The chamber was strewn with straw. A horse, a tall, powerful roan stallion, eyed her warily as she edged past it and began to climb the narrow, twisting stone steps that snaked up the opposite wall.

Bliss climbed carefully. There was no rail, no balustrade. One false step would send her tumbling toward the flagstone floor so far below. She looked up toward the top of the stairs— toward the landing and the door leading off it. Whatever was there—whatever secret Isaac had tried to protect—would be revealed in a matter of moments.

At the top of the stairs Bliss paused, pressing a hand to her pounding heart. She reached out toward the doorlatch, hesitated, then pressed it down. The door swung open soundlessly on greased hinges.

Before her Bliss saw a dimly lit octagonal chamber—the top of the tower. It was furnished sparsely, lit by a single candle. The windows, little more than slits to allow for the defense of the castle, had been blocked up. The heat in the room, meager as it was, came from a brazier in the middle of the stone floor.

A bed stood against one wall—a narrow four-poster whose threadbare brocade hangings were drawn against the chill. They were parted slightly on the side toward the brazier to catch whatever warmth there was. On a table flanked by a pair of rickety chairs lay the remains of a meal and a half bottle of wine.

Slowly, uncertainly, Bliss moved toward the bed. She stopped once, alarmed, as she saw the slight movement of the curtains. Someone was there, in that bed, listening to her footsteps, waiting for her approach. But who? And why?

Steeling her resolve, reminding herself that she was, after all, mistress of the castle with the right to know who was making a home in the unused tower, Bliss strode forward and threw back the draperies at the foot of the bed.

A little scream escaped her. She fell back a step, a hand raised to her throat, as she found herself staring down the gaping bore of a horse pistol held in the hand of the highwayman who had stolen her, taken her into the forest, kissed her, and who had haunted her dreams ever since.

Chapter 4

Bliss fell back a step, one delicate gloved hand raised to her throat. Her gaze was riveted on the gaping black bore of the pistol aimed at her face.

"You," the man in the bed breathed, his voice low and harsh. The pistol wavered in his hand, then fell to his side. "How did you find me here?"

"There was blood," Bliss replied, her wits returning now that the weapon was no longer poised before her. "On the snow outside. And hoofprints leading to the tower. Then I saw Isaac leaving the tower."

Sighing, his eyes closing as though overcome with fatigue, the man lay back on the pillows. His hair was thick and dark, a rich deep brown against the creamy pillowcase. His eyes, when he reopened them and fixed them on Bliss's face, were the color of fine mahogany. An unhealthy pallor had replaced the sun-burnished tones of his skin and a sheen of perspiration moistened his face.

He started, eying Bliss suspiciously when she stripped off her glove and laid a hand against his forehead.

"You have a fever," she said softly, feeling the heat of his dampened skin.

He shifted in the narrow bed, and Bliss saw the edge of a bandage wound around his lower chest.

"Stephen wasn't lying," she said, more to herself than to him. "He really did shoot you."

"Stephen?" the wounded man asked, slitting his eyes to look at her.

"Lord Villiers. He and his mother and sister came to the castle last night. He said they'd been robbed but that he'd shot the highwayman. He was certain he'd hit his mark."

"So he did," the man admitted, swallowing painfully, "damn his eyes!"

Bliss looked around. A jug of water stood on the table and beside it a cracked mug. Tossing her gloves onto the table, Bliss filled the mug and took it to him.

"Drink some of this," she told him.

The highwayman struggled to rise, wincing with the effort. His hand, large, rough, and callused, touched hers as he steadied the mug and drank thirstily.

"I thank you," he breathed, obviously taxed by the effort.

"You're very ill," she observed. "A doctor should be brought."

"No," the man interrupted. "The fever will pass. Isaac will tend the wound." He scowled. "It's so damnably hot in here."

Bliss had thought the air chilly but she knew his fever must make even the meager heat of the brazier seem like an inferno. Bliss took out her handkerchief and soaked it with the water that remained in the mug. Kneeling beside the bed, she gently wiped the sweat from the highwayman's fevered brow.

A shiver coursed through him as the cool water bathed his heated skin. His dark eyes searched her face as though he were wondering what could have prompted her kindness.

"Who are you?" Bliss asked, averting her eyes. His steadfast gaze discomfited her.

"Kit," he told her. "Kit Quinn." Bliss started to say something, but he went on: "What will you do—my lady?"

"Do?" Bliss countered.

"Will you send for your guardian? Will you tell him a criminal has taken refuge beneath your roof?"

"My guardian is in London," Bliss answered evasively.

"The castle is filled with his retainers. Or you could send for a magistrate."

Rising from his bedside, Bliss replaced the

mug on the table. She felt a glimmer of the emotion she'd felt on the night they'd met—the night when he'd carried her off into the forest. There was an edge to his voice, a glint of dislike in his eyes she did not understand.

"You would be hanged," she pointed out, turning back toward the bed. "Do you think I would willingly send a man to his death on the gallows?"

A sardonic smile quirked Kit Quinn's full lips. "Why not?" he demanded. "What does a man's life signify to the daughter of the Earl of Barthorp?"

"Explain yourself!" she demanded, bristling at the mention of her beloved father's name.

"This house," he replied. "Its contents. Your father did not mind taking them. He did not care that their loss broke a once-proud man and drove him to a despair so deep he died of it."

"Baron de Wilde's blood is not on my father's hands!" Bliss argued, eyes ablaze. "The man was a traitor to his King—his liege lord! He deserved his punishment!"

Fury blazed in Kit Quinn's dark eyes. Gritting his teeth, he pushed himself up, obviously meaning to go after Bliss. The blankets and sheets covering him fell back, exposing a wide expanse of tanned flesh. A scarlet rose blossomed in the once-white bandages—the stitches Isaac had sewn into his torn flesh to stop the bleeding had ripped apart. With a pained sound between a snarl and a groan, Kit Quinn sank slowly, angrily, back onto his bed.

Bliss snatched up her skirts and ran for the door. Heedless of the danger, she plunged down the steep, winding stairs and ran past the stallion that whinnied and pranced, startled.

The light of day dazzled her as she ran over the snow-covered ground toward the gate. The gatekeeper, dozing, looked up in amazement as the mistress of the castle tore by, her hood fallen back, her red curls tumbling over her shoulders, her cheeks chilled and glowing. He watched her as she crossed the courtyard, a flurry of blue velvet and white petticoats, headed toward the stables at the far end.

The stable was warm and dark, redolent of the mixed scents of horses and hay and old leather. Bliss paused, squinting into the darkness that seemed so complete after the brilliance of the daylight and the glistening white snow. A young groom, pausing in his labors over a handsome silver and leather bridle, glanced up. Realizing who it was who stood there, he rose and tugged nervously at the dark forelock that hung over his forehead.

"Milady," he said quietly.

"Isaac," Bliss replied. "Where is Isaac?"

"In the back, milady," the groom told her, pointing.

Bliss followed his direction and found the old head groom in the tack room where the air was rich with the scent of fine leathers.

"Isaac?" she called.

NIGHTRIDER

The old man looked up from his conversation with one of the stableboys. His white brows arched in surprise. His shrewd eyes, which missed little, took in Bliss's disheveled appearance and obvious agitation. Handing the delicately tooled lady's sidesaddle to the stableboy, Isaac came to Bliss's side.

"Aye, milady?"

"You must come with me," she urged, already turning to retrace her steps.

"This way, milady," he told her.

Moving off in the opposite direction, he left Bliss no choice but to follow him. They plunged deeper into the darkness, wending their way to the back of the stables. There, in the depth of the ancient building, Isaac led Bliss into the small, comfortable chambers that were his own quarters.

"What is it, milady?" he asked, an edge of fearful anticipation in his face and voice.

"It's Kit," Bliss told him. "You must come help him!"

Isaac stared at her, momentarily stunned by the realization that Bliss knew of Kit and his condition. Then, springing into action, he led Bliss through an iron-hinged door that took them out into the blinding daylight.

Isaac's door at the back of the castle left them no closer to Kit's tower than they would have been had they left through the front gate, but at least the back way afforded them some privacy from the prying eyes and gossiping tongues of the castle servants, most of whom owed their first loyalty to Lord Holme. Bliss and the old groom ran over the glittering snow and in a few moments they were climbing the stone steps to Kit's lair.

"What happened?" Isaac wanted to know, still bewildered by the simple fact of Bliss's knowledge of Kit and his whereabouts.

But Bliss was far ahead, already on the landing at the top of the stairs. She pushed open the door and entered the tower room without waiting for Isaac to join her.

Kit, his bandages stained crimson with the blood of his reopened wound, half-knelt on the floor. It was apparent that he had tried to reach the table across the room.

"Isaac!" Bliss cried, going to Kit's side. "Hurry!"

The old groom appeared in the doorway, his chest heaving. He stood there a moment before fully comprehending what had happened. When at last he did, he rushed across the chamber and lent his help to Bliss who was trying to get Kit back to the bed.

"Get the box from the table," Isaac ordered after they managed to return Kit to his bed. While Bliss obeyed, he began to peel the blood-soaked bandages away from Kit's reopened wound.

The rough wooden box Bliss brought him contained needles and threads and lengths of coarsely woven cloth torn into long strips. Isaac laid the box on the bed. Without waiting to be told, Bliss brought the jug of water to the bedside.

She gasped as the last layer of bandages was lifted away. The wound Stephen Villiers had inflicted on Kit was gaping, angry, and ragged where Isaac's stitches had been torn with Kit's efforts to rise. Bliss felt a twinge of guilt that she had made him so angry. It was true he had impugned her father's honor, but he seemed equally anxious to preserve the memory of the old Baron de Wilde. She should not have quarreled with a man in such dire condition.

Isaac bathed the wound, cleaning away the blood. "'Twill have to be sewn again," he muttered. "Ye did yerself no good tryin' to get up, my lad."

"Try to get the ball out," Kit hissed through gritted teeth.

"The ball?" Bliss repeated. "The pistol shot is still in the wound?"

"Aye," Isaac admitted. "He were in no state to have me probin' it last night. I'm not certain I should now."

"But the lead could kill him."

"Aye," Isaac agreed. "Light the candle, then, an' bring it here, milady. I'll be needin' yer help."

Bliss did as she was asked. While he cut away the torn stitches and probed the wound for the pistol shot, Bliss staunched the blood that continued to flow. Beads of sweat sheened Kit's body; his knuckles were white with the force of his grip on the bedclothes and straw tick beneath him. Bliss could imagine the pain he must be feeling, but she heard scarcely a sound escape between his clenched teeth and compressed lips.

"Wait," Isaac said after what seemed an eternity. "I think . . . aye, here it is."

From the wound he extracted a flattened lead ball. Examining it for a moment, he tossed it aside, his craggy face showing immense relief. "Now it'll heal cleanly. Milady? I'll be needin' you to hold the edges of the wound close so it can be stitched proper."

Bliss nodded. Leaning close, she pressed her fingers into the reddened, torn flesh to close the wound. She glanced at Kit but his eyes were shut tight. His breathing was shallow and quick.

"Hurry, Isaac," she said softly, feeling instinctively that Kit could bear little more and that he would loathe the thought of her witnessing his agony.

"Aye," Isaac agreed. With deft fingers he stitched Kit's wound much as he had treated injured horses during his long years as stableboy, groom, and head groom at Chatham Castle. When he had finished, he wound fresh bandages around Kit and stood back as Bliss drew the blankets up over him.

Together Bliss and Isaac left Kit lying quietly, though whether asleep or unconscious neither could tell.

"Perhaps someone should stay with him," Bliss mused as she descended the stairs.

"I'll look in on him," Isaac told her. "I'll bring him some broth later."

"I could have a tray sent for you both from the castle kitchen," Bliss offered. "They always make far too—"

"No, milady," Isaac interrupted. He saw Bliss's curious look. "Beg pardon, but the servants in the kitchen are all yer servants hired by yer guardian. Better that they not know Kit's in the tower. I have rooms of my own as ye've seen and I do my own cookin'. I'll bring him something."

"Tell me about him, Isaac," Bliss asked. "Why is he a highwayman?"

Isaac shrugged. There was a long pause before he replied. "Kit's family, milady, like my own, owed its livelihood to the castle. Many fell on hard times when Milord de Wilde died."

"But could he not have remained at the castle the way you did? I'm certain some position could have been found—"

Isaac shook his head, silencing her. "It was impossible, milady."

The old man said no more, and Bliss could see it would be useless to try and pry more information out of him. She sighed. "Well, then, I'll leave his care to you." She glanced up at the darkening sky. "Mrs. Lonsdale must be wondering where I've gotten to. I'd better go in. Isaac? You will let me know how he is, won't you? Tell me if he needs anything?"

"If you wish, milady," the groom agreed.

Bliss started away, but Isaac's question stopped her. "Milady?" Bliss turned back toward him. "Will ye be sendin' for the magistrate?"

"No," Bliss replied solemnly. "I will not have any man's blood on my hands . . ." Her face clouded. ". . . however bloodthirsty and treacherous Master Quinn seems to consider my family."

Bliss left Isaac and returned to the castle, where, as she had predicted, Mrs. Lonsdale was about to send a party searching for her. Bliss's explanation, that she had been exploring and had lost track of the time, did nothing to allay Mrs. Lonsdale's curiosity, but Bliss would say no more.

That night as she lay in her darkened chamber, Bliss thought about Kit there in the tower that rose in silhouette against the wintry night sky. She remembered the warmth of his flesh beneath her fingers as she had helped Isaac treat him, she remembered how he had refused to give in to what must have been excruciating pain. He was strong and brave and handsome . . . so handsome.

Unbidden, the memory of their first meeting returned to taunt her. That wild ride through the forest, that kiss, the strength of his body against her, his lips crushing hers, demanding a response.

Bliss trembled with the memory. But then another less tantalizing remembrance overshadowed it. She recalled the glint of fire in his eyes as he defended Lord de Wilde, the bitterness in his voice as he denounced her father and herself. His accusations that her father had gladly profited from Lord de Wilde's downfall.

He despised her and her family. Bliss turned on her side and huddled beneath the covers. From the moment he had discovered who she was, he had made his disgust apparent. Why then, she asked herself, did she not simply turn him over to the authorities? He was a criminal, pure and simple. He lived beneath her roof, hid there while he waited for the night to cloak his villainous activities. Why not simply call the magistrate and be done with Master Kit Quinn? Certainly she owed him no consideration, and he obviously bore no respect for his unwitting hostess.

But she knew, even as the thought swirled in her mind, that she could not give Kit over to the authorities. What she had said to Isaac was true—she could not be the instrument of another's imprisonment and death.

And there was something more. . . . Angry as

Kit made her, much as she resented his dislike of her family and his opinion of her father, she was drawn to him quite helplessly. Even now she longed to go to him, to bathe his brow, to tend his wound. It was an emotion she'd never felt before . . . and one she did not quite dare to analyze.

Chapter 5

In the days that followed it seemed to Bliss she thought of nothing but the highwayman, Kit Quinn, in the far tower of Chatham Castle. A dozen times and more she started to call for her cloak and boots, intending to visit him. She always changed her mind. She did not know exactly what it was that kept her from going, she only knew she could not seem to find the courage to wrap herself in velvet and fur and venture across the courtyard and out the gate.

For nearly three weeks while the winter softened and the promise of spring began to brighten the sunshine and warm the earth, Bliss confined herself to asking Isaac how Kit was faring. She watched for the old man and beckoned him to her when their paths happened to cross.

"How is he, Isaac?" she would say softly, feigning a casual interest that belied her anxiety.

"Mendin', milady," the groom would reply. "'Twas a grievous wound as ye well know. 'Twould have killed many men. But he's strong. He'll soon be well and whole again."

"Does he need anything?"

Isaac shrugged. "If ye have a blanket ye'll not be needin', milady . . . Though the days are milder, the nights are still cold and he has but the brazier to warm him."

"I'll see what I can do," Bliss promised.

A few hours later Bliss, a folded quilt beneath her billowing cloak, crossed the courtyard and entered the stables. She made her stealthy way to Isaac's rooms and, letting herself through them, left the castle via Isaac's outer door and went to the tower.

Her heart fluttered as she climbed the twisting stairs to Kit's tower room. Her mouth felt dry. At the top of the stairs she paused, unaccountably nervous.

"This is ridiculous!" she told herself. "I feel like a frightened little girl."

Taking a deep breath, she rapped at the door and heard Kit's muffled reply: "Come in."

Bliss's hand trembled as she opened the door. She leaned around it and found him seated on a chair, a sword in one hand and a sharpening stone in the other.

His dark eyebrows arched in surprise. "I thought it must be Isaac," he said. "Come in, my lady, and tell me to what I owe this honor."

Bliss entered the room and closed the door behind her. Parting the front of her cloak, she brought out the quilt she'd taken from the chest at the foot of her own bed.

"I spoke to Isaac," she told him. "He said you might need another blanket. The nights are still quite cold."

Kit's deep brown eyes swept Bliss from head to toe. "There are other ways to keep warm on a cold night, my Lady Bliss."

Bliss turned away to hide the flush that darkened her already pinkened cheeks. "I'll put it here on the bed," she told him.

Unfolding the quilt, Bliss spread it over Kit's narrow bed. As she smoothed it, she heard the clank of the sword as he laid it down and the click of his heels on the flagstone floor as he came to her side.

She looked up at him. His eyes were thoughtful. His face was set in stern lines.

"What is it?" she asked, wondering what could have driven the lazy good humor from his face.

"That quilt," he said softly. "My . . . my mother made it. Many years ago."

"Your mother?" Bliss looked down at the blanket. The stitching was fine and even, the workmanship intricate and exquisite. "She was a fine needlewoman," Bliss told him. "I found the blanket in the chest at the foot of my bed. Your mother must have sewn it for Lord de Wilde."

Kit nodded. "She did."

"Isaac told me that your family worked at the castle."

Kit looked at her, his eyes wary. "What else did he tell you?"

Turning away, Bliss walked to the brazier and held her hands out to its warmth.

"He said your family fell on hard times after Lord de Wilde's death. That was the reason you took to the highway." She looked back at Kit. "Is that true?"

"In essence," he admitted.

"Your parents are—"

"Dead," he interrupted.

"Have you no brothers or sisters?"

Kit moved away, returning to the table where his sword lay. "No," he answered shortly, leaving Bliss with the clear impression that he did not appreciate her interest.

"It's a dangerous life, the life of a highwayman," she went on, knowing she was treading on dangerous ground.

"That it is," Kit agreed, his tone wary. "But it suits me."

"How can it? You were shot, nearly killed. You could face the gallows if you are caught and brought to trial. There must be something else for you to do."

"Such as?" he asked, an edge of sarcasm and

impatience to his voice.

Bliss shrugged. There was a chill in the room that had nothing to do with the weather. She wondered if she should let the matter drop and leave. Instead, she plunged on.

"You could help Isaac in the stables, or something could be found for you in the castle. I—"

"I could put on livery and fawn on you and your fine guests, is that it, milady?" he snarled. "Be your lackey at your beck and call?"

Bliss swung toward him. "At least you'd be earning your living honestly! At least you wouldn't be a criminal having to hide by day!"

Kit's dark eyes flashed, and for a moment Bliss thought she might feel the edge of his gleaming sword against the tender flesh of her throat. His hand tightened on the hilt of the weapon; his face was tight and flushed with anger.

"Better to live like a criminal," he hissed, "than to grovel at another man's feet."

Bliss lifted her chin, struggling to hide the exasperation and frustration he caused her. She had come with the best of intentions. She had only wanted to help him, and now he was acting as if she had insulted him by offering him honest employment.

"I did not mean to wound your pride, Master Quinn," she said coolly, "and I shall not insult you again by trying to help you avoid the hangman's noose. In fact . . ." She paused, trying to control the tremor in her voice. ". . . in fact, I wish you all success in your life of crime. And when they come to hang you, rest assured I shall come to see you off . . . to hell!''

With a toss of her head, Bliss turned in a swirl of green velvet and flame-red curls. She marched to the door and, without a backward glance, stormed out of the room and down the tower stairs.

Behind her, alone in his tower lair, Kit's face was a study in contrasts. On the one hand his pride had indeed been wounded by the suggestion that he might accept employment in Chatham Castle. On the other hand, the girl who had just left, so haughty and angry, was by far the most beautiful creature he had ever seen. The combination of Bliss's beauty, her temper, and her spirit, aroused his admiration—and his desire.

Kit shook his head trying to rid himself of the thoughts that warred inside him. A decision would have to be made and soon. The girl aroused troubling emotions in him. There was danger for both of them as long as both remained at Chatham Castle. The best thing he could do, he knew, was leave. But the thought of leaving was hard for him to bear.

Kit's expression was grave, his mood pensive, as he gazed at the blanket Bliss had brought him—the blanket, he remembered now, he had not even thanked her for.

* * *

"Are you feeling well?" Louise Lonsdale asked, pressing a cool palm to Bliss's forehead.

Bliss started, jolted out of her reverie as she sat in a small parlor before a blazing fire. She mustered a wan smile to reassure the house-keeper.

"I'm perfectly well," she replied. "Only a little tired. I think I'll go up now. Will you send Mercy to me?"

Louise agreed, and Bliss left the warmth of the little parlor and climbed the stairs to her room.

Her maid arrived only moments after Bliss had entered her room where a fire had been kindled in the gaping stone hearth. No words passed between them as Mercy undressed her mistress and prepared her for bed. Bliss dismissed her with a weary wave as she sat before her looking glass, her brush in her hand.

In the quiet solitude of her room, Bliss gazed at her reflection in the golden light of the candles burning in the ormolu sconces of her dressing table. The girl in the looking glass seemed pale, her golden eyes were large in her heart-shaped face, her titian hair was a shimmering cloud that fell to the shoulders of her wolf-trimmed velvet dressing gown.

Bliss sighed as she pulled the silver-backed brush through her long red curls. What had she expected, she asked herself, when she had gone to the tower? Gratitude, perhaps? Kit Quinn seemed singularly unmoved by the fact that she had helped Isaac tend him or that she had raised no objection to his remaining a secret guest in what was, after all, her property. And today when she had taken him a blanket to help warm him in his tower lair, he had not welcomed her, made no attempt to be cordial or even tolerant. He made no effort to conceal his resentment of her. If anything, he was more hostile than ever when she had offered to employ him. He was impossible! All she'd been doing was trying to help him avoid meeting his end on Tyburn Hill at the end of the hangman's rope. And what thanks had she gotten for her pains?

Laying her brush aside, Bliss rose from the dressing table and blew out the two candles burning in its sconces. The tester bed had been turned down, and Bliss pulled off her dressing gown and tossed it over the foot of the huge bed.

But as she would have kicked off her high-heeled mules and climbed the bedsteps, she heard the noise . . . unidentifiable but definite, coming from the shadows at the far side of the cavernous chamber.

"Who is it?" she demanded, squinting toward the shadows that danced with the movement of the firelight around the soaring walls. "Mercy? Is that you?"

There was a movement in the shadows, and then he appeared, moving soundlessly into the light, like a ghost clad in black, his booted feet making no sound on the carpet-covered flag-stone floor.

Bliss gasped, backing away. Her eyes were wide golden pools in her pale face. Her heart pounded, pulsing in the scented hollow of her throat, as she watched Kit Quinn approach.

"You!" Bliss breathed. "How did you get in here? What do you want?"

Kit's dark eyes swept over her. Her nightdress of fine, sea-green, lace-frothed lawn clung to her. The firelight glowed behind her, casting her body into silhouette against the delicate fabric.

"I came to . . ." Kit began, his thoughts a jumble, his eyes, his mind, filled with the sight of her there, so vulnerable, so beautiful. He had been bemused, bewitched, watching her as she sat before her looking glass brushing those cascading red curls. A warning voice told him to leave, to slip out of the room as silently as he'd come, but he could not. He'd watched her, watched the play of emotions on her face as she gazed into the looking glass. He'd held his breath when she'd shed her robe and had known the moment had come when he must reveal himself or leave undiscovered.

"Well?" Bliss prompted, feeling naked and defenseless there in the solitude of her bed-chamber. "Why did you come?"

"To thank you," he managed, his mood, his emotions, unfathomable to her. "For the blanket and for what you did . . . helping Isaac."

Bliss drew a shaky breath. She had just been thinking of those things. Though she knew it was impossible, she wondered if he couldn't somehow fathom the secrets of her heart, the unspoken thoughts that lay in her mind.

"How did you get in?" she asked. "Did Mercy let you in here?"

Kit shook his head. "No one let me in. This is an ancient castle. The walls are very thick. They are honeycombed with passages, hidey-holes, secret rooms. I grew up here, don't forget, but I don't think even I know them all."

Bliss glanced toward the grey stone walls. Somehow she did not find the thought of his being able to make his way to any part of the castle particularly comforting. She trembled, gooseflesh rising on her skin.

"I did not come here to frighten you," Kit told her, moving closer.

"I'm not frightened," Bliss lied, her throat closing on the words.

"I think you are," he disagreed. "You cannot think I would harm you."

"Can't I?" she countered. "From the first moment I met you you've shown me your dislike. What should I think? What should I expect?"

Kit hesitated. It was true, he knew, he had not tried to conceal his resentment of Bliss's inheriting Chatham Castle and all its treasures. Still, he had his reasons . . . reasons that were too personal, too private for him to share.

NIGHTRIDER

"I'm sorry," he said, "for my churlishness. I cannot explain." He took a step toward her, his hand outstretched. "Can we not—"

Bliss stumbled backward, startled by his movement. Her foot, tangled in the trailing skirt of her nightdress, buckled under her and she began to fall.

With a single swift movement Kit was at her side. His arms went around her, catching her, drawing her upright, holding her close. Through the thin lawn of her nightdress he could feel the heat of her skin. His hands, holding her tightly, felt the hardness of her ribs, the first curve of her breasts. She was close to him, so close he could smell the warm scent of her flesh, the clean fragrance of that cloud of hair that spilled down her back.

Bliss did not dare look up at him. Her hands gripped the heavy woolen cloth of his sleeves. The crested brass buttons on his coat were cold against her skin as they stood together, breathless.

"Bliss," Kit said softly, his voice low, the word like a stolen kiss.

Trembling, Bliss raised her eyes to his face. The firelight played on it, casting shadows into its sharp planes, glistening in his dark eyes, shining on his sable brown hair.

Shivering, frightened, Bliss shook her head slowly from side to side. The attraction, the desire, that he had first awakened in her that night in the forest returned to her now a hundredfold. She knew she could not resist him. She knew that her senses, her emotions, would bow too readily to his will. And she knew, most of all, that they should not be there, holding each other, in the warm intimacy of her bedchamber.

"Please," she whispered, begging for his compassion, hoping he would release her before anything more could happen. "Please, go."

"You can't know what you're asking," he replied.

He drew her against him and Bliss melted in his arms, her body curving into his far larger one. Her desire, new, innocent, untested, was fired by his.

Her head fell back as he slipped a hand behind her knees and swept her into his arms. He lay her across the great tester bed and knelt beside her. His face was above hers; his eyes were filled with wonder and desire.

Bliss raised a trembling hand and touched his cheek. Whatever resentment, whatever hostility existed between them, it was banished, temporarily vanquished by the mutual need that had been there, in their hearts, from the first moment they'd seen one another. Bliss was lost, she was his, and they both knew it.

Kit leaned toward her. His lips brushed hers softly, gently. His hand caressed her, moving upward until it found her breast. He gentled her, kissing her, murmuring to her, when she started, frightened, her cries smothered by his lips on hers. And then . . .

"Milady?" The knocking at the door was like thunder, shattering the hazy, sensuous spell they had woven about themselves. "Milady? Are you asleep?"

"Louise!" Bliss hissed, struggling to rise.

"Who?" Kit asked.

"My housekeeper."

The knocking came again. "Milady, a messenger has arrived with an express from my Lord Holme. He says it's important."

"Just a moment, Louise," Bliss called. She looked at Kit. "You must go. Please."

"Go get the letter," he told her. "She needn't know I'm here."

"I can't. She'll expect me to let her in. Please, Kit, you must go. It was a mistake. We should never have . . . You and I . . ."

"The lady and the highwayman," he snapped. "I'll go. I wouldn't want to soil your lily-white skin with my highwayman's hands."

"Kit," Bliss said as he left her and crossed the room with swift, silent steps. "Kit, wait, I didn't mean . . ."

He lifted a tapestry hanging on the far wall and, in a moment, disappeared behind it. Behind him Bliss, feeling empty, bereft, slid off the bed and pulled on her dressing gown.

She wanted to run after Kit, bring him back, let whatever had been about to pass between them go on to its inevitable end. But she could not. She knew she should not. However it hurt

Kit's pride, what he said had been absolutely true. He was a highwayman. She was a lady. Love between them was impossible.

Feeling as if she would cry if she so much as thought of Kit, Bliss went to the door and opened it to admit her housekeeper.

"Did I wake you?" Louise asked. "I'm sorry, chick. I would have waited until morning, but the messenger insisted Sir Basil wanted his letter read the moment it reached you."

"You didn't wake me," Bliss assured her. "Give me the letter."

Breaking the seal, Bliss unfolded her guardian's letter and scanned the contents. It was short, impersonal, with no inquiries after her health or well-being. It instructed Bliss to make ready to receive him and several guests, to make certain that both Chatham Castle and herself were looking their best when he arrived in five days' time. It could mean only one thing.

"Oh, Lord," Bliss moaned.

"What is it, sweet?" Louise wanted to know.

"He's coming. Sir Basil. With guests. He's found me a suitor."

"Perhaps not," Louise disagreed. "Perhaps it's only visitors."

Bliss shook her head. She knew without having to be told that her guardian had chosen a husband for her, and she feared that she knew who it was.

"Lord Villiers," she said dully. "It must be."

"That popinjay," Louise growled. "Surely not."

Bliss thought of Stephen Villiers, thought of being held by him, touched by him, kissed by him as she'd just been held and touched and kissed by Kit Quinn. And the thought brought with it a wave of such repugnance that she burst into a torrent of tears that startled and puzzled her loyal and loving housekeeper.

Chapter 6

In the morning Bliss set the servants to preparing rooms for Sir Basil and his guests. Her heart was heavy with dread. She had no doubt that when her guardian appeared he would bring with him Stephen Villiers, his mother, and his sister. It seemed a foregone conclusion that Sir Basil would be enthusiastic about the match—with their rich and powerful connections the Villiers were the sort of glittering prospects he'd had in mind for her. There would be hell to pay when she told him she did not wish to marry Stephen. How could she explain to him that for all his heritage and breeding, Stephen Villiers simply did not touch her heart, her senses? And how could she ever tell him that she could only marry a man who could stir her affections, touch her heart, awaken her desires? Most of all, how could she explain that she knew what she wanted to find in marriage because she had felt those emotions, those stirrings—felt them in the arms of a highwayman her prospective bridegroom had tried to kill.

Kit. Bliss could not stifle a sigh as she thought of him. He had not come back to her room the night before as she'd thought he might. His pride was wounded, no doubt. Bliss bit her lip, wishing they need not be estranged. But surely he realized there could be no future for them together. Surely he could see that she could not live in his world, nor he enter the life her station and breeding had prepared her for.

She knew the best thing for her would be to leave Chatham Castle, to return to London and forget Kit Quinn and the new, thrilling, forbidden feelings he had awakened in her. She knew, repugnant as the thought was to her, that it might well be in her best interests to marry Stephen and leave Chatham and Kit forever. Most marriages among her set were, after all, based on titles, breeding and fortunes. Few men or women of the privileged class expected to find happiness, much less love, within the confines of their marriages.

The prospect of condemning herself to a loveless, "fashionable" match brought hot, stinging tears to Bliss's eyes. Resolutely she forced the thought from her mind. She would wait until Lord Holme arrived before she charted any course for the future. She would wait—and hope—that he had found another gentleman for her, a gentleman who could make her feel the way Kit did without the obstacles that stood between her and her high-wayman.

She thought of Kit in his tower room. He should be warned, she realized. He should be told that her guardian was returning and might be bringing with him the man who had come so close to ending Kit's life.

Seeing that the servants were all engaged in their various tasks, Bliss pulled on a satin-lined velvet cloak and left the castle.

But the moment she entered the tower, Bliss knew something was wrong. Kit's horse, the tall roan stallion, was gone. Where would Kit have gone, she wondered, in the middle of the day? He lived by night. His profession, after all, demanded it. It seemed to Bliss that he risked his very life by venturing boldly out in the daylight.

"Kit?" she called, wondering if Isaac might have taken the stallion to groom and exercise him. "Kit, are you up there?"

There was no reply, and Bliss started up the stairs thinking it was possible he did not hear her. But when she reached the top and stood on the landing at the head of the curving stairs, she saw that her hopes were in vain.

Kit's tower room was empty, stripped bare. There was not one stick of furniture, not one scrap of cloth to show he had ever been there. Even the brazier that had provided the only source of heat during those cold winter nights was gone.

Shaken, Bliss hurried back down the twisting stairs. Going by the back way, she went to the stable to search for Isaac.

"Where is he?" she demanded of the old groom when she found him.

Beckoning for Bliss to follow, Isaac led her away from the other groom who worked there. When they were out of earshot of everyone else, he turned back toward her, a solemn look on his wrinkled, kindly face.

"He's left the tower," he told her.

"I know!" Bliss replied impatiently. "I've just come from there!"

Isaac nodded. "It was for the best, milady, what with his lordship comin' back an' all."

"How do you know about that?" she demanded. "How did Kit know?"

Isaac shrugged. "The messenger told me. I told Kit. 'Twas too dangerous for him to remain in the tower. If his lordship had found him there . . ."

Bliss sighed. She knew it was true, but she hated the thought of Kit's being gone. "Where is he now?" she wanted to know.

Isaac hesitated, his eyes darting here and there, resting anywhere but on the questioning face turned toward his own.

"Isaac?" Bliss prompted.

"There's a cottage," the old man said at last, "in the forest not far from the village. Kit's gone there."

"Near the village?" Bliss repeated. "But who will look after him? Surely you can't take his food all the way—"

"He has friends in the village, milady," Isaac told her. "There are those there who Kit . . . well . . . he looks after them. They will be only too willin' to see to his needs."

"Will you tell me how to find this cottage? I'd like to visit him." Bliss saw in Isaac's face that he did not like the notion. Laying a hand on his arm, she said softly, "Please, Isaac. My guardian is coming in two days' time. He is bringing with him a man he means me to marry. I want to visit Kit now, while I am still able."

Isaac's eyes searched Bliss's face. At last he nodded. "Aye, milady, I s'pose ye do at that. Ye go to the village. Go south past the churchyard and into the forest. Follow the road until ye see an old stone wall. Look sharp for it, mind, 'cause 'tis half-buried with vines and weeds. When ye find the wall, leave the road and follow it. Straight on. 'Twill take ye to the cottage."

"I'm going in to change," she told him. "Have my horse saddled by the time I get back."

With a tug of his forelock Isaac agreed. But his eyes were troubled as he watched Bliss walk away. The catch in her voice when she spoke Kit's name—and the look in Kit's eyes when he talked of Bliss—boded no good for either of them.

Chatham village, which, like the castle of the same name, had been part of Bliss's inheritance, lay on either side of a pretty little river that appeared out of the forest and disappeared back into it after flowing through the village and beneath its arched stone bridge. It was a charming place of thatched roofs and stone walls. Its church was an ancient one dating back to the days of the Conqueror. The village green was dotted with grazing sheep and flocks of geese.

The inhabitants of Chatham, numbering about one hundred, went busily about their daily tasks, wheeling barrows, making repairs, buying and selling goods they grew in their fields or raised on their little patches of ground or sewed or spun in their cozy cottages.

A ripple of interest seemed to pass through the village as Bliss approached on the dainty white mare with the elegant, tooled leather sidesaddle. Her habit, of emerald velvet buttoned and braided with gold, was in startling contrast with the mare's snowy sides. Her plumed hat rested jauntily on her upswept curls.

It seemed to Bliss as she rode through the village that all of Chatham's inhabitants had come out to see her pass. Their combined stares were like a weight on her shoulders. Some were merely curious, some openly hostile. Bliss remembered Isaac's telling her that many of them had served Lord de Wilde at the castle but that they had been turned out by Lord Holme when he had sent his own servants to prepare the castle for Bliss's arrival.

It wasn't my fault! she wanted to cry out to them. I am not to blame for your dismissals! I am not to blame for Lord de Wilde's death! But she said nothing. To those villagers who dropped curtsies or doffed their hats to their mistress she gave a nod and a smile. The rest she ignored as she guided her mare over the bridge to the old church where she turned south as she passed the ancient churchyard with its jumble of moss-grown headstones.

She was deep in the forest when she saw the stone wall. Half-buried, broken, nearly tumble-down, it was hard to see in the shadows of the thick woods. But Bliss was looking for it—she'd begun to fear she'd missed it—and when she spied it there, its ivy and moss-covered stones blending so neatly with the undergrowth, she felt a sense of relief. Tugging at the mare's reins, she guided her off the narrow, rutted road and into the underbrush.

They picked their way carefully through the forest, both Bliss and the mare alert for holes and stones lying in the weeds waiting to trip them. It seemed they had gone too far—they had left the road far behind them—and had Bliss not trusted Isaac she would have begun to wonder if he had given her the wrong directions.

Then, at long last, she spied the cottage through the thickly growing trees and bushes. It was small, its stone walls covered with vines that would soon leaf out into a verdant wall of ivy. Its roof was thatched. Bliss knew it must be Kit's—his roan stallion was tethered outside. But there was another horse tethered nearby. Dappled grey and slightly swaybacked, the animal was clearly past its best years.

Bliss reined in her mare and sat, well concealed amidst the bushes and trees, wondering what to do. It might be, she knew, that Kit would not wish it known that Lady Bliss of Chatham Castle came to visit him in his forest cottage. On the other hand, he might not care who knew of her association with him.

As she sat there pondering, her dilemma was solved for her. The door of the cottage opened and Kit appeared.

Bliss's heart skipped a beat when she saw him. She leaned forward in the saddle, her eyes hungry for every detail, her breath caught in her lungs. She parted her lips to call to him, but the sound died in her throat.

Kit turned back toward the doorway, and his guest emerged. He stepped back to let the girl pass, then slipped an arm about her waist and walked with her to the waiting horses.

The girl, in her plain, linsey-woolsey gown, its short skirt showing a pair of shapely ankles, its lines molding to a form far more voluptuous than Bliss's, looked up at Kit. She said something and he laughed, then bent toward her and kissed her quickly, softly, on her full, parted lips.

Bliss felt breathless, as if the air had suddenly been sucked out of her. She watched as he lifted the girl onto the back of the swaybacked mare, then swung himself up onto the saddleless back of the roan.

While Bliss watched, pale, stunned, Kit rode off with the girl whose long blonde hair glistened in the dappled sunshine of the clearing around the little thatched cottage. They disappeared into the forest, and Bliss sat there for a long while, her eyes glazed and dead, her hands slack on the reins, her senses fogged and dull, until at last her mare's restless shifting brought her to her senses.

Turning the horse about, Bliss retraced their route back to Chatham village and to the castle beyond.

Chapter 7

Huddled in a chair, her knees drawn up, her pale face tucked into a corner of a high-backed wing chair, Bliss watched yet another dawn breaking over the grey walls of Chatham Castle.

It seemed to her she had not slept for the past four nights, she had not eaten, she scarcely noticed the bustle of the servants readying the castle for their master's arrival.

Her mind instead was filled with thoughts of Kit. Images of him tormented her day and night. She saw him again and again leaving his cottage in the forest with his arm about the beautiful girl. She saw him smiling at her, kissing her, laughing with her.

Oddly enough, it was the last that troubled Bliss most. The look on Kit's face was one of genuine pleasure, real affection. There was none of the wary mistrust, the scarcely veiled hostility Bliss recognized every time she and Kit met.

Well, Bliss mused to herself, not every time. She remembered the night he had come to her room. That had been real—his desire for her, his passion. Hadn't it?

Bliss's brow puckered. Had he come intending to seduce her? He must have known the possible consequences of such a liaison. She had not questioned their mutual desire on that night—until now.

"No, no!" she muttered. "It was only the night and our desire that spurred us. It was not deliberate. Not planned. I do not know what grudge it is Kit bears against me—why my inheritance of this castle so enrages him—but even that resentment could not be so bitter that he would seek to ruin me out of spite."

But the seed of suspicion was planted in her mind. What had been a sensuous, titillating memory was now reduced to something dark, treacherous. Bliss shivered at the thought of how near she had come to disaster. If Mrs. Lonsdale had not come to her door with the letter from Sir Basil, Bliss knew she would have allowed Kit to make love to her.

What would have happened then? she wondered. Would he have gone back to his blonde village girl? Would he have tried to hide what he had done, or would he have laughed with her over his vengeance on the heiress of Chatham Castle?

A pain, sick and gnawing, writhed in the pit of Bliss's stomach. Weak and limp in her chair, she closed her eyes, only to see Kit's dark, handsome face in her mind's eye.

"Kit," she whispered softly in the pink light of the breaking dawn, "would you have betrayed me? Would you have turned my own senses against me to be avenged for whatever evil I have done you?"

He was a highwayman—a thief of gold and jewels. Was he also a thief of love? Bliss longed desperately to know the truth. In the meanwhile, she could not help fearing the worst.

Bliss was still huddled in her chair, her wide, haunted eyes fixed on the horizon outside the castle walls, when Mrs. Lonsdale came to her room.

"Here, sweet," the housekeeper said, spying her mistress in the wing chair. "I've had water heated for your bath. His lordship was leaving London at daybreak, so he said. You want to be ready when he gets here with . . ."

She stopped, her words trailing off when she saw Bliss looking so small and pale.

"Merciful heavens!" she cried. "You look white as a ghost! Whatever is wrong?"

Shaking her head, Bliss stiffly left the chair she'd occupied for hours. "Nothing," she lied. "I couldn't sleep."

"Worried about his lordship and this would-be beau he's bringing with him?"

"Aye," Bliss agreed, "that's it." It was, she realized with a little pang of conscience, the first lie she could remember having told the woman who had raised her.

"Never mind, chick," the housekeeper cooed, laying a dressing gown about Bliss's shoulders. "Not even Sir Basil Holme, fond as he is of getting his own way, can make you wed a man you do not want."

Bliss said nothing as she was led off to the anteroom where a tub waited, its hot water steaming in the cooler chamber. But she knew, even as she followed Louise so meekly, that she had fallen in love with Kit Quinn. And she knew also that if he betrayed her, if the passion, the desire, that had fired her own, had been no more than his anger and bitterness in disguise, nothing would matter to her ever again.

Afternoon was giving way to evening when a lookout posted high on the castle's battlements called down that Sir Basil's traveling coach was approaching. The servants were assembled in the entrance hall, and Bliss, dressed in sea-green and pale yellow, her upswept hair threaded with matching ribbons, went to the door to greet her guardian and his guests.

The coach entered the courtyard, its coat of arms emblazoned on the sides barely clearing the narrow gateway, and circled around to come to a halt before Chatham's heavy, iron-banded main entrance. Two footmen hurried out to open the coach door, and Bliss stood framed in the doorway waiting for her guardian's appearance.

Sir Basil's hollow-cheeked face was wreathed in smiles as he stepped down from the coach. He beamed up at Bliss, and she imagined that his delight must surely come from knowing that his ward, whose guardianship had cost him so dearly, had proven to be a prize on the marriage mart.

Turning back toward the coach, Sir Basil held out his hand. A long-fingered hand in a violet glove took Sir Basil's hand, and a thin woman in violet and peach emerged from the coach.

Bliss averted her eyes. She did not need to see who else descended from the coach. She knew the woman who walked regally toward her— Daphne, Lady Villiers.

"How are you, my dear?" Sir Basil called when they were still some distance away. "You look pale. Hasn't Lonsdale been feeding you?"

"Welcome back to Chatham, my lord," Bliss said dutifully. She dropped a shallow curtsy to her guardian and his companion. "Milady," she said, her eyes focused somewhere just below Lady Villiers's chin.

"How are you, my child?" the older woman asked. There was a smug satisfaction in her eyes that told Bliss she expected her to fall in with the plans laid for her future—a future as Stephen Villiers's wife.

Behind his mother and Sir Basil, Stephen approached with his sister, Letitia. He smiled up at Bliss as they mounted the steps, and Bliss could see he was genuinely glad to see her.

A short, sharp pain stabbed Bliss's heart. If only she could return that smile. If only she could abandon herself to the prospect of the marriage her guardian desired for her, how much simpler everything would be.

"Welcome to Chatham Castle, my lord," she said, curtsying to Stephen as he reached her. "Welcome," she added, looking at the pinched, petulant face of Letitia Villiers. "I trust your journey was a pleasant one."

"It was not!" Letitia assured her. "The coach rocked and jolted! I don't know why you must needs live out in the wilds of the country! After you and Stephen are wed—"

"Letitia . . ." Stephen's voice was low and stern.

The girl glared at her brother from beneath the brim of her pale pink bonnet. She said no more and, tilting her chin haughtily, swept past Bliss and into the castle.

Stephen watched her go, then turned an apologetic smile toward Bliss. "You must excuse my sister," he said softly. "She did not want to leave London. She fancies herself in love."

Bliss's eyes widened in surprise. "Letitia?" she stuttered. Then, realizing how it must have sounded, Bliss flushed prettily.

Far from being insulted, Stephen laughed.

"My sentiments precisely," he confided. "But I fear the man she has chosen is not suitable."

"Why?" Bliss demanded, a bitter edge to her voice. "Is he a highwayman?"

"What was that?" Stephen asked, bewildered.

"Nothing," Bliss assured him quickly. "I hope your sister's love affair may end happily."

"I fear it cannot. My mother detests the man. She has high hopes of a brilliant marriage for Letitia, and Lord Cameron is a penniless Scot with all the rough-hewn charm of his countrymen."

Bliss thought Lady Villiers should be thankful to find any suitor at all for her sour-faced, whining daughter but was too tactful to say so. Instead she said:

"Even so, I shall continue to hope for the best."

"Your hopes would be in vain, I fear," Stephen warned. "Even if my mother could tolerate the man, he is, as I said, penniless. And Letitia's dowry . . ." Stephen shrugged. "It would not support them for long." Smiling, he dismissed the subject. "But come, let us go inside. I would not have you catching a chill."

Bliss laid her hand on Stephen's arm and he led her into the great hall. She was the picture of meek obedience, but inside she was thinking: Letitia needs a dowry to marry her penniless lover. Here is one more reason they will try to force this marriage upon me.

* * *

They were a merry party at dinner that night
—with one exception. Bliss, sitting in her place
at one end of the long dinner table, listened to
Lady Villiers with a sinking heart.

"It will be a brilliant marriage," the thin,
brown-haired woman in scarlet was saying.
"Quite a brilliant marriage."

"Indeed it will," Sir Basil agreed.

"Perhaps," the lady went on as though Sir
Basil had not spoken, "the King might be persuaded to attend. And the Queen of course," she
added hurriedly, her narrow face twisting into a
mask of disdain, "although it hardly matters if
the Portuguese is there. I'm certain dear George
and Barbara will be in attendance."

Bliss studied her food thinking what a fool the
woman was. "Dear George and Barbara," indeed! Bliss very much doubted whether George,
Duke of Buckingham, or Barbara, Countess of
Castlemaine, would have appreciated being re-
ferred to so familiarly by this minor member of
their family.

"Of course, our townhouse is too small to
accommodate such a gathering," Lady Daphne
went on. "But since Stephen and Bliss will live
in Barthorp House, the ceremony and ball can
be held there. After the house is refurnished, of
course."

Bliss's eyes narrowed as she cast a cold,
suspicious look at the woman. "What is wrong
with the furnishings?" she demanded. "My

mother furnished that house when she and my father were married."

"There is nothing wrong with it, Bliss," Sir Basil insisted placatingly. "It is a beautiful house. Merely a little—"

"Old-fashioned," Lady Daphne finished for him.

"The dark, heavy, so-English style is complete *démodé*, my dear. Styles are light now, graceful, gilded."

"We need not discuss this now," Sir Basil decreed, recognizing the warning in the mutinous set of Bliss's mouth. "There is time for such concerns after—"

"Not so much time," Lady Daphne argued.

"Mother," Stephen said coldly, his green eyes stern as they rested on his mother's narrow face.

Lady Daphne glared at her son, her face a picture of pouting pique. At last, with a sigh, she lowered her eyes. Stephen had won the round, but Bliss was certain the battle would go on.

A strained silence ensued until Stephen's sister, Letitia, broke it to say:

"After Stephen marries Bliss, I will be able to marry Angus."

"Angus!" Lady Daphne spat. "Why you wish to wed with that uncouth Scot is beyond all reason! We can arrange a much better match for you, my dear, leave it to me."

"I want Angus!" Letitia whined. "You said there was nothing truly wrong with him but that

121

he was penniless."

"Hardly a minor consideration," Stephen snapped.

"With all Bliss's money, she can provide an income for us!" Letitia glared at Bliss as though daring her to object.

"That is enough, Letitia," Stephen snarled. "I forbid you to say anything more on the subject."

"You're not my father!" Letitia argued. "And I will have Angus! I will!"

Bliss sighed, pushing away her plate. She rose, the footman behind her jumping to draw away her high-backed, carved chair.

"I have a headache," she told them, her eyes flickering between Sir Basil's face and Stephen's. "I must bid you good night."

The gentlemen stood as Bliss swept out of the room without a backward glance.

Bliss felt relieved to be out of the company of people she found so distasteful, but she had scarcely reached her room when a knock came on the door.

"Come in," she called wearily. She hoped it would be Mercy or Louise Lonsdale but was not surprised when Sir Basil appeared in her sitting room doorway. "It was not sham, my lord," she told him. "I have a monstrous headache."

"Lady Villiers was concerned," he told her. "You seem pale and—"

"And she was worried that I may sicken and die before she and her brood get their hands on my fortune!" Bliss cried bitterly.

"Bliss—"

"No!" She paused, the throbbing in her head taking her breath away. "I tell you, sir, you had best send those hideous people back to London for I will not marry Stephen."

"You will," Sir Basil disagreed.

"I will not!" she argued. "I tell you there will be no marriage and—"

"The contracts are already signed," he said softly.

"The con—" Bliss paled. Marriage contracts, she knew, were as binding as the ceremony itself. "But how can that be? I was not consulted."

"There was no need," Sir Basil said. "I am your guardian. You are not of age. The matter is settled."

"No!" Bliss protested as he turned to go. "Wait, come back, you must—"

The door closed behind Sir Basil with a thudding finality that seemed to Bliss the death knell of all her hopes—all her dreams.

Chapter 8

Bliss stared after her guardian. She was astonished, stunned, beyond words, beyond thought. It was not possible, she told herself. He could not have bartered her away to that loathsome woman's son without a single word to her.

But he had done it, she thought, heart sinking, a black morass of despair opening beneath her, threatening to swallow her. The contracts were signed. He was her guardian and she was not yet of age. Her present, her future, her very life was under his control. If only she were older—if her majority was a matter of months, rather than years, away, perhaps she could stall the marriage until her birthday and then declare her opposition to the match. But for now there seemed no hope of avoiding the wedding.

Retiring to her bedchamber, Bliss lay across the high tester bed. She stared, unseeing, at the canopy so far above. She felt numb; there were no tears, no anguished sobs, only the dull, sickening thudding in her temples that seemed to reverberate through her brain with her slightest movement.

The sound of the door opening made her wince. She half expected that Lady Daphne had come to berate her—or to reassure herself that the prize she had purchased for her son was not likely to expire before the wedding.

But it was Louise who appeared in the doorway. Her motherly face was filled with concern as she came to the bedside.

"Poor chick," she cooed. "Come, let me help you into your nightrail."

"I don't want to move," Bliss told her. "It hurts so."

"Then the sooner you are abed, the better. Come now, 'twill take only a moment."

Patiently, painfully, Bliss allowed the housekeeper to help her off with her gown and petticoats and on with her lace-trimmed lawn shift. As Louise had promised, it was only a few minutes before Bliss was tucked into the high, wide bed.

"There now," the housekeeper soothed, massaging Bliss's temples with gentle circular strokes. "That's better, isn't it?"

"Aye," Bliss whispered. Reaching out, she caught Louise's wrist. Her eyes were wide and haunted as she half rose from her pillows. "Have you heard?" she demanded. "He means to wed me to Stephen Villiers. Between him and Lady Daphne they have arranged it all."

"Aye, love," Louise confirmed. "I heard." She longed to comfort her charge, but there were no words that could ease Bliss's misery.

"I won't marry him," Bliss insisted, lying back into the welcoming softness of her pillows. "I won't. I'd rather be dead!"

"You don't mean that," Louise said hurriedly. "You can't."

"I do! I do!" Bliss cried, the tears, too long suppressed, welling into her eyes. "I hate Stephen! I hate that mother and sister of his! I don't want him! I want—"

Bliss bit back the name that sprang to her lips. Kit. She wanted Kit. But was he any better? He had tried to seduce her—to ruin her—and for what? To satisfy some vendetta he held against her family.

"Aye, chick," Louise asked. "What do you want?"

Bliss wiped away her tears with the backs of her hands. "Nothing," she murmured, turning her face away from her beloved Louise. "I only want to sleep now."

"Shall I bring you a draught? It would take but a moment to—"

"No," Bliss interrupted. "I think I can sleep now." Whether she could sleep or not she did not know. She wanted only to be alone. She knew that her pain, her wretchedness, hurt Louise and she knew she could not hold it inside much longer.

"Very well, then, I'll say goodnight." Leaning over Bliss, Louise kissed her gently where the red-tinged curls fell over the pale skin of her forehead. With a sympathetic smile and a murmur of concern, Louise left Bliss, leaving only one small candle burning to light the comforting darkness of the cavernous room.

Turning on her side, burying her tears, muffling her sobs in the thick feather pillows, Bliss wept. Though she'd already vowed to find some way, any way, to avoid the marriage her guardian had contracted for her, her weariness, her headache, and the shock of being presented with a fait accompli made her too vulnerable not to give way to despair just then.

It was when her tears had at last subsided that she became aware of the other person in the room. Until then she had been too caught up in her grief to notice the wavering of the candle flame as a door was opened, the soft footfalls crossing the flagstones, the shadows dancing across the tapestried walls. And even when she realized she was not alone, she could not have said how she knew. It was a knowledge born in her heart rather than her senses.

Sniffling, she looked up half expecting to find Louise there, come back to see how she was, or Sir Basil come to order her to reconcile herself to the marriage.

It was neither. Instead Kit stood there, swathed in black, his full, caped cloak flowing down over his thigh-high black leather boots. His face was shadowed by the wide brim of his black hat, but his eyes glittered, reflecting the candlelight, as he drew off his silver-studded, black leather gauntlets.

"What are you doing here?" Bliss demanded, pushing herself up from the pillows. "Are the highways deserted tonight? Could you not find any travelers to rob?"

Kit shrugged a shoulder. "All the world seems to have stayed at home tonight," he replied, matching her sharp-edged tone.

"You should have come earlier," Bliss bandied. "You could have robbed my guardian and the Villierses. Again."

Kit laughed without mirth. "I've tasted Master Villiers's lead once. It was enough. And I had little gain to show for my trouble."

When Bliss would have replied, Kit waved a hand, dismissing the subject. "Tell me what it is that troubles you, Bliss," he said softly.

Bliss looked away as he came to the bedside. He tossed his hat onto the coverlet and laid his gauntlets beside it. The candle flame threw the planes of his face into sharp relief, rendering him, if it were possible, even more handsome than Bliss remembered. But then she saw again in her mind's eye the picture that had greeted her that day at his cottage—the picture of Kit and his blonde village girl laughing together. Pain, like the stabbing of a needle-sharp stiletto, filled her heart.

"Go away," she whispered, a catch in her voice, a sob in her throat. "Just go away."

"Bliss." Kit reached for her. His hand encircled her delicate wrist and he turned her toward him. "Tell me."

"My Lord Holme," she said brokenly, "has contracted a marriage for me. I am to wed with—"

"Stephen Villiers," Kit finished for her. His heart seemed to stop in his chest. He felt suffused with hot, sweet hatred for the man who had once tried to kill him. Images flashed in his mind—images of Stephen touching Bliss, holding her, possessing her—and Kit was filled with a possessive fury that shocked him. He had not realized until that moment how much he wanted her, how fervently he longed to possess her—not only her body but her future, her life.

Her eyes averted, Bliss did not see the play of emotions that flitted across Kit's face. She was too sunk in her own misery to suspect the depth of his. She could not begin to imagine the emotions warring inside him.

But Kit, after that first shocking flare of emotion, brought his senses under a tight rein. His face assumed a mask of cool amusement, of casual indifference.

"My congratulations," he said, rising from the bed's edge. "Doubtless you shall be moving back to London soon."

Bliss stared at him, stung by his coldness. Could he not see how much the thought of this marriage hurt her? Or was it simply that he did not care?

She did not bother trying to decide which it was. She could not bear another ounce of pain. Not then. She had too much pain in her heart already.

"Oh, get out of here, damn you!" she snarled, fighting back the white-hot tears that welled to the surface so easily. "Go back to your cottage! Go back to your blonde doxy! I hope she gives you the pox!"

Bemused by the sudden change—both in the subject and in Bliss—Kit did not at first realize what she had said. When he did, Kit stared at her. "My what?" he asked.

"Don't pretend to be innocent!" she snapped. "I saw you. Oh, aye. I went to your cottage. I thought you might need something. But what did I find? You and your doxy! Doubtless she can give you anything you might need!"

"My doxy?" Kit thought back, mentally reviewing the visitors he'd had at the little cottage. "Ah! You must mean Bess. She's—"

"I don't give a damn what or who she is!" Bliss cried, seizing a pillow and flinging it at him. "Just get out, damn you!"

Kit smiled. Kneeling amid the tumbled bed-clothes, her cheeks flushed, her titian hair streaming, her eyes bright with unshed tears, Bliss was a fetching sight.

"Jealousy becomes you, my sweet," he said softly.

Bliss gasped. It was true! She was jealous! But to have him know it—to have revealed it to him—mortified her.

"Get out!" she growled, sliding off the bed and running toward the door. "Get out this moment or by God I'll tell my guardian you are here and he'll see you on Tyburn in a trice!"

Slipping on his gauntlets, Kit picked up his hat and swept her a grand, courtier's bow. "As you will—my Lady Villiers," he acquiesced, and was gone as silently as he'd come.

Bliss stood there, alone once more in her room. "My Lady Villiers." How cold his voice had sounded. How unconcerned. He did not care that she was to be another man's wife. He did not care that she was to be forced into a loveless marriage with another. He did not care at all.

And he had not, she noticed, denied his liaison with the girl she had seen at his cottage. He had only been amused by her jealousy.

Picking up the pillow she had thrown at him,

Bliss climbed back into bed and lay down, holding it close in her arms.

"He cares nothing for me," she whispered to the darkness at the corners of the dimly lit room. "He cares nothing for me at all."

And it seemed that, in that moment, her embattled heart shattered like crystal into a thousand glittering fragments.

When Kit left Bliss's rooms, he went to the stables and Isaac's cozy chambers where a warm fire and a mug of ale were always waiting for him.

Ale in hand, he sat before the fire scowling at the orange-red flames in the soot-tinged stone hearth.

"He's bartered her away, damn his eyes!" he muttered. "He's sold her for the Villiers name and position."

"Exchanged her fortune for their lineage and influence," Isaac observed. "'Tis the way of such things among the mighty, is it not?"

"Even so," Kit blustered. "This man Villiers is a fool. Doubtless he pictures himself playing the gentleman at the royal Stuart's court decked out in the satins and jewels Bliss's money will buy him, gambling away her fortune at the tables every night."

Isaac cast a sideways glance at Kit. "She will be very unhappy in this marriage," he observed. "If it could be stopped . . ."

"Stopped?" Kit drank deeply of his ale. "I doubt it could be. Holme would have to nullify the contract, and he is far too enamored of the notion of allying himself through Bliss with the Villierses to do that. He would not give that up."

"I was not speaking of Lord Holme," Isaac informed him. "If Lady Bliss does not want the marriage, could not the two of you, between you—"

"No!" Slamming down his mug, Kit pushed himself out of his chair. "What could I give her? A cottage in the forest? Food and clothing bought with stolen gold? Endless worry that her husband will end his days on Tyburn Hill leaving her behind with the stigma of his crimes?"

"But if you married her," Isaac pointed out, "Chatham Castle and all its possessions would be—"

"Enough," Kit growled, his face darkening. "I'll not gain Chatham that way."

"It does not trouble my Lord Villiers to gain Chatham 'that way,'" Isaac reminded him, hoping jealousy would overcome pride.

Kit clapped his hat atop his head. "At least 'my Lord Villiers' has a name, a family, to barter with. 'Tis more than I have to offer." He shook his head when Isaac would have objected. "No, my friend, 'tis impossible." He sighed. "And the way of the world. Good night."

Isaac's eyes were sad as he watched Kit disappear into the darkness. He knew there was little he could do to change Kit's mind once it was set for or against anything. He could only hope that time, circumstances, and the love he knew Kit and Bliss bore for one another in their secret hearts would overcome what seemed to be overwhelming odds.

Chapter 9

Bliss was still in her rooms the next day, bathed but not yet dressed, putting off as long as possible the moment when she must go down and face her betrothed and his family, when a message came from Stephen asking her to ride with him.

"What will you tell him?" Mercy wanted to know as she stood before the armoires containing Bliss's gowns. "You could say your headache is no better."

"No," Bliss disagreed. "Perhaps if I can speak to Stephen alone, away from his mother and Sir Basil, I can make him see that we would not suit one another. Surely there must be other heiresses who would be more welcoming of his suit.

He could find another woman to fill the Villiers family coffers.

"Go down to him, Mercy, and tell him I will join him in an hour's time. Then come back and help me dress."

The maid left and Bliss went to one of the armoires and pulled out a habit of cherry cloth braided with silver. In a box on a shelf rested a silver-plumed cherry hat to match. The color, Bliss knew, was not the most flattering shade with her red hair, but then she was not interested in appearing at her best. If Stephen found her less attractive in the harsh light of day, he might be more agreeable to the breaking of the contract her guardian had negotiated with his harridan of a mother.

When Mercy returned she wrinkled her pert, upturned nose at the red habit. "Oh, not that one, milady. The heather blue is so much prettier. Or the pale green."

"No, this one," Bliss insisted. "I have my reasons. Now come, pin up my hair for me. Has my Lord Villiers sent to the stables for the horses?"

It was little more than an hour later that Bliss descended the stairs and found Stephen waiting for her, a small hamper at his booted feet.

"I've had some things packed for us," he told her. "A bottle of wine, some cheese, bread. I thought we could stop somewhere, find some pretty spot, and get to know one another better."

Bliss nodded. "There are some things I must speak with you about," she told him. "Alone."

Offering Bliss his arm, Stephen picked up the basket and the two of them left the castle for the courtyard where Bliss's mare and Stephen's gelding were waiting.

It was a pity, Bliss reflected as they rode out of the courtyard and away from the castle, that her feelings were so set against Stephen Villiers. He was handsome, very tall and elegant in his buff and brown, his plumed hat resting on his light brown hair that fell in luxurious waves to his shoulders. His eyes, green like his mother's and sister's, were filled with admiration whenever they rested on her. In such moments Bliss could almost believe that, unlike his grasping female relatives, it was not wholly for her fortune that Stephen pursued her.

Still, however handsome and courtly Stephen might be, Bliss's heart belonged to another. Her foolish, treacherous heart had been stolen that first night in the forest by Kit Quinn.

Bliss sighed. What a willful, capricious thing a heart was. Common sense, practicality, nothing mattered. The heart did as it pleased and damn the consequences.

"What is troubling you?" Stephen wanted to know.

"I'm sorry?" Bliss said. "I did not hear you."

"I did not say anything. Nor did you. You seemed to be a thousand miles away and just now you heaved the most heart-rending sigh. What is wrong?"

"We'll talk about it when we stop," Bliss promised.

Stephen's fair brows arched. "I don't like the sound of that."

Bliss looked away. He would like it even less when he discovered she wanted to end their betrothal. She hoped against hope she could make him see how unsuited they would be as man and wife. It was her only hope of escaping the marriage.

"Is this Chatham?" Stephen was asking as they approached the village.

"Aye," Bliss confirmed. "Take care, though. The folk hereabouts are loyal to their former lord, the Baron de Wilde. I don't believe they care much for me."

"How could they not?" Stephen countered. "I cannot imagine anyone preferring anyone over such a beautiful mistress as you."

Bliss smiled wanly. His flattery was meant to beguile, to charm, she supposed. But in view of what she was about to say to him it was unwelcome.

As they entered the village, riding side by side, the villagers reacted to them much as they had to Bliss when she had passed through before. Some were curious, some sullen, some acknowledged their presence, some pretended not to notice. But one of them Bliss noticed especially, even before Stephen called her to Bliss's attention.

"I wonder who that pretty wench might be," he mused.

"I don't know," Bliss snapped, eyes narrowing when she saw it was Bess, the girl who'd been with Kit at the cottage.

"I'm surprised she does not work at the castle. Some of the maids there are dour-faced old jades. I dare say hers would be a welcome face and—"

"Maidservants are chosen to work," Bliss snapped, "not to please ogling masters!"

Stephen grinned, believing Bliss was jealous over his admiration of the girl. "As you say, sweetheart," he acquiesced, pleased.

Bliss gritted her teeth. She knew what Stephen thought. Soon enough she would disabuse him of the notion that she cared enough for him to be jealous of the girl. What was most unbearable was the thought of seeing Kit's pretty village wench day in and day out beneath her very nose at Chatham Castle.

Kicking her mare into a gallop, she left Stephen, and Chatham, far behind. As she passed the churchyard she unconsciously turned in the direction of Kit's cottage. Riding into the forest, her only thought was to put as much distance as possible between herself and Kit's doxy.

"Bliss!" Stephen called after her, his spurs digging into the glossy sides of the gelding as he tried to catch up with her. "Bliss, wait!"

But they were deep in the forest before he came abreast of her. Both Bliss and her mare were winded, and when Stephen asked her to stop she readily agreed.

"What is wrong with you today?" Stephen asked as he lifted Bliss down from her sidesaddle and tethered both horses in the shade on the banks of a small brook.

"I have a great deal on my mind," Bliss told him as he carried the basket to a shady spot beneath an ancient oak tree.

"Does it concern us?" he asked, taking a blanket from the basket and spreading it on the ground.

"It does," Bliss admitted. "I must speak with you most seriously, Stephen."

"I am at your disposal, milady," he said, his tone teasing. "But come, share some wine with me first."

Bliss sat near him on the blanket and accepted the wine glass he held out to her. He wasn't going to make this easy for her, but she had not expected him to. Still, she steeled her resolve, reminding herself that she had no reason to feel sorry for him. There was no question of breaking his heart. He did not know her well enough to love her. Surely his feelings could go no further than an admiration of her beauty, perhaps a budding affection. Better to nip it in the bud now than to let it drag on.

"Stephen," she said at last, shaking her head

to refuse the bread and cheese he offered her. "I have something to say to you."

"You don't wish to marry me," he said quietly, eying her over the rim of his glass.

Bliss stared at him, surprised. "I—but—how did you know what I was going to say?"

"Sir Basil told me you had misgivings about the marriage."

"Misgivings hardly describes it," Bliss told him frankly. "You must see that we would not suit, Stephen."

"I don't see that at all," he disagreed. "Bliss, this is merely fear. I understand. You are young. The thought of marriage must be frightening to you, but—"

"It is not fear!" Bliss insisted. "I hardly know you! You hardly know me!"

"Then how do you know we would not suit?" he demanded.

Bliss frowned, exasperated. "I know one thing," she told him, setting her glass aside. "I know I do not wish to marry you. I do not love you."

"As you have said," Stephen replied, apparently unperturbed, "you hardly know me. It takes time for love to grow between two people."

Bliss thought of the electricity that had crackled between herself and Kit from the first moment their eyes had met. That had been the first glimmering of love, though she had not known it at the time. It had been mutual, instantaneous.

It was that elusive, electric emotion she wanted in a marriage.

"Stephen, please," she said, rising. "I cannot marry you. That is all."

She looked back expecting to find him angry. But the look on his face as he rose and came toward her was one of patient serenity.

"Bliss," he said gently when he reached her. "You are young, innocent. You know nothing of the ways of men and women."

Bliss flushed, thinking of Kit and the feeling he aroused in her when he held her and touched her and kissed her. Nothing of love, indeed!

"I don't see what that has to do with this," she told him coldly. "It is simply a matter of—"

"Bliss," he said patiently, his hand sliding around her upper arm and drawing her toward him. "You must not be afraid."

"I am not afraid," she insisted, trying without success to draw her arm from his grasp. "Why will you not listen to me?"

"I think you are afraid," he persisted, his other hand capturing her other arm. "And I mean to show you there is nothing to fear."

Bliss gasped, pulling back as far as his too-tight embrace would allow. His face descended toward hers and she realized, too late, that he intended to kiss her.

"No, Stephen!" she cried, but he had pulled her against him, his long, lean body curving over her.

Bliss struggled in his arms but his strength

was too great to resist. She tried to cry out but his lips, slanted across her own, smothered her pleas.

"Don't fight me, Bliss," he hissed, using his height and weight to bear her to the ground. "Let me take you. I'll show you how well suited we are."

"Let me go!" Bliss shrieked, trying without much success to stem the rising tide of panic inside her. "You can't do this! You can't!"

"But I can," he cooed. "The contracts are signed. You are mine, Bliss, to do with as I please."

Bliss writhed beneath him, desperate to escape, knowing even as she did that her fear, her struggles, excited him even more. She felt the hot tears flooding her eyes, trickling down into the tangles of titian curls spread out about her head. She bit at the hands that held her wrists imprisoned on either side of her head, but Stephen only laughed. Holding both her wrists with one hand, he pulled them up above her head while with his other hand he tugged at the cherry skirts of her habit.

A moan of despair escaped her as she felt his hand on her thigh above the lace-gartered silk of her stocking.

"Please, Stephen," she sobbed, "please don't do this. Please, stop!"

Stephen's green eyes glittered as he looked down into her tear-stained face. "In a moment, beautiful Bliss, you'll know what pleasure is.

And then you'll beg me not to stop!''

Bliss sobbed as he forced her knees apart and moved between her thighs. There seemed nothing she could do; she was lost. He would have his way, and both her guardian and his mother would support him saying the contracts were, after all, as binding as the ceremony and she had no right to refuse him.

She heard Stephen's breath, harsh, rasping, in her ear as he moved above her, fumbling with his clothes. She was frightened, but it was not the same kind of fear she'd felt on the night Kit had come to her room. That night, despite her innocence, she had felt the sweet, fierce desire deep in the pit of her belly, the rising, melting heat inside her. She had not known what he meant to do to her, but some hitherto unknown emotion had spurred her forward, made her want it.

The fear she felt now was something far different. Darker. It was a stomach-churning, sickening kind of fear. She was being dragged against her will into a world she did not want to enter—a world from which there could be no escape. If only—

She screamed as Stephen pressed himself against her, trying to take her, trying to force himself past the untouched, unyielding barrier of her virginity.

"Let me go!" she shrieked, pounding at his shoulders with her fists, writhing beneath him, terrified. "Let me go, damn you!"

Stephen did not answer, but another, deeper voice did, saying:

"The lady said let her go!"

The words were swiftly followed by the kick of a heavy jackboot that sent Stephen sprawling into the weeds and freed Bliss from his loathsome embrace.

Bliss looked up and saw Kit, his face flushed with fury, his pistol poised, its gaping bore aimed at Stephen. His intention was clear.

Scrambling to her feet, Bliss ran to him. She stepped between him and Stephen, who was crouched on the ground fumbling to rearrange his clothing.

"Don't kill him!" she cried. "Please, please, don't!"

Kit's sable eyes shifted from Stephen to Bliss. They stared at her, incredulous. "Did you enjoy his rough wooing, then, milady?" he asked tightly.

"No! I hated it!" she whispered, fresh tears blurring her vision. Reaching out, she laid a trembling hand on his chest. "But if you kill him you will hang. I could not bear it."

A muscle trembled in Kit's cheek. His eyes went back to Stephen who took a step toward him. "Stay where you are!" he snarled. "Another step and it will be your last."

"You had no right to interfere," Stephen hissed, braver now with Bliss between them. "The lady is to be my wife!"

Kit's face flushed a deeper crimson. "'Twas

not the gentlest courtship I've ever seen," he growled. He trembled, and Bliss knew that only her presence, her entreaties, kept him from killing Stephen.

"Please, Kit," she said too softly for Stephen to hear. "He is not worth your life."

Kit's eyes searched her face. "Go back to Chatham," he told her. "Send someone back for him. I'll be gone before they get here."

"You won't kill him, will you?" she asked.

"Not if you don't wish me to, no," he acquiesced. "Though I'm damned if I know why." He sighed, gazing down into her upraised eyes. "No, I won't kill him—this time. Now, go on. Back to Chatham. He'll be here—alive."

Mounting her mare, Bliss rode away knowing Kit would do as he promised and spare Stephen's life and thanking whatever guardian angel had sent him to her to save her from Stephen —at least this time.

Chapter 10

Returning to Chatham, Bliss sought out Isaac in the stables. She drew him aside as a groom took the reins of her mare and led the animal away.

"You must send someone to get Stephen," she told him. "Kit . . ." She glanced around to be sure they were not being overheard. "Kit had him at gunpoint when I left. He said to send someone back for Stephen."

"Does he—does milord Villiers know who Kit is?"

Bliss shook her head. "I don't think so. I don't think Stephen recognized Kit as the highwayman he shot. At any rate, Stephen is in the forest at the edge of the road not far from the wall. Do

Sandra DuBay

you know the wall I mean? The one that leads to Kit's cottage."

"Aye, milady," Isaac nodded. "I'll go myself. I should be able to find him."

Thanking him, Bliss left the stables and went into the castle. To her chagrin, the first person she met was Lady Daphne.

"Ah, my dear, you've returned," she said, apparently not noticing Bliss's rumpled habit or the leaves and twigs clinging to her tangled curls. "Did you enjoy your ride?"

"Not particularly," Bliss snapped. "And I find your son's notions of courtship not at all to my liking, madam."

The smile on Lady Daphne's narrow face wavered. Her green eyes glanced toward the door behind Bliss.

"Where is Stephen?" she asked. "Still in the stables?"

"No," Bliss replied. "I left him in the forest. I sent a groom back for him, so doubtless he will be returning in due course of time. Now, if you will excuse me, madam . . ."

With the sketchiest of curtsies, Bliss swept past her would-be mother-in-law and mounted the stairs to her rooms.

Summoning Mercy, Bliss called for water and bathed herself, scrubbing as hard as she could, trying in vain to wash away the memory of Stephen's touch, of his body trying to possess hers. She shuddered as she remembered lying beneath him, remembered his kisses, his clutching caresses. The memories repulsed her, but she could not drive them from her mind.

Even after her bath when, dressed in a clean, soft nightdress and wrapper, she sat before the fire while Mercy brushed her drying hair, Bliss could not forget the look in Stephen's eyes when he had seized her, pushed her down. There had been no love there, no tenderness, only a fierce possessiveness and a grim determination to force her to his will.

Both Bliss and Mercy started when the outer door of Bliss's rooms flew open, then crashed shut. The heavy footfalls crossing the sitting room floor could belong to only one person, Bliss thought. Rising, she motioned Mercy away and drew herself up, ready to face her guardian's wrath.

Sir Basil stormed into her bedchamber without bothering to knock.

"What is this I hear, miss, about your leaving Lord Villiers in the forest? His mother is most upset."

"Doubtless she is," Bliss acknowledged. "But I care this much for her and her vapors!" She snapped her fingers.

Sir Basil's eyes blazed. "Leave us alone," he ordered Mercy.

The maid looked to Bliss, who nodded, dismissing her. With a curtsy to her mistress and a wary look at Sir Basil, Mercy retreated, leaving Bliss and her guardian alone.

"You try my patience, miss," Sir Basil snarled.

"By the heavens, you do! There are times when I could cheerfully strangle you!"

"There are times, my lord," Bliss countered, "when I would thank you for strangling me. It would spare me the fate you have condemned me to."

"Fate?" Sir Basil's eyes narrowed. "What the devil do you mean?"

"I mean, sir, the marriage you have contracted with that woman and her son."

"He is a Villiers," Sir Basil pointed out, "highly connected and well-favored."

"He is a monster!" Bliss cried. "And I would as soon wed with the devil as with him!" Tears sprang to her eyes and Bliss fought to quell them. She wanted no show of weakness now. She meant to fight this marriage, even if it be a hopeless fight, and she knew that weeping would only weaken her.

"Why do you say this?" her guardian demanded. "Explain yourself. Has he beaten you?"

"No," Bliss admitted. "But—"

"No!" Sir Basil interrupted. "He has not, much though you may deserve it."

Bliss's eyes blazed with indignation. "He has not beaten me, my lord," she retorted. "I could sooner bear a beating! He took me riding this afternoon with the intention of forcing himself upon me." Taking a deep breath, she forced down the repugnance those words evoked in her. "Aye, my lord," she went on. "He pretended to be all gallantry, all charm, and then when we were alone in the forest he tried to force himself upon me!''

She waited for her words to penetrate her guardian's mind. She expected outrage, indignation, expected him to denounce Stephen for a villain. But Sir Basil only stared at her as if she were mad.

''Is that what all this is about?'' he demanded scathingly.

''You seem mighty unconcerned,'' Bliss snapped. ''Did you not hear what I said? The man tried to rape me!''

Sir Basil sighed, regarding her with impatient disdain. ''You are a fool, my girl, a missish fool! The contracts are signed. You are as much his wife as if the ceremony had taken place. It is his right to have you when and where he pleases. You had no right to refuse him.''

''My God!'' Bliss cried. ''His right! To push me down on the ground! To tear at my clothes! To assault me like an animal!''

''Get used to it, my girl,'' Sir Basil told her, a smirk in his voice. ''You'll come to like it in time.''

''Never!'' Bliss shouted. ''Never! If he ever tries to do that to me again I'll kill him! I swear it!''

Her guardian ground his teeth. ''You'll be damned lucky if he doesn't beat you to within an inch of your life on your wedding night, you little fool! It's what you deserve! It's what I'd do if I were your husband!"

"He'll never be my husband!" Bliss snarled. "I won't marry him! I won't!"

"By God!" Sir Basil growled. Seizing Bliss by the arms he shook her. "You'll marry him or I swear I'll—"

The bedchamber door flew open and Lady Daphne, pale face flushed crimson, green eyes slitted with fury, swept into the room.

"My son has returned!" she cried. "Some wretch accosted him in the forest! Held him at gunpoint! And this chit left him there! Left him at the mercy of that villain!"

"Was he harmed?" Sir Basil asked with a concern that made Bliss want to scream.

"No," Lady Daphne admitted. "But the villain left poor Stephen there, tied to a tree. And what was more . . ." She pointed an accusing finger at Bliss. ". . . she knew the varlet!"

Bliss's heart seemed to stop in her chest. What if Stephen had heard what she'd said to Kit? Was it possible that—

"She spoke to him!" Lady Daphne was continuing. "She spoke with him and convinced him not to kill my son. What is more, the man told her to go, to ride off and leave my son in his clutches. And she obeyed him!"

"Well?" Sir Basil snapped, turning to Bliss. "Is this true? Did you know the man?"

"No," Bliss lied, relieved that Stephen had not, after all, heard what had passed between Kit and herself. "I did not know him. He came upon us by chance. He saw that Stephen was . . ." She blushed. ". . . what was happening and thought to rescue me. That is all."

"I don't believe you!" Lady Daphne cried. "I think you and this man are conspiring to do my son some harm!"

Bliss rolled her eyes, and even Sir Basil eyed the woman with impatience.

"It seems unlikely, madam," he said, "since by your own admission your son was not harmed."

"He might have been killed!" she argued. "And it would have been all your fault!" She waggled a finger in Bliss's face. "You are a horrid, selfish creature!"

"If I am so horrid, so selfish," Bliss told her, "surely you would not wish to have me as your daughter-in-law."

Lady Daphne stared at her, lips compressed in a tight line. But Sir Basil was not at such a loss.

"Your ploy will not work, miss," he told her severely. "The marriage will take place and you will reconcile yourself to it."

"Never!" Bliss hissed.

"Oh, I think you will," her guardian said confidently. "If you get hungry enough or thirsty enough you may begin to see more clearly." He smiled at Lady Daphne. "Come, madam, it is high time this little hoyden learned some manners."

With Lady Daphne on his arm, Sir Basil left Bliss's bedchamber. He pulled the door shut behind them, and Bliss heard the sound of the key turning in the lock.

Lifting her chin, Bliss glared at the locked door. What did she care, she asked herself, if he locked her in? If he refused her food and water? She would stay in her room till doomsday rather than agree to a marriage she did not want with a man she could not love.

But as afternoon gave way to evening and evening to night, Bliss's resolve began to waver. Her stomach growled, for she had had nothing save the glass of wine in the forest since breakfast. Her throat, parched, ached for water. She knew that before the night was over she would be pleading for a sip of water to wet her dry mouth, soothe her sore throat.

She felt powerless. Before the combined determination of Lady Daphne and Sir Basil, how could she hope to escape the fate they had planned for her?

The prospect was bleak. Tied for life to Stephen when her heart, her soul, her body longed for Kit. Forced to submit to Stephen's demands, forced to oblige him when and where he chose, to suffer the rough caresses of his hands, the invasion of her body by his, all the while remembering the brief, incomplete heaven of Kit's love.

Despite what he said, despite his apparent indifference to her plight when she'd told him of her betrothal, Bliss was certain Kit cared for her. When he had rescued her from Stephen he'd been ready to kill Stephen for trying to rape her. If only . . .

Sinking onto the foot of her bed, Bliss stared out at the moonlit night. If only she could be with Kit for even one night. If only she could know one precious night of true love, real love, perhaps she could bear the prospect of a loveless marriage with Stephen. At least she would have known the joy of love, she would have her memories to comfort her, to cling to, during the bleak years ahead.

But how? She glanced at the locked door. Even if she could leave her room, how could she make her way out of the castle undetected? She would have to be a ghost, flitting blithely through the thick stone walls and—

She gasped, remembering the nights Kit had come to her here, in this very room. He had appeared like a ghost and disappeared again. What was it he had said about the castle?

"The walls are very thick. They are honeycombed with passages, hidey-holes, secret rooms . . ."

"If I could find the door," she said softly, looking toward the tapestry behind which he'd disappeared.

She felt a nervous fluttering in her stomach. Even if she found the entrance, could she find her way outside? She did not even know where the passage led. She could lose her way within the thick stone walls and never find her way out. And how could Sir Basil, who did not even know the passage existed, find her? All he would know was that she was missing.

Cursing herself for a coward, Bliss marched toward the tapestry. She must be prepared to risk everything, she told herself sternly. After all, what had her guardian condemned her to if not a kind of living death? She should be prepared to risk everything to attain her heart's desire.

Behind the tapestry the wall appeared solid. Bliss felt the rough stones, tapped them, pushed at them. There seemed to be no seams, no cracks. But a door had to be there. It had to! Kit had appeared and disappeared with such ease. The latch must be there hidden among the stones.

But as she poked and prodded and nudged, her frustration grew. And then, when she was about to give up, to decide that the very Fates were against her, she balled her fist and struck a stone high above her head.

Soundlessly the wall moved, a section barely wide enough to admit a man separated from the rest. It swung open a few inches, pivoting on a rod running through it from top to bottom.

Bliss gasped, stepping back. The chilled air escaping through the opening raised gooseflesh on her arms and breasts. She stared into the darkness beyond the opening and wondered what she might find. The prospect of plunging into that unknown darkness frightened her. It would be so easy, she knew, to push the door shut again and resign herself to her fate, but then she would always wonder what might have happened had she taken the chance. She knew she might very well always regret her cowardice in staying safely in her room when everything she wanted most in the world lay in the darkness at the other end of the tunnel.

Hurrying to her wardrobe, Bliss pulled out a black cloak and a pair of fur-lined boots. Then, taking up a candle, she went to the passage behind the tapestry and plunged into the darkness that lay beyond.

Chapter 11

The passage stretched off into the invisible distance, only the patch of candlelight surrounding her revealing to Bliss the lost, moss-grown tunnel in which she found herself. Here and there as she made her way she could see evidence of doorways leading into other chambers, but she did not try any of them. She could not know where she might be but felt she had not gone far enough to be anywhere but well inside the castle.

She cried out, stumbling, as the passage dropped off seemingly into nothingness before her. Bliss crouched, holding the candle out, and saw that she stood at the head of a narrow set of steps. Taking a deep breath, the candle held before her, her other hand holding her nightdress and cloak well away from her feet to keep from tripping, Bliss gingerly descended the steps and resumed her trek.

In the darkness surrounding her, Bliss could hear the scratching of tiny claws, the scuttling of tiny feet. She was thankful for the darkness that concealed the creatures living in the tunnel and for their instinctive fear that sent them skittering out of her path, away from the light of the candle she held in her trembling hand. She shuddered, recoiling, at the gossamer caress of spiderwebs hanging like tattered lace curtains across the passage. The darkness yawned before her like an endless abyss.

Holding her candle high, Bliss looked back in the direction from which she'd come. Her courage was failing her. For all she knew, she might have gone in a circle—she might be back where she started. She might even be in a completely different part of the castle further from her goal than ever.

She pondered turning back. But then she noticed a sliver of light beneath a door off to her right. Perhaps if she could see where she was she might find she had come far enough—she might be nearly outside the castle.

Shielding the light of her candle, Bliss crept to the door. It was not hidden. No effort seemed to have been made to conceal it, at least not on the tunnel side. But what, she wondered, lay on the other side?

Ear pressed to the door, Bliss listened. She

longed for a voice, some clue as to what she might find if she opened the door. But there was nothing. There was no way to discover where she'd gotten to unless she took the chance and opened the door.

Extinguishing her candle, Bliss sat the candle-stick on the floor. Her hand trembled as she grasped the iron ring set into the thick planks. It turned easily in her hand and the door swung open.

Bliss's eyes were wide as she peered around the edge of the door. Her heart pounded, she held her breath. It was only when she saw where she was, when she realized where the tunnel had taken her, that she let out her pent-up breath and allowed herself to hope. She stepped into the room.

"Isaac?" she called softly, for she had emerged in the old head groom's quarters in the stables. "Isaac?"

The white-haired old man appeared in the doorway, a tankard of ale in his hand. He glanced up and saw her, started, and dropped the tankard to the floor.

"Sweet Jesu!" he breathed, ignoring the ale spreading across the worn boards of the floor. "Milady!"

"Isaac . . ." She went to him. "I'm sorry to frighten you. I came through the passage. I need your help."

"What can I do, milady?" he asked.

"You can help me get a horse out of this

castle. I want to go to Kit."

Isaac stared at her, surprised. "Tonight, milady? By yourself?"

"Aye." Bliss bit her lip. "My Lord Holme means me to wed with Lord Villiers. He has sworn not to release me from my room until I agree." She took a deep, calming breath. "I don't know how I can escape this marriage, Isaac. All I know is I must see Kit again, if only once more, before . . ."

Isaac's mind raced. He knew of Kit's feelings for Bliss, and he also knew that Kit would never try to prevent Bliss's marrying a man of title and position. It frustrated Isaac beyond measure to know that Kit would not try to make Bliss his own because he could not give her any of the things a woman of her birth and breeding expected from life. It did not matter to Kit that Bliss had inherited an enormous fortune—all that Kit knew was that he could not come to her on equal terms.

But, Isaac reasoned to himself now, if Bliss went to Kit, if her love for him and his love for her were forced into the open, surely then Kit would not stand by and watch as she became another man's wife.

He grinned. "Aye, milady, I'll help you. But you'll not go alone. I'll ride with you through the woods. I know a shorter route to Kit's cottage that goes round the village. And I'll wait and see ye safely back."

Bliss blushed. "There's no need for that," she

told him, not knowing how to tell him she intended to remain there all night. "I'm certain I could find my way—"

"I'll see ye back," Isaac insisted. "I'll get ye back by dawn, milady. Now I'll go see to the horses."

Bliss turned away to hide her crimson cheeks as the old man left. It was obvious that Isaac knew her intentions and apparently approved, but still she was embarrassed that he should know she meant to spend the night with Kit.

Going to the bucket of fresh water that stood on a table, Bliss lifted a dipperful of water and drank thirstily, feeling the cool, sweet water ease her parched throat and chill her empty stomach. A half loaf of bread lay there and she broke off a piece and ate it.

"Milady?" Isaac's voice, hushed so as not to waken the grooms sleeping in their quarters not far away, made Bliss turn around. "Open the outside door, if you please."

Bliss did as he asked, then stood back in amazement as he led two horses, saddled and ready, through his rooms and out into the night.

"We'd best be off," he told her. "The dawn won't wait forever."

Her booted foot in Isaac's hand, Bliss was lifted into her sidesaddle. The old groom swung up onto his own mount and they were off. They galloped through the night, and the wind blew through Bliss's streaming hair and made her cloak billow back over her horse's rippling tail.

NIGHTRIDER

Isaac led her with certainty through the forests he had known since childhood. When they came to the little river that ran beneath the bridge in Chatham village, Isaac took her reins and led her horse through the water, carefully choosing a shallow part where the water did not rise above the animal's haunches. And then they were off again, into the deep forest, without even the light of the moon to show them the way, heedless of whatever night creatures prowled there.

By the time they reached Kit's cottage, Bliss was too exhilarated by the wild night ride to be frightened. It was only when Isaac dismounted and came to help her down that she realized the time had come when she must face Kit, reveal her feelings, her desires, and face whatever consequences might result.

"I'll be here, milady, when ye want to go back," Isaac promised.

Bliss nodded. "Thank you, Isaac," she told him. "I . . ."

But there was nothing she could say, nothing that needed to be said. Pulling her cloak tight about her, Bliss went to the door and knocked.

There was no reply, and for a long, awful moment Bliss wondered if Kit might be gone, might be out plying his trade on the King's highway. Then again, she realized, he might not be alone. If his pretty village girl, Bess, were there . . . Bliss shut her eyes, feeling a nervous fluttering in her stomach. How could she bear it if she had escaped from her room, ridden through the night, only to find Kit ensconced in his bed with his beautiful doxy?

She raised her hand to knock again but could not. She did not know how she would bear the humiliation of appearing at his door and finding him with a lover. Perhaps, she told herself, she should simply turn away. Perhaps she should go back to Chatham Castle, accept her fate, and try to bury whatever feelings she had for Kit. It might be better—for both of them. It might be best—.

"Bliss?" Unnoticed by Bliss who was deep in thought, the door had opened and Kit, breeches and shirt hurriedly drawn on, stood there. "What are you doing here? You didn't come alone!"

"No." Standing there, Bliss felt suddenly tongue-tied. "No, I didn't come alone. Isaac came with me."

Kit looked over her head and saw Isaac sitting near the base of a tree. The horses were tethered nearby.

"May I come in, Kit?" Bliss asked. "That is . . . unless . . . unless you have . . ."

A hint of a smile touched the corners of Kit's mouth. "I'm alone," he assured her. Reaching out, he took her hand and drew her into the cottage. "You're freezing. Come by the fire."

The cottage was one low-ceilinged room. At one end an enormous fireplace yawned, housing a blaze that dispelled the night chill. To one side of the fireplace were a table and chairs, on the other side stood a tester bed with thick, heavily carved posts and worn, blue velvet hangings, its rumpled coverlets testimony to Kit's recent awakening. A single candle burned on the floor beside the bed, throwing shadows into the thick ceiling beams above. Threadbare rugs covered the floor, its planks worn smooth by the feet of generations of inhabitants. There was an intimacy, a coziness about the place that Bliss had never found in any of the grand manors and castles in which she had grown up.

"Was your guardian very angry when you returned without Villiers?" Kit asked as Bliss rubbed her hands and held them out to the fire.

"Furious," Bliss admitted. "He locked me in my room and swore not to allow me food or water until I agreed to the marriage."

"But you got out," Kit observed.

"I remembered the nights you came to me. I found the passage and followed it to Isaac."

Kit laughed. "So you won't be missed?"

"Not until morning," she said softly. "I . . . I had to come, Kit. They will force me to marry Stephen. I know they will. I can think of no way to stop them. But I hate the thought of . . . of . . ." Her cheeks flushed crimson. ". . . of belonging to him."

Kit's voice was low, tense as he said, "Why have you come to me, Bliss?"

Turning to him, she found she could not raise her eyes to his face. "I cannot bear to live a life without ever knowing true love, Kit, real love. I have to know, if only for this one night, what love can truly be. I know that I . . . I think that you . . ." She faltered, her cheeks blazing. With trembling fingers she undid the clasp of her cloak and let it fall in a black velvet cascade to her feet. "Don't send me away, Kit, please."

Kit looked down at her. The firelight behind her threw her body into silhouette against the thin lawn of her nightdress. Flickering gold and red lights of the fire danced in the silken curls that framed her face. He closed his eyes. He was suffused with desire for her, the desire that he had fought against since the first moment he'd seen her.

"Bliss," he said tightly, "are you certain . . ."

"Aye," she breathed, "never more certain of anything."

"But what if . . . afterward . . ."

"Hush." She pressed her fingers to his lips to silence him. "Don't think of afterward, Kit, think only of tonight, of this moment."

She placed a trembling hand on his chest where the deep vee of his open shirt laid his chest bare. As her eyes gazed into his, she drowned in their dark depths. She held her breath as he raised his hands and cupped her face. She trembled as he bent toward her and kissed her so softly, so gently. As their lips met she swayed, her legs threatened to give way beneath her, but Kit's arm snaked behind her knees and he lifted her, swept her into his arms, and carried her to the warm tester bed.

Kit's hands trembled as he undid the laces of Bliss's gown. Her skin was satin-soft as he pushed the gown from her shoulders. Gently, slowly, he drew it off her, uncovering the pearl and alabaster beauty that had haunted his days and nights.

Bliss blushed, shielding her body with her hands. Kit smiled down at her, understanding. "You should not be embarrassed," he told her. "I've never seen a woman more beautiful."

Standing beside the bed, Kit pulled off his shirt and breeches. Bliss gasped, looking away. "You mustn't be frightened of me, Bliss," he told her, lying beside her. "I'm only a man."

"I am frightened," she admitted. "And yet . . ." She shivered at the touch of his hand on her hip, her waist. She touched his cheek. His sable hair twined about her fingers as he lowered his head and kissed her lips, her chin, her throat, her breasts. His lips captured one petal pink nipple, already tight and tingling like a rosebud. A surge of pure sensation ran through Bliss. She arched toward him, unable to get enough of his kisses, his caresses. Her body seemed to be melting as the heat within her rose to a fever pitch. She ached for . . . for . . . for something she'd never wanted, something she'd never dreamt of in her maidenly bed.

Kit moved above her. His hands gently parted her legs as he lay poised above her. And then . . .

The pain took her by surprise, jolting her

mind back in time to the forest floor where Stephen had tried to rape her.

"No!" Bliss cried, struggling. "You're hurting me!"

Kit drew away from her. His face was moist, his breathing was quick, harsh. His eyes burned with desire, but he recognized her fear.

"Hush, love," he soothed, kissing her. "I do not mean to hurt you. The pain will last but a moment. It is always so for a woman. Trust me, Bliss. Let me love you."

Bliss gazed up at him. She wanted him, needed him. "Aye," she whispered. "Love me, Kit. Love me now."

Forcing herself to lie still in his arms, Bliss held her breath, biting her lips to stifle her cry as Kit took her. She arched, expecting more pain to follow the single, stabbing hurt. But there was no more pain, there was only pleasure, vague at first, tantalizing, elusive, then growing, blossoming inside her until she could feel nothing else, think of nothing else.

She moaned as Kit moved, his body against hers, deep inside her. His lips were on her throat, her cheek, he kissed her lips gently, savagely. His body was hard against her soft skin, his flesh was hot, moist, his movements slow, gentle at first then faster, harder, driving Bliss beyond fear, beyond pain, beyond everything but the pleasure . . . pleasure of a kind she'd never imagined existed.

* * *

Afterward, while Bliss lay in Kit's arms, he kissed her tenderly.

"It will get better," he told her. "When it's not so new, when you're not so nervous, it will be much better for you, Bliss."

Bliss smiled and caressed his cheek but she did not believe him. Nothing, she told herself as she lay there in the warm bed, Kit's arms around her, could possibly be better than what they had just shared.

Chapter 12

Bliss smiled tremulously as Kit brushed a soft red curl back from her cheek. "I'll have to go soon," she told him, her voice filled with regret. "Dawn cannot be far away."

"Will you get back in the same way you got out?" Kit asked.

"Aye." She toyed with the fingers of the hand she held in her own. "Isaac said he would wait and take me back. I'll have to be back in my room before Sir Basil comes to unlock the door. He mustn't know I've been gone."

"The bastard," Kit growled. "I suppose he means to starve you into submission."

"I think he does," Bliss agreed.

"I have some bread and meat. I'll wrap some for you to take back."

Bliss rested her cheek on his shoulder. Her arms slipped around him and she pulled him close. "Oh, Kit," she sighed, "I don't want to marry Stephen. If only there was a way to thwart their plans. I thought if I could have even one night with you I could bear the marriage. But now . . ." She shuddered in Kit's arms. "Now the thought of wedding Stephen, of lying with him, turns my blood cold."

Kit lay beside her, his eyes trained on the tester above. "I doubt your guardian is a man to change his mind, Bliss. And the Villierses, doubtless, are too fond of the notion of gaining your fortune to give up their plans easily."

"I know," Bliss admitted. "But Kit, I . . . I don't love Stephen. I don't even like him. I love you!"

She watched, perplexed, as Kit pulled his arm from beneath her and slid out of the bed. Taking his breeches from the floor, he pulled them on and went to the cupboard where he busied himself cutting slices of bread and cold meat.

"Kit?" Bliss said, confused by his sudden change of mood. "Did you not hear what I said? I love you."

"I heard you," he replied. Wrapping the bread and meat in a cloth, Kit placed them on the table ready for her to take with her. When at last he turned his attention back to Bliss, his eyes were unreadable, his expression cryptic.

"You must not love me, Bliss," he told her sternly. "It is impossible for us. You know that."

"I don't know that at all!" she cried, wanting to weep. "Why do you say that?"

"Because it's true." Kit shook his head. "You're a lady. The mistress of great estates. Your place is at court dressed in silks and velvet, bedecked in jewels. I'm a highwayman. I live by night. I rob and steal for my living."

"You could leave the highway," she told him.

"I cannot," he disagreed.

"But why?"

Coming to the bedside, Kit handed Bliss her nightdress. He waited until she had pulled it over her head and buttoned it before he went on.

"When you inherited Chatham Castle," he told her, "most of Lord de Wilde's family retainers were turned out. Many of them were old. They had no homes, no families to turn to. I was indebted to Lord de Wilde so I felt it my responsibility to provide for his faithful servants."

"So you took to the highway to provide for them," Bliss surmised.

"Aye," Kit affirmed. "I did. They depend upon me, Bliss, for the food they eat, the clothes they wear, the roofs over their heads."

"Isaac once told me something of this," Bliss told him, "and I said had I known of their plight, I would have helped them."

"They would not accept help from you," Kit replied. "Most of them would rather starve than take gold from . . ."

"The usurper," Bliss supplied bitterly. "They would not take gold from me, but they will accept stolen gold?"

Kit avoided looking at her when he answered. "They would consider gold from you stolen as well."

Sliding off the bed, Bliss pulled on her boots and snatched up her cloak from the floor. "And do you also consider me a thief, Master Highwayman?" she snapped.

"There was a time," he admitted, "when I looked upon you as an intruder, a usurper, an enemy. But I know it was not your fault that you inherited Chatham and—"

"Generous of you!" she snapped. "Particularly when one stops to consider that the Lord de Wilde you and these villagers adore was a traitor to his King and country!"

"You will not speak of Lord de Wilde," Kit said coldly, his face hard.

Bliss opened her mouth to reply but bit back the words. She did not want to fight with him, not now, not over something that should make no difference between them.

"Kit," she said softly, "let's not argue about Lord de Wilde. Instead, we should be finding a way to be together despite Lord Holme, despite the Villierses."

"I told you, Bliss," Kit reminded her, "it is impossible."

"No, listen to me," she entreated. "If the villagers will only accept help from you, so be it. I will give you the gold and you can give it to them. They need never know it is—"

"No," Kit interrupted. "I won't be kept by any woman. I won't be bought and paid for. I'll earn my living even if it be on the King's highway."

"Damn you, Kit Quinn!" Bliss cried. "We could be together! Don't you want to be with me?"

Kit steeled himself, hardening his heart. He wanted to be with her more than she could possibly know, but there were too many obstacles that could not be overcome. It was better, he told himself, to force Bliss to hate him than to see her heart broken over a love that could never be.

"No," he told her coldly, "I don't want to be with you."

Bliss gasped. After what had just happened between them he could not mean what he'd said. "I don't believe you," she whispered. "How can you say such a thing now, after . . ."

Kit turned away lest his expression betray him. "You offered yourself to me of your own free will, milady. I'm not made of stone. But that does not mean I want to spend my life with you."

"Liar," Bliss breathed, trembling. "Liar!"

A knock on the door startled them both. Isaac's voice, muffled through the door panels, warned:

"Milady? 'Tis nearly dawn. We've got to get back to Chatham."

"I'm coming, Isaac," Bliss called back. She looked at Kit who stood with his back toward her. Her hand rose and stretched out toward him, but she could not bring herself to touch him. He seemed so cold, so distant. She felt at that moment she could not bear another harsh word, another second's coldness from him. She was confused, bewildered.

Pulling her cloak tight about her, Bliss went to the door. She opened it and started out, pausing only to say:

"Good-bye, Kit. I doubt we shall meet again."

Kit closed his eyes. His hands tightened on the back of the chair in front of him. It took all his strength not to run after her, to call her back, to hide her there in his cottage forever, just the two of them alone.

He heard the hoofbeats of the horses as Bliss and Isaac rode off into the night, racing the dawn back to Chatham Castle and safety. Too late he noticed the bundle containing the bread and meat he had prepared for Bliss. Now he seized it and, crushing it in his fists, threw it into the dwindling flames in the fireplace.

Bliss said nothing during the long ride home. With Isaac beside her she rode in silence, forcing back the tears that blurred her vision, stifling the sobs that swelled, aching, in her breast.

It was not until she had made her way back through the tunnel, not until she was safely returned to her room, tucked into her bed, that she gave way to her heartbreak, and the tears, the sobs, she had held back overcame her.

* * *

Bliss was sleeping when the key turned in the lock. She had cried herself to sleep even as dawn painted the horizon in purple and pink. Sir Basil entered the room and crossed to look down at his ward. The marks of her sorrow were plain on her pale cheeks. The fine lawn of her pillowcase was still wet with her tears.

Sir Basil smiled. He hoped her spirit had been broken. He hoped she would see the folly of her pitting herself against him in a fight she could not hope to win.

He leaned down and touched her shoulder. "Bliss?" she said quietly. "Bliss, wake up."

Groggy, dazed, Bliss blinked, then opened her dark-shadowed eyes. Pushing herself up on one elbow, she stared up at her guardian in confusion.

"What . . . ?" she mumbled. "Oh, what do you want?"

"What do you think?" Sir Basil retorted. "Have you come to your senses, my girl, or do you need another day in this room?"

"I . . ." Bliss wanted to argue, wanted to shout that he could keep her there forever and still she would refuse to bend to his will. But the words would not come. Her mind was still too full of Kit, of his love, his passion, his coldness, his callousness in taking her to his bed and then dismissing her like some common doxy. How could she have loved him? How could she have thought him different, more noble, than Stephen Villiers?

A little voice inside her whispered that Kit's coldness and callousness had been a sham. There was something else there, another reason for his behavior, there had to be, but she could not just then imagine what it might be. She could not, at that moment, decipher Kit's words, divine his meanings. The pain was still too new, too keen.

How much better, her bruised heart told her, to keep her emotions safe, to hold herself apart, to guard her heart. With Stephen there would be no danger. He could not touch that tender, vulnerable place deep inside her that Kit had torn asunder. He could never hurt her as Kit had hurt her.

"You need not lock me in any longer, my lord," she told her guardian, eyes fixed on the coverlet. "I will do as you wish."

Sir Basil stifled the triumphant laughter that welled into his throat. He had won as he'd always known he would, and it had taken far less time and effort than he'd imagined it might.

"I will have some food brought up to you," he told her. "Then you must bathe and dress. Tell your maid to begin packing. We leave at midday."

Bliss said nothing as her guardian turned to leave. It was not until he had nearly reached the door that she realized what he'd said.

"Leave, my lord?" she called after him.

"Aye, we're going to London," he replied, halfway out the door. "We've put off this business long enough.''

Bliss stared at the door as it closed behind him. Her first thought was to escape, to run back to Kit and beg him to tell her what obstacle stood between them—what was so insurmountable that love could not overcome it. But she knew she could not face Kit again, not in the cold light of day, not after what had passed between them in his bed—and afterward. There was nothing she could do to resolve their differences. She was not certain anything could resolve them. Perhaps Kit was right—theirs were two different worlds and it might be that neither could enter the other's.

Pushing back the coverlet, Bliss rose from her bed. Her body ached, bringing back memories of the night before, of Kit's body and her own, together, one.

Ruthlessly she pushed those memories out of her mind, relegated them to the deepest, darkest corner of her mind where they could not torture her, where they could remain, forgotten yet not forgotten, unable to hurt her except for those unguarded moments when she remembered what she had risked—and what she had lost— for love.

Chapter 13

It was just after midday that the short procession of coaches left Chatham Castle and turned into the London road. The first carried Bliss, Stephen, and Sir Basil. Lady Villiers and Letitia rode in the second, and the third carried Louise Lonsdale, Mercy, and the maid who had come with Stephen's mother and sister.

Bliss and Stephen rode side by side facing Sir Basil. Bliss's mood was somber. She gazed out at the passing scenery saying nothing, doing her best to keep from thinking too much about what she was leaving behind. Sir Basil and Stephen seemed happy, almost jovial. And well they might be, Bliss reflected. They were satisfied she had at last come to her senses and realized she could not hope to fight against them and the fate they had planned for her.

Bliss did not look at Stephen as he reached over and took her gloved hand into his own. She did not care. Her thoughts were elsewhere.

What, she wondered, would Isaac make of her sudden departure? She had left no message for Kit. After her silence on the ride home from Kit's cottage, Isaac must wonder what had happened during those hours when she'd been alone with her highwayman lover.

Would Kit tell him? she could not help wondering. Would he tell his old friend that she had offered to give him the gold he needed to help Lord de Wilde's old servants in order that he might leave his dangerous profession?

In spite of herself, Bliss smiled wanly. It was just as well, she supposed, that Kit had not accepted her offer. Until her marriage or coming of age, Sir Basil controlled her fortune and she would have been hard-pressed to get the gold she'd offered Kit.

Kit. Closing her eyes, Bliss sighed. Everything came back to Kit. Her body was still sore from the night before—it seemed her every movement brought back tangible evidence of their night of . . .

Love? She wondered. For her it had been, but for Kit? What was it he had said? She had offered herself and he had merely availed himself of her offer. No more.

The memory of his coldness, his flippant

dismissal of her feelings, her offers, hurt and humiliated Bliss. Still, she could not bring herself to regret having gone to him. Those hours in Kit's arms had awakened her every sense, turned her from a dreamy, romantic girl into a woman who knew what love should be between a man and a woman. Even if she never knew those emotions, those sensations, again—and with Stephen at her side it seemed doubtful— she at least had known them for those brief, precious hours.

"Bliss?" Stephen was prompting. "Are you unwell?"

"Hmmm?" Bliss turned to look at him. "What did you say?"

"I asked if you were unwell," he repeated.

"I'm fine," she replied. "I slept badly last night, that's all."

"Come, then, try to sleep," he invited. Sliding an arm about her shoulder, Stephen drew Bliss against him. "We've hours before we reach London."

Bliss leaned her head into Stephen's shoulder and closed her eyes, slipping easily into a deep and mercifully dreamless sleep.

When she awoke it was to find the coach drawn up before the massive front entrance of Barthorp House in the Strand. The mansion, Elizabethan in design, its half-timbered walls heavily grown with ivy, its diamond-paned mullioned windows sparkling in the sunshine, was not the grandest mansion of those lining the thoroughfare that ran from the heart of London to Whitehall Palace, but it was gracious and elegant.

Bliss was relieved when the coach carrying Lady Daphne and Letitia Villiers went on to their own home, Villiers House in Great Russell Street. She wished that Stephen would follow his mother's and sister's example and go home, but he offered her arm and escorted her into the oak-paneled entrance hall of the mansion.

While Bliss paused to allow a footman to relieve her of her cloak, hat, and gloves, Stephen went into the parlor and looked around.

"It's a lovely house," he told Bliss who saw no alternative but to join him there. "You mustn't worry about what my mother said about redecorating. Nothing need be changed if you don't want it."

Bliss said nothing but she wondered how long Stephen's generosity would hold out against the wishes of his determined mother.

Sir Basil appeared in the doorway. He smiled, seeing his ward and her betrothed in such intimate conversation.

"I've ordered food," he said as he came into the room. "Will you stay, my boy?"

"Thank you, no," Stephen declined, surprising Bliss and pleasing her. But her pleasure dimmed as he went on, "I've much to do before tonight. I'll be back at nine to take Bliss to Whitehall."

"Whitehall?" Bliss looked at her guardian. Sir Basil obviously knew what was going on, but she had been told nothing.

"A small gathering," Stephen explained. "In my Lady Castlemaine's apartments. She was kind enough to invite us. I think she is curious to see her future cousin."

"Must it be tonight?" Bliss asked. That she'd agreed to the betrothal at all was a strain on her already overworked senses, but to be taken on approval to the King's notoriously temperamental mistress seemed beyond her just then. "Surely there will be other gatherings, Stephen, other evenings when we could go to—"

"Nonsense," Sir Basil interrupted. "Once the two of you are married I expect you'll spend a great deal of time at court. It's never too soon to begin making friends there, eh, my boy?"

"Just so," Stephen agreed. He smiled down at Bliss. "There is nothing to be nervous about," he told her, clapping his plumed hat onto his head. "I'll come for you at nine."

Bliss watched as Sir Basil walked to the entrance hall with Stephen. It was not that she was nervous about going to Whitehall or meeting Stephen's illustrious cousin. It was simply that she longed to delay as long as possible the moment when she would be officially presented to society as the future Lady Villiers. It seemed to her that the more public their betrothal became, the tighter the net drew around her, trapping her in a situation that was not appealing even though there seemed little more to attract her in any other possible solution.

That night, in the bedchamber that had been hers since she'd left the nursery, where beautiful tapestries depicting dreamy pastoral scenes formed the backdrop for furniture fancifully carved and upholstered in pink and gold striped silk, Bliss was dressed by Mercy and two other maidservants under the watchful eyes of Louise Lonsdale.

Bliss's gown was of periwinkle silk. The skirt and long, full sleeves were gathered back to show creamy silk frothed with yards of lace. The long, tightly fitted bodice was fastened down the front with pearls the exact size and color of the strand encircling Bliss's throat and the drops dangling from her ears. A strand of smaller pearls had been threaded through her upswept curls—they glistened there among the shining red locks.

"You look beautiful, my dear," Louise said, dabbing her eyes. "As lovely as your mother when she went to court. God rest her soul."

It was, Bliss knew, the highest compliment Louise could pay, for Bliss's mother had been one of the great beauties of Charles I's court in the days before the Civil War—before the Protectorate that had sent the dead King's son, now Charles II, into exile.

Bliss's smile was wan as she accepted the

painted fan the housekeeper pressed into her hand.

There was a knock on the door. Lord Villiers, a footman announced, had arrived. Bliss tried without much success to hide her unhappiness as she embraced Louise, who wished her all success, and went downstairs where Stephen, resplendent in lavender silk, lemon ribbons, and silver lace, waited.

They rode to Whitehall in silence. Bliss gazed out the window, and Stephen could think of nothing to say to her. He was not such a fool as to think that she welcomed the betrothal her guardian had forced on her—in fact he had been astonished when she had bowed to Sir Basil's wishes after but a single night locked in her room at Chatham Castle. There was more to her meek surrender than a mere night's isolation and hunger. Of that much he was certain. But what might have happened during that night that had affected her so radically? It was a mystery he could not begin to solve—and one he longed to explore.

The coach came to a halt, and Bliss and Stephen descended. They were escorted through the palace to the rooms, overlooking the Privy Garden, of the King's reigning— though by no means only—mistress, Barbara Palmer, Countess of Castlemaine.

Rumors abounded about the beautiful, flame-haired Countess. She had been the King's mistress since before his restoration, and her position, despite his marriage to a Portuguese infanta and numerous liaisons with ladies of the court and ladies of the streets, seemed unassailable. Each time a new young beauty appeared at Whitehall, rumors would have her supplanting Lady Castlemaine. But those beauties came and went, married off to some courtier or other, and Barbara remained, secure, haughty, and anything but serene.

She came forward now as Stephen and Bliss were announced. Dressed in emerald and gold, she was flamboyant, like some exotic, dangerous creature too beautiful to be quite real. She smiled as Bliss sank into a curtsy before her.

"So, you are my cousin's betrothed," she said, her voice low, dusky, as unusual as her beauty. "And such a pretty creature you are, too."

Bliss rose from her curtsy. She had the distinct, immediate impression that Lady Castlemaine had examined her and judged her no threat. For that reason, and, of course, for the wealth she would bring into the Villiers family, Barbara was disposed to be cordial.

"Your Ladyship is most gracious," Bliss said automatically. She had committed herself to this farce when she had acquiesced to her guardian's wishes at Chatham Castle, and unless or until she could find a way out, she was condemned to play her part.

"Come with me," Barbara invited, slipping a

hand through Bliss's arm. "You must come and meet George."

Bliss accompanied the King's mistress into a salon where the exquisite tapestries on the walls were nearly eclipsed by the breathtaking splendor of the furniture, much of which was of solid silver worked by master artisans. The pieces were, Bliss surmised, gifts from Barbara's royal lover. The benefits of being the favorite, it was apparent, were rich indeed.

"George." Barbara tapped the shoulder of a large, flaxen-haired man in yellow silk.

The Duke of Buckingham, George Villiers, turned around. He was florid of face, heavily jowled, with bloodshot pale blue eyes. An air hung about him, an air of decadence, of jaded boredom as though he had seen all there was of life and now looked only for some new diversion to brighten the wearisome sameness of his days.

He smiled, his eyes narrowing, as he gazed down at Bliss. "So," he drawled, his eyes lingering on the swell of Bliss's bosom above the lacy neckline of her gown. "You are to be my little cousin. Come, coz, let me welcome you into the family."

Before the amused eyes of Lady Castlemaine and the elegant assembly gathered in her apartment, the Duke pulled Bliss into his arms. Holding her tight against his portly body, he bent his head to hers. His lips covered hers in a savage, bruising kiss that left her feeling sullied, embarrassed, and ashamed.

As he released her, Bliss stumbled slightly. The Duke smiled, obviously assuming she had enjoyed the kiss as much as he had. Lady Castlemaine laughed and the others in the room followed her lead. As for Stephen, his face was flushed, his anger obvious, but he did nothing to rebuke his powerful relative. Bliss wondered how far he would allow the Duke to go before he protested.

Stephen and Bliss were drawn into the fawning crowd of sycophants who hung on Castlemaine and Buckingham's every word hoping that some of the royal favor in which the pair basked would shine on them as well. Their flattery and servility seemed blatantly insincere to Bliss, but both Barbara and Buckingham seemed to regard the attention as nothing more than their due.

Bliss, who had heard rumors of this lady or that who had captured the wandering eye of the so-called Merry Monarch, wondered how many of the ladies and gentlemen in that room would remain loyal to their hostess and her cousin were they to fall from their lofty height.

There was a commotion in the anteroom. A footman rushed up to Barbara and whispered in her ear.

"The King!" she breathed, her green eyes glowing with triumph. With a hissing sweep of her emerald skirts, she vanished into the anteroom to greet her guest, her lover.

NIGHTRIDER

"He was supposed to be supping with the Queen tonight," a pale, languid viscount said behind Bliss. "The Portuguese will be mightily out of sorts."

There were snickers and snide, sneering references to the Queen made loudly enough that the Duke who stood near Bliss could hear. Because the Queen was Lady Castlemaine's enemy, one could not champion her there, in Castlemaine's rooms, without jeopardizing one's place in the favorite's favor.

Bliss felt only compassion for the little Queen whose heart had been broken by the many infidelities of her charming consort. But Bliss's musings, her sympathy, were pushed aside as the King entered the room.

He had lost none of the lazy sensuality that had always struck her when she was still his ward. He was tall, over six feet, and his body moved with a loose-limbed grace. His eyes, dark and heavy-lidded, seemed lit by some ever-smoldering fires that threatened to burst into flame whenever his gaze came to rest on the face and figure of a pretty woman.

His features were irregular, unhandsome, and yet there was about him some indefinable allure that drew women to him, even in those long, lean years when it seemed he would forever remain a pauper prince without a country.

Barbara brought the King to where her cousins and Bliss stood. The two men bowed, and Bliss sank to the floor in a rustle of silk.

"Your Majesty," Barbara purred, her arms possessively twined about one of the King's, "You know Lady Bliss. But perhaps you do not know that she is to wed with my cousin Stephen, Lord Villiers."

"Indeed?" Holding out a long-fingered, heavily ringed hand, the King allowed Bliss to kiss him. Then, taking one of her hands in his own, he drew her to her feet.

His dark eyes studied Bliss's face as though he were seeing her in a new light. The almost imperceptible twitch of his lips beneath his narrow black moustache told Bliss that he liked what he saw.

The golden lace that frothed from the cuff of his crimson silk coat fell back as he lifted Bliss's hand to his lips. The kiss lasted a second too long, the light in the King's eyes shone a little too warmly. Lady Castlemaine's green eyes narrowed as she stared at Bliss's face, looking for something she had not sought there before.

"You are to wed with Lord Villiers, are you, my little beauty?" the King asked. "I begin to regret that you are no longer a ward of the crown."

Bliss smiled up at him, charmed as always by his lazy humor.

The King sighed, his large, dark eyes wistful as he glanced toward the Duke of Buckingham. "Ah," he breathed, "for the days of *droit du seigneur!*"

NIGHTRIDER

Everyone within earshot laughed—everyone except Bliss and Lady Castlemaine who was suddenly not quite so enchanted with the pretty little heiress her cousin had brought to the King's court—and back into the King's attention.

Chapter 14

Bliss forced a wan smile as the music ended and she sank into a curtsy before her partner— the King. She was weary of the seemingly endless round of dinners and balls she and Stephen had been invited to since their first appearance at Whitehall. And more than that, she was growing ever more uneasy. At first she had supposed that their sudden popularity was due to the fact that she would soon become a member of the Villiers family. But she soon discovered that was not the case. Rather, the invitations that started in a trickle and grew to a deluge came as a result of the King's obvious admiration. The knowledge surprised and discomfited her.

The King, so gossip said, had lost his heart to

NIGHTRIDER

Frances Stewart, a young, empty-headed beauty whose family was distantly related to the royal Stuarts. From the moment of her arrival at Whitehall, the King had pursued her. Her surrender seemed imminent. But to everyone's surprise, Frances had not surrendered. Heedless and foolish as she might have seemed, she had guarded her virtue, stubbornly refusing the King's persistent advances. She had risked his wrath rather than dishonor her family and herself by becoming the latest in the King's long line of mistresses.

Stung, his pride hurt by his failure, unused to rejection, the King was said to have turned his attentions to young Lady Bliss. Her flame-haired beauty, though not as full-blown and flamboyant as Lady Castlemaine's, had undoubtedly attracted him. Speculation had already begun as to whether Bliss might be the one to finally tumble the imperious and seemingly indestructible Countess of Castlemaine from her lofty perch as preeminent mistress at Whitehall.

For Bliss's part, she was relieved to see Barbara swooping down on them as the music ended. The Countess moved with feline swiftness to extricate her lover from the clutches of the beautiful young girl she had been prepared to like but now looked on with resentful suspicion.

Still breathing heavily with the exertion of the dance, Bliss sank into a curtsy to the Countess. When she rose, the King smiled down at her. With his green-eyed mistress staring daggers at them both, Charles lifted Bliss's hand to his lips and, turning it over, kissed the soft white palm.

As the King turned away, Barbara clinging to his arm, Bliss took advantage of her momentary solitude to escape from the room to the relative quiet of the Stone Gallery.

The Gallery was the heart of Whitehall, the hub around which the wheels of court revolved. It was the place to see and be seen, to make contacts and assignations, to gossip and scheme and flirt. But just then, with the ball in progress, with the King inside, the Gallery was quiet, its candles burning low, its corners shadowy and private.

Which, Bliss reflected as she sank onto a cushioned windowseat, was precisely what she needed just then. Relaxing the stiff, elegant posture that had carried her so gracefully in the ballroom, Bliss allowed her back to curve, her chin to drop. With one hand she massaged the back of her neck below the pearl-threaded knot of hair from which carefully curled tendrils had been allowed to escape.

She hated the court. It seemed impossible that she could loathe the glitter and glamour of such a life, but she did. When she thought of her chagrin at having been taken away to Chatham Castle by Sir Basil a few short months before, she wondered at the changes those months had wrought in her. Now she longed for nothing so much as to be back at Chatham, away from London, from the court and the King and his pack of gossiping, intriguing courtiers.

Bliss's smile was filled with self-mockery. Was it really that she longed to be away from London, or was it that she yearned to be back at Chatham, to be near Kit, to risk the hurt and heartbreak he might give her on the chance there was love somewhere beneath all that mistrust and resentment?

"Kit," Bliss whispered, wanting to speak his name, to hear the sound of it in her ears once more. Unbidden her mind flew back to that night in his cottage. She felt a quivering in the pit of her stomach, remembering his touches, his kisses, the love he had given her and taught her to return in kind.

Bliss shivered with the memories. There would never, she told herself, be another night like that. She would never find love like that with Stephen or, she feared, with any other man. It was Kit, only Kit, who held the keys to her heart, her senses. He—

Suddenly, without knowing how, Bliss became aware that she was not alone. She glanced around and finally saw him.

He was tall, broad-shouldered. His dark coat and breeches blended with the shadows surrounding him. The full-bottomed wig he wore with its shoulder-length tumble of thick, dark curls was like those worn by nearly every man at court. Only his face would have identified him, but this was hidden, concealed by the darkness where he stood—the alcove whose candles had guttered out.

Bliss felt a cold chill snake up her spine. He stood there so silently, watching her. She could almost feel his gaze upon her. It had a weight, a tangible touch that unnerved her. And yet there was nothing threatening in his presence; he did not seem menacing or evil. It was only his silence, his stare, that disconcerted her.

Bliss was about to rise, to challenge the man, when a voice hailed her from the doorway of the ballroom.

"Bliss." It was Stephen. "Here you are. I've been looking everywhere for you."

"Where have you been?" Bliss demanded. Stephen had left the ballroom early on, after sharing the opening dance with her, and she had not seen him from then until now.

"I was in the cardroom playing Hazard," he replied. "Luck was not with me tonight, I'm afraid."

Bliss bit back a sharp retort. Since her betrothal to Stephen had been made public, he had been courted by every gamester in and out of Whitehall. And of course they were all only too happy to allow him to play on credit. The size of his future wife's fortune was well known, and his promises to pay were welcomed. Bliss wondered how many thousands of pounds it would take to settle Stephen's debts once they were married. But, since a woman's property became her husband's upon their marriage, there was little Bliss could do about it and even less point in starting a row then and there.

She remembered the man who had been staring at her. He was behind her as she stood facing Stephen. In a low, conspiratorial tone, she said:

"Stephen, look behind me. Is there a man, dressed in dark clothing, standing in the shadows?"

Stephen looked over her head. "There was. He left as I came out of the ballroom."

"Who was he?"

Stephen shrugged. "I'm not certain. I did not pay much attention. I think it might have been Lord Newcastle."

Bliss sighed. Glancing around, she saw that the man had vanished. She hadn't a notion as to who it might have been, but she did not think it was Lord Newcastle. It didn't matter, she supposed, but her curiosity had been piqued.

"Let's go back to the ball," Stephen urged.

Bliss shook her head, her face troubled. "Please, Stephen, can't we go home?"

"Home?" He stared at her. "It's only midnight, Bliss. The ball will last for hours."

"I don't care. I don't like it here."

"You are greatly admired," he pointed out, feeling not a little annoyed with her. He knew he was envied for being the betrothed of such a beautiful—and rich—young woman and he enjoyed flaunting her before the court. For too long he had been merely an inconsequential twig on the mighty tree of Villiers. Now all the signs pointed to his becoming far more than that—when he married Bliss he would be rich indeed, and with those riches he could buy power, influence. And with Bliss's beauty enhancing those riches, that power, there seemed no heights to which he could not aspire.

"Admired!" Bliss spat. "Stephen, doesn't it trouble you that gossip already places me in the King's bed!"

"Has the King—" Stephen began, his green eyes—not, now that Bliss noticed it, so different from those of Lady Castlemaine herself—alight with jealous fire.

"No," Bliss answered quickly. "But his attentions have been much observed. Even Lady Castlemaine suspects he means to bed me."

Stephen laughed. "Does that surprise you? It should not. I don't doubt every able-bodied man in that ballroom would like to bed you, Bliss. You are very beautiful, and no one is more susceptible to a beautiful woman than the King. It is not for nothing that they have nicknamed him after the prize stud in the royal stables—Old Rowley."

"Even so," Bliss argued, her distaste evident.

"Bliss." Stephen's tone was patient, fond. "You know little of men and their ways. Men don't look at love the same way women do. Oh, we'll court a woman with pretty words and gallantry if that's what she wants, but all we really want is to bed her. If it's offered freely, so much the better."

Bliss recoiled as if stung. That smacked too closely of Kit and what he'd said about their night together. Was that really all it had been to him? A night of passion freely offered and eagerly accepted? She couldn't bear to think so.

"Stephen," she said softly, hiding her emotion. "Once we are married, I would like to leave London. Not for Chatham," she assured him quickly. "Perhaps we could go to live at Barthorp Hall and—"

"Yorkshire!" Stephen said it as if she had suggested they go to live on the moon. "You want to live in Yorkshire!"

"It's not the end of the world," she defended. "Granted, it is distant and perhaps a bit harsh and—"

"Desolate?" he suggested. "Don't you understand, Bliss, we have a brilliant future ahead of us here, in London, at court!"

"A future as what?" she countered. "A gamester's dupe and the King's newest whore?"

Stephen flushed, though whether he was more upset about Bliss's portrayal of herself as the King's doxy or himself as a failure at the card tables she could not tell. He opened his mouth to argue but was cut off as a deep, too-familiar voice said:

"Enjoying yourselves?" The Duke of Buckingham stood beside them.

"Of course, Your Grace," Stephen answered automatically.

"Actually," Bliss replied, ignoring Stephen and the uneasy look he gave her at her tone of voice, "I was about to ask Stephen to take me home. I fear fatigue has gotten the best of me."

"The King will be disappointed," Buckingham drawled. "Doubtless he will miss holding you in his arms for another dance."

"There are so many ladies longing to dance with the King he will hardly miss me."

"You underestimate yourself," Buckingham replied, "if you think any of those others could take your place."

"I fear they will have to do," Bliss told him, "for I do not intend to remain long at court after Stephen and I are married."

"What is this?" the Duke asked, turning to Stephen.

Stephen shrugged, withering before his cousin's look. "Bliss has taken it into her head that she wants to live at Barthorp Hall when we are married. In Yorkshire."

"Yorkshire!" The Duke was as horrified as Stephen had been. "We cannot allow that!"

"Nevertheless, my lord Duke, it is my wish," Bliss persisted.

The Duke recognized the determination in her eyes. Arguing with this stubborn little chit would only steel her resolve.

"Perhaps for a while," he allowed. "But only a while. We cannot have such beauty and charm rusticating in the country. And now, my boy, you should take your lady home. She is fatigued, remember?"

Bliss gazed up at the Duke, surprised. That he should take her part and tell Stephen to take her home astonished her. Could it be the Duke would be an ally? If so, he would be a most unexpected one.

She bobbed a curtsy. "Thank you, Your Grace, and good night."

The Duke of Buckingham watched as Stephen and Bliss moved away. His eyes were thoughtful, his expression solemn. Over the music and the din of the crowd in the ballroom, he could hear Barbara Castlemaine's voice. It was too shrill, her laughter was strained and forced. The woman, for all her beauty, was a fool. She tried to pretend, to herself and everyone else, that nothing had changed since those halcyon days just after Charles's restoration. But she knew—as did everyone else—that Charles had grown tired of her avarice, of her tantrums and tirades. Even her beauty, once so dazzling, had begun to fade. She saw every young woman newly arrived at court as a rival. And she knew, moreover, that once her downfall was complete she would find her "friends" deserting her, her creditors hounding her; she would find herself at the mercy of the many powerful enemies she had made during her reign as Charles's haughty and imperious favorite. And that knowledge was made all the more galling by the fact that the

beauty in the forefront of those pegged to replace her was her own cousin's betrothed.

Buckingham glanced back toward the now-
empty Gallery where he'd last seen Bliss. There
were many advantages to being related to the
King's premier mistress. Revenues from taxes
flowed into the Villierses' coffers, the King
granted them rights and privileges that enriched
them and gave them the power to enrich themselves. Land, estates, offices—the bounty flowed
like a torrent. But what if Barbara were sup-
planted? Might not that torrent dwindle to a
trickle? Even to nothing? Buckingham knew the
King had toyed with the notion of divorcing his
barren Queen and marrying the recalcitrant
Frances Stewart. The thought of that head-
strong, priggish girl as Queen sent shivers
through Buckingham.

No, if Barbara fell from her lofty post, she
must be replaced by someone sympathetic to
Villiers interests. Preferably someone who *was* a
Villiers. And who could that be?

Bliss. Buckingham smiled. The girl's reluc-
tance he put down to maidenly prudery. She
would come to her senses, he was certain, and
then . . .

Smiling, Buckingham turned back toward the
ballroom. That was the answer, he was certain:
if Barbara fell, and certainly she was likely to
soon, he must see to it that Lady Bliss Paynter—
Bliss, Lady Villiers, he corrected himself—was
there to step into her place so that the rich

reward belonging to the family of the royal favorite would not pass out of Villiers hands.

"Ah, here you are," the King said as the Duke entered the ballroom. "Where has your cousin disappeared to? And his lovely lady?"

"I fear the lady was fatigued, sire," Buckingham replied. "She is used to life in the country. Early to rise, early abed."

"I could not agree with her more," the King chortled. "Early mornings are the best part of the day. As to early abed—were Lady Bliss mine, I would see that she was abed early indeed!"

The courtiers surrounding the King laughed appreciatively, and the Duke of Buckingham joined in. Suddenly the future—which had seemed clouded with uncertainty—seemed much brighter.

Chapter 15

"Milady?" Mercy was peering around the door of Bliss's bedchamber.

"Come in, Mercy," Bliss invited. "What have you got there?"

"A letter, milady," the maid replied, holding out a folded sheet of paper. "For you."

"A letter for me?" Bliss frowned. "From whom?"

Wordless, Mercy held out the missive to her mistress. Bliss took it, opened it, and glanced at the closing near the page's bottom.

"Isaac!" she breathed. "Mercy! Where did you get this!"

"He sent it to me, milady, folded inside another letter. He asked me to give it to you when you were alone."

Heart pounding, Bliss leaned over the letter and read:

"May it please your ladyship. Forgive me for interfering in a matter that rightfully is none of my concern . . ." Bliss's whispered voice trailed off. Her eyes, unbidden, scanned the page and picked out Kit's name in several places. Foreboding swept over her. She went on, her voice hushed, her words inaudible even to Mercy who stood nearby.

"I was not surprised when your ladyship left the morning after your ride to Kit's cottage. Nor was I surprised when the news reached Chatham that you were to be married to Milord Villiers. I suspected you would not be able to hold out against my lord Holme's wishes.

"When I went to Kit with the news, he seemed to think there were other reasons for your going off to London and to marriage with Lord Villiers. What these reasons might be he did not say and I did not ask. But none of this is the true reason I write.

"It is Kit. After your ladyship left, he took to the highway with a vengeance. He took dangerous and foolish risks. It was as though he wanted to be captured even knowing what that would mean."

Bliss shuddered, her eyes drifting away from the page. ". . . even knowing what that would mean." Death. That was what it would mean. Kit's exploits were already well known. Were he to be captured it could well mean the hangman's rope. But now, it seemed, he had ceased to care.

"Kit," Bliss breathed. Much as the memories of their night together still hurt, keen as the pain of Kit's coldness still remained, Bliss could not bear the thought of his embarking on a life of reckless danger. She read on:

"What I have written to say, milady," Isaac went on, "is that not long after your ladyship returned to London, Kit disappeared. No one hereabouts has seen him or heard from him. There were rumors that he had been captured, that he was in prison, or had been transported, or was dead. But no one knows. If your ladyship has heard anything, or if you have seen or heard from Kit, I pray you write and tell me so. We here in Chatham are worried for him.

"Your loyal and obedient servant."

Bliss looked up and found Mercy watching her expectantly. She shook her head.

"It's Kit," she told the maid, knowing that the girl, like everyone else in Chatham village, knew Kit Quinn and harbored deep respect and affection for him. "He's disappeared. Isaac asks if I've seen him or heard from him." She scowled, biting her lip.

"Have you, milady?" Mercy ventured to ask.

Bliss sighed. "Not at all. I wish I could tell Isaac Kit was well, but I know less about it than he does. If only we had parted . . ." Then, remembering Mercy's presence, Bliss silenced herself. "I'll have to write back and tell Isaac I know nothing." She looked up at her maid. "Surely if Kit had been captured there'd have been some mention of it in the gazette."

"Doubtless, milady," Mercy agreed, but she, like Bliss, sounded distinctly doubtful.

A tap at the door startled them both. Mercy hurried to open it.

"My Lord Villiers is here, milady," a footman announced.

"My Lord Villiers is always here," Bliss muttered. More loudly, she replied: "Tell him I shall attend him directly."

Rising from her dressing table, Bliss stood while Mercy laid a taffeta cloak over her aqua-blue and pale yellow gown. She was to accompany Stephen and his sister, Letitia, to a play in Drury Lane.

On the way out of the room, she stopped. Smiling back at Mercy, she asked:

"Would you like to come, Mercy?"

The girl's eyes widened. "Me, milady?"

"You. Get your things. Hurry now."

It was by no means unheard of to have one's maid accompany one, Bliss knew, particularly a young, unmarried woman venturing out in the company of a young man. Of course it could be argued that Letitia Villiers would have satisfied any need for a chaperone, but Bliss preferred having someone she liked in the party.

Together Bliss and Mercy descended the stairs

and found Stephen and Letitia in the front parlor. Stephen, as usual, wore the height of fashion, his suit of sky blue trimmed with scarlet, his neck and wrists awash with lace. Letitia, likewise, wore a gown of the latest mode, but her pale complexion and light brown hair faded into mousey nothingness beside the gown's brilliant crimson.

"I've asked Mercy to join us," Bliss announced in a tone that brooked no contradiction. "We should go. We'll be late."

"The King is attending today," Stephen told her as they walked toward the door. "The play is always held up until the royal party arrives, and the King is always late."

Climbing into the carriage, they set out for the theater. Had Bliss not been preoccupied with thoughts of Kit, she would have noticed Letitia's unusual animation. Usually sullen and quiet, the girl prattled on about the weather, the play, fashions, anything and nothing.

It was not until they reached the theater and took their places in the box that Stephen had bespoken for them that the reason for Letitia's high spirits became apparent.

"Oh!" Letitia cried, leaning over the railing to point down into the raucous, crowded pit below where gallants stood on the benches to flirt with the ladies in the boxes above and orange girls circulated, dodging grasping hands as they sold their wares. "Look there! It's Angus!"

Stephen rolled his eyes as she motioned for her suitor to join them. "Really, Letitia," he chided. "Mother would not approve."

Letitia's answering pout was all the reply he received. For Bliss's part, she was curious to see this penniless Scot who had wooed Letitia Villiers.

When he appeared, Lord Cameron was not what Bliss had expected. He was tall, handsome, dressed fashionably in scarlet and grey, with merry blue eyes that twinkled down at Bliss.

"With your permission, milady," he said, taking a hurriedly placed chair between Bliss and Letitia.

"Lord Cameron," Bliss said. "I have heard much of you."

"I return the compliment," the Scotsman replied, his speech betraying the fact that he had spent little time in the northern climes where his estates lay. "Letitia has spoken much of you."

Bliss turned her attention away from him. She did not doubt for a moment that Letitia had told Lord Cameron about her—no doubt Letitia had told him that once she and Stephen were married, Bliss's fortune would provide a means for them—Letitia and Angus, Lord Cameron—to wed.

"The King!" Stephen hissed.

With the rest of the audience, Bliss rose as the King appeared in the doorway of the royal box.

The Queen, small and swarthy, her jet black hair curled and twined with pearls, followed him into the box. Her ladies and his gentlemen filed in to sit behind them.

The Duke of Buckingham sat on the King's left. The Duke of York, James, Charles's brother and heir, sat to the Queen's right. Behind the King and Queen, Lady Castlemaine and Frances Stewart sat side by side.

There was shuffling and jostling as the audience resumed its seats and the play began. A lithe, pretty woman in a billowing white shirt and tight black breeches appeared on stage, bowed low to the royal box, and began to speak the prologue to the play.

"Peg Prynne," Stephen whispered to Bliss. "They say she wears a ring worth eight hundred pounds that the King gave her. There are rumors that he means to buy her a house and take her off the stage."

Bliss glanced toward the royal box. Charles was leaning forward, his full-lipped mouth smiling beneath the thin black moustache. His dark eyes were fixed on the lovely woman on the stage. He was completely oblivious to the pain in the dark eyes of the adoring woman on his right.

Sitting there watching, Bliss felt compassion for the Queen. It was obvious that she was hopelessly in love with her husband. It was equally obvious that, aside from a rather tepid fondness, her husband felt little for her. He preferred women like Barbara Castlemaine with her flamboyant, volatile beauty; women like Frances Stewart, breathtaking, unattainable; women like Peg Prynne, lively, bold, unashamed of her lowly origins, sassy and amusing. The Queen was neither beautiful nor lively. She was quiet, devout, long-suffering. It would not have occurred to her to fight for her husband against his mistresses. Had it, it might have piqued her errant spouse's wandering interests.

The play wound on, but Bliss saw little of it. She thought of Isaac's letter. Of Kit. Where could he be? She sighed. How she longed to be back at Chatham where she could discuss the matter with Isaac, where she could go to Kit's cottage and see if he might have left some clue behind that would give an indication of his destination when he'd left. But it was all useless. She was trapped in London. And it was obvious that Stephen wanted nothing of country living. He coveted the glamour of the court and the excitement of high-stakes gambling, and once Bliss's fortune was in his possession, he would have the means to indulge both desires.

At long last the play ended. As they rose from their seats, a messenger came to invite Bliss and Stephen to the royal box so Bliss could be presented to the Queen.

They were on their way there when Bliss noticed a man in the crowd who seemed to be the same man she had seen at Whitehall. The man in the shadows who had watched her. His back was turned toward her, but there was something about him, some indefinable quality that reminded her of . . .

"Stephen," she said excitedly, "wait. That man over there, the man in deep green. I must speak to him. Come—"

"Bliss!" Stephen was exasperated. "The Queen is waiting. What are you thinking of?"

"It will only take a moment. Stephen. Stephen!"

Despite her protests, Bliss found herself nearly dragged along the corridor. She had no alternative but to enter the royal box and make her curtsy to the little Portuguese Queen, who was coolly gracious. She had spent too much time at her husband's court not to be apprehensive when yet another beautiful young girl appeared. She recognized the light in her husband's eyes and was not so insulated by her cadre of loyal and protective ladies that she had not heard the gossip concerning her husband's admiration of this lovely young heiress.

Though it seemed an eternity, it was only a few minutes before Bliss and Stephen left the royal box. Bliss scanned the corridor, but the man in green had disappeared, as she'd known he would. She was pensive as they went back to rejoin the rest of their party. Had it really been Kit there, in green, or was she simply imagining things because of Isaac's letter? She wondered if she would ever know.

Chapter 16

Bliss was pleased when the time came to leave the theater. But her pleasure was short-lived. Angus, Lord Cameron, showed no inclination to leave them, and Stephen showed no inclination to go home.

"Shall we go visit Captain Maxwell?" Angus suggested, climbing into the Villierses' carriage.

"Today?" Stephen asked. "Is there time?"

"Indeed, it was fixed for five. We've time enough."

"Who is Captain Maxwell?" Bliss wanted to know.

She glanced at Mercy, who shrugged in reply.

"You don't know?" Angus exchanged an amused glance with Letitia, who sat beside him clinging to his arm.

"Don't tell her," Letitia urged. "Let her be surprised."

"Aye," Stephen agreed, "you've a surprise in store for you. One I think you might find interesting."

The carriage inched forward along Drury Lane, hemmed in by others as the audience thronged the street to watch the royal party depart, then climbed into their own carriages to drive home.

As the carriage left Drury Lane and rolled on past St. James's Park, Bliss began to feel edgy. She didn't know why, perhaps it was the smug smile on Letitia's lips, perhaps it was the looks that passed between Stephen and Angus. All she knew was that when they finally reached their destination, she was horrified.

"Tyburn Hill!" she cried, face pale, as the carriage approached the swarming mob that ebbed and flowed around the gallows in the center. Carriages ringed the mob, many of them bearing elegant and ornate coats of arms. The taste for executions as an entertainment was by no means limited to the lower classes.

Both Angus and Stephen laughed. "Aye, Tyburn!" Stephen told her. "Come, Bliss, you're no milk-and-water miss. Why so white-faced?"

"This Captain Maxwell," she managed, one hand gripping Mercy's arm as the maid sat beside her, "is he the man being executed?"

"He is," Angus confirmed. "And not past time! The wretch made the Dover road all but impassable."

"He was a . . ." Bliss began, a sick feeling starting in her stomach.

"Highwayman," Letitia finished for her.

Bliss felt as if the carriage had tilted beneath her. She felt giddy, faint. Her hand trembled as she laid it on Stephen's arm.

"Take me home, Stephen, please," she asked, her voice tremulous.

"Oh, no," Letitia argued. "Do let's stay! Bliss, don't be such a bore."

"Please, Stephen," Bliss repeated, ignoring her betrothed's sister.

"It's too late to leave," Stephen told her as a roar went up from the crowd. "Here comes the cart."

Stephen nodded toward the window. The crowd was parting to let the cart bearing the condemned man pass among them. "Captain Maxwell," Stephen said aloud.

Bliss gazed at the man. In breeches and a shirt, he waved and smiled as he rode toward his death. Men cheered, ladies wept. It seemed macabre to Bliss that such a serious event could be treated as lightly as the play they had just left.

The cart halted beneath the noose that dangled from one arm of the three-sided gallows. The crowd quieted to hear Captain Maxwell's last words.

The highwayman's shoulder-length black hair

was ruffled by the breeze as he drew himself up. His teeth flashed white in the sun as he smiled, seemingly unconcerned by the fate that would be his in a matter of moments.

His voice reached Bliss's ears, borne on the hot summer breezes:

"I've come here before ye," he announced, "to pay for my crimes, and 'tis justly I've been condemned. But I tell ye all, I'd not trade a day of it for a life of dull respectability. I've no regrets, except, haply, all those lovely ladies I'll never love . . ." He waited until the appreciative laughter of the crowd died down. ". . . and now, I bid ye all farewell. May the Lord bless my friends, and may my enemies be damned!"

Bliss closed her eyes as the hangman stepped forward and slipped the noose about the highwayman's neck. She would not, could not, look, but her imagination supplied the details as she heard the thunder of the horse's hooves as it was driven forward, pulling the cart with it, leaving the highwayman to dangle in the air, feet kicking, until he strangled.

"Is it over, Stephen?" she asked weakly.

"Not yet." It was Angus who replied. "He's putting up a game fight."

Feeling sick, Bliss leaned against Mercy. The maid-servant understood Bliss's distress. In Bliss's mind it was Kit hanging there, Kit struggling against the rope that was slowly—too slowly—ending his life.

Her pallor was so stark, her trembling so

violent, that Stephen leaned toward her.

"Bliss," he said, his tone confused. "I don't understand this. The man is a criminal, condemned and executed. He does not deserve your concern. He does not merit—"

"Get me out of here, damn you!" Bliss hissed, feeling that at any moment she would distress herself by being sick. "Take me home now, or by God, you'll regret it!"

Shouting to the driver, Stephen ordered the carriage away from Tyburn. A tense silence reigned in the carriage and lasted until they drew up before the entrance of Barthorp Hall in the Strand.

"I'll come in with you," Stephen offered as Bliss took a footman's hand and stepped down from the carriage.

"No you won't!" Bliss snapped as Mercy left the carriage. "Go away, Stephen! Just go away!"

Whirling away from the carriage, Bliss ran into the house closely followed by Mercy. The door slammed behind her, and there was little Stephen could do but order the driver to take them away. He would not risk the humiliation of going to the door only to be denied entrance.

"Well," Letitia mused as the carriage passed between the ornate gates of Barthorp House and turned into the Strand, "what do you suppose is the matter with her?"

"Shut up, Letitia," Stephen growled, not looking away from the window. He had the distinctly uncomfortable feeling he had just made a serious mistake with Bliss.

In Bliss's dream she was traveling through the Kentish countryside with Stephen beside her. They had married and were going to Chatham. As they approached the castle gates, Bliss saw something hanging above the gates.

"What is that?" she wondered aloud, leaning toward the window.

"That damned highwayman," Stephen told her. "Your highwayman. Your lover."

"No!" Bliss cried, falling back. They were drawing closer now. She could see Kit there, his body wrapped in chains, hanging over the main gate, at the mercy of the elements, the ravens. "No," Bliss whispered, sickened.

"There it is," Stephen told her, "and there it will remain. You will see it every day, Bliss, until it rots and falls."

As the carriage approached, Bliss saw Kit, or what remained of him. He was no longer the dashing, rakishly handsome man she had known, had loved, had touched and kissed. He was . . . was . . .

Bliss awakened with a scream. She sat up in the dark, warm confines of her pink taffeta-hung tester bed. Tears trickled down her cheeks, her heart pounded beneath her beribboned nightrail.

Trembling, she lay back against the pillows. It

had been only a dream brought on by that hideous scene at Tyburn Hill.

She sighed, thinking of Isaac's letter. If only she knew Kit was safe. The horror at Tyburn would not have affected her so were it not for the uncertainty over Kit. Isaac had said Kit had taken foolish risks, had grown reckless. It was only too possible that one of his victims had shot him. Stephen had, after all.

Bliss closed her eyes. The thought of Kit lying somewhere, mortally wounded, was too hideous to contemplate. It could not be true. He must be alive and well somewhere. He must be in hiding. Still, she could not overlook the fact that Isaac, who knew him best of all, had been concerned enough to write to her.

She felt helpless in London. There was nothing she could do. If only she were at Chatham. Surely between them she and Isaac could solve the mystery.

In the darkness she cursed Stephen, his sister, and Lord Cameron. All this was their fault! If they had not insisted on going to Tyburn she would not be lying here now, at the mercy of these grotesque imaginings. They were, the lot of them, insensitive, grasping, and avaricious. Letitia and her penniless suitor looked on Bliss as their future income. Not only was she to bolster the sagging finances of their branch of the Villiers family, she was to support Letitia and her threadbare lover. The closer the wedding date came, the less she wanted to be allied with that family.

After tossing and turning until nearly dawn, Bliss finally fell into a deep, undisturbed sleep. It was mid-morning when Mercy shook her awake.

"Milady?" she said, "I am to wake you. You are to go with milord Villiers, his lady mother, and his sister to the country."

"The country . . ." Bliss squinted in the bright sunshine that flooded the room through the opened draperies. "Oh, now I remember."

They were to go to the Duke of Buckingham's country house. Bliss groaned. The thought of spending time not only with Stephen and his mother and sister but with the Duke, whom Bliss not only disliked but distrusted, was more than she could bear.

"I'm not going," she told the maid.

"Sir Basil—"

"Can go to the devil!" Bliss told her. "I will not go!"

Mercy left, and, as Bliss expected, it was not long before Sir Basil stormed into her bedchamber.

"What is this nonsense?" he demanded. "Your maid says you refuse to go out today."

"I do," Bliss retorted. "After yesterday, I cannot bear the sight of Stephen and his sister. Do you know where they took me?"

"Aye, to Tyburn," Sir Basil replied. "What of it?"

"What of it?" Bliss pushed herself up in the

bed. "It was hideous! I thought I would be sick then and there!"

"Squeamish," Sir Basil sneered. "You realize whose home you are invited to, don't you?"

"The Duke of Buckingham," Bliss confirmed. "I don't like him. He's a lecher and a hypocrite."

"He is a great and powerful man!"

"He is a hypocrite! He pretends to be the King's most loyal subject, but he married the daughter of one of Cromwell's generals to save his estates! He pretends to represent the Puritan interests, but he ogles every woman he sees. His vices and debaucheries are legendary!" Sir Basil was about to speak, but Bliss went on: "And if you force me to go today, I shall tell him so to his face!"

Sir Basil paled. "You would, too, wouldn't you? Damn you! You could ruin everything! All right, then, stay home if you must. I'll send word to the Villierses that you are ill. But by God, I'll not tolerate much more of this foolishness!"

Bliss smiled as he stomped out of the room. It felt good to win even this small battle against her guardian. It was, she determined, only the first of what she hoped would be many such victories.

Climbing out of bed, she tugged the bell rope to summon Mercy. When the maid arrived, Bliss outlined her plan to the girl, knowing as she did that her faithful maid would be only too happy to help her.

"I mean," she told Mercy, "to leave London. I

mean to go back to Chatham."

"Has Sir Basil—" the girl began.

"Sir Basil knows nothing about it. And he must not suspect, Mercy. He will stop us." The maid nodded, drawing closer to her mistress. Bliss went on: "Will you come with me?" Mercy nodded again. "Then I must tell you, it will be dangerous. It must be done at night—tonight if we can manage it—and you know traveling at night is dangerous. We must have a coach and driver. We cannot use Sir Basil's coachman, obviously, so we must find someone else. Hire someone."

"I know someone," Mercy volunteered.

"You do?" Bliss was frankly surprised. "Who is it, Mercy."

"A friend, milady," the maid replied cryptically. "If your ladyship will trust me to arrange it."

Bliss sat back in her chair. "You surprise me, Mercy, truly you do. But I do trust you and I will leave it in your hands."

Smiling, Mercy curtsied. "Tonight, then, milady?" she said. Bliss nodded. "Then, with your leave, I'll go speak to my friend. I can tell anyone who asks that you've sent me to the 'Change to buy you some ribbons and scent."

The maid turned to leave the room, and Bliss, suddenly alert, leaned forward.

"Mercy?" she called. The maid stopped and turned toward her. "Don't you need some money to give this friend of yours? Surely he will expect to be given at least part of his gold in advance for such a risky undertaking."

To Bliss's surprise, Mercy shook her head. "No, milady, that won't be necessary. As you trust me, so does he."

"Very well, then, go to him now," Bliss told her. "And Mercy? I won't forget this, I swear I won't."

Smiling, the maid curtsied to her mistress and hurried out of the room. Behind her, Bliss sat back in her chair. She felt, for the first time in a long time, that she could afford to hope things might work out for her after all.

Chapter 17

Though Bliss knew she needed to be alert for the night to come, she could not force herself to rest during the day. She was too excited, too nervous. She could not believe she was actually taking the step. To run away from London, from Sir Basil, from Stephen. It seemed inconceivable. And yet . . . what other choice did she have? She had to take the risk.

Mercy had returned in a surprisingly short time. She came up to Bliss's room, her cheeks flushed with excitement.

"Did you speak to your friend?" Bliss asked urgently.

"Aye, milady. He has a coach and horses— fast horses. He will drive us to Chatham tonight.

We must meet him near St. Martin's Lane at midnight."

"And the gold?" Bliss asked, praying she would not be expected to produce a large amount on such short notice.

Mercy shook her head. "He said he would take it up with your ladyship at Chatham."

"Very well." There was nothing Bliss could do but agree. It was too important that she get to Chatham to waste time worrying about how to find the gold to compensate the coachman.

For the rest of the day, Bliss forced herself to behave as if nothing unusual was afoot. She read, she worked at the needlepoint firescreen she'd been making for Louise Lonsdale, at dinner she sat with Sir Basil making polite conversation, all the while willing the hours to pass more quickly until she could retire to her room and plan her escape.

"Oh, my," she murmured, yawning expansively as the tall case clock in the hall chimed ten. "I must bid you good night, sir."

"You know, don't you, that Stephen sent four messages today inquiring about your health?"

"Did he?" Bliss forced herself to sound interested. "What did you tell him?"

"I told him you were feeling better. I promised him you would accompany him to the Honors Ball at court on Thursday."

"And so I shall, my lord," Bliss promised, certain she would not be in London to be held to her promise.

NIGHTRIDER

For the next two hours, Bliss and Mercy waited together in Bliss's bedchamber. They waited in near darkness, afraid to leave more than one small candle burning lest someone passing Bliss's door see the light and wonder that she was still awake.

"Should you not pack a bag to take, milady?" Mercy asked.

Bliss shook her head. "I have things at Chatham—enough to tide me over. I don't want to be burdened with a bag while we are going to St. Martin's Lane."

Mercy glanced at the clock on the mantel. "It won't be long now, milady. Less than an hour."

Bliss sighed. "I pray that your friend . . . what is his name?"

"Christopher, milady."

"Christopher. I pray that your friend Christopher will be there with his coach."

"He will, milady," Mercy assured her. "You've no need to worry."

But Bliss did worry. She worried for the next three-quarters of an hour while she waited to leave the mansion. She worried as she and Mercy slipped soundlessly down the staircase and crossed the dark entrance hall. She worried as she and her maid hurried across the courtyard of Barthorp House and out into the Strand, and she worried as she and Mercy ran toward St. Martin's Lane, two dark shadows in the night.

"Where is he?" Bliss asked as they neared

their destination. "He's not here, Mercy! He's not—"

"There he is, milady," the maid pointed out. "He's waiting just as he promised."

Bliss squinted into the darkness. There was indeed a coach standing in the shadows. It was not the most elegant vehicle Bliss had ever seen and the four horses hitched to it were a motley lot, but just then they were the answer to Bliss's prayers.

She looked up at the coachman sitting high on the box, the reins held in his gloved hands. "You are Mercy's friend Christopher?" she called up.

His only reply was a nod of his head that set the bedraggled plumes of his black hat astir.

Bliss would have said more, but Mercy touched her arm, urging: "Come, milady, 'tis hours to Chatham. We haven't time to lose."

Bliss could not argue. With Mercy following, she climbed into the coach and sat back against the cracked leather squabs. From the box she heard the crack of a whip and the slap of the reins. The coach rocked and creaked as they started off. On their way to Chatham, Bliss told herself, on the way to freedom. To Kit.

The rocking of the coach lulled Bliss to sleep. Stretched out on the coach seat, she slept as they rolled through the countryside putting London and the Villierses farther and farther behind her.

An hour before dawn they came in sight of Chatham Castle. Mercy, who had dozed and awakened, let down the window and peered ahead, trying to pierce the darkness that shrouded the castle ahead of them. She knew they must be nearly there—so much time had passed. She looked at Bliss who slumbered so soundly and smiled. How relieved she would be to reach Chatham. If only everything could work out for her—and for Kit. If only—

Mercy's thoughts were interrupted as the coach reached the gateway. The portcullis was lowered and the horses whinnied as the coachman hauled on the reins to stop his team.

"Here, now, what d'ye want?" the grumpy gatekeeper shouted, annoyed at being awakened so suddenly and so early.

"Open the gate!" the coachman called down. "Your mistress is here!"

"My mis—"

Mercy leaned out the coach window. "Hurry! Open the gate! My Lady Bliss is inside."

Jarred into action, the gatekeeper tugged at the chains to raise the portcullis. With a creak and a groan, the spiked gate rose, jerking a few inches at a time until it was high enough to admit the coach and coachman high on the box.

"Milady?" Mercy jogged Bliss awake once the coach had halted near the entrance of the castle. "Milady. Wake up. We're here."

"We're . . ." Bliss sat up carefully, her muscles stiff. At once, she realized what her maid had said. "We're here! At Chatham?"

"Aye," the maid confirmed. "At Chatham!"

Scarcely daring to believe it was true, Bliss climbed down from the coach. The doorway of the castle stood open. Footmen spilled out, hurriedly fastening their livery. Fanshawe, the butler who was in charge of the household in Louise Lonsdale's absence, appeared, his periwig askew.

"Milady!" he cried, meeting Bliss halfway to the doorway. "We had no idea . . ."

"I know it's sudden, Fanshawe," Bliss told him. "There are no bags."

"My Lord Holme . . . ?"

"Is not with me. I am alone but for Mercy and the coach—" She gestured toward the coach box, but it was empty. Assuming that the driver had gone inside with Mercy, Bliss waved the thought aside. "I'm going up to my room, Fanshawe. We'll discuss this further in the morning."

"As you say, milady," the butler acquiesced.

Considering that she had slept for the better part of the past four hours, Bliss felt surprisingly tired as she mounted the stairs to her rooms. It was to be expected, she supposed. She had lived in such a state of nervous excitement for so long that now, when things seemed to be going her way, she felt exhausted. In the morning, she would speak to Isaac—in the morning she would begin trying to find Kit.

Entering her bedchamber, Bliss found a candle already burning on the bedside table. Mercy was not there, but Bliss was certain she would be along in a moment to help her undress.

Sitting at the dressing table, Bliss pulled the pins from her hair and let the curls cascade down her back. Untying the ties of her cloak, she let it fall in a puddle of black taffeta to the floor. Her reflection in the looking glass was pale, drawn, but that, she promised herself, would change. Once she was away from Stephen Villiers, once she found Kit, she would feel better—look better.

A movement in the reflected depths of the looking glass startled her. She was not alone in the room.

"Mercy?" Bliss swiveled on the dressing table stool. "I did not see you there. I was wondering where you—"

But it was not Mercy who stood there. Instead, swathed in shadows, enveloped in his caped coachman's cloak, his plumed hat still atop his head, was the coachman, Christopher, who had driven them from London.

Bliss felt a flicker of fear in the pit of her stomach. He was an ominous figure there in the darkness. But surely, since he was a friend of Mercy's, she had nothing to fear from him.

"Oh, it is you," Bliss said. "I suppose you wish to be paid? Mercy said you did not discuss payment. I am afraid I have not much gold here at the moment. But never fear, you will be paid well for your kindness tonight."

The man said nothing as he stood there. Bliss shivered, thinking she could see the glitter of his eyes in the shadow of his brim that hid his features.

"Will you not speak to me?" Bliss asked. "Tell me your price for tonight's work. If I haven't gold enough to meet it, I have some few jewels with me. They are not worth a great deal, but I am certain they will please . . ."

"Bliss," the man said softly, stepping forward out of the shadows. "Why did you wish to come here? Why did you not stay in London with your betrothed?"

Bliss began to tremble. It could not be! It was not possible. And yet . . .

"Who are you?" she demanded.

"You know who I am, Bliss," the voice replied.

Bliss swallowed hard. "I don't believe it. I don't . . ."

"You do," he contradicted. "You know the truth. Why do you refuse to believe it?"

"Kit." Bliss's eyes filled with tears that overflowed to trickle down her pale cheeks. "Kit! It was you. You! You drove the coach tonight. You brought me home to Chatham."

"Aye." Pulling off the concealing hat, Kit gazed at her from across the chamber. "It was me, milady." He bowed, sweeping the hat grandly before him. "Your loyal and obedient servant."

"It can't be . . . it can't . . ." After all the worry, all the uncertainty, he was there, with her, alive and well.

Bliss took one step toward him. Another. But then the enormity of it all, the shock, overcame her. Without warning she pitched forward, and Kit rushed to her, arms outstretched.

Mercy entered the room just as Kit caught Bliss in his arms. Gasping, the maid ran to Kit as he knelt on the flagstone floor with Bliss cradled in his arms.

"Is she . . . ?" the maid asked anxiously.

Kit smiled. "She's fainted, Mercy, that's all. Come, help me get her undressed and into bed."

"Undressed?" Mercy gazed at Kit, eyes wide. "Help you? But—"

"It's all right," Kit assured her. "Come now and help. She'll be fine. I give you my word."

Uncertain, not a little shocked, Mercy followed as Kit carried Bliss to the bed. Between the two of them they undressed her down to her shift and tucked her between the sheets of the huge tester bed.

"Stay with her," Kit directed. "If she wakes up she should not be alone."

"Where will you be?" Mercy asked as Kit retrieved his hat.

"I'm going to speak with Isaac," Kit told her. "He should be awake. Doubtless the coach horses have been taken to the stables."

"He's been worried about you," Mercy told him. "He wrote her ladyship a letter asking her to let him know if she heard anything about you. He was afraid you'd been captured and thrown in prison or . . ." Remembering the hanging that she, like Bliss, had been forced to witness, Mercy could not bring herself to say "hanged."

". . . or worse," she finished lamely.

"I know," Kit admitted. "I was sorry to cause him distress. I'll explain it to him as best I can." His eyes lingered on Bliss still unconscious on the bed. "Take care of her, Mercy," he said softly.

"Aye," the maid agreed, smiling as Kit disappeared through the hidden panel behind the tapestry. "That I will."

Chapter 18

Bliss awoke with a start. Sitting up in the tester bed, she gazed at her surroundings as though momentarily unable to remember how she had gotten from Barthorp House in London to Chatham Castle in Kent.

Mercy was at her side a moment later. "Milady?" the maid said, bending solicitously over her. "Shall I bring you anything?"

Frowning, Bliss brushed back her tumbled curls. "No, I . . ." She looked toward the window where the mid-morning sun glowed behind the heavy draperies. "Kit!" She looked at Mercy, an expression of near panic in her eyes. "Kit! He was here, wasn't he, Mercy? It wasn't a dream! He was . . ."

"He is here, milady," the maid assured her. "I

helped him put you to bed after you fainted. He's gone to have a word with Isaac."

"Isaac," Bliss murmured. Her eyes narrowed with suspicion. "Did Isaac know Kit was in London? Was his letter to me all part of some scheme to—"

"No, milady," Mercy interrupted. "Isaac did not know where he was. No one knew excepting—"

"You." Bliss's tone was accusing. "You knew all along where he was. That much is obvious. When I said I wanted to come to Chatham, you went to Kit and arranged for him to drive us here, didn't you?"

"Aye." The girl hung her head. "I didn't want to lie to you, honestly! It was only that . . ."

"That Kit told you not to tell me," Bliss finished for her. Not for the first time she marveled at the loyalty the people of Chatham bore for Kit. Mercy's family lived in the village, and it was clear she shared their feelings for the highwayman who dwelt among them.

The maid sniffled, apparently expecting to be dismissed from Bliss's service. "I am sorry, milady," she whispered. "Truly sorry."

"It's all right," Bliss told her. "I don't know why all of you bear such allegiance for Kit, but you do. Come along now, fetch me some water to wash in and then help me dress. I'm going to Isaac's to speak with him and Kit."

Relieved to find she was still Bliss's maid, Mercy hurried to do her mistress's bidding. Less than a half-hour later, Bliss let herself through the concealed panel in her bedchamber and made her way down the long, dark tunnel to Isaac's quarters in the stables.

At the same time, having finished a hearty if plain and homey meal, Kit and Isaac were sitting in front of Isaac's cold, empty hearth sharing ale.

"I still don't see the sense of it, my lad," the old groom was saying. "Ye say ye went to London and never saw the girl. What then, if I may ask ye, did ye go there for?"

"I saw her," Kit corrected. "I saw her at Whitehall, I saw her at the playhouse, I saw her at Tyburn . . ."

"Tyburn?" Isaac spat into the ashes in the fireplace. "What in the devil's name was that lass doing at Tyburn?"

"Villiers and Cameron took her to see a highwayman executed."

"By Christ! Could they not find a gentler entertainment for her? And who is Cameron?"

"Executions in London are high sport," Kit told him. "They come in their thousands to see the most famous criminals. And Cameron is Lord Cameron. A Scot. He's nearly penniless—a gamester. He's courting Villiers' sister, Letitia."

"Pah!" Isaac wrinkled his nose. "He has no great taste in women to court that sour-faced little shrew."

Kit laughed. "He has tried to court every

heiress in London. Now it seems he's set his sights on wedding into the Villiers family."

"These Villiers haven't a deal of money," Isaac reasoned. "That girl is no heiress."

"No," Kit allowed. "But her brother is betrothed to a great heiress."

"Ye don't mean to say—" Isaac sat forward, his eyes ablaze. "Ye don't mean they expect the young mistress to support the lot of them?"

"I think they do," Kit assured him.

"Damn them all!" Isaac muttered. "What will ye do about it?"

Kit said nothing, and Isaac went on:

"Come now, ye don't mean to let them have the girl, do ye?"

"No," Kit assured him quickly.

"Ye've done precious little to stop them this far," the old man reminded him.

"I thought perhaps Bliss could be happy with Villiers," Kit told him. "He could give her everything I couldn't—a life at court, respectability. That is why I didn't want Bliss to know I was in London. I wanted to see her there, with Villiers, and see if she was happy. If she was, I'd have gone away, out of her life, forever."

"But she wasn't happy?" Isaac asked.

Kit shook his head. "No, she wasn't. And every time I saw her with Villiers she looked more unhappy. Then there was Buckingham." Kit scowled. "I'll tell you something, Isaac, the Duke has designs on Bliss. I'm not certain just what . . . Perhaps he wants her for himself."

"The old goat," Isaac cried, feeling an almost paternal rush of protectiveness for his mistress.

"When Mercy came to me and said Bliss was determined to run away from London, I knew the time had come for me to take her away."

Isaac nodded approvingly. "But ye cannot stay here," he pointed out. "That guardian of hers and Villiers'll be comin' after her. Ye know that."

"Aye, I know," Kit agreed. "As soon as Bliss is ready to travel, we'll have to go on."

"Aye, that's the answer. Take her away from here. Take her where they won't find her until it's too late."

"Too late?" Kit asked.

"Aye. Too late for Villiers to marry her. Too late for Lord Holme to stop you. Ye do mean to wed the girl, don't you?"

Kit scowled, troubled. "I don't know if it would be fair—"

"God's blood, lad!" Isaac exploded. "What does fair have to do with it? Ye love her, don't ye?"

"Aye," Kit agreed softly, eyes faraway and wistful. "I love her, Isaac, more than you can know."

Neither man heard the small door in Isaac's chambers opening, neither man noticed Bliss standing there. It was not until Kit had spoken that they saw her, cheeks flushed, eyes awash with tears.

Kit rose and went to her. Taking her into his

239

arms, he held her gently, tenderly. Whatever mixed emotions he had had about revealing his feelings to her were banished from his mind. He had come so close to losing her, he did not intend to let anyone take her away from him again.

"You love me," Bliss whispered, tears trickling down her cheeks as she gazed up at him.

"Aye," he admitted, his eyes gentle as he smiled down at her. "I do."

"Why did you not tell me? Why did you send me away from you after . . ." She drew a deep breath. The memory of that night still pained her. "You seemed so cold . . . so cruel."

Neither noticed as Isaac discreetly rose and left the room, closing the door behind him.

Kit sighed. "Ah, Bliss, how can I explain? Villiers could give you everything I could not. A powerful and influential family, entree to court, all the glamour and excitement of London . . ."

"Love?" Bliss prompted. "Could you truly imagine I could love him?"

Kit shook his head. "I hoped you could learn. I did not want you to be unhappy, Bliss."

"But I was unhappy, desperately unhappy," she murmured.

"I know," he admitted. "I saw you."

"You saw—" Bliss's eyes widened. "It was you! That night at Whitehall! And at the playhouse! I thought . . . but why did you not come to me?"

"I had to see you, to watch you, without your

knowing I was there," he explained. "That was the only way I could know how you truly felt about Villiers and your future with him. When Mercy came to me and said you meant to run away, I told her I would help."

"Will you still help?" Bliss asked.

"What do you mean?"

Leaving his embrace, Bliss walked across the room. "You must know I cannot stay here." She looked toward the window. The sun rode high in the sky. "By now Sir Basil must know I've gone. The logical place for him to look for me is here, at Chatham. I must go on, Kit. I mean to go north, to Barthorp Hall in Yorkshire."

"Surely after he discovers you're not here," Kit suggested, "he'll look there next."

"Aye," Bliss admitted. "He will. But by then . . ." She toyed with an old bridle Isaac had been mending and had left lying on a table. "By then it could be impossible for him to force me to wed with Stephen."

"How?" Kit wanted to know.

Bliss hesitated. If she said what was in her heart and Kit refused . . . But there was no time for hesitation, no time to worry about consequences. "If you and I were married before he found us . . ."

Kit said nothing. Bliss stood with her back to him, obviously waiting for his reply. He could see the tension in her, could almost feel the breathless anticipation with which she waited for his answer.

Sandra DuBay

Going to her, he put his hands on her shoulders and turned her toward him. He slipped a finger beneath her chin and tilted her face up. His eyes were gentle as he gazed down at her.

"Bliss, you might regret this," he told her. "There is much you don't know about me. Too much. If you knew . . ."

"Shhh." Bliss laid a finger across his lips. "It doesn't matter, Kit. None of it matters. Don't you understand? I love you. I don't care about your past. All that matters is the future—our future."

Kit tried to smile but he was troubled. For all Bliss said, he believed that if she knew the truth about him it would matter very much. Still, he could not bring himself to tell her . . . not now. . . not yet. But soon, he promised himself, very soon.

Ruffling her hair, he pulled her into his arms and held her fast. "As you wish, brat," he teased. Leaning back, he touched her face gently. "Ah, Bliss, you can't imagine how it tortured me, thinking of you belonging to Villiers. And after we were together that night—" He closed his eyes as though in pain.

"You don't need to think of it any more," she told him. "We'll be together, Kit, forever."

The light in her eyes, the warmth of her in his arms, the soft scent of her skin, her hair, made Kit almost giddy. "We have to go," he told her. "Doubtless Holme will be here in a matter of hours. We must be on our way. But if we have the time . . ."

Bliss blushed prettily. "Aye?" she teased. "If we have the time?"

Moving away from her, Kit slapped her lightly on the backside. "Go on, you little baggage," he ordered. "Get back to your room and gather together whatever you mean to take with you. I'll see to the coach. It's a long drive to Scotland, you know."

"Scotland?" Bliss asked. "But Barthorp Hall is in—"

"Yorkshire, aye," Kit agreed. "But we've got to go to Scotland first, brat. Where do you think couples go when they elope? Now go!"

Giggling, Bliss dropped him a curtsy. "Aye, sir," she acquiesced. With a smile and a teasing kiss blown across the room, she disappeared into the tunnel that would take her back to her room. Eloping! With Kit! It seemed too wonderful to be true! At that moment she felt that she could fly to Scotland.

"Mercy!" she cried, bursting into her room and nearly scaring the unsuspecting maidservant out of her wits. "Hurry and help me pack a few more things. We're going to Scotland!"

"Scotland, milady?" the girl repeated, perplexed.

"You and me and Kit! We're . . ." She bit her lip, almost giddy with excitement. "Kit and I are to be married!"

"That is . . . I . . . congratulations, milady," the maid said, strangely subdued.

"What is it, Mercy?" Bliss asked. "You don't seem at all happy for me."

"Oh, but I am," the maid assured her. "I am, milady."

"Come, hurry and help me," Bliss urged. "And bring some things for yourself. You did not take everything to London with you, did you?"

"No, milady," Mercy answered dully.

Bliss bustled around the room peering into drawers and armoires to see what she had left behind that she could take with her. She was too excited to notice and wonder about the peculiar reaction of her maid. All she knew was that she was eloping with Kit—that the man she loved loved her in return and was going to be with her—forever.

Chapter 19

It was mid-afternoon when Stephen Villiers's coach drew up before the entrance of Barthorp House in the Strand. Normally he would not have waited so long to call on Bliss, particularly when he had had a message the previous morning saying she was indisposed and so would not be able to join Stephen and his mother at the Duke of Buckingham's estate.

But Stephen did not believe that Bliss's "indisposition" had anything to do with her health. She was angry with him, he thought, over his insistence that she go with him to the execution of the highwayman at Tyburn.

It was odd, Stephen reflected as he stepped down from his coach, pausing to fluff the fall of lace at his throat and cuffs. His suit of sky blue satin was more subdued than his usual taste, and that too was a concession to Bliss, whom, he had noticed, eyed him strangely when he wore his usual peacock hues. Aye, it was definitely odd, Bliss's reaction to the highwayman's death. Surely she could not sympathize with the wretch. He was a criminal. He robbed innocent people unfortunate enough to be on the road after dark. And it was not as if he had not been warned. Captain Maxwell—the villain whose execution they had witnessed—had been burned on the thumb, the usual warning that the man's next offense would be his last.

And yet Bliss had seemed almost overcome at the thought of his death. She was a complex woman, Stephen reflected. He did not understand her. Sometimes he wished she were some featherpated little chit who would simper and giggle and flutter her eyes and think of nothing more than her gowns and jewels. And yet he was fascinated by the mystery that hung around her. She baffled him and intrigued him. He had the feeling she could slip through his fingers at any moment like a will-o'-the-wisp, and that feeling only made him want to hold on to her all the tighter.

Climbing the steps, Stephen rapped on the door. A footman opened it and bowed as Stephen entered. Mrs. Lonsdale, hurriedly summoned, came to meet him.

"Good morrow, my lord," she said, curtsying.

"Good morrow, Lonsdale," Stephen replied.

"Fetch Lady Bliss down, if you please."

"My lady has not rung yet today, my lord," the housekeeper told him.

"Not rung?" Stephen looked at the tall case clock near the staircase. It was nearly two thirty. "Surely she is not still abed? Is she truly ill, Lonsdale? I thought, yesterday . . ."

"She was not ill," the older woman admitted. "Even so, I do not disturb her before she rings in the morning."

"This is not the morning." Stephen scowled. "Where is Lord Holme?"

"Gone out. To Whitehall, I believe. He should be returning soon, my lord."

Stephen sighed, growing more exasperated by the moment. Both he and Mrs. Lonsdale heard the sound of coach wheels and horses' hooves in the courtyard. Lord Holme had returned.

Sir Basil appeared in the doorway. He looked from Louise to Stephen and back again. The looks on their faces made him ask:

"What is this? Is something wrong?"

"Lonsdale says Bliss has not yet rung."

Sir Basil looked at the housekeeper. "Have you looked in on her yet today?"

"No, milord," the housekeeper told him. "I do not disturb her before she rings."

"Where is her maid? What's her name . . . Mercy? Call her down. If she's been in to see Bliss . . ."

"Now you mention it, my lord," Louise told him, "I've not seen Mercy today either. Strange.

She usually comes down to see to the water for milady's bath.''

Stephen and Sir Basil looked at one another. At once the light dawned. Their faces paled. Leaving Louise Lonsdale to stare after them, they raced up the stairs toward Bliss's room.

"Empty!" Sir Basil snarled, standing in the doorway. "Damnation! The little chit has run away!"

"But why?" Stephen asked, perplexed.

"Why d'ye think, you young fool?" Sir Basil growled. "She doesn't want to marry you!"

Stephen stared at him. Normally Sir Basil was all fawning attention. Clearly the man was a better actor than any on the stages of Drury Lane.

"Where would she go?" he ventured, hoping his innocent question would not provoke another outburst from his companion.

"Chatham," Sir Basil muttered. "I'd stake my life she's gone to Chatham." He entered the room. "Look about, lad. See if you can find any clue as to her reason for going now."

The two men began methodically searching the room. Ribbons and jewels were scattered over the floor. Powders and paints were knocked askew. The chairs and carpets were soon awash with Bliss's gowns and petticoats as Stephen and Sir Basil rummaged through chests and armoires.

"Here!" Stephen said at last. In the bottom of

the chest at the foot of Bliss's bed he had found the letter Isaac had written to her.

He handed it to Sir Basil, who scanned it, his ruddy complexion growing mottled with the fury that rose inside him.

"Quinn!" he growled. "Kit Quinn! God's teeth! I should have known it!"

"Kit Quinn?" Stephen asked. "But who—"

"The highwayman!" Sir Basil snarled. "The highwayman who robbed us on our way to Chatham! He's the same one who robbed you the night you met Bliss. I'd stake my life on it."

"But I shot him," Stephen protested. "I'm certain I hit him."

"I wish to hell your aim had been better, then," Lord Holme snapped. "Because according to this letter he was alive and well long after that."

He handed the letter back to Stephen, who read it.

"But according to this," he told Sir Basil once he'd finished, "this highwayman is missing. The old man thinks he might be in London."

"Perhaps Bliss thinks she can find him," Sir Basil speculated. "Or perhaps . . ." He scowled. A new, even more provocative thought entered his mind. "Perhaps he found her."

"Are you saying she might have run off with this wretch?" Stephen demanded. His mind reeled. All he could think of was his mother's rage at his allowing Bliss—and her fortune—to escape and his own mortification when people learned that his betrothed had run away with a . . .

"Highwayman!" he breathed. "That was why she was so upset over the execution at Tyburn. Captain Maxwell was a highwayman like this . . ."

"Quinn," Sir Basil supplied. Wheeling, he stormed from the room, Bliss's letter still clutched in his hand. He bellowed for Louise and when she appeared ordered:

"Have a hamper packed, Lonsdale, and get my traveling coach. The chit's run off to Chatham!"

Louise stared at him dumbfounded for several long moments and then hurried off to do as she'd been told. Behind her, Sir Basil turned back to Stephen. "You'd best go home and gather a few things, Villiers. I'll be along within the hour to collect you."

"Me?" Stephen repeated, not relishing the thought of hours spent cooped up in a coach with a blustering Lord Holme.

"Of course, you, you damned young—" Sir Basil caught himself. "You had a hand in driving her away. You can damned well help me get her back. Now go!"

Dreading the prospect of explaining to his mother the reason for his sudden departure from London, Stephen nevertheless hurried away to go home and pack a few changes of clothes for the journey to Chatham and however long it might take to convince Bliss to return with him.

Standing in the corridor outside Bliss's door, Sir Basil glared at the crumpled letter in his fist.

"Kit Quinn!" he muttered, his heart filled with hatred for the dashing rogue who threatened all his plans for Bliss and himself. "By God, I'll see the wretch hanged if it's the last thing I do!"

Bliss leaned forward eagerly as the coach turned into the courtyard of Barthorp Hall. She knew that by now Sir Basil would have discovered she'd run away. She knew that he could well have reached Chatham already and discovered that she'd been there and left. She even admitted that he might well be on his way to Yorkshire to look for her at her family's ancestral seat. But she did not care. It was too late. For she and Kit had made their way across the border into Scotland. They had driven through the night, through the day, heedless of the hour, stopping only to change horses at various coaching inns along their route. They had been exhausted by the time they had reached their destination, but it had been worth it.

As Bliss stepped down from the coach, she laid her hand into the hand of the man who stood before her, her lover, her husband.

"Well, Master Quinn," she said, sweeping a hand toward the house that rose before them.

"What do you think?"

Kit looked at the building that sprawled all around them. It had been built in the reign of Henry the Eighth on the site of an ancient fortress. Shaped like an H, it had front and rear courtyards, and the gallery running between the east and west wings had so many diamond-paned windows that it seemed entirely made of glass.

"It's beautiful," he admitted. There was a grandeur about the place, a feeling of solid security that made him uneasy. He had known that Bliss was a great heiress who had inherited Chatham Castle and its lands along with the house in the Strand in London, but this . . . this tangible proof of Bliss's fortune made him all the more aware of how little he had brought into their marriage.

Bliss sensed his mood and easily fathomed the reason for it. She wondered if it had been a mistake to bring Kit here, but quickly dismissed the thought. He knew she was an heiress. He knew her father had left her a great fortune. He would simply have to accept the fact and learn that his love was more than equal in her eyes to her fortune. She would have traded it all to become what she now was: Mistress Quinn.

"Come inside," Bliss invited. "Though I warn you, it might be in dreadful condition. I haven't been here in more than two years. Father left only a few servants to care for the house. They might have let it decay with no one to watch over them."

Linking her arm through his, Bliss led Kit to the iron-studded front door. It opened as if by magic when they approached, revealing a footman hurriedly fastening his livery.

"Milady!" he said, bowing awkwardly as he worked the fastenings of his blue and white jacket.

"Where is Valentine?" Bliss demanded.

"Here I am, milady." A tall, spare man dressed in black appeared. His face was hollow-cheeked, his lips pursed. His blue eyes, alert under his close-clipped white hair, scanned Kit from head to foot before returning to his mistress's face. "This is a pleasant surprise."

"And so is this," Bliss said, looking around. The low-ceilinged entrance hall and the rooms that lay off it seemed immaculate.

"I do not tolerate sloth, milady," the butler informed her.

"Indeed, I should have known you would not," Bliss admitted. She dimpled as she smiled up at Kit. "Valentine, this gentleman is Master Christopher Quinn. He is my husband. And your new master."

The only sign of the butler's surprise was a slight widening of his blue eyes. Collecting himself immediately, he bowed before Kit. "Sir," he said reverently.

"Valentine," Kit replied. "How do you do."

"Valentine," Bliss said, "I should like water heated for two baths. And a small supper. We'll have them in the master's suite, I think. We will be retiring early." She blushed and hurried on: "We've been on the road several days."

"As you wish, milady," the butler said and turned to leave.

Night had fallen when Bliss and Kit lay in the glow of a single candle that burned on the table beside the huge, carved four-poster standing in the cavernous bedchamber traditionally belonging to the lord of Barthorp Hall. Bliss gasped as Kit swept a hand up along the smooth, pearly flesh of her thigh and over her hip. She felt warm, drowsy in the aftermath of their lovemaking, but at Kit's touch her body trembled, the sweet ache started inside her again.

Kit lifted himself on one elbow and smiled gently down at her. "Aren't you tired, sweetheart?" he asked, even as his hand cupped one trembling breast.

Bliss shook her head, her body arching as his thumb teased the hard pink peak of her breast. She reached up to touch his face. The emotions he aroused in her were so new, so deep. Their intensity astonished her, even frightened her.

She twined her fingers in his dark hair and drew his head down. Their lips met in a tender kiss, a lovers' kiss. Their lovemaking before had been urgent, almost frenzied, but now there was a languid sensuality to their movements. Their bodies, already moist, melted against one another, their flesh warm and wet as Kit moved over Bliss. His lips were teasing as he kissed her cheeks, her throat, her breasts. Bliss moved restlessly as he traveled down her body pressing lingering, caressing kisses on her belly, her hip, her satiny smooth thighs.

"Kit," Bliss whispered. "Now, please now."

He moved above her. Bliss parted her legs for him, her eyes dark with desire. She moaned as he took her, as he entered her slowly, filling her with his love.

The pace Kit set was leisurely. He smiled down at Bliss, watching her eyes. Her pleasure was his pleasure and it grew inside her, the sweet, heavy languor stealing over her, taking her unaware, building until it burst within her, making her shudder in Kit's arms, her heart pounding against his.

She cried out his name and he gathered her into his arms holding her long after her body had ceased its trembling, long after fatigue had overtaken her. He watched her until she slept, her breasts rising and falling slowly, evenly, her breath soft and gentle, her lashes twin fans of auburn silk on her flushed cheeks.

Naked, Kit rose from the bed and walked to the diamond-paned window. For a long time he gazed out into the moonlit night. The silvery light shone through the window, a shimmering beam that fell across the bed where Bliss lay.

Kit looked back at Bliss. She was so lovely, so

innocent, bathed in the moonlight. His eyes were troubled, his expression solemn.

They were meant to be together, he believed, but first they must part. He meant to make her happy, but first, he knew, he would bring her pain.

Chapter 20

The great black traveling coach bearing the arms of Lord Holme rumbled along the road, the hooves of the eight black horses pulling it sending up a cloud of dust that made the coach's occupants keep the windows closed despite the stifling heat.

"Are you sure Bliss will be at Barthorp Hall?" Stephen asked, not relishing the prospect of a trip to Yorkshire at all and particularly not if they found their quarry was not there once they arrived.

"I'm certain of it," Sir Basil replied. "She loves the place. She was born there, raised there. It's where she'll go."

"With . . . him?" Stephen went on, unable to

force himself to say the name of the man who had stolen Bliss from him.

"Aye, she'll be with him. I'd stake my life on it."

"Do you think she knows about him?" Stephen wondered. "Do you think he's told her?"

Sir Basil shook his head. "I doubt it. The man is a rogue, a villain. He'd not tell her.

"Isaac—" Stephen began.

"He'll live," Sir Basil interrupted impatiently. "At least I think he will."

Stephen gazed out the window at what little he could see of the passing countryside through the haze of dust. "Perhaps we should not have had the lackeys beat him so," he said softly, the image of the old man bloodied and bruised haunting him from the depths of his conscience. "He is old, after all."

"It was the only way," Sir Basil reasoned. "He could have saved himself had he told us what we wanted to know in the first place."

"Even so, it was not Isaac who told us the truth about Quinn. It was the young groom."

"Aye." Sir Basil smirked. "These country people are all sentimental. It is a fault they have. He could not bear to see an old man beaten and so he told us exactly what the old man did not want us to know. Fool!"

Seeing the doubt and guilt still plain on Stephen's face, Sir Basil slapped him lightly on the arm. "Come on, lad, it doesn't matter, one old man! We have the information we need, and

NIGHTRIDER

when we reach Bliss, she'll soon learn the truth about her precious Kit Quinn!"

"But why must you go?" Bliss demanded not for the first time as she and Kit stood in the long, sunlit gallery of Barthorp Hall.

"I cannot tell you, Bliss," he replied patiently.

"Where are you going? Can you at least tell me that much?"

Kit shook his head. "Not now. Not yet."

"You don't trust me!" she accused, hurt.

"Bliss, please," he asked. "Can't you believe me when I tell you this is something I must do? When I come back, I will explain it all to you. You'll understand then, I promise you."

"I want to understand now!" she argued. "I want to go with you!"

"No," he refused flatly. "I must do this alone."

"Is there someone else?" she asked. "Is that it? Do you have to go to some woman and tell her you've married me? You're going to that blonde doxy of yours, aren't you? The one in Chatham—"

"Bliss . . ." Kit interrupted.

"Bess! Wasn't that her name? If I find out you've gone to her I'll—"

"Don't threaten me, Bliss," Kit warned. "I've told you I'll explain everything when I get back, and I will. Until then, let me remind you that I am your husband, madam, and you promised to obey me!"

Bliss eyed him mutinously but held her tongue. She did not want to argue, but neither did she want him to leave her so soon after their marriage and particularly not when he would not tell her where nor why he was going.

"How long will you be gone?" she wanted to know. "Is it permitted to ask that much?"

"It should not be more than a few days," Kit replied. "I'll come back as soon as I can."

"Promise?" she asked, moving to him and sliding her arms about his waist.

"I promise," Kit told her, enfolding her in his embrace. He leaned down to kiss the luscious little mouth that was tipped up to him and chuckled when she kissed him back, her body moving against his.

"Don't try to tempt me to stay, minx," he said, releasing her.

Bliss pouted prettily. "It does not hurt to try," she reasoned. "And maybe you'll want to come back sooner."

"I'll come back as soon as I can," he promised again. "But before I can come back, I have to leave. Come now, sweetheart, smile for me. I'll be back before you have time to miss me."

Bliss forced a smile and returned his kiss. She walked to the door with him and watched as he mounted the horse that had been saddled at his order and brought to the courtyard.

Swinging up into the saddle, Kit smiled at Bliss and blew her a kiss before riding out, his horse's hooves ringing on the cobblestones of the courtyard.

Bliss sighed, watching until he disappeared up the wooded lane. "I'll be back before you have time to miss me," he had said. He was wrong. Bliss's heart ached, and she bit her lip, feeling as if she wanted to cry.

"I miss you already," she said softly as she turned back and went into the house.

The rest of the day passed slowly. Bliss wandered through the house like a lonely little ghost. She had always loved Barthorp Hall. When she'd been at Chatham and in London she had longed to be here. But now it seemed so large, so cold, so empty. Kit's absence had left a void in her life, her heart, that not even the dear, familiar atmosphere of her beloved family home could begin to fill.

Though she would not have thought it possible, the night passed even more slowly than the day. She lay in the huge four-poster, its sprawling emptiness reminding her all too keenly of the hours she and Kit had spent there. Her fingers ached to touch him, her arms ached to hold him, her body yearned for the touch of his.

With a groan of yearning, of frustration, she rolled on her side and tried to force herself to sleep.

But her eyes were darkly shadowed with fatigue when she rose the next morning. She had dozed again and again only to dream of Kit and had awakened feeling more lonely than before.

"He'll be back soon," Mercy assured her mistress when she brought Bliss's morning cup of chocolate.

"I hope so," Bliss replied listlessly. "I don't know why he could not tell me where he was going or why."

"I'm certain he has his reasons, milady," the maid told her, taking the empty cup and saucer from her mistress.

Bliss eyed the maid suspiciously. "Do you know anything about this, Mercy?" she asked, remembering that the maid had known of Kit's presence in London when she herself had had no idea of it.

"Me, milady?" the girl hedged, clearly nervous.

"Aye, you!" Bliss snapped. "Kit is my husband, Mercy, I have a right to know anything there is to know about him!"

"Aye, milady," the girl agreed, "but . . ."

"But he told you not to say anything, is that it?" Bliss demanded.

"He means to tell you everything, milady, when he comes back. I'm certain of it."

"Damn you!" Bliss cried. "Why are you more loyal to him than to me! All of you from Chatham were like that! You! Isaac! Everyone!" Bliss's heart was filled with a jealous resentment of Mercy and every person in and around Chatham who knew more of her husband than she did. What was it, this deep, dark secret of his they all protected so well?

"Get out!" she snarled, suddenly unable to bear the sight of the girl. "Get out of my sight, damn you, or I'll send you packing!"

Emphasizing her order by flinging a pillow at Mercy's head, Bliss rolled over in the bed and abandoned herself to tears of anger, jealousy, and frustration.

Her eyes were still puffy and red when she descended the stairs early in the afternoon. She had had Valentine send up one of the parlor maids to help her dress, for she still did not want Mercy near her.

"Has there been any word from your master?" she asked the butler who came to greet her at the bottom of the stairs.

"No, milady," Valentine replied. "Will your ladyship be wanting something to eat? I will have the cook bring—"

"Nothing," Bliss interrupted. "I'm not hungry." She sighed. "I shall be in the library, Valentine. Send someone to me if my husband returns."

Valentine bowed and watched with troubled eyes as the young mistress he'd known from babyhood wandered off toward the library at the far end of the east wing overlooking both the rear courtyard and the wooded park surrounding the hall.

Bliss went to the library and plucked a volume

from one of the long shelves lining the walls. She did not look at the title. It did not matter to her what the book might contain.

Curling into a chair, she gazed out the window, the book resting on her lap. She was still sitting there when the door opened and Valentine appeared.

"Milady?" he said softly.

Bliss started. The shadows in the room had lengthened. She had no idea how many hours had passed since she'd entered the room, but afternoon was giving way to evening. The room was softly lit in the mauves of twilight.

"Milady?" Valentine repeated.

Bliss uncurled her legs, wincing at the pain. The long hours sitting cramped in the chair had tied her muscles in knots.

"What is it, Valentine?" she asked. Then, suddenly, she drew a deep breath. "Kit? Is it Kit? He's back, isn't he?"

"I do not know, milady," the butler told her. "But a coach was just seen turning into the park."

"Oh!" Certain that Kit was returning at last, Bliss dropped her book. Snatching up her skirts, she ran past Valentine and out the door.

"Kit!" she whispered, her heart singing. "At last! At last!"

Her heart sang, she was going to see him again! She was going to know the truth! Everything would be clear at last and there would be no more shadows to cloud the happiness she was sure would be theirs.

Ignoring the footman who was about to open the door, Bliss seized the polished handle and pulled the heavy door open. Her pale green skirts rustled around her, her loose red curls bounced on her shoulders, as she ran down the steps just as the coach stopped before her.

It was not until the door opened and the first occupant stepped down that she realized her mistake. "No," she whispered, looking up into the smirking face of her guardian. "Oh, no."

"Bliss," Sir Basil said. "How kind of you to come out to greet us."

Stephen, looking embarrassed, climbed out of the coach and stood slightly behind Lord Holme.

"What are you doing here, Stephen?" Bliss demanded.

"Should he not be here?" Sir Basil countered. "He is, after all, your betrothed."

"Go away!" she cried. "Get off my land!"

"Not just yet," Sir Basil told her. "We're here to talk to you, Bliss."

"I don't want to hear anything you have to say!"

"Oh, I think you'll want to hear this," Sir Basil said, the sneering smile on his face making Bliss's flesh crawl. "It's about a friend of yours, a certain highwayman. One Kit Quinn."

"Kit . . ." Bliss knew a moment's terror. Had they somehow captured Kit? Was he even then languishing in some dank, damp cell awaiting the same fate as the man whose execution she'd unwillingly witnessed?

She looked from Sir Basil to Stephen and back again. "What do you know about Kit?" she demanded. "Where is he?"

"He's not here?" Lord Holme asked. He exchanged a surprised glance with Stephen. "You surprise me, my dear. I thought he was with you."

Bliss felt a moment's relief. If they did not know where Kit was, that meant they did not have him.

"He's coming back," she told them. "He's promised to come back soon."

"I wonder if you'll be so eager to see him," Sir Basil mused, "once you've heard what I have to tell you."

Bliss longed to order them away, to send them packing. But a voice inside her told her they knew whatever secret was being kept from her, that somehow they had penetrated the conspiracy of silence that surrounded Kit. She had to know, even if it meant hearing it from the two men she loathed.

"Come in, then, and say what you've come to say," she told them. "And then I expect you to go!"

Sir Basil and Stephen followed her into the hall. And though Stephen dreaded being present when Bliss learned the truth about her highwayman lover, Sir Basil found himself looking forward to the moment when "Kit Quinn" was exposed for what he truly was, the moment when the blinders that love had put on Bliss's eyes were torn off and she knew the truth about the thief who had stolen her heart. The man she had taken into her heart—and her bed.

Chapter 21

Sir Basil and Stephen followed Bliss into the hall. She led them into a drawing room off the glass gallery and faced them impatiently.

"Very well," she said, her chin high, her air defiant. "Have your say, then go."

"Come now, Bliss," Sir Basil chided, enjoying the suspense he knew she was feeling. "You are mistress of this house. It is for you to show hospitality to your guests."

"You are not my guests," she reminded him coolly. "I do not remember inviting you—either of you."

Stephen looked away, embarrassed by the mere fact of being there. He wished Sir Basil would do as Bliss asked—simply tell her what they'd come to tell her. He longed to be away, back in London, finished with this business.

"Bliss," Sir Basil said, his voice smooth, his expression smug. He was enjoying the game. He had the upper hand with his beautiful, haughty ward and he intended to play it for all he could, "Stephen and I have been running after you for days. We are dusty, we are tired, we are hungry. You are behaving like a spoiled child."

Knowing she was not likely to be rid of them easily or quickly, Bliss summoned Valentine.

"Have a supper prepared," she told the butler. "Have Lord Villiers' and Lord Holme's things taken up to rooms for them. And have water heated for their baths."

The butler bowed and left, and Bliss turned back to her guardian. "Will that suit you, my lord?" she asked.

"Admirably," Sir Basil told her. "After we have bathed and changed and eaten, we will talk—all of us."

Chafing, Bliss waited below while Stephen and Sir Basil were shown up to the rooms prepared for them. Heated water was brought to them and their needs seen to by footmen pressed into service as valets for the occasion.

When supper was served, Bliss picked at the roast venison and the carrots and peas while Sir Basil ate heartily exclaiming over the venison as well as the roast beef, lamprey pie, rice pudding, vegetables, and wine.

"Excellent," Sir Basil pronounced when he finished, long after both Bliss and Stephen had allowed their own plates to be cleared away. "Excellent, my dear. My compliments to your cook."

"I will convey them later," Bliss promised. "For now, might we get down to your reason for being here?"

"Indeed. Shall we retire?"

Impatient, Bliss rose and led the way out of the dining room where the walls were covered with tapestries and the sideboard gleamed with plate that had been in Bliss's family for generations. She led the two men into a drawing room whose windows faced out onto the park now swathed in shadows, lit only by the glow of the moon.

"Where is Kit, by the bye?" Sir Basil asked as he reclined on a chaise-longue. "Why is he not here with you?"

Bliss looked away. It embarrassed her to admit that Kit had left her but it could not be helped. "He . . ." she began haltingly. ". . . he had to go away for a while."

"Oh?" Sir Basil fairly purred. "And why was that?"

"I don't know!" Bliss snapped. "He did not tell me."

"Where did he go?" her guardian persisted, intent upon causing her as much discomfort as possible.

"I do not know!" Bliss hissed. "What matter, my lord? He had to go away. He will soon be back. That is all that counts."

"Humph." Sir Basil cast a smug look toward Stephen. "With any luck, he won't come back at all."

"He will come back!" Bliss snapped. "I know he will. He promised to come home as soon as he could."

"Home?" Sir Basil snarled. "This is hardly his home."

"It is now," Bliss said defiantly. "He is master of this house, my lord." She looked from her guardian to Stephen and back again. Drawing a deep breath, she blurted:

"Kit and I went to Scotland before coming here. We were married there."

"What!" Sir Basil thrust himself to his feet, his face mottled with fury. "You stupid little fool! You could not have done such a thing!"

"I tell you it's true," Bliss insisted. "Kit is my husband."

Sir Basil's fists clenched and unclenched. He longed to strangle the haughty creature who stood before him. "I don't believe you!" he snarled. "Where is the marriage certificate?"

Marching to the bell rope, Bliss tugged it. When Valentine appeared, she sent him to fetch her maid.

"Mercy," she said when the girl stood before her. "Go to my room and get my marriage certificate."

Mercy hesitated, looking from Bliss to Sir Basil who glared at her and to Stephen who sagged in his chair, his face ashen. Nervously, she bit at her lower lip.

"Well?" Bliss prompted. "Go and get it."

"It is not there, milady," the maid told her.

"What do you mean?" Bliss demanded.

"The master took it with him."

"Took it—" Bliss frowned, confused. "But why would he do that?"

"I don't know, milady. He asked me for it just before he left. I took it out of your dressing table."

"It does not matter," Sir Basil decreed. "That will be all, girl. Leave us alone."

Sketching a shallow curtsy, Mercy hurried from the room, leaving her mistress alone with her tormentors.

"It does matter," Bliss disagreed. "I will prove to you that Kit and I were—"

"I said it does not matter, Bliss," Sir Basil interrupted, wearing of his game. "This 'marriage' will be dissolved as soon as we get back to London."

"Dissolved!" Bliss blanched. "You could not!"

"Indeed I could," Sir Basil assured her. "And I will."

Bliss knew only too well that her guardian might well be able to have her marriage declared invalid. She was pre-contracted to Stephen. She was underage to contract her own marriage. There were myriad excuses to declare such a union null and void. And, if all else failed, Sir Basil had access to her considerable fortune.

He could bribe the right officials and have his way.

"Please," she said softly. "I beg you. Just leave us in peace. I love Kit and he—"

"You love Kit," Sir Basil sneered. "You don't even know Kit! He's lied to you, you little fool! He's lied to you from the first. And you, besotted ninny that you are, you believed him! You played into his hands as he knew you would!"

"Explain yourself!" Bliss demanded, trembling. "I won't have my husband insulted in his own home!"

"After we discovered you'd run off, we searched your room. We found the letter from Isaac."

"Isaac," Bliss breathed. "You went to Chatham, didn't you?"

"Aye, we did. You'd gone on by then and no one wanted to tell us where you'd gone. We questioned Isaac. He was reluctant, but after a little persuasion he told us about 'Master Quinn.'"

"And what is the truth?" Bliss could not resist asking.

Sir Basil shot a triumphant look at Stephen, who avoided his glance. "The truth," he said, looking back at Bliss, "is that Kit Quinn, the highwayman you've taken to your bed, is really Christopher Quinn de Wilde, son and heir of the late Baron de Wilde, the traitor whose lands you inherited from your father."

Sandra DuBay

"De Wilde!" Bliss breathed. "Kit is the Baron de Wilde?"

"Aye," Sir Basil admitted. "Though his lands were forfeit, the King could not take away his title. The man is Lord de Wilde. Much good may it do him!"

Shaken, Bliss reached out toward a chair. Her face was pale, her hands trembling. Stephen rose and went to her side to guide her to the sofa he had just left.

"It can't be true," Bliss whispered. She looked at Stephen sitting beside her, and found a surprising depth of sympathy in his eyes. "It can't!" she whispered.

"It is true, Bliss," Stephen told her. "Isaac told us. And some of the villagers told us as well."

"That was why Kit took to the road," she murmured. "The family retainers turned out of the castle were his father's servants. That is why he felt he had to provide for them."

"Noble of him," Sir Basil sneered. "Considering that it was his father's treachery to his King that caused all their troubles in the first place."

"But . . ." Bliss shook her head. "I still can't believe it."

Tugging the bell pull, Sir Basil summoned Mercy to help Bliss to her room. The maid appeared, eyes downcast, as if knowing that Kit's secret was a secret no longer.

Bliss looked at the maid, her eyes accusing. "Is it true, Mercy?" she asked. "Is Kit truly Lord de Wilde? Is he the son of the old Baron de Wilde?''

Not daring to meet her mistress's eyes, Mercy nodded. "Aye, milady. We all swore to tell no one. I wanted to tell you. I did! But Master Kit . . . Milord de Wilde . . . said he would tell you. When the time was right.''

"When the time was right!" Sir Basil scoffed. "And when was that? After he'd duped the little fool into marrying him? After he'd charmed her, beguiled her by leading her to believe he was some sort of noble rogue, stealing by night to provide for some old men and women? After he'd married her and regained possession of his lands?''

"No!" Mercy cried. "It was not that way! He was going to tell her." She looked at Bliss, her eyes tearful. "He loves you, milady. Truly he does.''

"He has an odd way of showing it," Sir Basil sneered. "He's gone off and left her alone after only a few days of marriage.''

"He'll come back!" Mercy insisted. "He would not simply leave her! You don't understand him!''

"Bah! You're romantic fools, the pair of you! The man is a villain, a liar and a thief. Doubtless he'd be a traitor, too, like his father, given the chance. He doesn't love Bliss! He loves Chatham and all it contains. Doubtless he's back there even now, a mug of ale in his hand and a doxy on his knee, laughing up his sleeve at the way he fooled Bliss and cheated her out of part of her inheritance.''

''Enough!'' Bliss cried, rising. She was bewildered, confused. Kit had lied to her from the beginning. That in itself was hard enough to bear. But the thought that he might have planned it all, feigned a love he did not feel, drawn her into a love that, for her, was all too real, was simply too much.

Picking up her skirt, Bliss ran out of the room. Through the open door, they heard her heels on the carved wooden staircase. Mercy went to the foot of the stairs. She longed to go to her mistress and comfort her, reassure her, but just then she did not know if she would be welcome.

Stephen started after Bliss, but Sir Basil caught at his sleeve to stop him.

''Leave her be, my boy,'' the older man counseled. ''She's had a shock. Give her time. She'll come to see what a rogue it is she's tied herself to. And she'll come willingly when it's time to go back to London.''

Smiling, Sir Basil clapped Stephen on the shoulder. ''Don't despair,'' he told him confidently. ''I've a feeling she'll be yours yet.''

Chapter 22

Bliss passed the rest of the day in her room in stunned silence. She felt humiliated, mortified and betrayed. She felt as though she'd been exposed, not only to Sir Basil and Stephen but to herself as a foolish, gullible girl taken in by a dashing villain who'd played on her innocence and inexperience.

Suddenly it all seemed so clear. Suddenly she understood. She remembered Kit's hostility from the night they met. That night in the forest he had been so charming, so romantic—until he discovered who she was. Then his manner had changed. He'd become cold, harsh. She had not understood at the time; she'd been bewildered, perplexed. But now, she realized, he had seen her as a usurper. She had inherited the estates that had been in his family for centuries. The family heirlooms, the treasures, Chatham Castle itself . . . all these things Kit had grown up with. He had taken for granted his right to inherit the castle, its lands and contents. One day, he had believed from childhood, he would be Baron de Wilde, master of Chatham. But then had come the war, and his father had taken Cromwell's side against a monarch he saw as a tyrant, under the domination of his French Queen. It had been the old Baron's downfall and that of his son.

Bliss gazed up at the carved wooden tester above her. She wondered how she would have felt if their situations had been reversed. Certainly she would have been bitter, she would have resented the person who had inherited everything she considered her own. But to pretend to be someone else—to wed that person without telling him the truth. No, Bliss did not believe herself capable of such deception.

She wondered where Kit could be. He had taken their marriage certificate with him. Was it, she wondered, valid? He had signed it "Christopher Quinn." Or had he? She frowned. She could not remember. She had signed the certificate first and then—The wife of the parson who had married them had engaged her in conversation. She had not seen Kit sign the certificate. Nor, now that she thought of it, had she looked at the certificate itself after the ceremony. It had been signed, sealed, and rolled up, tied with a scarlet ribbon. Kit had given it to her and she had simply tucked it into her trunk.

Had he, she wondered, signed it with his true name? If he had, their marriage was valid. She was now Baroness de Wilde, and he, as her husband, was master not only of his own ancestral home but of Barthorp House in London and Barthorp Hall as well. And her fortune, with the exception of that small portion that was hers by dower rights, was under his control.

Even now, she knew, he could be busily signing drafts worth thousands of pounds. He could be at her goldsmith's depleting her fortune as quickly as he wished.

But no, she told herself. Kit would not do such a thing . . . Would he? She smiled bitterly. She would not have thought Kit would deceive her over something so basic as his identity, but he had. What else might he be capable of? In his own way, was he any less devious, any less grasping and avaricious than Lady Villiers and that whey-faced daughter of hers? All any of them wanted was her fortune.

"Damn them!" she muttered. "Damn them all! I'm tired of being a pawn for them. Sir Basil bought my guardianship to advance his ambitions, Stephen and his family want to enrich themselves with my gold, and now Kit . . ." Bliss closed her eyes, feeling an ache in her heart she knew that even time would not heal.

Kit. Of them all, Kit's betrayal was the worst for he had turned her own senses against her. He knew she was in love with him and he had used that to sway her. How he must have laughed at her! She had offered to help him, tried to get him to leave the highway. She had thought it was his pride that had made him refuse, but now she wondered . . . might it not have been all part of his scheme?

Bliss's cheeks flamed at the memory of how she had fled back to Chatham, back to Kit. She had asked him to marry her! How triumphant he must have felt! He had set his trap and bided his time, and she had willingly fallen into it. What a stupid, credulous fool she was!

"Never again!" Bliss vowed to the room around her. "I'll never allow myself to be duped again! I'll be cold, calculating, hard-hearted. No one will ever control my heart, my senses that way again!"

There was a timid tapping on the door.

"Come in!" Bliss called, sitting up on the edge of the wide bed.

One of the housemaids entered the room and bobbed a curtsy. "Milord Holme sent me up to see if your ladyship needed help with your gown . . . or anything, milady."

"Where is Mercy?" Bliss asked.

"Downstairs, milady. She did not think you would want to see her just now."

Bliss thought of her maid, of how the girl had

known all along who Kit really was, of the fact that Mercy had known Kit was in London and had gone to him when Bliss needed a coachman to drive them back to Chatham. The girl, like the rest of those in Chatham village, gave their loyalty to Kit, the man they considered their lord and master. She was as much a betrayer of Bliss's trust as Kit himself.

"She was right," Bliss muttered. "I don't wish to see her. Especially now." She looked at the maidservant. "What is your name?"

"Patience, an' it please your ladyship."

"Come then, Patience," Bliss told her, stepping down on the bedsteps, "help me into my nightrail. I'm exhausted!"

In the morning, Bliss's resolve was firmly set. As she strolled across the rolling lawn behind the hall, she solemnly promised herself that from that moment on, she would be as coldly calculating as Lady Daphne herself. She would do nothing according to the dictates of her heart, her senses. Her actions would be based solely on cold, hard logic.

Rounding a long, high hedge, she nearly collided with Stephen. He was dressed simply in brown cloth and to Bliss's eyes looked better than he did in his London rainbows of silks and lace.

"Good morning, Stephen," she said, surprising him with her pleasantness.

"Good morning," he replied. "I was not following you, Bliss. Indeed, I did not know you were about. I'm certain you'd rather be alone, so I'll just—"

"Don't ramble so," Bliss told him. "And I would not necessarily rather be alone. Come, walk with me. We should talk, I suppose."

Stephen fell into step beside her. He looked down at her, wishing he could gauge her mood, but her face was hidden by the wide brim of her feather-laden, green velvet hat.

"I am sorry, Bliss, about what happened."

"You are?" She looked up at him, curious. "Why should you be?"

"You must think me a monster," he chided. "I do care for you, you know. My proposal of marriage was not based entirely on greed."

Bliss would have argued that, but the note of hurt in his voice stopped her. Perhaps he did harbor some sort of feeling for her. It was possible, she supposed, however unlikely it seemed.

"In any case," he went on, taking her silence for skepticism, "I am sorry. I know you . . . cared for Quinn . . . de Wilde . . . and I know you must be terribly hurt by what happened."

"Aye," Bliss admitted. "No one likes to think they've been a fool for someone they . . ." Her voice dropped to a whisper. ". . . loved."

"What will you do now?" Stephen wanted to know.

"What *can* I do?" she countered. "Sir Basil says the marriage can be dissolved. But, Stephen, I did not see the certificate. If Kit signed his true name, his title, is it not valid?"

Stephen shook his head. "Perhaps. But there is the matter of your betrothal to me. It was approved by the King. The contracts were signed. You were pre-contracted to me, Bliss, and so your marriage to Kit can be invalidated. It will take time."

"I need time." Stopping, Bliss turned and looked up at Stephen. "After this marriage is dissolved, you and I will still be betrothed. Will we not?"

"Aye," Stephen agreed. "We will."

"If you wish to end our betrothal, I will agree. After all, this," she winced, "marriage with Kit. It was . . ." She blushed at the memory of lying in Kit's arms. "He and I . . . we . . ."

"I understand." Stephen felt a painful stab of jealousy shoot through him. They had consummated their "marriage." De Wilde had held her, made love to her, while he, Stephen, had been fortunate if she allowed him to kiss her. The resentment he had felt toward the highwayman Kit Quinn turned into the beginnings of a burning hatred for Christopher, "Kit" de Wilde, Baron de Wilde of Chatham—Bliss's husband. Bliss's lover.

"In any case," Bliss was continuing, "even if this marriage is dissolved, I could not quickly enter into another."

"I do understand, Bliss," Stephen told her. "You will need time. I will wait."

He had little choice, Bliss thought, unmoved by his patience and understanding. In his own words it would "take time" to invalidate her marriage to Kit. If he truly wanted to marry her, Stephen would have to wait, and even after the marriage was annulled, it would be awhile before she would be prepared to consider entering into another such union.

"Let's go back into the house," she told him, turning back toward the hall.

Together they returned to the manse. In one of the rear windows she could see Sir Basil watching them. His face was wreathed in smiles. It was obvious that he was delighted that she and Stephen could be so civil with one another. Bliss's eyes narrowed. Let him enjoy this moment. He would soon learn that she was not so easily swayed as he might think.

"Here you are!" Sir Basil boomed as Bliss and Stephen entered the glass gallery through the rear entrance. "And here I thought you were still shut up in your room, Bliss. But you were with Stephen!"

"We happened to meet in the garden," Bliss told him, lest he think they had purposely gone on an intimate stroll together.

"What matter?" he said jovially. "You are together, and how pretty you look! I vow, m'dear, your cheeks are blooming!"

Bliss handed her hat and gloves to a footman and faced her guardian solemnly. "I have decided, sir," she told him matter-of-factly, "to accompany you and Stephen back to London."

"Wonderful!" Sir Basil grinned at Stephen as if congratulating him.

"It was entirely Bliss's decision," Stephen told him quickly. He felt there might once more be hope that Bliss would be his and he was anxious that her guardian not spoil things between them.

"And this 'marriage' of yours?" Sir Basil prompted.

"Once we return to London," Bliss told him, "you may see to having the marriage dissolved. I will make no protest." She lifted her chin, masking the pain her words caused her. "Now, if you will excuse me, sir, I will see to my packing. I should like to be away from this place as soon as possible."

"Certainly, certainly, my dear," Sir Basil agreed. "We'll leave whenever you say."

He smiled triumphantly as Bliss sailed past him and climbed the stairs. He had won, far more easily that he'd ever dared to expect. He could afford to be magnanimous in victory.

Patience, the housemaid who was now serving Bliss, folded Bliss's clothes and packed them into the trunk that stood open in the middle of the bedchamber. She looked up as a knock sounded on the door.

"Never mind," Bliss told her, going herself to answer it.

Mercy stood there, her cheeks flushed, her eyes puffed and red. It was obvious she had been crying. Sniffling, she dropped Bliss a curtsy. "May I speak with you, milady?" she asked meekly.

Bliss stared at her for a moment, then nodded. "Come in," she invited, stepping back. "Patience, leave that for now. I'll call you when I need you."

Curtsying, the girl left the room and Bliss closed the door and turned to her lady's maid.

"Well?" she prompted.

"They say you are going back to London with Sir Basil and Lord Villiers, milady," the maid began.

"Gossip travels quickly," Bliss observed. "But it is true. I mean to go back. And I mean to see this marriage dissolved, Mercy."

"Oh, no, milady! You mustn't! If only you'll wait until milord comes back—"

" 'Milord' is it now?" Bliss snapped. "Before it was merely Kit."

"Please, milady," Mercy whispered, "I did not want to lie to you—"

"But Lord de Wilde held your loyalty," Bliss finished for her. "You gave him your allegiance; you helped him to deceive me."

"You do not understand—"

"No, I do not!" Bliss snapped. "I trusted you, Mercy! You betrayed me!"

"You do not understand—"

"No, I do not!" Bliss snapped. "I trusted you, Mercy! You betrayed me!"

Weeping, Mercy fell to her knees at Bliss's feet. "Forgive me, milady," she begged. "It is only that my family . . . for generations we have served the lords of Chatham Castle and—"

"I am the mistress of Chatham Castle!" Bliss reminded her. "Or at least I was until you helped Kit trick me into this marriage."

"He did not mean to hurt you, milady," Mercy told her. "He only—"

"Don't defend him to me!" Bliss ordered. "Hear me, Mercy. Mark my words. I will not have a servant near me who defends that man! If you still feel you owe your first loyalty to him, you can stay here and wait for him to come back—if he ever does!"

"Please, milady, I want to stay with you!"

"Then swear to me now, on peril of your immortal soul, that you will be loyal to me, first and foremost. Swear it!"

"I swear it, milady," she vowed fervently, "before God Himself!"

"Very well, then, get up. Go and pack whatever you need. We're leaving for London as soon as I'm packed. Hurry, now." Bliss watched the maid rise and go to the door. "And, Mercy?" she called after her. "Send Patience back in to finish my packing."

It was early afternoon when Bliss, Sir Basil, Stephen, and Mercy gathered in the hall of Barthorp Hall waiting for their coach to be loaded with their trunks and brought to the door for them. A hamper containing cold roast meat, cheese, bread, and wine had been packed in the kitchen and brought for them.

"We'll drive until nightfall," Sir Basil decreed, "then stop for the night. It's a pity we did not start earlier."

"We still would not have reached London in one day," Stephen reminded him.

"No, but the inns are better to the south. Ah, here is the coach."

"Milady?" Valentine came to Bliss's side as Mercy, Stephen, and Sir Basil went out to the waiting coach.

"What is it?" Bliss asked, eager to be gone.

"What shall I do if . . . the gentleman . . . returns?"

Bliss felt a twinge of pain at the thought of Kit coming back and finding she had gone back to London with her guardian and her betrothed. No! she chided herself, there was no time for doubt, no room for pity.

"Have his belongings packed," Bliss decreed, "and if he comes back, throw him—and them—out!"

The butler bowed, and Bliss, without a backward glance, went out to join the others in the coach.

Chapter 23

Kit rode like a man possessed. The horse beneath him practically flew, his hooves a dark flash, his iron shoes striking sparks off stones in the road that took them south, toward Chatham Castle.

He thought of Bliss back at Barthorp Hall. It had been hard—very hard, he thought longingly—to leave her. He had wanted to stay, to lose himself in her beauty, to spend every day and every night making love to her. But there would be time enough for that when this other business was behind him.

Now that he and Bliss were married, he intended to go to London and petition the King to restore Chatham and her lands to the de Wilde family. After all, Bliss was Lady de Wilde now; there would be no question of her losing anything. It would merely remove the stain on Kit's family name, his honor. He did not want Bliss to be ashamed when she found out he was not simply a reformed highwayman. He wondered what she would think if she knew she had married the Baron de Wilde, a man whose father had been condemned, stripped of his lands, his honor, as a betrayer of the King Bliss so admired.

He would go to London, show the King the marriage certificate, assure him of the love between Bliss and himself. But first he would return to Chatham Castle. He wanted Isaac to know that all was well. He wanted the man who had been a second father to him to know that there would once more be a Lord de Wilde installed at Chatham Castle.

Kit smiled to himself as he thought of the rejoicing his news would bring to Chatham village. Though Bliss had done nothing to earn the enmity of the villagers, they still gave their first loyalty to their traditional lord. Now they would learn to love her as he loved her. Now she would truly be their lady, the wife of their rightful lord, and all the mistrust, all the resentment would vanish. They would love her as he loved her. There was not a doubt in his mind on that score.

Straightening in the saddle, he tried to banish some of the aching in his back and legs. He'd been in the saddle for hours, stopping only once to eat and change horses at a coaching inn. Now that his goal was finally in sight, now that Bliss was his and there seemed the real possibility that he could repair the damage to his family's honor, he was eager to have the matter done and be back at Barthorp Hall, back in Bliss's arms.

Thinking of Bliss, the pain in his back and his legs was forgotten only to be replaced with another ache, an ache not so easily banished, an ache not so easily assuaged, an ache that lasted as long as it took him to reach Chatham Castle long after night had fallen.

He dismounted behind the castle near the door that led into the stables. With stealthy steps he made his way to Isaac's door. He reached for the door latch but a noise behind him made him whirl around.

A young groom, drowsily rubbing sleep from his eyes, appeared from an empty stall. He stared at Kit as if he were seeing a ghost.

"My lord!" he cried, taking a step toward him.

"There is a horse outside, Jeremy," Kit told him, recognizing the boy. "He's tired and hungry. See to him at once. I'm going to speak with Isaac."

"He's not there, my lord," the boy said, his tone nervous.

Once more, Kit turned from Isaac's door. "What do you mean?" he demanded. "Where is he?"

The boy kicked at the straw near his feet. "Well, my lord, he . . . we . . . we . . ."

"Out with it boy!" Kit prompted.

"We took him to your cottage in the forest," the boy finished in a burst.

"But why?" Kit demanded.

"In case they came back, my lord!" The young stableboy trembled at the thought. "They might kill him the next time!"

"Kill him! What the devil are you talking about?" Kit came back to the stableboy's side and glared down at him. "Explain yourself!"

The boy was trembling. "They were here, my lord. They were looking for you . . . and for my lady Bliss."

"Who was here!" Kit knew he was frightening the already nervous boy but his impatience was overcoming his compassion.

"My Lord Holme," the boy managed finally. "And that other one, Lord Villiers."

"Holme! And Villiers! When were they here? What did they want?"

"They came looking for you and for my lady Bliss. They asked Isaac where you were but he wouldn't tell them. They . . . Lord Holme . . . he had his lackeys beat Isaac. They were big, hulking fellows." The boy shook his head, cringing at the memory. "Sweet Jesu, my lord, I thought they would kill him!"

Kit felt a white-hot rage building inside him. To think of that bastard's villains laying violent hands on Isaac! He'd kill Holme for this! By God, he would!

The boy was sniffling. Only his masculine

pride held back the tears that welled into his eyes and threatened to trickle down his cheeks.

"I told them, my lord," he confessed, shame-faced. "I told them where you'd gone. I betrayed you . . . But I thought they would kill Isaac. I knew he would never tell them—he'd die first! But I told them. I wanted them to stop. I'm sorry, my lord."

Kit sighed heavily, laying a comforting hand on the boy's shoulder. "You did the right thing, Jeremy," he assured him. "I'll deal with Holme and Villiers later. But what about Isaac? Will he live?"

The young groom shook his head. "The doctor doesn't know, my lord. He says it will take a few days before he can be sure."

Kit looked at the wall above the boy's head. His fury writhed inside him like a living being, but he had to think clearly. He had to force himself to think rationally, to act rationally, not to act on reckless impulse.

"Saddle me a fresh horse, Jeremy. I'm going to see Isaac."

"But Lord Holme and Lord Villiers!" Jeremy protested. "They've gone north! They've gone to Barthorp Hall!"

"I know." Kit scowled. "But there is nothing I can do to stop them just now. I'll see to Isaac first and then worry about Holme and Villiers."

Kit waited impatiently while Jeremy saddled a fresh horse. Then, vaulting into the saddle, he rode away from the castle and into the forest, skirting the village. He wanted as few people as possible to know he was back in Chatham.

He thought of Basil Holme and Stephen Villiers no doubt riding even now into the courtyard of Barthorp Hall. Had he not ridden cross fields a good part of the way to save time getting to Chatham, he might well have encountered them between here and Barthorp Hall. Somehow he might have been able to stop them from getting to Bliss, or . . . But no, he wouldn't think of that now. He wouldn't worry about Bliss. She was his now—his! She would never allow her former guardian and that snake, Villiers, to part her from him.

It was with trepidation that he entered the cottage he and his father had occupied in the forest. Bess, the village girl who had cooked and cleaned for him, turned from the kettle boiling over the fire in the hearth. Her eyes were wide with fear, her mouth an 'o' of surprise.

"My lord!" she cried, relieved. "It's you! I was afraid it was—"

"Holme's lackeys?" Kit finished for her.

"Aye," she admitted. "Have you brought milady back with you?"

"No, she's still at Barthorp Hall in Yorkshire."

"Oh, my lord! That's where they're going! My Lord Holmes and my Lord Villiers! They're going to—"

"I know," Kit interrupted. "Jeremy told me."

"Jeremy told them about you as well," she

Sandra DuBay

muttered disapprovingly.

"Now, Bess," Kit chided. "He told them to save Isaac. He said he was afraid for Isaac's life."

"I suppose that's the truth of it, my lord," she relented, glancing toward the bed with the half-drawn curtain.

"How is he?" Kit asked, half dreading her answer.

"The doctor says he thinks he'll live, though Isaac's not as young as he once was."

Kit went to the bed and gazed down at the groom who lay on his back, the quilts drawn up to his chin. What Kit saw as he gazed down at his old, dear friend sickened him.

Isaac was scarely recognizeable. His face was bruised and swollen, his nose obviously broken. Both eyes were blackened and when he turned his head on the pillow, he winced, even in his sleep.

"His left arm is broken," Bess told him. "And one of his legs. The doctor says he'll limp for the rest of his days."

"Has he any medicine for the pain?" Kit asked.

"Aye, the doctor left some. It's there, in the flask on the mantel. I don't know what's in it, my lord, but it stinks to high heaven."

Kit smiled in spite of his anger. "But does it seem to help him?"

"Oh, aye, it makes him sleep and that's what's best for him. I try to get him to eat something. There's gruel in the pot there, at the edge of the grate. With his face the way it is, he cannot chew anything much. But he can get the gruel down, at least."

"You're a good girl, Bess," Kit told her, taking her hand, "to care for him this way."

"Well, how could I not, my lord?" she said simply. "We care for our own here in Chatham."

"Aye," Kit agreed. "That we do." Kit noticed the pallor of her usually rosy cheeks and the dark circles under her eyes. "You're exhausted," he said. "Why don't you go home for the night? I'll sit with him."

"But my lord!" she objected. "You should not! It's not right—"

"Come now, Bess." He smiled. "How long did I live among you? Am I above such things now? Simply because I am wed to the mistress of Chatham Castle?"

"Wed?" Bess's eyes widened. "Are you? My lord! You and Lady Bliss—"

"Aye, Bess, we are. There's to be de Wildes at Chatham once more!"

The girl's face split in a wide, delighted grin.

"Well now, you go home and rest. I'll sit with Isaac tonight then start back to Yorkshire when you return. Good night, Bess."

"Good night, my lord." Pulling her woolen cloak over her dress and tying her pattens over her shoes, she left the cottage and started off into the wintry night.

"Bess!" Kit called after her. The girl looked back at him. "Tell your mother I'm here with

Isaac but no one else should know."

"Aye, my lord," the girl agreed unquestioningly, then disappeared into the night.

It was shortly after dawn the next morning that Kit rode away from Chatham, retracing his route back to Yorkshire and Bliss. He felt easier in his mind about Isaac now. The old groom had awakened in the night and taken great comfort in Kit's presence. He'd been overjoyed that Kit and Bliss were married and had seemed reassured when Kit promised him he would go back to Barthorp Hall in the morning and see that Sir Basil and Stephen Villiers did no mischief there. Above all, he promised Isaac that he would soon see another Lord de Wilde installed at Chatham Castle with his beautiful, beloved Bliss at his side.

But Kit's confidence in the future was abruptly shattered when he arrived at Barthorp Hall. The place had an empty, deserted air that boded ill. Kit felt wary, anxious, as he dismounted in the courtyard. Surely Bliss should have been watching for him. Where was she? Why didn't she come to him?

The door was locked. Kit pounded on it and it opened to reveal the butler, Valentine. But rather than opening the door to admit him, he blocked the way.

"I am sorry, my lord, but I have orders not to admit you."

"Orders?" Kit was mystified. "What are you talking about, Valentine? Where is Lady de Wilde?"

"My lady is gone, my lord. She has left for London with my Lord Holme and my Lord Villiers."

"Holme and Villiers took her!" Kit blustered. "Why didn't you stop them, man!"

"She wanted to go, my lord. And it was she who ordered that you not be admitted. I am sorry, my lord. Your belongings have been packed. They are waiting in a coach in the stable."

"But, Valentine," Kit argued, "I cannot believe that Bliss would—"

"I am sorry, my lord," the butler apologized uncomfortably. "But I have my orders. Good day, my lord."

Kit stood there, astonished, as the heavy front door of Barthorp Hall was closed firmly in his face.

Chapter 24

"**I** have set matters in motion," Sir Basil announced over dinner one evening not long after their return to London.

"How long will it take?" Bliss asked softly, her eyes fastened on her untouched meal lest they betray her emotions.

"The courts move slowly," her guardian admitted. "But it should not take too long. You should thank God you were betrothed to Stephen. Because of that we can obtain a decree of nullity on grounds of pre-contract. Had you not been betrothed, you would have had to obtain a divorce, which requires an act of Parliament." He shook his head sadly. "Even so, it will be expensive."

Laying her napkin aside, Bliss rose. "If you

will excuse me, sir . . ."

"You have not touched your dinner," Sir Basil observed. "You have not been eating enough to keep a sparrow alive."

Bliss made a dismissing gesture with one hand. She turned to leave, but Sir Basil stopped her.

"Bliss?" He laid down his knife and fork. "Stephen tells me you have agreed to marry him once the decree of nullity is obtained."

"Aye," Bliss admitted. "I have."

"Good." Sir Basil smiled benevolently on the ward he believed had finally come to her senses. "It will be a good match."

Nodding, Bliss left the dining room. A good match. She supposed it would. Each of them brought something to the marriage—in her case, wealth; in Stephen's case, his name and connections. As marriages among the aristocracy went, it was indeed a good match.

It had one added attraction, Bliss thought as she started up the stairs to begin dressing for the ball Stephen was to escort her to. There was no love. She felt little for Stephen. He did not touch her heart, did not stir her senses. Therefore, she reasoned, he could never hurt her as Kit had. There was, just then, a very real security in that thought.

The ballroom of Rutland House was lit by a hundred candles. The long, oak-paneled room had a marble floor in black and white. In the musicians' gallery, the private players of the Earl of Rutland played for the dancing couples below.

"Do you want to dance, Bliss?" Stephen asked as he came to her side with a glass of ratafia.

Bliss shook her head. "I'd rather not. I think I'll just sit here, near the doors." She indicated the bank of gilded chairs where the dowagers sat and gossiped over their fans and their sewing. Outside the French doors the lantern-lit garden ran down to the Thames and the water stairs by which Bliss, Stephen, and others who lived on the river had arrived for the ball.

"As you wish," Stephen acquiesced, sitting down beside her.

Bliss smiled. "You needn't keep me company," she told him. "I heard Lord Rutland saying there was a gaming room there, off the other end of the ballroom. Why don't you go and amuse yourself?"

Stephen looked with unmistakable longing toward the carved double doors of the adjoining salon where the ardent gamblers among the guests had retired almost immediately upon arriving.

"Well," he hedged, knowing he should stay with Bliss yet drawn by the excitement of the gaming tables, "perhaps just for a moment. I won't be long, I promise. If you decide you want to leave, simply send someone for me."

"I will," Bliss assured him. "Now go. Enjoy yourself."

She watched as Stephen crossed the long room. He was being so solicitous of her feelings it almost made her feel guilty. After all, she, his betrothed, had eloped with another man, married him, bedded with him . . . And now here was Stephen behaving as if she were some delicate creature who had to be coddled and pampered.

Bliss smiled as she smoothed the peach silk skirts of her gown. The petticoat showing at the front where the skirt was draped back was of heavy ivory silk embroidered with tiny pearls. Lace frothed the elbow-length sleeves and the low neckline where a single baroque pearl hung from a heavy gold chain. It was pleasant, she supposed, to be treated so gently. How long it might last, she couldn't guess, but for now . . .

"My lady?" A man stood before her.

Bliss looked up. The young man was handsome with black hair and brilliantly blue eyes. The scarlet and gold of his suit set off his coloring to perfection.

"Sir?" Bliss replied.

"I am the Viscount Bastwick. William. Will you dance with me?"

Bliss was about to refuse, but the young man was very handsome and the admiration in his blue eyes was a balm to her wounded heart. She had been rushed by her guardian from the schoolroom into her betrothal with no time for flirtations, for innocent dalliances. She smiled.

"Of course, my lord," she agreed, holding out her hand to him.

Together she and the young Viscount took their places on the crowded dance floor. The musicians in the gallery above struck up a minuet, and Bliss, her hand resting on that of the young Viscount, circled the room.

The dance was not half finished when the usher at the door struck the parquet floor with his staff and announced a late arrival:

"The Baron de Wilde!"

At first, Bliss did not realize what he had said. The music was loud, and the Viscount, her partner, was speaking. The truth did not strike her until she saw Kit appear behind her partner.

"Excuse me," he said, nudging the handsome young man, "I should like to dance with my wife if you don't mind."

The Viscount stopped in mid-step. His bright blue eyes widened with surprise and confusion.

"But . . ." he said, staring at Bliss, "I thought you were . . . that is . . . I do beg your pardon, my Lady de Wilde."

Flustered, the young man retreated. Kit took Bliss's hand in his own and fell into step with the dancers about them.

"What are you doing here?" Bliss hissed under cover of the music. Her cheeks were flaming. From the corner of her eye she saw the Viscount Bastwick in conversation with a half dozen young ladies and gentlemen. She could just imagine what was being said—she, the betrothed of Lord Villiers, the wife of Lord de Wilde? And wasn't this Lord de Wilde the son of the Baron who had been disinherited by the King for his traitorous support of the regicides who had plotted the downfall of Charles I?

"I might ask you the same," Kit countered. "As I recall, I left you at Barthorp Hall where you were to wait for me. When I returned . . . well, you know what I found when I returned."

"Then you must know why I left," she retorted.

"Indeed, I cannot imagine," Kit told her.

"Enough!" The music ended and Bliss jerked her hand away and fled from him. Heedless of the hundreds of curious eyes watching her, she ran from the ballroom into the concealing darkness of the garden.

At the far end of the garden where the Thames glimmered in the moonlight, the boatmen waited to ferry their masters and mistresses back to their riverside manses. If she could reach them, Bliss told herself, she could be taken home—home to Barthorp House— where she could order the gates locked against the man in dark blue silk who was even then following her into the garden.

"Bliss!" His voice was stern, angry. His footfalls on the graveled walk were swift, determined.

"Go away!" Bliss hissed over her shoulder, quickening her steps. "Leave me—"

Kit's hand closed on her arm and jerked her to

a halt. In a flurry of silk and lace, she was spun around to face the man who glared at her, his dark eyes glittering beneath furrowed brows.

"Let me go!" she demanded, trying to pull her arm out of his bruising grasp.

"Bliss," he began, growing exasperated by her struggles. "Listen. Listen to me!"

"I won't!" she snapped. "I listened to you before! More fool I!"

"You should have waited for me," he told her. "I told you I would be back and—"

"You know why I didn't wait!" she snarled. "I found out that everything about you was a lie!"

"I was going to tell you the truth—"

"Were you, my lord?" she growled. "When? On our fifth anniversary? Our tenth?"

"Truly, Bliss," he went on patiently, "I did not want to lie to you."

"You managed rather well," she countered spitefully.

Closing his eyes, Kit sighed. "Listen to me, Bliss. Hear me out, that is all I ask. If only you waited—"

"No, no! I won't listen to you!" Bliss averted her face to hide her emotions. "I don't care what you say! I don't want to hear any more of your lies!"

"Damnit, Bliss!" Kit snapped, his patience giving way to a desire to shake her to her senses.

"It was all planned, wasn't it?" Bliss cried. "From the first, I expect. This stupid little fool, you must have thought, dazzled by the highwayman who appeared and carried her off into the forest. I can make her care for me, I can play the rogue, the romantic, tragic figure, until she falls in love with me and then dupe her into marrying me. That way, I'll regain my father's estates. I'll be lord of Chatham Castle."

"It wasn't that way," he insisted tightly.

"Liar. Liar!" she hissed. Feeling the tears welling into her eyes, Bliss turned away from him. "You must have thought me the stupidest little fool in the world!"

Kit reached out to her. He knew she was in pain, he knew she'd been hurt far more than he'd imagined she might be. He should have known that her guardian and Stephen Villiers would somehow ferret out the truth and come after her. But he'd never thought they would get to her before he could get back and explain why he had not told her who he was.

"Come here, Bliss," he said softly. "Don't cry."

"I'm not crying!" she snapped, evading the hand that would have pulled her into his arm. "And don't touch me!"

They stood there in the darkness, the lanterns that were the garden's only illumination casting a shadowy glow around them. Bliss trembled, her body remembering their night together even while her mind tried to block out the memory. She had thought him handsome before, with his dark, glittering eyes, his sharp-planed, classic features, the air of strength, of power that emanated from him. But now, dressed as befitted the Baron de Wilde rather than the highwayman Kit Quinn, there was an elegance about him that only added to his dashing masculinity.

Even as she stood there, even as her mind told her she should hate him, she longed to melt into the embrace he offered. What was wrong with her that he should affect her so? Why couldn't she hate him as he deserved to be hated?

Sensing her confusion, Kit moved closer. "Bliss," he said, his voice nearly a whisper, "I know I've hurt you. But I did not mean to, if nothing else, you must believe that."

"I . . ." Bliss murmured. "I don't know . . ."

Her head, her mind, told her to flee. Her body, her heart, urged her to listen. The temptation that had seemed so easy to resist before—the temptation to listen to him, to hope it had somehow all been a hideous mistake—welled inside her, defeating all her best efforts to quell it.

"Come sit down," Kit invited, motioning toward a bench in the shadows.

"No," Bliss breathed.

"Come," he repeated, taking her hand.

A shiver coursed through her as he took her hand in his. He drew her gently toward the bench, his eyes gentle, his smile tender.

"I can't," she whispered, her resistance melting.

"Just for a moment," he promised.

NIGHTRIDER

Unable to resist, Bliss sank down onto the bench beside him. But even as she did, the voice of reason chided her for a fool. She was falling under his spell once more, surrendering without a fight. Was she so weak, her own conscience asked her, that she could ignore the pain that was still so keen in her heart of hearts? Run away! the voice urged inside her. He'll only lie to you again, hurt you again!

But when she looked into Kit's dark eyes, her heart turned over in her breast. "Kit," she began, the word like a sigh in the warm, scented intimacy of the garden, "I can't . . . you can't begin to understand how it hurt me—"

"I'm sorry," he said softly, his hand cupping her face. "I'm so sorry. Bliss—"

Bliss shivered as he leaned toward her. Her lips trembled waiting for the touch of his. She leaned toward him waiting . . . waiting . . .

"Bliss?" Stephen was framed in the doorway of the ballroom. "Bliss! Where are you!"

Gasping, Bliss came to her senses. She blinked, staring at Kit as if confronted by the devil himself.

"Ignore him!" Kit urged.

"Bliss!" Stephen called again, moving out into the darkness of the garden.

Evading Kit's grasp, Bliss left the bench, backing away, eyes wary, shocked at how close she had come to disaster. Kit rose, reaching out to her, and Bliss whirled away, curls flying, and fled toward the mansion, toward Stephen.

"Stephen!" she cried, flinging herself into his arms. "Take me home! Please, now!"

"They said de Wilde was—" Stephen began. Then he saw Kit standing in the shadows. "So you are here," he muttered coldly. "What do you want?"

"My wife," Kit snarled. "Let her go."

Stephen lifted his hands from Bliss. "I am not keeping her prisoner," he retorted.

"Bliss, come here!" Kit ordered.

Shaking her head, Bliss buried her face in the pale green silk of Stephen's gold-embroidered coat. Her hands crushed the delicate fabric as she clung to him.

"Take me home," she pleaded, her tears staining Stephen's jacket.

"As you wish," Stephen agreed, his voice unmistakably triumphant.

His arm about Bliss's waist, Stephen led her past Kit and down the graveled path leading to the river and the gilded boat that had brought them from Barthorp House. Without looking, Stephen knew that Kit was furious, his face flushed with rage.

Kit watched them go. He made no move to stop them. It would only upset Bliss more and put more distance and distrust between them. But he would not give up. She was hurt, more hurt than he had feared she might be. It would take time to win her back—it would take time, he realized, to convince her to listen to his explanation. But from her reaction tonight, from the way she trembled when he touched her, the way she had come so near to letting him kiss her, he believed her love for him still burned beneath the hurt, beneath the pain, and he meant to reach out to that love and soothe the hurt.

She was meant to be his, he believed, she belonged to him, and no one, least of all Stephen Villiers, would take her away from him!

Chapter 25

From the night of the ball at Rutland House, Bliss became a prisoner of Barthorp House. She would not leave, would not accompany Stephen on so much as a drive in the park for fear of seeing Kit.

"This is ridiculous, Bliss," Stephen chided one sunny afternoon when they strolled together in the gardens behind the house. "The court is gone to Newmarket. We could have gone. There's no reason—"

"There is a reason," Bliss argued stubbornly.

"De Wilde," Stephen muttered. "You cannot spend the rest of your life within these walls because you might see him."

"After the marriage is annulled, it will be

different," Bliss promised.

"Will it?" Stephen wondered. "You are obsessed with the man. Don't deny it. You think of him constantly."

It was useless to argue, Bliss knew. It was the truth. Kit was like a ghost who haunted her days and her nights. She thought about him during her waking hours; she dreamed of him at night. Too often she awoke confused, dazed, thinking herself back at Barthorp Hall lying in the great tester bed where she and Kit had spent their wedding night, those all-too-brief hours when she'd thought her dreams had come true but when she'd really only entered a nightmare from which she could not seem to awaken.

"I'm sorry, Stephen," Bliss murmured. "I cannot explain—"

"I can," he interrupted. "You're in love with the man."

"No!" Bliss paled. "It's not true!"

"It is," he argued. He saw the tears flooding her eyes, threatening to spill down her cheeks. "But hush, now, I should not have said it. Come here."

He took Bliss into his arms and held her. Her arms went about him, returned his embrace, but Stephen knew only too well that even as they stood there in one another's arms, Bliss was thinking of the wretch who had stolen a kiss on that wintry night in Kent, then gone on to steal her innocence, and her heart.

Stephen looked up to find Mercy approaching along the graveled walk. "Bliss," he said softly.

She looked up at him and he nodded in the direction of the approaching maid. Bliss stepped away from Stephen, and he could not help wondering if it was because the maid was an ally of Kit's and might report the tender scene in the garden to him.

"What is it, Mercy?" Bliss asked as the maid reached them and curtsied.

"A summons, milady, from the palace. The King wishes to see you."

"The King?" Bliss glanced up at Stephen. "I thought the court had removed to Newmarket."

Stephen shrugged. "They have. I don't know why he would return."

Mystified, Bliss returned to the house with Mercy and changed her gown. A boatman rowed her to the water stairs of Whitehall Palace, where she was met by William Chiffinch, the Keeper of the King's Closet.

"Follow me, if you please, my lady," he bade her and led her up the Privy Stairs.

Bliss felt a moment's unease as they emerged into the King's bedchamber. It was not unusual, she knew, for ladies who had attracted the King's attention to be summoned here. But surely she had not given him reason to believe she would welcome his attentions. She liked the King, thought him charming, witty, attractive in a sensuous way that had nothing to do with looks or rank. But she had no ambitions to replace Barbara Castlemaine—or his dozen other mistresses—in his bed.

"Master Chiffinch . . ." she said, holding out a hand to him as the man bowed his way out of the room.

In reply, the man pointed to a door leading off the room. He disappeared back the way they had come, and almost immediately the door he'd indicated opened and the King appeared.

Bliss sank to the floor in a curtsy. She remained there, tense, nervous, until the King bade her rise.

"I have not seen you in a long while," he said, smiling. His dark eyes, so expressive in his long, heavy-featured face, betrayed his admiration of her beauty. "I have missed you."

Bliss studied the floor. "I am surprised Your Majesty noticed my absence."

"Are you?" Reaching out with one beringed finger, the King tilted Bliss's face up toward his. "Look at me, Bliss. Why are you so shy suddenly?"

Unbidden, Bliss's eyes strayed to the huge bed that dominated the room. Its beaten silver shimmered in the dull light glowing behind the drawn draperies. The tall ostrich plumes decorating the ornate finials high atop the posts nodded with the drafts that swept through the chamber. She swallowed, biting her lower lip.

The King's laughter startled her. "God's

Sandra DuBay

body!" he chuckled. "You thought I had you brought here for—" His laughter rumbled in the room. "Beautiful as you are, my little Bliss, much as I admit to desiring you, seduction was not my reason for wanting to see you here, privately. I want to know the truth of these rumors I have heard."

"Rumors, sire?" Bliss hedged.

"I have heard a confusing tale, my dear," he said, sitting down in a great carved armchair and motioning Bliss into another near him. "They say you are wed—to the son of the Baron de Wilde, young Christopher."

"It is true," Bliss admitted. "But it was a mistake."

"Tell me," the King invited.

Haltingly, tearfully, Bliss told him everything from the moment of their meeting to the horrible hour when Sir Basil and Stephen told her the truth about the man she had married.

By the time she finished, Bliss was dabbing at her eyes with a handkerchief offered her by the King.

"Sir Basil has petitioned the court for a decree of nullity," the King told her. "Is that what you truly want, Bliss?"

Sniffling, Bliss nodded. "Aye," she told him. "It is what I want."

"Have you spoken with your hus—with Lord de Wilde?" he amended.

"Not really. We spoke once. At Rutland

House. He said he did not mean to hurt me. But he lied, from the beginning. I cannot forgive him and I cannot believe he did not do it deliberately."

"That is a harsh accusation," the King told her.

"Aye," Bliss admitted. "Still, I believe he married me only to regain his family home—Chatham."

The King smiled. "I will not believe that any man would marry you merely to regain an estate. Still, I think you should speak with him. Hear his side of it, Bliss. That is why I have had him brought here as well."

"No, sire, please!" Bliss cried, half-rising from her chair.

"Aye, Bliss, it is a command. I will be in there." He pointed to the door of his Privy Closet, his inner sanctum which no one could enter without his express permission.

Rising, the King went to the bedchamber door and spoke to William Chiffinch who was waiting outside. He turned back to Bliss, his face stern.

"I cannot," she whispered, her eyes pleading.

"You must," he decreed, and left her there, alone.

Bliss clenched her hands in the folds of her azure skirts. Behind her she heard the door open and close. She heard the footfalls crossing the room. But still the voice that shattered the silence was like a stiletto piercing the very heart of her.

"Bliss?"

Heart pounding, she turned and found Kit standing before her. "Kit," she said softly. "The King commands I must hear your . . . excuses."

The two of them sat in the chairs Bliss and the King had occupied. Her knuckles were white, her breathing quick, erratic, but she forced herself to sit there as Kit began.

"When I left you," he said, "I intended to go to London, to petition the King's pardon of my father. I did not want his disgrace to taint our life together. I did not want you to be ashamed to bear the name de Wilde. But I went first to Chatham. There I found that Isaac was near death—" He paused as Bliss gasped. "Aye. He was beaten by your guardian's lackeys."

"But why?" Bliss demanded.

"Because he would not tell them where we had gone. In the end, one of the young grooms told them, to save Isaac's life. Had he not—" Kit shook his head. "In any case, I remained there until it was certain Isaac would live. And then I returned to Barthorp Hall. I hoped I could get there before Lord Holme and Villiers turned you against me, but I was too late. You know what reception met me when I arrived."

Bliss blushed at the thought of Kit's being refused entry to Barthorp Hall on his return. She had ordered him thrown out, and that was what had happened.

"That was why I left you," Kit told her. "If only you had waited."

Shaking her head, Bliss rose. "It makes no difference," she told him. "Our marriage was based on lies. It is best to end it."

"You are my wife, Bliss," Kit told her, leaving his chair. "No one can part us. No one!"

"Sir Basil has asked for a decree of nullity," Bliss revealed.

"Damn him!" Kit snarled. "The bastard—"

"I agreed to it," she told him.

"You can't!" Crossing the space between them, Kit seized her arms. "You can't do this, Bliss!"

"I can!" she cried, pulling free of him. "And I will! I hate you! Do you hear me? I hate you!"

Kit recoiled. His expression changed to one of stern, hard anger. "And after?" he asked, his voice cold as ice.

"After," Bliss told him, "I will marry Stephen Villiers."

Kit's eyes glittered as he leaned close to her. His breath was warm on her cheek, his voice low, menacing in her ear as he said:

"Do that, my Lady Bliss, and you will find yourself a widow before the week is out!"

The door of the King's Privy Closet opened and the King appeared. Both Bliss and Kit swung toward him, Bliss sinking into a curtsy, Kit bowing.

Sandra DuBay

"Well?" the King asked, striding into the room followed by his ever-present pack of spaniels. "Did you hear him out?"

Bliss nodded. "I did, sire," she replied.

"And do you still want the marriage annulled?"

Bliss did not dare to look at Kit. She knew his eyes would be filled with fury, she could feel the rage emanating from him, seeming to fill the bedchamber. Trembling, she nodded.

"I do," she whispered.

"Well, then, the petition will go forward."

"May I leave now?" she asked, uncertain how long she could retain her composure.

"Aye. Go home, Lady Bliss." The King nodded toward the door through which she'd entered. "William is there, waiting to take you down the stairs."

Curtsying, Bliss disappeared, and the King moved to stand beside Kit. "My sympathies," he said softly. "To lose such an exquisite creature . . ."

Kit's eyes were cold, his air one of icy determination as he turned to the King. "I have not lost her yet, sire," he said softly. "And I will kill the man who tries to take her from me."

Bowing, he left, not waiting for the King's permission to retire. Behind him Charles watched him go. He had not heard the last of this matter, he knew, and he felt certain it would

320

end tragically for one of them. But which one, he wondered, returning to his Privy Closet. For Bliss? For Kit? Or for Villiers?

Chapter 26

It was frustrating to Kit that he could not seem to get close to Bliss. After the meeting at Whitehall she had immured herself at Barthorp House in the Strand. The gates were closed and guarded, the water stairs watched. Bliss did not go to the theater or the shops. As far as he knew, she did not so much as venture into the garden to take the air.

It was, perhaps, Bliss's own idea. Their encounter at the palace had no doubt shaken her, perhaps frightened her. But Kit believed she was encouraged in her seclusion by her guardian and the Villierses. They meant, no doubt, to keep her from him, to fill her mind with poison against him, until she was married to Stephen and beyond his reach.

Kit's face hardened with hatred. More fools they if they believed he would give up merely because they had used their influence and Bliss's money to have the decree of nullity rushed through the courts.

Turning back toward his desk, Kit saw the papers lying there, the documents attesting to the fact that Bliss, so briefly his, was no longer Lady de Wilde. The marriage had been annulled, so the papers said, owing to her pre-contract to Stephen, Lord Villiers.

Pre-contract! Kit paced across the small floor of his parlor whose windows overlooked Suffolk Street. That may have been the excuse for the annullment but it was not the reason. The reason? He smiled a smile full of bitterness and self-mockery. Bliss had left their marriage because the husband she believed to be a highwayman, a criminal, had turned out to be a baron.

No, he forced himself to admit, it was not entirely that. It was the lie. He had let her go on believing he was nothing more than a highwayman when everyone else at Chatham knew who he was. But how could he have told her? She was outspoken in her opinion of his father as a traitor. Had she known it was not only Lord de Wilde's estate but his own patrimony she had inherited, it would have affected their relationship from the start.

Damn. Damn! Kit thought. It was useless to brood on the past, to wonder how things might have turned out had he acted differently. The only thing he could do was concentrate on the future. Bliss was his. His! And he would kill any man who tried to keep her from him. And that included Stephen, Lord Villiers.

Several times each year the court removed to Newmarket where the King could indulge his love of horseracing. Tents and pavilions were erected for the courtiers while the King himself stayed at Audley End, the country home of the Earl of Suffolk.

Bliss arrived in Newmarket with Sir Basil five days after the court had followed the King. The Villierses were already there, having left London with the Duke of Buckingham, who, once the King's preference for the place had become apparent, had built a large and imposing house as near to Audley End as possible.

"Here we are, my dear," Sir Basil said as the coach passed between the gates of the Duke's mansion.

Bliss looked up at the imposing brick manse. It was large, impressive, built for show, and, in keeping with the Duke's character, slightly larger than Audley End.

"How long must we stay?" Bliss asked as a footman appeared and came to open the coach door.

"As long as the King remains, of course. Come now, smile, Bliss. No long faces in front of the Duke, if you please."

Obligingly, Bliss painted a pretty, if artificial,

smile across her lips. Linking her arm through her guardian's, she mounted the steps to the front door, where the Duke himself had come to greet them.

"Here you are at last," George Villiers said, taking Bliss's hand from her guardian's arm and slipping it into the crook of his own. He cast a single brief glance at Sir Basil. "Holme," he acknowledged dismissively.

Bliss longed to break away and run. She did not like the Duke. Though he had never been other than cordial to her, there was something about him that made her skin crawl. It was more than the stories they told about him, more than the rumors of his debaucheries and perversions. But she could not quite pinpoint the source of her dislike. It was as if she sensed that he wanted something from her that she did not wish to give.

"Stephen is not here," the Duke told her. "He has gone with the King to watch the training runs. But Lady Villiers and Letitia are still here."

"How nice," Bliss murmured dutifully, but the grimace on her face told a different story.

The Duke laughed, his long blond curled wig bouncing as he did. "I agree with you," he told her confidentially. "The woman is a harridan, and that whey-faced daughter of hers a whining schemer. You know she has set her heart on wedding that Scottish gamester, Angus Cameron?"

"Aye," Bliss admitted. "And they mean me to give them the gold to live on."

"And will you?" the Duke wanted to know.

Bliss shrugged. "It will not be for me to say, Your Grace. After Stephen and I are married, my fortune will be under his control."

"Perhaps we can do something about that," the Duke said cryptically.

"What do you mean?" Bliss asked.

Smiling a sphinxlike smile, the Duke shook his head. "All in good time, my beauty. For now, come say good day to Lady Villiers and Letitia and then I will take you to Stephen. And the King."

An hour later Bliss rode beside the Duke toward the hill atop which the King, Stephen, and several other gentlemen sat on horseback watching the jockeys exercising their mounts. One of the men noticed them and drew his companions' attention to their approach. With the exception of the King, the gentlemen doffed their hats to the Duke.

"Ah, George!" the King said, at last tearing his gaze away from the riders below. "The bay gelding you sold me goes well. See there?" He nodded toward the track. "That's Roswell astride."

"A good man," Buckingham murmured.

"Aye." The King's blinding smile flashed as his large, dark eyes rested on Bliss. "Lady Bliss," he said, his voice softening to the low, drawling tone he used with pretty women. "Well met. Your beauty is a refreshing change from all this ugliness."

His companions laughed dutifully and reined their horses aside to allow Bliss to move to the King's side.

"I expected to find my cousin here," the Duke said.

"My Lady Castlemaine seems to spend longer at her toilette these days," the King remarked.

"Then perhaps it is best she does not appear so early. The harsh light of morning is cruel. Particularly when there is so much fresher beauty so nearby."

The Duke lifted Bliss's hand to his lips as those around them chuckled. Venturing a glance in the King's direction, Bliss found him watching her, his eyes heavy-lidded with speculation.

Good God! Bliss thought, the realization suddenly dawning on her. Buckingham knows the King is tiring of Castlemaine. He means me to replace her! He means me to be the next Villiers to occupy the King's bed!

She looked toward Stephen, wondering if he knew of his cousin's plans for her. But Stephen was looking away, his gaze doggedly fixed on the riders below. The only outward sign of any agitation on his part was the flushing of his normally pale face.

He would do nothing, Bliss told herself. He would bend to the wishes of the Duke and give his wife to the King! Sweet heaven! Was there no end to the lengths these Villierses would go to in order to bolster their fortunes?

Bliss shuddered, feeling sick to her stomach. Was that the fate they had consigned her to? Royal whore? Did Stephen already know of the Duke's ambition for her? Did Sir Basil? Was there no one who could protect her from them? No one who would save her from the fate—

She drew a sharp, hissing breath as she noticed a man on horseback riding among the colorful tents and pavilions set up on the flat, wide expanse of land in the distance. He was much too far away to allow her to make out his features, but Bliss was certain who it was. Kit. Kit! Her hus— No, she reminded herself, no longer her husband. Kit had vowed to kill any man who tried to possess her. By that, she knew, he meant Stephen. But what would he do if she were pushed into the King's arms? What could he do? Charles was the King . . .

The King. Bliss felt a wave of fear wash over her. Would the fact of his being King temper Kit's jealousy? Lessen his possessiveness? After all, it would not be the first time a de Wilde pitted himself against his sovereign.

"Bliss?" Stephen had come to her side without her noticing. "Are you all right? You're so pale all of a sudden."

"Can we go back to Buckingham House?" she asked softly. "Please, Stephen."

"If Your Majesty will excuse us," Stephen

ventured. "I would take Bliss home now."

"Eh?" The King looked at Stephen blankly. Then, noticing Bliss's pallor, nodded. "Aye, take her home, lad. The sun is too strong for her, I fear." He smiled and lifted Bliss's hand to his lips. "Rest, my beauty," he said, "we will see you at Audley End tonight, I hope?"

"She'll be there," the Duke promised before Bliss had a chance to reply.

Wheeling their horses, Bliss and Stephen set off toward Buckingham House. As they did, Bliss glanced back toward the city of colorful tents, her eyes scanning the scene looking for Kit. But he was gone. Perhaps, she told herself hopefully, she had only imagined him there. Perhaps it was not Kit but only someone who resembled—

But no, she was forced to admit. It had been Kit. She was certain. And she was sure of one other thing. Kit had come to claim her. He had come to confront Stephen. And the matter would be settled one way or another before they left Newmarket.

The hour was late when the Villierses returned from Audley End. Murmuring her good nights, Bliss hurried up the stairs to her room. She was silent as Mercy undressed her and prepared her for bed. When the maid took up Bliss's brush, Bliss waved her away, dismissing her, wanting only to be alone.

The candleflames danced as the door closed

behind the maid. Alone in her room, Bliss stared at her reflection in the looking glass. Did she look different? she wondered. Had the past few hours somehow marked her? They should have.

Bliss shuddered with the memory of what had happened at Audley End. It had been a conspiracy, she was certain. The Duke and Lady Villiers and, no doubt, Stephen and Sir Basil as well, had taken her to Audley End with the idea of contriving to leave her alone with the King.

Actually, she had to admit, nothing dire had happened. The dinner had been a small, intimate gathering. And after dinner, when the King had expressed a desire to show Bliss a portrait of a horse he had just bought, the others had declared they had already seen it.

So Bliss and the King had gone alone into the tiny anteroom. The chamber had been lit by only a pair of candles burning on either side of the portrait. Bliss had dutifully admired it, all the while feeling uneasy because of the King's nearness. And then . . .

And then she was in his embrace. His arm had snaked about her waist and pulled her to him. His mouth covered hers, his hands caressed her, tugging at the sleeves and shoulders of her gown, pulling at it, drawing it off her shoulders. His lips had been moist, his breath hot against the skin of her throat, her breasts.

"No, please!" she had begged. "Please, don't!" She struggled in his arms until, at last, her pleas reached him. The King stood back, releasing her, his face hard, his eyes cold, as he looked down at her.

"I beg your pardon, my dear," he said, "I did not realize I was so repellent to you."

"You are not repellent," Bliss assured him. "It is only . . ." She felt the heat of her cheeks as she blushed. "I am not Lady Castlemaine."

The King's face relaxed. "No, I should have realized that. But I thought perhaps . . . I assumed you knew of Buckingham's ambitions for you."

"I suspected," Bliss admitted. "But I did not believe . . ."

"And I have frightened you," the King said gently. "You are young. More innocent than I thought. Come, Lady Bliss, we will go back. The time is not right for us."

Now, as she sat there in the privacy of her own room, Bliss realized the folly of her relief when she and the King had returned to the others. He had not given up the idea of making her his mistress, he had merely postponed it. As she replayed his words in her mind, she believed he thought that once she was married to Stephen —an older, wiser woman—she would be more amenable to replacing her husband's cousin in the post of royal mistress.

The bleakness of her future overwhelmed her, and Bliss saw in the mirror the tears that began to trickle down her cheeks.

The voice in the silence of her room took her by surprise:

"Why are you crying, Bliss?"

Gasping, Bliss thrust herself to her feet. In the far corner of the room, Kit stood, watching her, his eyes alive and glittering in his shadowed face. His hair, drawn back and tied at the nape of his neck, looked as black as his clothing in the shadows that enveloped him.

"Kit," she whispered, not quite daring to believe he had come to her there, in the Duke's house. But he was there, so tall, so strong, the concern plain in his handsome face.

"Why are you crying?" he asked again, his voice like a caress to her frayed nerves.

At once he seemed to offer both danger and safety, peril and protection. He opened his arms to her and Bliss ran to him and found herself closed in the strong embrace that was like a shield between herself and the cruel, glittering world that threatened to consume and destroy her.

Chapter 27

Although he'd meant to be cold, hard, impervious to her beauty, Kit found himself concerned, almost frightened by the vehemence of her sobs as she stood in his arms. He had come to her to tell her once and for all that he'd had done with her—that if she preferred Villiers to him she could have him, and be damned to her. He'd almost convinced himself that he meant it. But now—

"Bliss," he murmured, his face against the thick titian curls that fell in luxuriant waves down her back, "Bliss, hush now, tell me what's happened?"

Sobbing, Bliss leaned against him. Her tears soaked into the black cloth of his coat, dampening the creamy linen of his shirt. "I . . . I cannot," she wept.

"Of course you can," he argued. "Tell me, sweetheart. Nothing can be that bad."

"It can," Bliss disagreed. "Or don't you think it's bad to be the King's whore?"

"The King's . . ." Kit frowned, confused. "What are you talking about?"

Sniffling, Bliss left Kit's arms. Her arms wrapped about herself, she turned her back to him. Haltingly, she said:

"They mean me to replace Castlemaine in the King's bed."

"They . . ." Kit stared at her. "Who?"

Bliss shrugged, shaking her head. "Buckingham, the King . . ."

"Stephen and Sir Basil?"

"I don't know." Bliss put a hand to her head. "Sir Basil, I think, would sell me to the devil himself if there was gain in it for him. As for Stephen . . . he will not go against Buckingham's wishes. If the Duke and the King were determined, Stephen would merely look the other way."

"The bastards!" Kit muttered. "And is this what you want as well?"

Spinning toward him, Bliss glared, her golden eyes ablaze. "How can you ask such a thing? Do you imagine I would willingly lie with the King? Damn you, Kit! I hate you!"

"No you don't," Kit disagreed, coming to her as she dissolved into tears once more. "And I am sorry I asked the question. It's only . . ." He looked around the room. "I hate seeing you here, under the Duke's roof. In the clutches of the Villiers family. You know what they are—Buckingham, Castlemaine, Lady Daphne. All of them. They're greedy, avaricious, stupid people and they measure the worth of a person by how they can profit from him or her. Castlemaine is losing her hold on the King, soon Charles will be looking for a new mistress. If you are that mistress, the benefits will remain in the Villiers family."

"Do you think Castlemaine is part of the plot?" Bliss asked.

"I doubt it. She's far too vain to believe the King's interest is waning. No, I think Buckingham probably means you to replace her before she knows she's being replaced."

Bliss shuddered. "I could not, Kit," she whispered. "I could not be the King's doxy."

"I know," he agreed, "which only shows how little they know you." Pulling a handkerchief from his pocket, Kit wiped Bliss's tear-streaked face and made her blow her nose. "Come now," he said, lifting back a strand of her hair that had stuck to her cheek, "Get into bed. There's nothing we can do about it now."

Obediently, Bliss climbed the bedsteps and snuggled under the coverlet. Kit stepped up on the steps and sat on the edge of the bed beside her.

"How did you get in here?" Bliss demanded suddenly.

Kit laughed. "I wondered when you'd get around to asking. Mercy—"

"Mercy!" Bliss sighed. "Is there no end to the girl's meddling?"

"She's only trying to help," Kit told her. "She thinks we should be together."

"Explain to her why we can't," Bliss told him sharply.

"I would," Kit replied, toying with one of her curls, "but first you'll have to explain it to me."

"Oh, Kit," Bliss chided. She could have reminded him that their entire relationship had been based on a lie—she could have told him she believed he had married her only to regain his ancestral estates—she could have called him a villain, a liar, a seducer. But just then it was so good to have him there, his presence comforted her, soothed her, made her believe she could somehow escape the fate the Villierses had in store for her, that she said nothing at all.

Leaning over her, Kit kissed her softly, gently, on her cheek where the soft skin was still damp from her tears. He kissed her cheek, her chin, finally her lips, quick butterfly kisses that seemed so much more intimate, more romantic, than the hard, savage onslaught she'd endured in the King's arms.

Kit's eyes were soft with tenderness as he leaned away from her. He knew he should go—this was not the moment to confront her, and he could bear little more of this intimacy when he knew they could not be lovers. But Bliss sighed as he left her. Her arms came up and wound themselves about his neck and she drew him back down, her eyes fixed on his lips, her own lips trembling with anticipation.

Kit felt her shiver in his arms as he kissed her again. He buried his lips in the warm hollow of her throat and heard the soft moan she could not suppress. A warning voice inside him told him to leave now, while he still could, but he did not hear it—and neither he nor Bliss heard the soft tapping at her bedchamber door.

"Bliss?" Stephen whispered as he opened the door. He'd known she was upset when they'd returned home. Concerned for her, he'd come to see her. When she hadn't answered his knock, he'd feared she was ill. "Bliss, are you—"

The scene before him looked like something out of a painting—the softly lit bedchamber where the candles were nearly guttered out, the lovers on the bed, the woman held in the man's arms, her eyes glowing as she gazed at him, his face a mask of desire as he kissed her.

Stephen stood there, struck dumb, unable to believe his own eyes. As he moved into the room he stumbled, and the door struck the wall behind it, alerting Kit and Bliss to Stephen's presence.

"Stephen!" Bliss breathed. A cold terror engulfed her. All Stephen would have to do was shout and the Duke's lackeys would run to his aid. Escape would be all but impossible, even for Kit.

But Stephen did not shout. Even as Kit left Bliss, even as he moved to face Stephen, ready for whatever happened, Stephen stepped into the room and shut the door behind him.

"What the hell are you doing here?" Stephen snarled. He glared at Bliss. "What's going on here?"

"I am visiting my wife, Villiers," Kit said coldly, disdain oozing from him, disgust for the weak-willed man before him.

"She's not your wife any more," Stephen reminded him. "I am going to make her *my* wife."

"And what else do you want to make her?" Kit demanded. "The King's whore? One royal whore isn't enough for the Villiers family? Oh, I forgot, two—there was your grandfather, wasn't there?"

Stephen flushed scarlet. It was no secret that the first Duke of Buckingham had risen to his exalted rank by being one of the pretty male favorites of the King's grandfather, James I.

"Damn you to hell!" Stephen growled. "If we were not in my cousin's house I would—"

"Aye? What would you do?" Kit taunted. "Nothing, I expect, just as you'd do nothing while your cousin played the pimp and laid your wife in the King's bed!"

"Are you calling me a coward?" Stephen snarled.

"Aye," Kit admitted, "you're a coward and worse, Villiers!"

Stephen knew there was nothing he could do. He had no choice. This man had humiliated him in front of Bliss, had insulted him and his family. Swallowing hard, he said:

"You will answer for what you've said, my lord!"

Kit's hand went to the hilt of his sword. "Gladly," he replied, ready to fight then and there.

"In the morning. At dawn. In the meadow beyond the stream. Do you know where I mean?"

"Aye, I know the place. At dawn, then."

The two men glared at one another as Bliss climbed out of the bed.

"You can't do this!" she cried, running to Kit, clutching at his coat. "Don't fight, Kit, please!"

Kit tore his eyes away from Stephen and looked down at her. "It had to come to this," he told her, "there was no other way." Smiling, he kissed the top of her head. "Don't worry for me, Bliss." His scornful eyes swept over Stephen. "There's no need."

He smiled as Stephen growled. With a mocking bow, Kit turned and strode out of the room, seemingly unconcerned that anyone might see him, a stranger and an enemy to the Villiers family, leaving their house at that hour of the night.

"I'll kill him!" Stephen snarled. "By God, I'll kill him if it's the last thing I ever do!"

Bliss stood there as he turned and stormed from the room. She knew Kit felt the same way, and she knew that for one of them it would, indeed, be the last thing he ever did.

Bliss watched from her window as Stephen rode out in the misty half-light of morning. She was already dressed in her riding habit—Mercy had come to her before dawn to help her dress.

"I'm going," she told the maid. "Did you tell the groom to have my mare saddled?"

"Aye, milady," Mercy confirmed. "I gave him the gold. He said he will take you to the meadow."

Leaving her room, Bliss tiptoed down the hall and down the stairs, exiting the house through a side door and making her way to the stables. There a young groom waited with two horses saddled.

"Hurry," Bliss urged as the groom helped her into her sidesaddle, then swung himself up onto his own horse, "Lord Villiers is far ahead of us."

"Aye, milady," the groom agreed. "This way."

They spurred their horses and rode out of the stableyard and across the flat, empty park surrounding the mansion. The trees that bordered the stream seemed so far away—and the meadow was beyond them. Bliss wished they could fly so they could reach the meadow before anything could happen.

But it was not to be. By the time Bliss and the groom reached the meadow, Kit was standing over Stephen. His sword, held loosely in his hand, was stained with Stephen's blood.

Bliss dropped to the ground and ran to Stephen's side. "Is he—?" she whispered, looking down at Stephen's prone body.

"Aye," Kit confirmed. "Dead. I did not mean to kill him, Bliss. I offered him his life if he would relinquish all claim to you. He refused. I had no choice, Bliss."

"I believe you," Bliss told him, knowing full well that Stephen would only have fought all the harder after Kit's offer.

Kit saw the groom approaching, his face pale with the shock of seeing his master lying dead.

"You'd better go with the groom to take Stephen's body home," he told her.

"No, Kit!" Bliss protested. "I—"

"Listen to me," he ordered. "Tell them what happened. Tell them Stephen challenged me."

"You're going away, aren't you?" she murmured.

"Only until I can manage to speak to the King. Until then, I imagine everybody will say I murdered Stephen. You are the only witness to the challenge, Bliss. You have to be with them to tell them."

"All right," Bliss agreed reluctantly. "I'll go."

Kit stayed only long enough to help the groom drape Stephen's body over his horse. Then, not daring to kiss Bliss in front of the groom, Kit mounted his horse and rode off in the opposite direction from Newmarket and the Villiers mansion.

Buckingham House was in chaos. Lady Daphne's wails echoed through its cavernous chambers, an eerie, keening sound that set Bliss's nerves on edge. Letitia, too, sobbed inconsolably, though Bliss believed her grief was less for her brother than for the knowledge that without Bliss's fortune in her family there would be no gold to allow her to wed her Scottish lover.

Bliss longed to run to her room, to be away from the mourning in which she could not wholeheartedly share. But she could not go. She remained in the drawing room where the Duke sat with Sir Basil planning revenge on the man they swore had murdered Stephen.

"Stephen challenged Kit," Bliss told them yet again. "He challenged him last night!"

"While the wretch was in your bedchamber!" the Duke snarled. He glared at Sir Basil. "Your ward's morals leave something to be desired, sir."

Bliss bit back the words that sprang to her lips. Buckingham, the greatest rake in the country, impugning her morals!

"She will be punished!" Sir Basil vowed. "She will pay for her part in this tragedy." His look was venomous as he stared at Bliss. "She will pay. But first we will avenge Stephen's death. Kit de Wilde will pay for this murder. Rest assured, Your Grace, he will pay with his life!"

Chapter 28

"**I** told you," Bliss repeated for what seemed like the thousandth time, "I don't know where Kit is!"

"Think about it," Sir Basil ordered. "Try to think where he might be."

Bliss watched as her guardian left the room, locking the door behind him. She knew that Sir Basil believed she knew where Kit was hiding, but in fact she did not. Weeks had passed with no word from him. She had no clue where he had gone on that morning when he'd left her there with Stephen's body.

Mercy did know, Bliss mused, a pang of jealousy piercing her heart. Bliss knew that the girl would tell her if she asked, but Bliss thought it better not to know—that way she could honestly plead ignorance when her guardian questioned her.

With a sigh, Bliss took up the book she'd been reading to pass the time. But she could not concentrate—the events of the past few weeks crowded her mind, blocking out all other thoughts.

News of Stephen's death had spread quickly through Newmarket. He had been murdered, they said, by Lord de Wilde, son of the old Baron—the traitor. Murdered, they declared, ignoring Bliss's protests that there had been a duel—a duel that had resulted from Stephen's challenge.

But no one listened, no one believed her. Murder, after all, was far more sensational and the Court of England thrived on scandal.

Bliss closed her eyes, remembering the days after Stephen's death. She'd been forced to endure the ordeal of Stephen's funeral, to accept condolences from ladies and gentlemen who eyed her curiously, then retired to gossip about her.

Her annulment from Kit was no secret—nothing remained a secret in London for long. And that knowledge, when combined with Stephen's death, made for a delicious tale of secret desires, betrayal, and death.

It had been a relief when they had returned from the country—from watching Stephen being entombed with the Villierses of the past. She had never been so happy to see Barthorp House as she had been that day. But then the inquisition had begun.

Sir Basil forbade her visitors—she was too deeply grieved, he told anyone who came to call. Bliss saw no one save Mercy and Sir Basil himself, who came again and again to demand that she tell him where Kit could be found.

Tossing her book aside, Bliss rose and went to the window. The garden stretched down to the Thames, and Bliss watched the boats being rowed along past the water stairs. She sighed. If only she could go to the river, climb into one of those boats, and be rowed away to some green garden where she and Kit could be together.

She smiled in spite of herself. Not so very long ago she had vowed she hated Kit; she had sworn she would hate him forever. But then had come the night before the duel—the night when she'd feared he might be killed—and she had known then that her life would never be complete without Kit. Oh, it might be more peaceful, there might be less hurt, less risk, but there would be less joy as well. And she believed with all her heart that whatever pain life with Kit might bring her, it would be worth it.

She turned when she heard the sound of the key turning in the lock. The door opened and Mercy appeared.

"Milady," the maid said, curtsying to her mistress.

"Have you been outside, Mercy?" Bliss asked. "Is it warm?"

"'Tis a beautiful day," the maid told her.

Bliss sighed. Whatever the weather, no day could be completely beautiful without Kit.

"Tuppence for your thoughts, milady," Mercy said lightly, then laughed. "You're thinking about his lordship."

"Aye," Bliss admitted. "I seldom think of anything else. Oh, Mercy, where can he be?" She held up a hand. "No, don't tell me. 'Tis better that I not know. Sir Basil will be back soon to question me again. It's like the Inquisition."

"In fact, milady," the maid said, drawing close to Bliss's side, "I've seen him."

"You . . ." Bliss gaped at her. "When! Today?"

"Aye. I told my Lord Holme you wished me to go to the 'Change. But 'twas not true."

"You went to see Kit?" Bliss envied the girl. "Is he well? How did he look?"

"Well," Mercy assured her. "Handsomer than ever. He is worried about you."

"Worried about me!" Bliss's laugh was strained. "He is the one who is accused of murder! He is the one being hunted!" She took a deep breath. "What did he say, Mercy?"

"He wants to see you, milady," the maid revealed.

"He can't come here!" Bliss felt panic rising inside her. It would be just like Kit to try and come to Barthorp House. "He's not going to try—"

"No," Mercy soothed her. "He wants you to

come to him. I'm to bring you. He says he wants to see you once more."

"Once . . ." Bliss frowned. "I don't understand."

"He said," Mercy went on, not relishing what she had to tell her mistress, "he said that he does not know how he can prove his innocence. He knows that no one believes you when you say Lord Villiers challenged him. He says he will forever be branded a murderer. He says he will not ask you to share his disgrace."

"Oh, God!" Bliss moaned. "Mercy! He's going away, isn't he?"

"Aye, milady. He says after he's seen you he's going to America."

"America!" Bliss tried to imagine life without Kit, separated from him by the endless expanse of the ocean. "But he can't go! He is innocent! Why won't they believe me?"

"They believe you are protecting him," Mercy told her. "And there is the groom."

"The groom? What groom?" Bliss asked.

Mercy hesitated. She had not wanted to tell Bliss, knowing it would upset her, but she had to know.

"The groom who took you to the meadow that morning," she said, not able to bring herself to meet Bliss's eyes. "He says he saw milord kill Lord Villiers."

"What!" Bliss trembled with rage. "He's a liar! Stephen was dead when we got there!"

"I know," Mercy agreed. "But he swears he

saw milord run Lord Villiers through—from the back."

"The back!" Bliss paled.

"Aye. He says Lord Villiers turned to go and milord ran him through."

Her legs wobbled and Bliss sank down into her chair. "And they believe him," she whispered. "They would not believe me, but they believe him! Why?"

But she knew why—they believed the groom because he was telling them what they wanted to hear.

"It's hopeless," she murmured, her already low spirits sinking even further.

"Come, milady," Mercy comforted, "milord wants to see you. Tonight."

"Where?" Bliss asked.

"Suffolk Street. I'm to take you there—after Sir Basil retires."

"All right," Bliss agreed. "I'll be ready."

It was nearly midnight when Bliss and Mercy, enveloped from head to toe in black, slipped out of Barthorp House and made their way into the Strand. Though it was dangerous to walk the streets of London by night, they would not risk taking a carriage lest the sound attract attention.

Together they hurried to Charing Cross, then turned into Suffolk Street.

"Here, milady," Mercy whispered, leading Bliss to a house set back from the others, its door swathed in shadows.

Bliss entered. The house was dark, only a few candles burned, and the heavy draperies were drawn tightly across the windows. Bliss pushed back her hood.

"Where is he, Mercy?" she asked. There was no answer. "Mercy?"

"I told her to leave us alone," a voice said from behind Bliss.

"Kit!" In a swirl of black silk, Bliss rushed into his arms. "Oh, Kit! I've been so worried about you. So frightened."

"Come, sit down," Kit invited. "Mercy will come back later to take you home."

"I don't want to go home," Bliss told him. "I want to stay with you."

"No." Kit shook his head. "I couldn't . . ."

"Listen to me!" Bliss urged. "Mercy told me you said you're going to America. Take me with you, Kit! We'll go there together."

"You don't know what you're asking," Kit told her solemnly. "America is not like England, Bliss. It's a wild, untamed place. Oh, there are settlements, towns, but not like here."

"I don't care!" She felt herself near tears. "I don't care! I only want to be with you. I love you."

"Bliss," Kit murmured, moved. He slid his arms around her and drew her to him. "I've dreamed of hearing you say those words. If only it could be . . . if only we could be together."

"We can be! We can!" she declared. "Don't

leave me, Kit, I beg you!"

Kit gazed into her eyes. Lost in their golden depths, he could almost believe there was hope for them, that there was some way they could be together. But he saw no hope of proving his innocence in England, and he could not, in all conscience, ask Bliss to leave everything she had in England and follow him into exile in the great wilderness of America.

"Bliss," he said, wondering how he could make her see that she was better off without him. "Listen to me. I'm going—"

Whatever he'd been about to say was lost as the door crashed open and the dancing flare of torches lit the shadowy room. Kit leaped to his feet, intent on defending Bliss from whatever intruder had come, but his efforts were wasted.

A company of the King's guards stormed into the room and surrounded them. There was no escape.

The ranks parted, and Sir Basil appeared with the Duke of Buckingham. Between them they supported Mercy who sagged, weeping, her legs scarcely able to support her.

"I caught the chit sneaking back into Barthorp House," Sir Basil told Bliss. "It took a little persuading, but she told us where she'd taken you. It did not take much thought to know why she'd brought you here."

Both the Duke and Sir Basil released their hold on the maid, and she fell to the floor. The back of her gown was torn open and her tender flesh was scored with welts.

"You've whipped her, damn you!" Bliss hissed, hurrying to kneel at Mercy's side. "You are monsters! Both of you!"

The Duke gazed at Bliss unconcerned. Her hatred, her loathing, could not touch him. He was about to get what he wanted—revenge— and nothing else mattered at that moment.

"Captain," he said to one of the guards, "go about your duties."

The guard stepped forward. "My Lord de Wilde," he said to Kit, "you are under arrest for murder. My orders are to take you to the Tower."

"Am I to be given a trial?" Kit asked.

"You'll have your trial, de Wilde," the Duke said, "much good may it do you."

"Trial or no," Sir Basil snarled as the guards closed ranks about Kit, "you're going to hang, d'ye hear me? Hang!"

Flanked by the guards, Kit was ushered toward the door. They were nearly to it when Bliss left Mercy's side and ran after him.

"Kit!" she cried.

A pair of arms encircled her and yanked her back. Pinioned against the Duke's body, Bliss heard his voice hiss into her ear:

"Don't waste your tears on that varlet. He's going to die. But you need not fear—I'll be more than happy to comfort you in your grief."

Bliss watched as Kit disappeared into the

night. The room seemed to spin about her, the shadows lengthened, the colors melded into a swirling eddy, and the last thing she heard before she descended into darkness was the mocking laughter of her guardian and the Duke of Buckingham.

Chapter 29

Kit was confined in the Tower of London, that grim, dreaded bastion that had seen so much misery, so much suffering and death. Bliss thought of him there, wondered if he was lodged in decent quarters or thrown into one of the damp, rat-infested dungeons.

The mere thought of him there made her queasy. At night she dreamed of him, saw him cold and hungry, tormented by his jailers. She invariably awakened only to weep with frustration and anger at his plight.

Sir Basil reassured her that Kit would, after all, have a trial. But that was no comfort to her. What sort of a trial could he have? He'd been judged and condemned by society already. And the Villierses, with their powerful connections and influence at court, could sway Kit's judges. With their gold they could buy witnesses who would willingly lie for them. It would be all to simple for them to conspire to send Kit to the gallows.

"There must be something I could do," Bliss told Mercy again and again.

"I don't see what," the maid replied. She sat in Bliss's room keeping her mistress company. Though Sir Basil had wanted her dismissed for helping Bliss go to Kit on the night he'd been arrested, Bliss had stubbornly refused to allow the girl to be sent away. "The Duke of Buckingham is determined to see his lordship hanged—as determined as Milord Holme and Lady Daphne. They'd never change their minds."

"No," Bliss admitted. "They won't be happy until he's dead. And they are so powerful. No one, saving the King, dares refuse them anything."

"Perhaps the King will pardon him," Mercy suggested. "But then, Lady Castlemaine is his mistress, isn't she? I don't suppose he would—"

"What did you say?" Bliss asked. "About the King pardoning him?"

Mercy shrugged. "He could, couldn't he? If the King pardons milord he could go free, couldn't he?"

"Aye," Bliss breathed. "He could! That's it, Mercy! I must go to the King!"

"Will he see you?" Mercy asked, awed by the prospect of simply deciding to go and see the

King of England.

Bliss shook her head. "I don't know. I hope so. There's only one way to tell."

The following morning Bliss rose with the dawn. With Mercy's help she dressed carefully in a gown of leaf green silk ruffled in cream and silver. Her hair was a mass of gleaming curls peeping out from the wide brim of her plume-laden hat. Her gown was cut low, and the narrow lace ruffles formed a frame for the exquisite emerald pendant that fell to nestle in the valley of her breasts.

"I've never seen you look lovelier," Mercy told her. "Surely His Majesty will give you anything you ask for."

Bliss said nothing. Charles was swayed by beauty, it was true, and was generous to women he desired. Her only worry was what he might ask in return for such a prodigious favor.

"I hope so," she murmured to herself, and turned for the door.

Every morning, whatever the weather, the King rose early and walked in St. James's Park. His pace was swift, and since his legs were longer than those of nearly all his gentlemen, he frequently finished far ahead of any of them.

Bliss knew he seldom stopped for anyone. Petitioners who sought to waylay him were frequently disappointed in that by the time they rose from their curtsy or bow the King was far past them and their opportunity gone.

Butterflies fluttering in her stomach, Bliss

hurried along the paths of St. James's Park hoping to catch the King after he had outdistanced the pack of courtiers and toadies who always tried to follow him.

"There he is!" Mercy said as she followed her mistress along the walkway.

"I see him," Bliss replied. He was not alone, but those few gentlemen who were still manfully trying to keep pace with him were beginning to lag. Let him be alone, Bliss prayed as she stationed herself in his path.

Bliss trembled as he approached. What if he did not notice her? What if he merely bestowed one of his customary "God Bless you"'s and went on his way? What if, even if he deigned to speak to her, he would not help Kit? He might be tiring of Lady Castlemaine, but would he want to do anything so completely against the Villierses' wishes?

As the King drew nearer, Bliss's nervousness grew. What if she spoke to him and he refused her? Wouldn't that be worse than if she had not gone to him at all?

The King had nearly reached her when Bliss's courage failed her. In a rustle of silk and lace she turned and was about to flee.

The King's voice stopped her. "Bliss? Lady Bliss, is that you?"

Shivering, her palms sweaty, Bliss turned back toward him and sank to the ground, head bowed reverently.

"Aye, sire," she said softly.

"You wished to see me, did you not?" He chuckled at the surprise on her face. "Come now, it's not so difficult to know that. You've come to the park at the break of day, dressed like an angel. You meant to attract my attention."

"I did, sire," she admitted, still not daring to look up at him.

"Then come, walk with me."

Linking her arm through his, the King moved on. A glance over his shoulder kept his courtiers at bay as he and Bliss walked on toward the canal where, in the winter, the King enjoyed "sliding" on the ice.

In deference to Bliss, the King slowed his pace. They walked slowly through the verdant beauty of the park where cows grazed and the King's collection of exotic birds and animals were looked after with greater care than many of the fine lords and ladies who followed in the wake of Bliss and the King.

"I can guess what it is you wish to speak to me about," the King said. "De Wilde is in the Tower."

"Aye," Bliss agreed. "But he is innocent, sire. Innocent!"

"He killed Stephen Villiers," the King reminded her. "Even he does not dispute that fact. He has admitted it."

"He was forced to confess?" Bliss whispered, paling.

"He admitted it," the King repeated. "He is quite comfortable in the Tower, Bliss. He's not being starved or racked. His quarters are finely furnished and he is well taken care of."

"May I—" Bliss began.

"No," the King interrupted, "you may not go to him. He is a prisoner, Bliss, and a crafty one at that. I want him left alone there."

"He is innocent," Bliss repeated. "The duel was Stephen's doing. He challenged Kit."

Stopping, the King sat on a bench at the edge of the walk and motioned for Bliss to join him. "Tell me what happened," he invited.

"At Buckingham House in Newmarket," Bliss explained, "Stephen came to my room and found Kit there. He challenged Kit to a duel. I begged Kit not to fight, but he said he had no choice. He said it had to come to that."

"Doubtless he was right," the King admitted. "But why, may I ask, was Kit in your bedchamber at Buckingham House?"

Bliss blushed. "I'm not certain," she replied. "He had not told me before Stephen appeared."

"I see," the King murmured. "You went to the duel?"

"Stephen forbade me, but aye, I went," Bliss confessed. "By the time I got there, Stephen was already dead."

"A groom has said he saw Kit kill Stephen. He says Stephen had turned and was walking away when Kit ran him through from behind."

Sandra DuBay

"It's a lie!" Bliss cried. "That groom saw nothing! He was with me! He showed me the way to the meadow where the duel was to take place. He saw nothing more than I saw!"

The King shook his head. "I believe you, Bliss, I don't think de Wilde is such a coward that he would murder a man in cold blood. But the trial must go forward."

"No! Please, sire!" Bliss felt hope slipping away. "The Villierses and Sir Basil are determined to see Kit hanged. They will buy witnesses, like this groom, to swear to whatever lies they concoct. How could Kit hope to have a fair trial when they are so thirsty for his blood?"

"Bliss," the King explained patiently, "a gentleman has been killed. Another is accused of his murder. There must be seen to be a trial. You know my feelings against dueling, Bliss. Even if Kit is innocent of murder, he must be punished for flouting my wishes."

"The challenge was Stephen's," Bliss reminded him hopefully.

"I know," Charles admitted. "But Kit fought."

"Could you not pardon him?" Her eyes shimmered with unshed tears. "Please, sire, pardon him. Free him. I would—" She blushed, lowering her eyes. "I would give anything to save his life."

"Even yourself?" the King asked softly, suddenly realizing the reason for the beautiful gown cut skillfully to reveal more of her luscious bosom than it concealed, the heady perfume that wafted into his nose, the artfully curled titian hair that danced on her creamy shoulders.

"Aye," Bliss replied, so softly he could scarcely hear her. "Anything Your Majesty asked."

"Ah, Bliss," he sighed, tilting her chin up with one long finger. "You don't know how tempting it is to test that statement. But I could not."

"Kit . . ." Bliss whispered, feeling on the edge of tears.

"Listen to me," the King said, "I will speak to Barbara Castlemaine. Perhaps I can persuade her that Stephen's death was not murder. I will prevail upon her to convince Buckingham not to pursue this trial. If I can do that, and they will agree, I can pardon your Lord de Wilde."

Bliss shook her head. "They will never agree," she predicted gloomily.

The King smiled. "They might," he disagreed. "I think they might."

Lady Castlemaine stood before her mirror scrutinizing her appearance with ruthless attention. The first faint lines had begun appearing about her eyes and she bent close to examine them.

No! she decided, brushing a fold from her rich royal blue and emerald green gown, she did not look a day over twenty. Her beauty was as lush, as startlingly vivid as ever. She was as desirable

Sandra DuBay

as she had ever been and she had the proof of it.
Was not the King coming to sup with her
privately?

She had been alarmed when the gossip of his
talk with Bliss reached her ears. She had spies
everywhere, and they had rushed to tell her that
the lovely young Lady Bliss had met the King in
the park. He had walked with her, sat with her,
spoken with her so intimately that not one word
had been overheard. What could it mean?

A footman scratched at the door, then entered. "The King, milady," he announced.

With a last pat to her flame-red curls, Barbara
went out to meet her royal lover.

Together they dined in Barbara's rooms overlooking the Privy Garden. Their conversation
was light, inconsequential, until Barbara could
no longer resist asking:

"What is this I hear about your being accosted
in the park by Bliss Paynter?"

The King smiled. He knew it must have been
on her mind but he wanted her to be the one to
bring it up.

"Aye," he admitted casually. "She wished to
speak to me."

"About Kit de Wilde, I suppose?" Barbara's
smile was smug. "She'd better get used to the
fact that the varlet is going to hang. He murdered Stephen."

"She says he did not," the King told her. "She
swears the challenge was Stephen's."

362

"She'll say anything to free him," Barbara scoffed. "But it won't save him."

"I suppose not," the King agreed. He sipped his wine. "She'll be devastated by his death."

"Would she had spared so much concern for her betrothed!" Barbara snarled.

The King smiled. "She is a beautiful young woman," he commented. "An angel. I think, perhaps, I may try to find some way to comfort her in her grief."

"What do you—" Barbara began.

"I think she should stay here, at court," the King went on. "Apartments could be found for her. Off the Stone Gallery."

Barbara gasped. The Stone Gallery, on the opposite side of the Privy Garden from her own rooms, was the heart of Whitehall. The King's own apartments were off the Stone Gallery.

"Perhaps she will not wish to stay at court," Barbara suggested.

"Oh, I may be able to convince her." He grinned at his mistress. "It may be just as well that you and your family want to see de Wilde dead. If Bliss were allowed to be with him, they would doubtless retire to Chatham and the court would lose a beautiful ornament."

Before Barbara could reply, a knock on the door interrupted them. A footman in royal livery appeared.

"A messenger for Your Majesty," the man announced. "From France."

"Alas, I must leave you," the King said, rising. "I have enjoyed our evening, Barbara. We must sup together again soon."

With a smile and a chuck under the chin the King left his mistress, who watched him go, her beautiful face thoughtful and troubled.

Chapter 30

"**A**re you mad!" The Duke of Buckingham eyed his cousin incredulously. "Have you forgotten that the wretch cost us a fortune? Do you have any idea of the size of Bliss Paynter's inheritance?"

"It's not the size of her inheritance that interests the King," Barbara snarled.

"What are you talking about?"

Barbara sank onto a stool in the Duke's drawing room. "The King came to my rooms last night," she told him. "We spoke of de Wilde being in the Tower. Charles said Bliss would be devastated by de Wilde's death and that he would comfort her, as he put it. You know what that means, George! I think he means to make her his mistress! He spoke of giving her rooms off the Stone Gallery!''

The Duke scowled. He had schemed toward just that end. When it seemed that Bliss would marry Stephen, he had planned to make Bliss the King's mistress. He had thought to place Bliss in the King's bed so that the power of a royal favorite—the power Barbara was rapidly losing—would remain safely in Villiers hands. Charles desired the girl, that much was abundantly clear. If she were to lose de Wilde, might she not turn to the King for comfort? And something more . . .

"It could be dangerous for us, Bucks," Barbara told her cousin.

"Aye, too dangerous," Buckingham agreed.

"A young, beautiful girl, new to the King's bed . . . She would have too much influence with him."

"And she would bear us a grudge," Buckingham suggested. "She would blame us for de Wilde's death."

"And she would be in a position to be avenged on us. But the King believes that if Bliss and Kit were together they would go to Chatham to live," Barbara told him.

Buckingham paced the floor. It was galling to be forced to abandon his plans. He'd been furious that Stephen had been killed. It was not that he bore any great affection for the cousin he regarded as a fool, under the thumb of his domineering mother; it was that he had seen Bliss as a means not only to enrich the Villiers family with her gold and vast estates but also to continue the not inconsiderable control Barbara had held over the King. If Barbara lost her position as favorite—and she seemed to be doing just that—her replacement must be another Villiers. And Bliss, with her beauty, her innocence, had seemed the perfect candidate.

But his plan had succeeded too well. The King desired the girl. He had desired her when she was to be Stephen's wife, and now that Stephen was dead he still desired her.

If Bliss became the King's mistress—if she gained the power that position held—what vengeance might she not wreak on the people who had caused her such grief?

He nodded gravely. "I don't see that we have a choice," he told Lady Castlemaine. "But you and I cannot be the ones to go to the King. It has to come from Daphne."

"She won't do it," Barbara predicted.

"She'll do it," he vowed, "or I'll whip her and that silly cow of a daughter of hers to within an inch of their miserable lives! Send a messenger to Villiers House. Tell them to come to your rooms tonight."

"Oh, not tonight!" Barbara protested. "I'm having a guest for dinner."

"One of your young, penniless gentlemen?" Buckingham sneered. "Or one of the acrobats from the fair?" His laughter was filled with disdain. "You've fallen far, coz. They say you're paying them now."

"Go to hell!" Barbara snarled, thrusting herself up off the stool.

"Doubtless we'll both be there one day!" the Duke called after her. "Have Daphne there tonight! At eight!"

Swathed in black, Lady Daphne and Letitia Villiers curtsied low before their illustrious cousin, Lady Castlemaine.

"We would not have come out for anyone but you," Lady Daphne told her, dabbing at her eyes with a black handkerchief. She eyed Barbara's scarlet and yellow gown as if offended by its gay colors.

Barbara smiled condescendingly. As if Daphne Villiers had so many invitations! She lived quietly, taking advantage of whatever friends she had, hoping to be invited to Lord This's country house or Lady That's estate in order to be spared the ruinous cost of maintaining a full-time London residence.

"Come, sit down," she invited. "Buckingham will be here shortly. There is a matter we must discuss with you."

They made small talk for the next quarter of an hour until the Duke appeared. Buckingham came in smiling pleasantly.

"My dear," he said, pecking at Daphne's upturned cheek. Letitia curtsied deeply and the Duke raised her up and bade them both sit down.

"We want to speak with you about Kit de Wilde," the Duke began.

"That bastard!" Daphne spat. "Hanging is too good for him! He should be drawn and quartered!"

"He should be left to starve in the deepest dungeon in the Tower!" Letitia added.

The Duke cast a glance at Barbara as if to say: "This is not going to be easy."

"We have discussed the matter at length," he went on, "and we feel it would be best if Kit were pardoned."

"Pardoned!" Lady Daphne leaped to her feet. "Never! He murdered my—"

"Be quiet!" the Duke roared. "If de Wilde is executed, Bliss will want to be avenged on us. She will blame us for his death."

"What do I care what the little bitch thinks?" Daphne hissed. "This is all her fault! She was with de Wilde, you know, in your house!" She waggled a finger toward the Duke. "In your house!"

"And your son was fool enough to challenge the man to a duel!" Barbara snarled.

"He had to defend his honor!" Daphne argued.

"Much good may his honor do him in his grave!" the Duke snapped. "Now sit down, Daphne, and shut up. I grow weary of this endless arguing."

Lips pursed, face flushed, Daphne resumed her seat. "You want me to excuse my son's

Sandra DuBay

murder because of some wanton little chit?"

"The King desires to make that wanton little chit his mistress," Buckingham pointed out. "That was fine when she was to be a Villiers. The power would have been kept in the family."

"What about me?" Letitia whined. "I am a Villiers! Why could I not—"

"Don't be ridiculous!" the Duke growled. "Now listen. If de Wilde is hanged, Bliss will hate us. She's no fool; she knows we are behind the charges against him. I was with Lord Holme when we went to arrest him. If she becomes the King's mistress after de Wilde's death, she will do all she can to ruin us. All of us."

"And what makes you think she will not try to ruin us even if de Wilde is pardoned?" Daphne asked.

"If de Wilde is freed, I do not believe Bliss would consent to become the King's mistress. Barbara, and the King, believe that Bliss would leave London and retire to Chatham with Kit. It would be best for us all."

Daphne eyed them resentfully. They would, she knew, prevail in the end. They would get their way as they always did, these cousins of her late husband. It was galling to be a poor relative, but particularly when one's rich relatives held so much power—and derived so much enjoyment from wielding it.

"Mother!" Letitia breathed when her mother remained silent. "You're not considering agreeing to this, are you?"

"We have no choice," Daphne told her.

"But you can't! I want Bliss to suffer! She promised, promised! She said she would give me an income so I could marry Angus and—"

"Shut your mouth, girl!" the Duke snapped. "You little fool! You're not going to ruin us all simply because no one now will buy you a husband!"

Letitia sulked while Daphne, unhappy but resigned, nodded her agreement.

"Very well then, it shall be as you wish. I will ask the King to pardon de Wilde."

Barbara and the Duke exchanged triumphant smiles. They had won as they'd fully intended to do and they'd enjoyed their victory as they always did.

It was late morning of the following day when Lady Daphne Villiers, flanked by Lady Castlemaine and the Duke of Buckingham, curtsied before the King in a small anteroom of his apartments.

"My lady," the King said, knowing full well what was coming but willing to play his part, "rise. You asked to speak with me."

"Aye, sire," Daphne said. "I wish to speak with Your Majesty about Lord de Wilde."

"Go on, my lady," the King invited.

Though the words burned her tongue, Lady Daphne said:

"I have decided that no good would come of executing him, sire. The challenge, so they say, was issued by my son. He fought. He was bested. There is no point in shedding more blood."

"What is it you wish me to do, my lady?" the King asked.

"Pardon him, sire," she murmured, hating each syllable. "Free him and let us be done with this loathsome business."

"You are a true Christian, ma'am," the King commented, wondering just how in the devil Barbara and Buckingham had convinced the woman to do this. "I will send word to the Tower that Lord de Wilde is to be set free without delay."

Rising, Lady Daphne sank into another deep curtsy before taking her leave. The King watched her as she made her way to the door. Her indignation, her resentment, was plain in the way she held herself, the stiffness of her walk. She had come to him under duress, he was certain, but it did not matter. The end result was the same—de Wilde would have his freedom and Bliss would have de Wilde.

Sighing, the King went to his Privy Closet to write out the order freeing Kit. He envied the man—to have a woman like Bliss willing to sacrifice anything and everything for his sake must be a wonderful feeling. He did not believe any of his mistresses had ever felt that way about him. Oh, they vowed undying love, to be certain, but all they gave was whatever it took to reap the rewards of being the royal favorite. The Queen loved him, to be sure, but her love made him uneasy, made him feel guilty, because he knew he hurt her with the behavior he could not—and would not—change.

The pounding at the door startled him. Generally his Privy Closet was sacroscanct—no one interrupted him there.

"What is it?" he called, annoyed.

The door opened and William Chiffinch appeared. His face was flushed, his eyes wide.

"A messenger, sire, from the Tower!" he blurted.

"The Tower? Good. He can take back this order freeing Lord de Wilde."

"But the message is about Lord de Wilde!" Chiffinch cried.

"Well? What about him?" Charles prompted. An uneasy dread gripped him. "He's not dead, is he?"

"No, sire, at least they don't think so."

"Don't think so? What the devil are you talking about, man!"

"My Lord de Wilde! When the guard went to see to him this morning he was gone."

"Gone!" Charles gaped.

"Aye, sire, gone! He's escaped from the Tower!"

Stunned, the King sagged back in his chair. Escaped! De Wilde was out there somewhere, doubtless hiding, not knowing that freedom had been a mere hour away. How was he going to tell de Wilde he was no longer a prisoner? How was he going to explain that Kit need not hide? And God's blood! How was he going to tell Bliss that her lover had vanished from his prison?

Chapter 31

It was late when Bliss found herself being ushered up the privy stairs to the King's inner sanctum. The summons had come to Barthorp House—a liveried messenger had arrived at the door and not even Sir Basil could have denied this royal command.

Mercy followed close at Bliss's heels. Her eyes were wide with wonderment. To her the King was a mythical being, someone not quite human for all his very human faults. To think that she was being led up the private narrow stairs to the most private chambers in England awed her and even frightened her.

William Chiffinch led her through the King's bedchamber. He rapped at the door of the Privy

Closet and, when the King's muffled voice replied, opened the door for Bliss.

Bliss entered the small hideaway that few had ever seen. It was here that the King retired for a moment's peace to escape his ministers, his mistresses, courtiers seeking favors, and ambassadors wrangling over treaties.

The room was littered with books and papers, letters and small, intimate objects collected during the wandering days when he was first a Prince of Wales without prospects and then, after his father's execution, a King without a kingdom. A letter, unfinished, lay on the desk. It began "My dearest Minette" and was for his sister, Henriette, now married to Philippe, brother of Louis XIV of France.

The King stood as Bliss hesitated on the doorsill. "Come in," he told her. "Sit down. What I have to tell you is both good and bad."

Bliss perched on the edge of a chair. "What is it?" she asked. "Is it Kit?"

"Aye," he admitted. "This——" He held up the pardon, signed and sealed, he had written for Kit. "——is a pardon. It was made at the request of Lady Daphne Villiers."

"Daphne!" Bliss stared at him. "But how in the world did you convince——"

"How is not important," the King told her. "What is important is that Kit is pardoned for Stephen's death. I give this to you."

Bliss clutched the precious document to her

breast. "Your Majesty," she whispered, "I don't know how to thank you. I will go to the Tower now and show this to the warder there. Then Kit can—"

"Sit down, Bliss," the King ordered. "That was the good part of what I must tell you."

Bliss sank bank into her chair. "Something has happened to him?" she asked, breathless. "What?"

"Even as I was writing the pardon, a messenger came from the Tower. Kit has escaped."

"Escaped!" Bliss sagged back in her chair. "But why? If he is pardoned . . ."

"He escaped before he knew he'd been pardoned. He's disappeared, Bliss, still believing he's going to be tried for murder."

Leaving her chair, Bliss went to the door and called for Mercy to join them. The maid came in, her eyes like saucers as she gaped at the King sitting there in shirtsleeves, a man, no more no less, for all his mystical monarchy.

"Mercy," Bliss said. "Mercy!" She poked the maid to jolt her out of her awestruck stupor. "Do you know where Kit is?"

"His lordship?" Mercy was perplexed. "He's in the Tower."

"Not any more," the King told her. "He escaped a few hours since. He got hold of a rope and lowered himself out a window into the moat."

"The moat," Bliss breathed, thinking of the

filthy, stinking expanse of water that frequently claimed both drunken revelers and lost cattle.

"It's been dragged with grappling hooks, Bliss," the King assured her. "Your Lord de Wilde is gone—but not to his eternal reward. He made good his escape from the Tower."

"But he doesn't know he has been pardoned," Bliss murmured, more to herself than to the King. "Poor Kit! He must think he's being hunted. He could be hiding anywhere."

"I'm sorry, Bliss, truly sorry," the King told her sincerely. "If I hear any word of where Kit might be—"

"Thank you," she whispered, rising. "I'll find him, sire, and when I do, he'll be grateful for this." She held up the pardon.

The King walked with Bliss to the privy stairs and watched as she and Mercy descended, their way lit by William Chiffinch.

When Bliss returned to Barthorp House it was with a lighter heart, a more buoyant step, a new hope for the future.

"Oh, Mercy," she said as she alighted from the coach and started toward the front door. "I'm certain Kit would go to Chatham. The people there would hide him, protect him, help him to clear his name. If I could go there and find him I could tell him he has been pardoned and might come out of hiding!"

"But will milord let you go?" Mercy asked.

Bliss shrugged. "Certainly not if he knows Kit has escaped."

Together they entered the house. Candles burned in the drawing room. Sir Basil was there, waiting. Bliss tried to slip past the door unnoticed, but her guardian called out to her as she passed the open door.

"Bliss?" he shouted. "Come here. What did the King want?"

"Nothing of import," she replied, praying the news of Kit's escape had not reached his ears.

"Missed you, eh?" A greedy gleam glittered in Sir Basil's eyes. "I think our royal Stuart stallion has plans for you, my beauty."

Bliss longed to claw the leering smile from his face, but she was grateful he did not know the real reason for her summons to the palace.

"I wonder, my lord," she said softly, "if I might be allowed to leave London for a little while. A week or two. No more than a month."

"Give the King a chance to miss you, eh?" Sir Basil laughed. "Where would you go? Yorkshire?"

Bliss shook her head. "Chatham. Yorkshire holds some rather unpleasant memories for me now."

"As well it might," he agreed. "Though I should think the memories of Chatham are scarcely more pleasant."

"May I go, then, my lord?" Bliss's heart was pounding. He did not know Kit was free! If only

Sandra DuBay

she could be away from London before he found
out!

"I suppose so. I doubt you can come to harm
with de Wilde safely locked in the Tower."

"Thank you, sir," she said meekly, feeling
triumphant. "Mercy and I will leave at first
light."

Climbing the stairs to her room, Bliss sent
Mercy to pack. The hour was late, but dawn
seemed so far away.

The sun was barely above the horizon when
the coach rolled out of the courtyard of
Barthorp House. Bliss leaned back against the
seat with a sigh.

"Thank God no one told Sir Basil about Kit's
escape," she told Mercy. "He would have locked
me in my room!" She gazed out the window as
they left the city behind them. "Please, please,
Kit, be at Chatham! I'm so afraid, Mercy, that he
might have gone to the Continent to escape
being tried for Stephen's death. But I'm hoping
he'd go to Chatham first to see to Isaac." She
sighed, gazing out the window as the hustle and
bustle of London gave way to the verdant pas-
tures and lush woodlands of the English countryside. "I've got to find him, Mercy, and tell
him he's free—free to come back to Chatham,
to London, to me."

As they rode along, Bliss willed the coach to
go faster, the miles to pass more quickly. The

sun rose higher in the sky and they stopped at a coaching inn to rest and see to one of the horses.

"Can't they hurry?" she asked the coachman who was watching as the inn's groom saw to the horse.

"If he's not cared for, milady, he'll come up lame," the coachman replied.

"Well, can't we get a horse from the stable here and then send someone back for this horse?" she persisted.

"Aye, we could," the coachman agreed. "Or John could wait and bring this horse along later."

"Good. That's what we'll do," Bliss decided.

In short order John, the footman who'd ridden on the box with the coachman for Bliss's protection, was ordered to remain behind and wait for the horse while a replacement was harnessed to the coach.

As they left the inn, Bliss glared up at the sun, now starting its descent toward the western horizon.

"We've wasted so much time," she sighed. "We'll be lucky if we reach Chatham by dark."

"We could be attacked by a highwayman," Mercy told her, her eyes twinkling.

Bliss smiled wistfully. "I would not mind—if it were the right highwayman."

They lapsed into silence as the coach raced through the afternoon sunshine. Chatham was not very far away, but Bliss's impatience and worry made the miles seem double. She gazed out the window, almost hypnotized by the greenery that surrounded them. It was not until she heard the shouts and the neighing protests of the horses as the coachman hauled on the reins that she realized they were being waylaid.

"Get down from the box!" a masculine voice ordered. "Throw down your weapons!"

Bliss looked at Mercy, her heart in her throat. "Kit!" she breathed, her pulse leaping wildly. "It's Kit!"

"No, milady," Mercy disagreed. "I don't think it is—"

But Bliss did not hear her. Certain that Kit had found her, she threw open the door and leaped down from the coach in a swirl of pink silk.

She knew at a glance that the man standing beside the tall roan was not Kit. He was garbed in black and his face was masked, but there was nothing about him that even vaguely resembled her lover.

"Ah, here she is," the man drawled. "Milady." He made her a mocking bow, the pistols he held in either hand never wavering.

"I have no gold," she told him. "Nor many valuable jewels. I have these ear bobs and a string of pearls. Take them and let us go in peace."

The man's blue eyes twinkled above the edge of his mask. "It is not your jewels I want, my beauty. It is you, yourself. I mean to take you with me."

"The hell you will!" the coachman growled, launching himself forward.

The crack of the pistol reverberated through the forest, startling the horses who shied in their traces and whinnied nervously. The coachman fell in a heap at the highwayman's feet, a crimson stain spreading over the front of his coat.

"Damn you. Damn you!" Bliss hissed, dropping to one knee beside the fallen man. There was nothing to be done, she could see. His eyes were glassy, unseeing.

"Murderer!" she hissed.

"Get back in the coach, milady," the highwayman demanded. "I will drive you."

"Go to the devil!" she snarled. "If I refuse, will you kill me as well?"

"You, my beauty, are worth far more to me alive than dead," he told her. "I would not kill you. But I will kill her!"

Before Bliss could react, the highwayman swung toward Mercy, who was charging directly at him. The second pistol barked and Mercy fell, eyes wide and staring, blood gushing from her breast.

"Mercy!" Bliss's wail echoed through the forest. Running to her maid, Bliss knelt. "Oh, Mercy!" she whispered, tears streaming down her cheeks.

In her horror, her grief, Bliss did not hear the

highwayman's approach. She did not look up in
time to see him raise his arm. She scarcely felt
the pain as the pistol butt descended against her
skull and rendered her unconscious.

Chapter 32

Bliss awoke slowly, her head throbbing. She tried to sit up but the pain in her head took her breath away.

Where was she? she wondered. What had happened? The last thing she remembered—

Mercy! Bliss's eyes filled with tears. The highwayman had shot Mercy. He had murdered the girl in cold blood, and for what? For trying to protect her mistress from a villain who meant to take her prisoner.

And he had done just that, Bliss reflected, forcing herself to banish the thought of Mercy from her mind long enough to assess her surroundings.

The room around her was small, simply furnished, a cottage by the looks of it. Doubtless they were hidden deep in the forest where the searchers Sir Basil would undoubtedly send to look for her would be hard put to find her.

There was a sliver of light beneath the door. She could hear muffled voices—a man's and a woman's—behind the door.

Gingerly standing, Bliss left the narrow bed and went to the door. Pressing her ear against it, she heard the woman say:

"You should not have killed them!"

The man replied:

"It was the only way. The coachman came at me, and that maid—she was a little hellcat, determined to protect her mistress."

"But now," the woman pointed out, "it will be more than kidnapping. It will be murder!"

"With no witnesses?" the man asked.

"Bliss! Bliss is a witness!"

The confrontation went on, but Bliss heard little of it. She was shocked, stunned. She knew those voices only too well. Without a thought for the possible consequences, she threw open the door.

"Letitia!" she snarled, glaring at the girl who stood before the fireplace.

Letitia Villiers turned toward her. "So, you're awake. I had begun to worry that Angus had hit you too hard."

"As if it would matter to you," Bliss hissed.

"It would matter a great deal," Letitia contradicted.

"The lives of my coachman and my maid did not matter."

"True enough," Letitia allowed, "but they interfered. They should not have."

"What is all this about?" Bliss demanded. "Vengeance over your brother?"

"Not entirely. You owe me something, Bliss, and I mean to have it."

"Owe you?" Bliss stared at the girl. "What do I owe you?"

"Gold. You promised me enough gold to allow me to marry Angus."

Bliss felt sick. "Is that what all this is about? My God! You've killed two innocent people over this . . . this . . ." She waved a hand toward Angus Cameron who stood on the other side of the room.

"You promised!" Letitia cried.

"That was before Stephen died," Bliss reminded her. "That was when we were going to be sisters. Now I will have no more to do with your family!"

"Before Stephen died," Letitia murmured. "And how did he die? He was murdered! By your lover!"

"The duel was Stephen's doing," Bliss snapped. "Kit was only defending himself."

"Liar!" Letitia cried.

"Kit was pardoned by the King and—"

"And why was he pardoned?" Letitia interrupted. "Because Castlemaine and Buckingham forced my mother to ask for it!"

"Why should they do that?" Bliss asked, skeptical.

"The King went to Barbara," Letitia told her, repeating the story that Barbara's footman had told Lady Daphne's maid, "and told her that if Kit were hanged he would 'comfort' you, as he put it. Barbara was afraid he would put you in her place."

"But he must have known I would never—" Bliss began, then stopped. Of course the King had known she would not become his mistress, even if Kit had been hanged. But he had known his mistress well enough to know that Barbara would believe he might. And her insecurity was enough to make her fall into his trap.

In spite of herself, Bliss laughed. Letitia moved toward her, fists clenched.

"Do you think it's funny?" she demanded. "An innocent man murdered? A guilty man set free? A promise—your promise—broken?"

"All right, Letitia," Bliss said, weary, her head pounding. "What do you want of me? Do you intend to keep me here until I promise to give you the gold you want? All right, I promise. Now let me go."

"Oh, no, I'm not that foolish," Letitia snapped. "I know you don't control your fortune. Sir Basil holds your purse strings."

"Then why didn't you kidnap Sir Basil?" Bliss asked sarcastically.

"We're going to hold you," Angus Cameron spoke up. "We're going to write to Sir Basil and ask for a ransom."

"What makes you think he will pay it?" Bliss demanded.

"He'll pay it," Leitita said confidently. "Surely he'll want you back. You are very valuable to him."

"You're mad," Bliss told them. "Both of you."

Angus and Letitia exchanged a look. Bliss saw she would have no choice but to let them play out this charade, and hope that help would find her before their schemes took an even more murderous turn.

Even as Bliss retired to her room in the cottage, a light rain began to fall. On the road, on the spot where Bliss had been abducted, Mercy stirred. Weakly she brushed away the raindrops that spattered her pale face.

She felt dizzy, confused. Turning her head, she saw the body of the coachman lying nearby. The memories flooded her mind . . .

"Milady!" she whispered. Pushing herself up, she looked around. The coach was gone. Bliss was gone. The highwayman had taken her, damnation take his foul soul!

Trying to rise, Mercy gasped at the pain in her left shoulder. The flesh was torn, angry red, caked with blood that matted her hair and stiffened her gown. She did not know what damage the highwayman's shot might have done. At that moment she did not care. She had only one thought—she had to reach Chatham and let them know what had happened to Bliss.

Slowly, painfully, she pushed herself to her feet, only to stagger and fall. She had no strength, and her head reeled with the effort to stand. But still she tried. At last she made it, balancing herself, taking first one, then another wobbling step. The rain, falling lightly, cooled her feverish brow. She leaned back her head and felt the cool water trickle down her throat.

It was dark and the moonlight danced in dappled patterns on the road ahead. Mercy forced herself to go on. She would reach Chatham, she vowed. She would get help for her mistress, or she would die trying.

Chapter 33

Sir Basil stepped down from his coach in the courtyard of Chatham Castle. His hollow-cheeked face was fixed in a sour grimace as he looked up at the stone edifice. Damn Bliss! he thought not for the first time. If he thought he could get away with it, he would beat the little chit senseless.

It was not until Bliss was well away from London that Sir Basil had heard of Kit's escape from the Tower. He had allowed the girl to leave for Chatham believing de Wilde safely locked up. And then to discover that not only was he free but that Bliss had known of his escape before she'd even asked permission to go to Chatham . . . When he had purchased the girl's guardianship he had never imagined it would be such a frustrating, maddening business. If he ever became guardian to another well-born orphan, he'd damned certain make sure she was a meek, biddable creature who would keep her mouth shut and do as she was told!

Determined to put the troublesome girl in her place once and for all, Sir Basil stormed up the steps past the footmen who had hurriedly opened the door and come out to fetch their master's baggage.

"My lord!" Fanshawe, the butler, scurried into the entrance hall. "We had no word! We were not expecting—"

"Bother what you were expecting!" Sir Basil snarled. "Have Lady Bliss brought to the drawing room immediately!"

"Lady Bliss?" Fanshawe asked. "I do not understand, my lord."

"Lady Bliss!" Sir Basil snarled. "Have you lost what few wits you ever possessed? Have my ward brought to me at once!"

"But, my lord, she is not here."

"Not here?"

"No, my lord." The butler began to wring his hands. "Oh dear, then you did not get the message."

"Message? What message?"

"It must have reached London after your lordship had left." Fanshawe turned mournful eyes on his master. "My Lady Bliss did not reach Chatham Castle, my lord."

"What!" Sir Basil's face flushed scarlet. "She ran off, didn't she, with that bastard de Wilde?"

"No, my lord!" the butler insisted.

"Damnation take them both!" Sir Basil blustered, not listening to his servant. "I'll hunt them down if it is the last thing—"

"My lord! My lord!" Fanshawe cried. "Lady Bliss has been captured. She has been seized by brigands."

"I'll have de Wilde sent back to the Tower!" Sir Basil raged. "Damme if I won't!"

"My lord!" Fanshawe shrieked at last.

"Well? What is it?" Sir Basil snarled.

"I am trying to tell you, my lord, that milady Bliss has been abducted!"

"Abducted? Explain yourself!" Sir Basil demanded.

"Lady Bliss's maid, Mercy, appeared at her parents' cottage in the village, milord. She'd been shot. It was a miracle she was not dead. She said Lady Bliss's coach had been stopped by a highwayman—"

"Likely de Wilde up to his old tricks," Sir Basil muttered.

"No, milord, it wasn't. This brigand shot the coachman when he tried to protect her ladyship. The coachman is dead. Then, when Mercy tried to help, he shot her as well. When she awoke, Mercy says the coach—and Lady Bliss—were missing."

"Missing . . ." The breath seemed to have left Sir Basil's body. "And there's been no word from her? From her abductor?"

Fanshawe shook his head. "None, my lord. I sent word to you in London. I had hoped the villains had contacted you."

"No, I'd heard nothing," Sir Basil admitted. "Where is Mercy now?"

"In the village, milord, with her family."

"Tell the coachman not to stable the horses. I'm going to see her."

Sir Basil's presence seemed to dwarf the small, cozy cottage where Mercy's family dwelt. He stood over Mercy, who lay in a narrow bed, pale and weak from her ordeal. Her mother hovered over her, too concerned for her daughter's health to be awed by the presence of Lord Holme in her home.

"Tell me exactly what happened," he told Mercy, his voice softer than she had ever heard it.

Haltingly, pausing often to rest, Mercy related the tale she'd already told both her family and Fanshawe, who had come when word of Mercy's dramatic arrival—and Bliss's disappearance—had reached the castle.

"When I woke up," the girl finished, sniffling, her eyes awash with tears, "milady was gone. The highwayman had taken her. I should have saved her," she whispered. "I should have—"

"You did everything you could," Sir Basil assured her. "You nearly gave your life for your mistress. No one could have expected you to overpower an armed man. Rest now."

Turning from the bed, Sir Basil walked to the door. He stopped just inside it and said to Mercy's mother:

"If she needs anything, send someone to the castle for it."

The older woman curtsied. "Aye, milord," she agreed.

She watched as the Baron left and went to his horse tethered outside. Imagine! A lord. In her home! And very nice he'd been, too, though of course not as kind as Lord de Wilde.

Mercy's mother went back to her daughter's side and sat beside the bed. Stroking her daughter's forehead, she tried to quiet her when the girl opened her mouth to speak.

"Hush now, pet," she said softly. "Ye've nothing more to say that can't wait awhile. Rest."

"Milord," Mercy croaked. "Milord, he—"

"He's gone, sweeting, back to the castle," her mother assured her.

"No." Mercy shook her head though the motion pained her. "Milord de Wilde. He must know—"

"He will," her mother promised. "Isaac will tell him. Never fear, sweeting, milord will find his lady even if no one else can."

Satisfied that her mother must be right, Mercy lay back against the pillows and fell asleep.

The ransom demand arrived at Chatham Castle late the following day. It had been sent to Sir

Basil in London, passing him as he made his way to the castle. Arriving at Barthorp House, it was sent back to Kent, to Chatham.

"Ten thousand pounds," Sir Basil muttered, crumpling the letter in his hand. "The varlets want ten thousand pounds or they say they will kill Bliss."

"Monsters!" Fanshawe breathed. "Vile, unspeakable monsters!"

"Aye," Lord Holme agreed absently. "Monsters indeed."

Leaning back in his chair, Sir Basil pondered the matter. Ten thousand pounds, while an enormous amount of gold, was a sum Bliss could easily afford. He could send a draft to Bliss's London goldsmith and have the gold at Chatham within a few days. The ransom demand instructed him to have the gold left at the ruins of an old church some miles distant. Once it was picked up, Bliss would be freed. A message would be sent to Chatham telling them where to find her.

But would she be unharmed? Sir Basil wondered if the kidnappers might not simply take the gold and kill Bliss to keep her from describing them. Certainly they would be foolish to let her live. And then what would he have accomplished by paying the ransom?

And what, he wondered, would happen if Bliss were murdered? She was the last of her family —she had no near relations on either her mother's or her father's side. Her fortune, her properties, would revert to the Crown—and the King would be very happy to have them, too, Sir Basil thought with a sour smile.

But might not Charles be persuaded to grant some small part of Bliss's fortune to her bereaved guardian?

It was a tantalizing prospect and one that, for the moment at least, made Sir Basil hesitate in sending out search parties to find the lair of the brigands who had kidnapped Bliss and now threatened her life.

The beating he had suffered at the hands of Sir Basil's lackeys had left Isaac with a limp and a permanent ringing in his ears that did not seem to diminish as time went by and his less serious injuries healed.

He had left Chatham Castle after the beating and gone to live in the little cottage in the forest that Kit had occupied after leaving the castle tower.

He'd been stunned when Kit had arrived, fresh from his escape from the Tower. He'd listened while Kit told him of his elopement with Bliss, their all-too-brief stay at Barthorp Hall. Kit told Isaac of returning to the hall after he'd come to visit the injured groom and of being told that Bliss had gone back to London with Sir Basil and Stephen. He told his old friend of following Bliss back to London, of dueling with Stephen, of being sent to the Tower on a charge of murder. Lastly, he told of his escape and how he had made his way back to the cottage, where he thought he would be safe until he found a way to prove his innocence.

The story had astonished Isaac—and saddened him. He believed with all his heart that Kit and Bliss were meant to be together, but now—with Kit a fugitive—how could they live in peace?

It was when Isaac had gone to the village that he heard about Mercy's being shot. Overhearing two men talking about Lord Holme's visit to Mercy's family's cottage, Isaac asked why he'd been there.

"Do ye not know?" the man asked. "Young Mercy's there. Shot she was. By a highwayman."

"Shot! Will she live?"

"Oh, aye, they say so."

"Why was she coming to Chatham?" Isaac wanted to know.

"Comin' with her ladyship, so they say. Ye do know 'bout her ladyship, don't ye?"

Isaac shook his head. "What about her?"

The two men exchanged a curious look. "Ye've been in them woods too long, man. She's been taken by brigands! Holdin' her for ransom, they are."

"Ransom!" Isaac felt the blood draining from his face.

"Aye! His lordship's at the castle. The villains sent 'im a note askin' for ten thousand pounds. They'll kill 'er, 'er ladyship, if the gold's not paid."

"Has anyone been sent out to look for her?" Isaac asked. "Surely Lord Holme has sent out search parties."

The men shrugged. "Haven't seen no one. Haply he'll pay the gold and be done with it."

Isaac murmured an agreement, but privately he could not imagine Sir Basil Holme simply turning ten thousand pounds over to anyone— not even ten thousand pounds of Bliss's gold.

Leaving the men, Isaac went to visit Mercy. The maid's mother admitted him, saying:

"'Tis hard for her to sleep, poor lamb. She's in such pain."

Isaac approached the bed, and Mercy smiled weakly. "How are you, my girl?" he asked, sitting in the chair at the bedside.

"Well enough," she managed. Reaching out, she caught Isaac's hand. "Milord de Wilde! Do you know where he is?"

Isaac cast a sideways glance at Mercy's mother. Like all the villagers in Chatham, she would protect Kit. "Aye," he admitted. "I do."

"Tell him," she urged. "Tell him what's happened to milady."

"I will," Isaac promised. "I should go now," he said, sensing that she was becoming too upset and it would do her no good.

"Wait!" Mercy cried, struggling to rise. "Wait! Tell him . . ." She gasped, falling back onto her pillows.

"Aye, tell him what?" Isaac wanted to know.

"Tell him milady was coming to Chatham to

find him—that she had come to bring him his pardon."

"Pardon?" Isaac looked at Mercy's mother, but the woman only shrugged.

"The King pardoned him. He gave the pardon to milady when he told her milord had escaped from the Tower. I was there when he gave it to her," she added, a note of pride in her voice.

Her tongue flicked out to wet her lips and her mother immediately brought her a cup of water.

"Tell him," Mercy urged after she'd taken a sip of the water.

"I will," Isaac assured her, eager to get back to the cottage and let Kit know he was no longer a fugitive. "I will!"

Leaving the cottage, Isaac forgot the errands that had brought him to the village. He hurried back to Kit and repeated everything he had heard.

"Pardoned!" Kit breathed. "Thank God! But why would the King pardon me? Surely the Villierses have not had a change of heart."

"It is a mystery," Isaac agreed. "But a welcome one."

"Welcome indeed," Kit agreed. "But what of Bliss? Basil Holme has not sent out search parties? Is he doing nothing to save her?"

Isaac shook his head. "They say in the village that the kidnappers are asking for ten thousand pounds."

Kit laughed wryly. "Basil Holme would as soon part with his left leg as ten thousand pounds. What can he be about, lagging this way? He'll wait too long, and who will pay for it? Bliss!

"It could be that is what he's hopin' for," Isaac murmured.

Kit stared at him, appalled. "Even Holme could not be so ruthless."

"Doubtless yer right," Isaac agreed.

But the thought was planted in Kit's mind, and the more he thought of it, the more dire the possibilities seemed.

"Do you think Mercy could bear to answer any more questions?" he asked.

Isaac nodded. "She'll do anything to help her ladyship."

"Then I'll go and speak with her. Perhaps she can remember more details than she told Lord Holme."

Pulling on his coat, Kit started for the door. "Don't worry, Isaac," he said. "If Bliss can be found alive and well, I'll find her."

Isaac nodded. He had every confidence in Kit, but he could not help wondering if he would ever see Bliss again.

Chapter 34

Kit sat beside Mercy's bed, her hand held in his. His smile was soft, reassuring, his voice low and gentle.

"I want you to describe the highwayman to me, Mercy," he said. "Think about it. Tell me what he looked like, what he sounded like, how tall he was. Anything you can remember. Perhaps I knew him when I was a highwayman."

"Oh, no, milord," the maid replied. "He wasn't a highwayman. He was a gentleman."

"A gentleman? What do you mean? He seemed educated? Cultured?"

"Well." The girl frowned. "I've been thinking about it ever so hard. At the time I was so scared, I did not even notice. But now that I recall it . . ."

"He looked like someone you knew?" Kit prompted when she remained silent.

"No, milord, I did not see his face. He wore a mask that covered him to the eyes. It was his voice. I'd heard it before." She shook her head. "I racked my brains trying to remember where. And I think I have remembered."

"Where did you hear it?" Kit asked eagerly. "Was it someone from here? From Chatham. Or in Yorkshire, perhaps?"

"No, milord. It was in London. It was the gentleman who made milady go to the hanging."

"The hanging?" Kit looked at Mercy's mother, but the woman only shrugged.

"Aye," Mercy went on. "In London. One day, Milord Villiers and his sister came to take milady to a play. She asked me to go as well. At the playhouse, a gentleman came and joined us. He wanted to go to the hanging on Tyburn. A highwayman, it was. Milady was so upset."

"And the gentleman," Kit persisted. "His name?"

Mercy sighed. "I can't remember it, milord. But he was Milord Villiers' sister's beau."

"The Scotsman? Cameron?"

"Aye!" Mercy's face lit with relief. "That's it, milord. Lord Cameron! Lord Villiers' sister went on and on at milady about how after milady and Lord Villiers were married, milady was to give her enough money to let her marry her gentleman."

"Oh, Lord," Kit sighed. "So that's what it is!" He looked at Mercy. "Letitia had planned on Bliss's giving her enough money to let her marry Cameron. Then Stephen died, so the wedding would not take place. And Letitia would not get her money. Now, Letitia is determined to get the gold."

"Lord Cameron and Mistress Villiers have taken milady!" Mercy breathed.

"So it would seem," Kit murmured. Bending down, he kissed Mercy gently on the forehead. "You're a good girl, Mercy, a brave girl. Rest now, and get well."

Kit rose and Mercy called to him. "My lord?" She bit her lip when Kit looked back at her. "You won't let them hurt her, will you?"

"I won't," Kit promised, though he did not feel nearly as confident as he sounded. "I'm going back to the place where Bliss was taken and I'm going to try and find her."

Mercy lay back on her pillows feeling better than she had since she'd been shot and Bliss kidnapped. Kit would find Bliss, she was certain of it. He would find her and save her. And they would be happy together again as they had been so briefly at Barthorp Hall before Kit had gone away and Sir Basil and Lord Villiers had come for Bliss.

In the main room of the little stone cottage in the forest, Letitia Villiers paced the tiny floor, nearly tripping over Angus's feet each time she passed.

"There should have been some word by now," she hissed. "Are you certain the ransom demand reached him?"

"Aye," Angus confirmed. "The servants at Barthorp House in London say it got there after he'd left for Chatham. They sent it on and it reached him the next day."

"Then why hasn't he done anything?" Going to the bedroom door, Letitia threw it open. "Bliss!"

Bliss looked up from the book she'd been reading. "What is it now, Letitia?" she asked, bored.

"We sent our demand to your guardian. He hasn't done a thing! He can order your goldsmith to deliver ten thousand pounds to Chatham, can't he?"

"Ten thousand pounds!" Bliss laughed. "He's never going to hand you ten thousand pounds, Letitia. You've no idea what a skinflint Sir Basil is. Did you threaten to kill me if he doesn't pay the ransom?"

"Aye," Letitia admitted. "We did."

"Doubtless Sir Basil has been too busy trying to decide who would inherit my fortune if I died to do anything about the ransom."

Letitia glared at Bliss, then slammed the door shut once more.

"That woman infuriates me," she snarled to Angus.

The Scottish lord leaned back in his chair. "He's not going to pay us the ransom," he told Letitia, voicing the suspicion he'd held for days.

"He has to!" Letitia insisted, paling.

"He's not going to." Angus rose, kicking back the chair he'd been sitting in. "What are we going to do, Letitia? We've kidnapped a young woman who is not only a great heiress, she is a woman the King likes. Desires. Do you think he is going to pardon us as easily as he pardoned de Wilde?"

"De Wilde!" Letitia spat. "This is all his fault! If he had not killed my brother—"

"If your brother had been a better swordsman," Angus snarled, "he would not have died."

"You will not speak of Stephen that way!" Letitia snapped.

"And you will not speak to me that way!" Angus growled. "I tire of your tantrums, Letitia. I will not have a wife who screams like a fishwife!"

He stormed out the door and Letitia scurried after him, catching him by the arm before he could reach his horse.

"I'm sorry, Angus," she whimpered meekly. "Forgive me. I did not mean to sound like a harpy."

Angus looked down at her and wondered what madness had ever possessed him to let her talk him into this scheme.

"It's not going to work," he told her quietly. "You know that, don't you? Holme is not going to pay the ransom."

"I know," Letitia admitted. "Damn the man!"

"We should leave, get out of here before someone finds us. We could go to Scotland. My estates there—"

"Scotland?" Letitia was horrified. "Go to live in the wilds of Scotland?"

"It's not the end of the earth," Angus pointed out defensively. "We surely cannot stay in England! Once Bliss is freed she'll tell everyone who it was who killed her coachman and her maid—who kidnapped her. Our lives won't be worth a tuppence's purchase."

"She won't tell if she cannot," Letitia pointed out.

"What is that supposed to mean?" Angus demanded impatiently.

"She can't tell anyone who kidnapped her—if she's dead."

"Dead!" Angus stared at her. "You are mad!"

"It's our only chance," Letitia persisted. "If Bliss is dead, who can prove who kidnapped her?"

"I don't like it," Angus hedged. "There's been enough killing. And for what?"

"We haven't any choice," Letitia went on. "We could make it look like an accident. That way, if we are connected to it, we could say we freed her but there was a tragic accident on the way back to Chatham."

"I don't know." Angus shook his head. "Let me think about it."

"All right," Letitia agreed. "But don't wait too long."

That night in her bed, Bliss lay staring into the darkness thinking of Kit. Was he at Chatham? she wondered. Did he know what had happened to her? Did he know that he'd been pardoned? That he was free?

She turned on her side wishing this farce was over, wishing she were at Chatham where she could find Kit and tell him the nightmare was over.

She went to sleep thinking of Kit, and her dreams centered around him. He was there, handsome, loving. She saw him in a hundred moods, a thousand settings. She heard his voice, felt his touch.

She sighed as Kit kissed her, his lips gentle on her temple, her cheeks, her lips. She parted her lips to receive his kiss and trembled at the touch of his hand on her thigh beneath the light chemise.

His touches grew bolder, his kisses more demanding; she felt his weight upon her as his body pressed hers down into the straw tick on the bed.

Bliss started, waking. This was no dream! she realized, shocked. This was real! But it wasn't Kit.

"No!" she cried, struggling beneath the man who held her, the man who even then tried to possess her.

NIGHTRIDER

A hand clamped over her mouth. "Be quiet, you little fool," Angus Cameron snarled. "Do you want to awaken Letitia?"

Bliss stared at him. Of course she wanted to awaken Letitia! How else was the foolish girl supposed to know that her fiancé was trying to ravish their victim?

She struggled, but Angus's weight held her down. His blue eyes glittered as he scowled down at her.

"Listen to me," he growled. "I'm trying to help you."

Bliss's eyesbrows arched. If Angus Cameron was trying to help anyone, it seemed to her, he was trying to help himself.

"You are in danger," he told her. "Your life is at stake. But I can help you. If I take my hand from your mouth, will you be quiet and listen?"

Bliss nodded, and the hand was lifted. Gasping, she pushed up against him. "Will you get off me, please?" she asked impatiently.

Reluctantly, Angus did as she asked. He sat on the edge of the bed, one hand clamped on her wrist.

"Letitia believes your guardian will not pay the ransom," Angus told her.

"I should have been surprised if he had," Bliss told him frankly.

"She does not want us to be punished for your kidnapping. Nor for the deaths of your maid and your coachman."

Bliss closed her eyes trying hard not to see the

409

image of Mercy and the coachman lying in the road.

"How can you think you would not be punished?" Bliss asked.

Angus hesitated. "She means for there to be no witnesses," he said quietly.

"She means to kill me," Bliss breathed, shivering.

"Aye," Angus confirmed. "She means you to die so that you cannot tell anyone who did this."

Bliss drew a ragged breath. "She's mad," she said quietly. She looked into Angus's eyes. "And do you agree with her? Are you willing to kill me for her?"

"I do not want to kill you," Angus said.

"Then set me free," Bliss asked. "Let me go. Now. By morning I could be back at Chatham."

"And by nightfall I would be in the Tower," Angus murmured.

Bliss sighed. "Why do you tell me this?" she asked. "If you are determined to kill me—"

"I did not say that," Angus corrected. "I am willing to bargain with you for your life."

"Go on," Bliss told him.

"Very well. I will tell Letitia I am taking you out to kill you. You and I will ride away from here. I will free you on the road to Chatham and ride away. You will go on to Chatham. You will wait one day before you tell them where this cottage is. By then I will be well on my way to the Continent."

"So you will be safely on your way to France or Holland before anyone comes looking for you. Is that it?"

"That is it," Angus agreed.

"And Letitia? What will happen to her when they come for you and find her here?"

Angus shrugged. "She is mad—and she is a Villiers. At the worst she will be given to her mother and confined in the country."

Bliss laughed wryly. "You've given this a great deal of thought, haven't you?"

"I have," he admitted. "Tell me now, do you agree?"

"Not yet," Bliss told him. "You haven't told me what you will expect from me in return for so generously sparing my life."

Angus's eyes glimmered. His hand left her wrist and fell onto the smooth, soft flesh of her thigh. "I think you can guess," he said softly.

"My God!" Bliss hissed. "You don't really expect me to lie with you, do you?"

Angus smirked. "And why not? You were de Wilde's lover—"

"I was his wife!" Bliss corrected.

"For a moment or two," Angus admitted. "You were betrothed to Stephen. Don't try to tell me you didn't lie with him. And the King—he did not pardon Kit out of the kindness of his heart."

"The Villierses convinced him to pardon Kit," Bliss told him.

"If you wish. Enough of this. Are you willing to bargain?"

Eyes narrowed, Bliss slapped his hand away from her leg. "I'd rather die than lie with a miserable bastard like you," she snarled.

Anger glittered in Angus's blue eyes. His face was flushed as he rose from the bed. "The decision was yours," he said tightly. "You will not live long enough to regret it!"

Turning on his heel, Angus went out, leaving Bliss to stare after him, a sick feeling of dread and fear in her stomach. The thought of letting Angus Cameron touch her sickened her, but the thought of dying filled her with fear. She looked around the room. There were no windows. The only exit was the door through which Angus had just left. And Bliss knew he and Letitia slept on a trundle bed in the room beyond. There was no escape.

In the other room, Letitia pushed herself up on her elbow. "Angus?" she said, seeing him standing near the window gazing out into the darkness. "Why don't you come to bed?"

"I was just thinking," he told her, turning away from the window. "It may be that you are right after all."

"Right about what?" Letitia asked, her head foggy with sleep.

Angus came and sat beside her on the bed. "Right about Bliss," he said. "I think it would be a mistake to let her live."

Letitia's smile seemed feral, like a she-wolf

who senses she has her prey exactly where she wants it.

"I think you're right," she cooed. "And the sooner the better. Tomorrow?"

Grimly, Angus nodded. "Tomorrow," he agreed, and, pulling off his clothes, slid into the bed beside her.

Chapter 35

"**G**ood morning, Bliss," Letitia said as she entered Bliss's room. "Did you sleep well?"

"Very well," Bliss thought, adding to herself: once I managed to get your lover to leave me alone!

"I've brought you your breakfast."

Bliss eyed the dish with trepidation. Letitia was no cook and everything she'd brought her so far was either underdone or burned.

This morning it was two pieces of doughy bread slathered with what looked like old butter. A glass of wine stood beside the dish.

"Thank you, Letitia," Bliss said dutifully. "Will you help lace my gown before you go?"

"Of course." Letitia picked up Bliss's rumpled gown and helped Bliss settle it in place. Standing behind her, Letitia laced up the back and tied it for her.

"Enjoy your breakfast," Letitia said, smiling as she left the room.

Bliss gazed after her thoughtfully. Why was she being so pleasant, Bliss wondered. What had happened to put her in such a good mood? Surely Sir Basil had not actually paid the ransom.

She eyed her breakfast with distaste. The bread and whatever covered it was inedible. Perhaps the wine would be palatable and would still the pangs of hunger in her empty stomach.

She sipped the wine absently, wondering what Letitia could be so happy about. Letitia, she knew, was happiest when making others miserable. So what unfortunate thing could have happened to brighten her day?

She was still pondering the matter when the first wave of dizziness struck her. Head reeling, she tried to stand. The room swayed before her eyes, and she sat down heavily on the bed.

"Letitia?" Bliss called, her voice sounding strangely distant in her ears. "Letitia!"

The door opened and Letitia stood there, smiling, her lips pulled back over her teeth in a smirking grimace. Angus Cameron appeared behind her, his expression less pleased but no less grim.

"Feeling giddy?" Letitia asked, her voice a mocking purr.

"What have you done to me?" Bliss demanded. "It was in the wine, wasn't it?"

"Aye," Letitia admitted. "It was."

"Poison, by God! You murderer!" Bliss fought the darkness that was engulfing her. She was dying, she was sure.

"It's not poison," Letitia corrected. "It will not kill you. It will only render you unconscious."

"Why? Letitia, why?" Bliss gasped.

"So that when Angus kills you," she replied, a chilling laughter in her voice, "you won't feel a thing."

Bliss slid helplessly into the abyss that yawned for her. Her last thought was of Kit—of the days and nights they would not spend together, of the years she had thought they had ahead of them, of the joys, the pleasures they would not share.

Angus stepped around Letitia as Bliss collapsed onto the bed. Gathering her into his arms, he carried her out to the coach, Bliss's coach, that stood waiting behind the cottage.

"Take care," Letitia cautioned as Angus laid Bliss on the seat and closed the door. "Come back safely, my darling, so we can leave for Scotland."

"Aye," Angus agreed. Bending, he kissed Letitia quickly, as if eager to be done with it. "Wait here for me," he instructed.

Climbing onto the box, Angus slapped the reins and the coach rolled away, following the twin-rutted path that curved away from the main road, through the forest, and back again, joining the road on the opposite side of Chatham village.

Angus cast a last look at Letitia as the coach disappeared into the forest. He never intended to see her again. He would dispose of Bliss—a pity, that, for the girl was truly beautiful—then go on to the coast, to France, to safety. By the time Bliss's body was found, by the time the searchers found the cottage and Letitia, he would be safely aboard the packet bound for freedom.

Even as Angus was driving away, leaving his unsuspecting ladylove to face the consequences of Bliss's murder alone, Kit was standing in the road at the spot where Bliss's coach had been stopped, where her coachman had been murdered, where Mercy had been shot.

They had taken the coach, Kit remembered. That meant they had either followed the main road or taken the faint, two-track path scarcely visible in a narrow gap in the trees. Since the main road led to Chatham Castle and the village beyond, it stood to reason that the bandit must have driven Bliss's coach on the narrow track.

Mounting his horse, Kit rode into the forest, sure he was getting closer to recovering Bliss from the clutches of Letitia and her lover.

He saw the cottage through the trees long before he reached it. It was old, ramshackle, the thatched roof ragged, the stone walls crumbling. But smoke rose from the chimney. Kit felt excitement rising inside him.

As he rode up to the door, it opened and
Letitia Villiers appeared. Her green eyes narrowed with hatred when she saw him.

"You!" she hissed. "What do you want here,
murderer?"

"You know what I've come for," Kit growled.
"Where is Bliss?"

"You killed my brother!" she shrieked. "You
should have been hanged!"

"Where is she?" Kit demanded.

A hideous smile parted Letitia's lips. "You'll
find out in due time," she smirked. "When it's
too late! Then you'll know how it feels to lose
someone you love."

"Damn you!" Kit snarled. Swinging down
from his horse, Kit went after her.

With a shrill little scream, Letitia wheeled and
ran for the cottage. But Kit was faster. His hand
closed about her upper arm and jerked her
around.

"Tell me, damn you!" he snarled. "Where is
Bliss?"

"Dead," Letitia hissed. "She's dead. Angus
took her out this morning to kill her."

"Where?" Kit repeated, shaking her until her
curls bounced on her shoulders.

"You don't have to worry, though," Letitia
assured him. "She won't feel a thing." She
giggled. "We put the potion in her wine."

"Where is she?" Kit bellowed, wanting nothing more than to wrap his fingers about the girl's

scrawny neck and squeeze the life from her.

Letitia pointed down the narrow trail that swept past the cottage. "There," she answered vaguely. "Angus took her down there. But it's too late . . . by now she must be dead."

Shoving her away, Kit swung up into the saddle and kicked his horse into a gallop. As he rode away, Letitia's high, shrieking laughter echoed in his ears, raising the hairs on the back of his neck and sending a shiver of fear down his back.

The lane was narrow, the trees crowding it on either side. Kit was only too able to imagine Angus and Letitia's scheme.

He pictured Bliss lying unconscious in the coach. Cameron would be driving it at breakneck speed along this narrow lane. At the proper moment, he would leap from the box letting the horses run free. The coach would careen into the trees, and Bliss, helpless, would be killed.

When her body was found, it would seem as if her death had been accidental. Letitia and Cameron could still be held responsible for the kidnapping, but it would be hard to prove that the crash of the coach had not been accidental.

Unless, of course, Letitia admitted as much. Kit thought she might, particularly when she realized what seemed perfectly obvious to him —that Angus Cameron, scoundrel though he might be, was not such a fool as to return to Letitia, who was rapidly completing her final descent into madness.

The distant rumbling of coach wheels and the pounding of hooves made Kit's heart jolt in his chest. He kicked his horse into a faster gallop and rounded a sharp curve.

There! Ahead, swerving, narrowly missing the trees on either side, Bliss's coach rumbled through the forest. No one sat on the box—Cameron must already have made his leap for freedom. The reins dragged on the ground, trailing behind the speeding vehicle.

Using his own reins as a whip, Kit spurred his horse forward. It was only a matter of time, he knew, before the traces broke or the coach hit one of the trees that grew so close to the narrow trail.

There was no room, he knew, to ride up beside the coach. There was only one way he could try to stop it.

His horse strained beneath him, white foam from his lips flying back to spot Kit's breeches. The horse's slender legs were a blur as he strove to do his master's bidding.

Kit waited until the coach was only an arm's length away, then, dropping his horse's reins, he leaped from the animal's back onto the back of the coach where the lackeys rode.

His horse slowed, following at a growing distance, as Kit climbed gingerly atop the swaying vehicle. He longed to look inside, to see to Bliss, but knew that a moment's inattention could spell disaster for both Bliss and himself.

On hands and knees, Kit moved across the

roof of the speeding coach. It swayed and bounded, threatening at every bump, every curve in the road to throw him to his death among the trees bordering the lane.

Holding his breath, Kit climbed down onto the box. His heart was pounding so, he could scarcely breathe, but there was no time to rest, no time to think. The reins were trailing far below, on the ground, between the flying hooves of the four matched greys who ran, frightened, confused, heedless of the danger to themselves and Bliss. Their eyes rolled in their heads, foam flecked their muzzles and sides.

Kit steadied himself, poised, muscles tensed. The road ahead was fairly straight. God willing, the traces would hold together, the horses would not break free just yet.

Taking a deep breath, Kit launched himself off the box. He landed astride the back of one of the horses and clutched desperately at the harness as he began to fall down between the horses.

Balancing himself, Kit gathered the leather reins and pulled, dragging them back with all the strength left in him.

It seemed at first that the horses were too frightened, too wild, to respond, but then, as the coach neared a sharp turn, they began to slow. Tossing their heads, prancing in the traces, they responded to Kit's hands on the reins. The coach slowed as it approached the curve, ceased its swaying, and finally came to a halt scant yards from the spot where it almost certainly would have been destroyed and with it, Bliss.

Leaping off the horse, Kit ran to the door. He was almost afraid to open it. What if Bliss, unconscious, had been killed by the jouncing of the coach over the rough trail? What if all his effort, all his dangerous work, had been in vain?

He twisted the handle and threw open the door. Bliss was there, a tumbled pile of green silk and white lace on the floor of the coach.

"Bliss?" Kit pawed through the silk and lace trying to find her. "Bliss!"

Uncovering her face, he saw first the spattering of blood that marred her temple. Red splotches that would become angry bruises spotted her shoulders and arms. Holding her, Kit pressed his fingers into the tender flesh at the hollow of her throat. He held his breath waiting . . . waiting . . . And then he felt it, the faint but steady thumping of her pulse beneath the bruised flesh. She was alive.

Carefully, Kit lifted her out of the coach and took her to the side of the trail to lay her in the soft, cool grass. She was still unconscious, though whether from the potion Letitia had given her or the tumbling she'd taken in the coach he didn't know. All he knew was that she was alive—she was safe—and he would take her back to Chatham and safety before he went back to see to the capture of Letitia and her lover.

* * *

NIGHTRIDER

Bliss lay in the wide bed in her bedchamber in Chatham Castle. Her body was bruised, and an angry cut marred the soft pale flesh of her temple, but she was otherwise unhurt. She smiled as the door opened and Kit appeared.

"Here you are," she said, stretching out a hand to him. "I was wondering when you'd come and tell me the news. What of Letitia and Cameron? And what of Sir Basil? They say he has gone."

Kit sat on the side of the bed and took Bliss's hand in his own. Raising it to his lips, he kissed it, his dark eyes twinkling at her.

"Angus Cameron is dead," Kit told her. "His body was found in the forest. Apparently he broke his neck leaping from the coach."

"And Letitia?" Bliss asked. "Was she still at the cottage when you returned?"

"Aye." Kit nodded. "Still waiting for Angus to return. She's mad, Bliss, completely, hopelessly. Her mother has taken her into the country. She'll be kept at Villiers House in Derbyshire for the rest of her life."

Bliss nodded. "It was the fate that Angus forecast for her," she said softly. "And Sir Basil?"

"Sir Basil has gone," he told her. "He's fled to France. He was seen boarding the packet at Dover. He knew he would be disgraced for not trying to rescue you. He knew the King would punish him."

Bliss smiled at Kit. "So Sir Basil will no longer be my guardian," she pointed out. "That means I will be a ward of the Crown once more. Do you think we might persuade the King to allow us to marry?"

Kit laughed. "I think he might be persuaded. I think he just might."

Chapter 36

The festivities celebrating Bliss and Kit's marriage lasted far into the night. Inside the great hall of Chatham Castle toasts were drunk, the bride was kissed, the groom was sighed over by ladies, married and unmarried, who imagined themselves in Bliss's place.

Outside the castle, in the courtyard and in the park beyond, the villagers and tenant farmers who owed their loyalties to Chatham and its lord danced and drank the ale that flowed freely. Bonfires burned and songs were sung. There was much to celebrate, after all. Lady Bliss was safe and Kit, their Lord de Wilde, was in his rightful place as lord of Chatham Castle with the woman he loved at his side.

Sandra DuBay

At midnight Bliss and Kit came out to the cheers of the villagers. They walked among them, sharing their happiness, accepting their good wishes.

Bliss let herself be drawn into a circle of dancers ringing a bonfire. When the dance ended she found herself near Mercy. She looked around.

"Where is Kit?" she asked the maid, squinting toward the groups dancing and drinking.

"He's over there, milady," Mercy told her, pointing toward the edge of the forest. "He told me to tell you he has a surprise for you."

"A surprise?" Bliss looked toward the darkness, intrigued.

Leaving the revelers, Bliss walked into the darkness where the park gave way to the woods. The moonlight filtered through the trees, painting the forest in silver and blue.

It was the whinny of the horse that caught Bliss's attention. Turning toward it, she saw them, the tall roan stallion and the man, dressed in black, standing beside him. Tall and broad-shouldered, he wore a plumed hat pulled low over his eyes. A black cloak fell from his shoulders to the ground.

"Goodness!" Bliss cried, giggling. "A highwayman!"

"Will you come peacefully, milady," a low, velvety voice asked. "Or must I use force?"

"I must warn you, sir, my husband is a

very jealous man."

"As well he should be, sweetheart," the high-wayman countered, "married to a beauty like you. But come, the night is waning."

Swinging into the saddle, Kit rode up to Bliss. He leaned down and lifted her into the saddle before him. Kicking his horse into a gallop, they rode off through the forest.

"Where are we going?" Bliss asked.

"To the cottage," Kit replied. "We'll never be left in peace if we stay at the castle."

Together they rode through the night, Bliss cradled against him, his cloak billowing out behind them, borne on the wind. Bliss closed her eyes; it reminded her of the first night they'd met, the night Kit had stolen a kiss—and her heart.

A fire was burning in the hearth at the cottage when Kit and Bliss reached it. Bouquets of wildflowers had been placed about the single long, low chamber. The bed was made, with sheets bearing the arms of the Baron de Wilde worked into their lace trimming and the em-broidered petals of a hundred roses strewn across them. Wine and cheese sat waiting on the table with two fragile Venetian goblets.

"Who did all this?" Bliss wanted to know as Kit pulled off his hat and cloak and tossed them over a chair.

"Bess," Kit replied.

Bliss's eyes narrowed. "Bess! The blonde from

the village?" A picture of the girl and Kit flashed in her mind's eye. "You let that little—"

"She is Isaac's niece," Kit told her. "She cleaned for me and brought food to me from her mother."

"Nothing more?" Bliss asked suspiciously.

Kit laughed. "Nothing more, my jealous beauty. Come here, my Lady de Wilde. I have you alone, at last."

Bliss trembled as she felt Kit's fingers undoing the laces of her silver-tissue, jewel-encrusted gown. It slipped from her shoulders and down over her hips to fall in a glittering heap on the rough floorboards. Her chemise and petticoat followed.

She leaned back against Kit as he caressed her. The brocade of his coat was soft against her bare skin. Her head fell back and his lips grazed the tender flesh of her throat. She leaned against him, her passion firing his, her desire enhanced by the sound of his harsh, quickened breaths, by the trembling of his hands as they stroked the round softness of her breasts.

Kit lifted her, carried her to the bed, and lay her across it. He pulled off her shoes, leaving her clad in long, white silk stockings gartered with pearl-studded ribbons above her knees.

Bliss watched, enthralled, as Kit pulled off his own clothes. She held out her arms to him and he came to her, gathering her against him.

NIGHTRIDER

Searing, urgent passion drew them together. Every ache, every need that suffused Bliss's trembling body was mirrored in Kit's face. He covered her flesh with kisses as Bliss stirred beneath him, driving her to something akin to madness.

Bliss moaned softly, moving beneath the exquisite onslaught of his hands, his lips. In turn, Kit's body quivered with the need of her, tautened with desire for her. Fervently, adoringly, he stroked her, caressed her, his hands, his lips feasting on the incomparable beauty that was his lady, his love.

Bliss arched against him, wanting to feel more of his skin, his body, against hers. Her hands clutched at him, pulling him closer, closer. "Kit," she whispered, her hands on his shoulders, his arms, her fingers in his thick, dark hair, drawing him up to her, "now, Kit, please, now!"

Poised above her, Kit's dark, glittering eyes gazed down into the misted golden pools so wide in Bliss's face. The time had come, he knew, for him, for her. He drew her to him, his hard callused hands sliding up the long, satin-soft length of her thighs, parting them, slipping under her small, rounded buttocks, lifting her.

He took her, his body becoming one with hers, giving her his love, taking hers with a mounting urgency, a raw, primal passion.

Bliss gasped, arching against him as his body

possessed hers. She knew, as he loved her, as he took her to the heights of passion—of pleasure —that she belonged to him, her lord and master, her highwayman, her nightrider, forever . . .

HEART'S LAIR

A Futuristic Romance
By Kathleen Morgan

Author of *The Knowing Crystal*

THEY WERE AFTER HIM.

Karic knew it, though no sound stirred the deep forest quiet, no enemy scent intruded on the damp sweetness of leaf mulch and wild violets. He could *feel* them coming, a sixth sense as innate to a Cat Man as his lithe limbs and boundless stamina. This sense melded with a strong ability to cloak his presence from most humanoids, but little good it would do him since his trackers had nonhuman help.

They'd pursued Karic for horas now, but he'd easily outdistanced them, maintaining a comfortable lead. It gave him time for breathing space, which he wanted to spend in this sun-lit glade, near the water-splashed pool, watching her.

She was small, and her long black hair, glinting like dark glass in the sunlight, fell from a center part into soft cascades down her shoulders and back. She was ethereal. Serene. A fragile beauty.

Karic wanted her.

That decision had been quick, simple. His mission was twofold, one part of it being to bring home a breeding female of some humanoid species. Whether he chose to give her to one of the other young Cat Men, or to keep her for himself, was not the issue. Karic knew he'd take her for himself. The problem, rather, lay in the other part of his mission. For the first time in his life, Karic's sense of duty warred mightly with an equally strong sense of desire.

She did nothing to ease his conflict. In an infinitely sensual motion, the female slowly stretched her arms over her head, the soft mounds of her breasts straining against her thin blue shift. Then, before Karic could inhale another breath into his tightly constricted chest, she slipped the gown from her ivory shoulders.

It fluttered to the ground in a long, agonizing flow of cloth, and Karic thought he'd never breathe again. For what seemed an eternity of heart-stopping tension she stood there, exquisitely, unashamedly, naked. Then she strode into the pool.

Karic's breath returned with a painful shudder, followed swiftly by a hot, heavy tightening in his loins. Sweat beaded his brow, glistened on his powerful arms and chest. He watched her, his body little more than a quivering, knotted mass of muscles.

She was his. He had known that from the first instant he'd seen her. Yet, for the moment, he could do nothing about it. It was bitter reality, but Karic faced it.

His people needed him. Too long had they been at the mercy of the Bellatorian invaders, inhabitants of the distant warrior planet, Bellator. Too long had those greedy usurpers of Agrica's agricultural wealth been permitted free rein, his people the only resistors on the peace-fully bucolic planet. And now, even their rebellion could well be at an end, if his mission failed.

No, there was still too much to be done. First, he must seek out the mysterious weapon fearful tales spoke of, and ascertain the full extent of its powers. Then, and only then, could he return to her, take her home with him. . . .

An eerie baying wended its way through the peaceful forest. Karic and the female froze. It was the cry of the dreaded search canus, vi-ciously hot on a scent. His scent.

Karic disappeared as silently as he'd come. Time enough to return for the lovely female. For now, he must set his sights on the Bellatorian-held fortress of Primasedes, infiltrate its defenses—and find the horrible weapon said to lie within.

* * *

Shadows darkened the hall, the fading summer sun throwing dancing fingers of light through the tall arched windows of Primasedes. Necator tightened his grip on Liane's arm as he led her down the long corridor, explaining her latest assignment.

"We've captured an Agrican, a very special one. Our new alarm system worked beyond my wildest imaginings, catching one such as he. We finally have a live Cat Man to study." His grin widened into one of wolfish pleasure. "And you, my talented little Sententia, are going to read his mind."

Relief washed through Liane. "It's but my job, my lord. It will be as you wish."

"It may not be as easy as you think with this one."

"Not easy? But how is that possible? No one can resist a Sententian mind-seek."

"And how many Cat Men have you had the opportunity of using it on?"

Liane shrugged. "None. But they are of a humanoid species. Why should there be any problem?"

"Cat Men are only half humanoid. Their other half is pure animal. And they have purported psychic powers of their own. We know for certain they possess the ability to cloak their presence from most people. That's why, up until this moment, we've been unable to capture one alive. But our trackers were out today with their search canus and, when it became evident the

Cat Man was headed for Primasedes, we had enough time to turn on our new alarm system. Seems though they can slip past our guards without them knowing, these Cat Men have little effect on a machine. But then, he didn't even know of its existence until it was too late."

At the mention of the search canus, Liane involuntarily shuddered. She'd heard their baying today, as she bathed in the forest. What if that Cat Man had been nearby? What would have happened to her then? She'd heard tales, revolting tales, of their uncontrollable sexual urges.

Necator's grip tightened as they walked down the hall. "Listen closely to my instructions. I care little for the usual information you obtain from your mind-seeks. I want specific details on where the Cat Men's lair is. I have nearly succeeded in annihilating this odious race of Agricans. If you discover their lair. I can eliminate the final obstacle to our complete domination of this planet. The Cat Men are the last of the rebels."

"Will it bring peace to Agrica?"

The Lord Commander similed at Liane's naivete. "Of course, my little Sententia. And isn't that what we all want?"

He halted Liane in front of a door marked "ANALYSIS." A strange light flared in his eyes. "He's a hard one, this Cat Man. So far even our most sophisticated tortures have failed to elicit the whereabouts of his lair. Unless you can get it from him, I fear he'll die with the secret. Will you try your best for me?"

Liane forced a wan simile. "Of course, my lord. I am a loyal Bellatorian, after all."

Though Necator warned her the scene in the room might be gruesome, nothing he said could have prepared Liane for the sight that met her eyes. Until now all her experience, both as psychic healer and research scientist, had been directed toward compassion and healing, not cold objectivity and torture. It required all her strength for Liane to follow the Lord Commander across the cold, stone-tiled laboratory toward the Cat Man.

He hung there, stark naked, in the middle of the room, his wrists and ankles bound with beryllium manacles that electronically suspended him in a spread-eagled position. Two scientists worked on him, one drawing a blood specimen from a bulging forearm vein, while the other obtained a biopsy of skin off the Cat Man's thigh for further microscopic study. And all, Liane thought, without any consideration to his dignity or comfort.

She was nearly overcome with the urge to turn and run from the room. If it hadn't been for her Bellatorian sense of duty, she'd have immediately recanted her earlier agreement to involve herself in this study. That, more than even the fear for her life if she refused to cooperate, kept her there.

Liane comforted herself with the realization that her part in the study was painless. In fact, she could easily anesthesize the Cat Man temporarily when she finished with the mind-seek. For at least a few horas, he would be pain-free, no matter what they did to him. And no one would be the wiser.

The thought motivated her to action. She turned to Necator. "I need total silence and the lights dimmed for the mind-seek. And I must be alone with my subject."

Her companion's eyes narrowed. "Don't toy with me, femina."

She sighed in exasperation. "These requirements are not whim, my lord. The mind-seek is a delicate art. Other thought patterns can distract from capturing those of my subject. And you said this Cat Man might be a difficult subject. Would you make my task all the harder?"

"Just be sure you succeed," he growled. "My patience is wearing thin."

"Yes, my lord."

Liane watched as the room was cleared and the lights dimmed, except for the small circle of illumination around the Cat Man's suspended form. She stood there in the shadows for a short while, preparing herself, studying him.

He was not quite what she'd imagined a Cat Man to look like. He was young, in his late twenties, tall, his shoulders massive, his body tough and athletically muscular. On his finger-tips she noted the sites of retractable claws.

That much confirmed the few photo prints available of the elusive species. But he wasn't as hairy. Granted, there was crisp, dark gold fur-ring on his well-formed body, but no more so than on many Bellatorian males. And his sexual organ, Liane noted with a scientist's detach-ment as her eyes slid down his body, was quite the norm, if a trifle large.

His face, set off by a thick, unruly mane of sun-streaked brown hair that fell to his shoul-ders, was also a surprise. His sun-bronzed skin had little facial hair other than dark brows, lashes and the shadow of a beard. That aspect of his appearance was in direct contradiction to the prints, which had always depicted a copi-ous amount of hair extending far from the hairline on all sides.

Though his head was lowered in exhaustion, his eyes closed, Liane was still able to catch a glimpse of his rugged features. His nose was slightly flattened, his browline a little more pronounced, but it did little to detract from his good looks. Exotic species though he was, the Cat Man was still a virilely handsome man.

Liane could admit that from a purely scientif-ic viewpoint, trained as she was to make astute, totally objective observations. And she also knew, with the same keen sense of observation, that this was no pure-blooded Cat Man. Half-humanoid blood ran in his veins, evidence that one of his parents had definitely been human.

But that wasn't surprising, either. Many were the tales of Cat Men abducting human females, ever since the successful massacre at their forest lair over thirty cycles ago. A large contingent of the males had been away hunting, so the story went, when an armed Bellatorian force fell on the hapless lair.

To a man, woman and child, nearly all the Cat Men were slaughtered. Only a few managed to escape, to reach and warn the returning hunters. It was the last time the Cat Men made their lair in their beloved forest, choosing instead the cold, barren safety of the distant Serratus Mountains. And, determined to ensure the propagation of their species to carry on the unending war against the Bellatorian invaders, the Cat Men turned to other breeding females.

Harsh times necessitate harsh measures, Liane thought, *but to be forced to mate with someone against your will. . . .* With a small shudder, she directed her attention back to the subject at hand.

The Cat Man moved slightly in his shackles, as if trying to find some position to ease his discomfort. His bruised body glistened with a fine sheen of sweat. Bellatorian tortures, Liane knew, were highly effective in their ability to incite pain that went on for hours after the initial stimulus was applied. It was their simple beauty—and perversity.

But even their power could be measurably eased during the mind-seek. Liane stepped forward. She could do little for him, but she would do what she could. She moved until she was but a breath away from the Cat Man and gently took his drooping head in her hands.

His lids slowly opened and Liane found herself impaled by an intense pair of green-gold eyes. They were defiant yet, at the same time, probing, at if he needed something from her. She felt her resolve melting.

Liane jerked back in surprise. Well, Necator had warned her of the Cat Man's powers.

A weak smile tipped the Cat Man's mouth. "Do I frighten you?"

The rasp of his voice, harsh with pain, clawed down Liane's spine, setting her nerves on edge. Even now, without benefit of the mind-seek, she felt herself merging with him, assuming some of his pain. There was a strong psychic link which made her uneasy.

She shook her head, in an effort to shake off the strange feelings as well as to deny his question. "No."

He cocked a dark brow. "I don't believe you."

Anger welled in her at the absurdity of the situation. There he was, bound, weak from torture, about to have his deepest secrets wrenched from him, and he had effectively taken control. Well, pity could only go so far.

"I don't want your pity."

Liane sucked in an exasperated breath. It was obvious she'd have to guard her thoughts from him so she tightened her mental control.

Momentary confusion flickered in his striking green eyes. Then his smile widened. "Your powers are strong, when you care to use them. But are they stronger than mine?"

She smiled for the first time. It was easier to rise to a challenge than be weakened by compassion. "We shall soon see, won't we?"

Her fingers moved into positon on his temples and forehead.

"What's your name?"

His unexpected question both irritated and nonplussed her. "What?"

"Your name. If I'm to be mentally assaulted, I thought it only fair to know my assailant's name. My name's Karic."

"I don't care to know your name!" Liane hissed through clenched teeth. She closed her eyes and began to concentrate.

"Are you always such a heartless bitch?"

Liane's eyes snapped open. For the longest moment she just stared at him. He was clever. She did her best work when she was indifferent to the recipient of her mind-seek, yet in the course of just a few moments, he had managed to stir compassion and anger within her. It had to stop.

"Do not fight me," she intoned the ritualistic instructions, "and you will feel no pain. Follow where I lead and it will be over before you realize. . . ."

Even before he felt an insidious warmth flow into his mind, Karic knew he had lost the first skirmish and steeled himself for the far more important battle to come. He forced himself to relax his painfully tensed body, gathering all his strength where he would soon need it the most. He knew what she wanted. It could only be the same secret his other tormentors had so diligently endeavored to extract from him ever since they'd electronically overcome him inside the city gates. If only he'd known about the alarm system, about the incapacitating force field, he could have prepared, avoided them. But it was too late now.

He let her mind join with his, allowed her to flow through the layers of inconsequential thoughts and memories, delaying her with questions, attempting to distract. He caught the fleeting mention of her name before she clamped down on further replies, and used the sound of it to tease and tantalize her.

Ah, Liane, so beauteous, so heartless. Why do you hate me, hate my people, to seek so avidly our destruction? Karic mentally bombarded her. *They will kill us, wipe us from the face of this planet, if you reveal our hiding place. Is that what you wish?*

She heard it all and relentlessly forged on, ignoring, as best she could, the forceful images of the man, brave, strong and proud. Of his people and his deep, abiding love for them. It was almost too easy, his too generous permission to enter his mind, but she doggedly plummeted inward, toward the deepest recesses of his being. His secret would soon be hers.

In the next instant, Liane slammed into something so hard, so immovable, that it sent a psychic jolt through her body. The pain of impact made her gasp, and her eyes fluttered open to career with his. His eyes held her as she stood there, suddenly pressed against him. For what seemed the longest time, neither could think nor breathe.

Reality returned like the slow, sensuous movement of warmed honey. Heavy, sweet and thick. She'd hit his mental wall, Liane realized, and it was like no other she'd ever encountered. She inhaled a fortifying breath and began a relentless psychic hammering against him. He was strong, but her powers were stronger. She knew it was but a matter of time.

The heat between them grew. Their bodies, molded so tightly together, dampened with the shared struggle, until Liane could feel every rippling muscle of his body straining against hers. Fire burned between them. A tiny ember flared to life in her mind, stoked by the insistence of the masculine intellect that held her just as firmly as she held him.

She was back in the forest, in the sunlit glade, by the water-splashed pool. This time, however, she was not alone. The Cat Man, Karic, was with her and he watched with his strange, hungry eyes. Watched as she slipped her gown from her body, watched as she made her way to him.

He took her in his arms. His mouth, sensuously full and wanting, covered hers. She went mad then, her arms entwining about his neck, her fingers burying into his thick mane of hair, their tongues meeting in a fierce, sweet, wet union. Mad—but the madness was but a fleeting escape from the true reality.

Liane wrenched free of his psychic manipulations, and looked up into eyes hot with passion.

The angry accusations burning in her eyes elicited no apologies from Karic.

"You were there with me as freely as I was," he muttered "I felt your body respond, felt your heart quicken beneath mine. It was real, no matter how much of it was of the mind. Admit it!"

"Never!"

Before Karic had a chance to react to the change in her, Liane's mind-seek slammed into him, forcing open a chink in his inner wall. She was half in, catching a glimpse of a distant mountain peak, before, with a gasp, Karic shoved her out. She fought back with all the power within her. For the longest time, they struggled, neither certain who the victor would be.

Pain tightened their features as one feinted, then attacked the other, sheer desperation fueling Liane's assault, bitter determination upholding Karic's. Even in his physically weakened state, the Cat Man managed to fend off every attack, even as he knew he had little left to give. If there'd been a way for him to self-destruct or to drive himself into incoherent madness, he'd have done it while he still had the strength— anything, to prevent him from revealing his people's hiding place. But that small favor was denied him. All that was left was for him to continue to fight.

Liane saw it, felt his rising desperation, yet the realization failed to sweeten her sense of victory. If he'd been stronger, not so cruelly weakened by the neural torture, she'd have never prevailed this far. Yes, the victory was within her grasp, but she knew now she'd have to kill him to gain it. Only in his dying would she at last penetrate his defenses, and that knowledge was almost more than she could bear.

Never, in all her cycles as a Sententia, had she ever done harm in a mind-seek, much less killed someone. Yet failure would be hers if she didn't kill him. Was it worth the price?

Duty and strict obedience to the will of higher authority, instilled in her since birth, were as much a part of her as the air she breathed, the water she drank. But those virtues were suddenly of little comfort in the face of seeing a brave, indomitable man die in her arms. She didn't think she could live with herself.

The conflict grew to crazed proportions. Life . . . death . . . right . . . wrong. The words, mingling with the confusing pleasure of the mental moments shared in his arms, rose to become a whirling maelstrom in her mind. Pain, worse than any she'd felt in her life, stabbed through Liane, sending sharp, bright, blinding shards of light into her brain.

Suddenly, it seemed too difficult to go on, to fight through the maze of choices. With a small cry, Liane fell to the floor.